God's Eye: Awakening

By

Dr. Aleron Kong

Table of Contents

Dedication

This book is dedicated to my uncle Koichi.

We lost him in the beginning of this year. He was a man who lived loudly, lived hard and who never forgot the importance of family.

You are not forgotten uncle.

From the Author

I am so honored that you would share your precious time with me. Thank you so very, very much. I hope you enjoy God's Eye. I gave it my all and I think it will be another amazing series for you to fall in love with!

I'm an indie author, which means I don't have a publishing company behind me. It's just me, a laptop and awesome fans like you!

Please leave a review at the end and click "like" on the reviews you agree with. You're amazing!!!

Now please enjoy!

Prologue

617,827,053 breaths.

That was the original measurement of Remington's life.

At the time of his birth, the Fates of the Skein had determined exactly how much time he would be allotted and what he would do with it. His would be a life of honorable achievement. Of sadness, true, but of far more joy. Of children and warm hearths, and finally, after a life well spent, he would be gifted with a dignified death.

It was true that predicting the weave of Fate's strings was harder on Earth due to the Chaos in every Earthling. Still, the predictions of Fate could be relied upon. For even in a system of the greatest Order, there is the possibility of Chaos, and even in a world of pure Chaos, Order can be found.

Put another way, Fate's plans went FUBAR when a bolt of pure Higher Energy struck the world. The Wyrd Skein was torn asunder, and the three immortal sisters found their own fates to be at risk. In the days following the Forsaking when the sky turned a roiling grey, some lived that should have died, and many, many more died that should have lived.

Threads were cut short, and countless new threads were woven into the story of Earth. No being, no matter how powerful, could now predict the future of the planet. The destinies of billions were set free to float on the winds of Change and Chance. One such soul was now running for his life.

***

Screams filled the night and the sour tang of vomit filled the air. Remy's heart beat harder than ever before. Though neither he nor any other being could know, he was gasping the final breaths of his tragically shortened life.

107 breaths remaining.

Sweat ran down Remy's face and plastered his shirt to his back. He didn't even notice. His heart also thudded hard enough to cause physical pain. Even that didn't capture his attention. All he was thinking about were the living and the dead.

Two hundred and fifty-nine of them had fled the city. Every one of those hundreds of souls had agreed to run to the dubious safety of this old army bunker. Only sixty-eight remained. Fifty-five had made it into the fortified structure that would hopefully be their new home and salvation. Twelve more prayed to any deity that would listen while they tried to make it to the fortified door. One stood at the threshold.

Remy stood in the doorway, one hand braced against its frame, and bellowed, "Run! Run! They're coming after you!"

105 breaths remaining.

The only answer was the agonized scream of a woman. Sara was an overweight suburban mom that had managed to survive when so many others had died. You wouldn't have thought she would make it through the last days of hell on Earth, but she had discovered a strong will to live. Where others had succumbed, she had fought tooth and nail to survive. She had gained the respect of everyone in the group. Within eyesight of safety, however, her story came to an end.

A mutated cat, black with red claws, jumped out of the darkness. It was no mere housecat. It had the size and physique of a mountain lion and easily bore her screaming figure to the ground. The two rolled in a violent struggle, but there was no doubt as to the outcome. Within the first few seconds, Sara's red blood splattered in broad arcs across the grass. In the twilight it looked black. The shadow cat gouged, bit, and clawed while she screamed and begged for mercy.

Remy watched with a tight jaw, but did not leave the safety of the doorway. When a group of people survived days of death and hopelessness, they could form bonds strong enough to last a lifetime. Her screams for help echoed through the night, but not one of the other eleven slowed down or even looked back.

No one was coming to help her.

In this new world, no paltry bond of friendship would protect you when monsters prowled. Misplaced mercy would kill you as quickly as a fang or claw.

They weren't men and women of the Western Confederation any more. Nations, gender, and race no longer mattered. Idealism was for fools. Most idealists had died out in the first few days of monster attacks. Those that survived lived only to feel those soft feelings crushed by the weight of reality. They were all Forsaken now. All that mattered was survival.

Instead of stopping or helping, they just used her agonized screams as motivation to run faster. Their legs pumped like pistons.

They all heard the yowling screeches of more monsters closing in. When given a choice between heeding the threatening roars of monsters or the begging of a woman who was already almost dead, the answer was obvious. The most kindhearted of the eleven just wished her a quick death. The more pragmatic of them hoped that she suffered as long as possible. Her screams might distract some of the monsters and provide the rest of them with precious time.

Remy watched as the woman went down, as more blood sprayed across the ground, as Sara continued to fight, frantically pushing at the partially insubstantial body of the shadow cat. Her efforts accomplished nothing. The only reason she was still alive was because the monster hadn't gone for the kill yet. Mutated or not, the beast still had the personality of a cat. It was playing with its food.

The dark skin on Remy's face stretched as his jaw clenched even tighter. Still, he didn't leave the doorway. He knew the same thing the remaining eleven runners did. She was already dead. Her body just hadn't caught up to that fact yet. Instead, he looked at the men and women he could still save. Remy's eyes locked onto the man lagging the farthest behind. Jay was a father, a good man. He was the kind of guy you would be lucky to have at your back. The only reason he was lagging behind was that he held his little boy in his arms. Even at fifty paces, Remy could see the whites of the man's fear-swollen eyes.

100 breaths remaining.

Remy shouted for him to run faster, but it was obvious Jay was at the end of his stamina. He was falling farther behind the others with every second. Exhaustion was putting lie to the belief that parents could do anything to save their children. The monsters crooned in excitement at seeing weaker members of the herd struggle and fall behind. The sound deepened Jay's fear into terror. Froth appeared at the corner of his lips, and his son sobbed into his chest.

I can't look back! I can't let go! Those two thoughts were on repeat in Jay's mind as he gripped his small son to his chest. Don't look back. Don't let go. Don't look back. Don't let go!

With fell, inevitable cruelty, two shadow cats emerged from the darkness and leaped. Their combined weight easily overwhelmed Jay and drove his body to the ground. One swipe of red talons opened up three jagged wounds in his back. His back arched and he shrieked in agony.

Most people would be surprised that such a large man would make such a high-pitched sound. Remy was not. He'd seen hardened soldiers cry for their mothers as they bled out far from home. To him, there was neither surprise nor shame. Everyone went out in their own way. In the end, it just didn't matter. Dead was dead.

In Jay's pain-addled state, he lost his grip on his son. The second cat sank its teeth deep into the boy's shoulder. The three-year-old cried out in pain and fear. He screamed for his father, the invincible figure that had always kept him safe. He screamed it over and over while the shadow beast mauled him. The only blessing was that the cries did not last long. He died still believing he would be saved. Jay howled, "No!" as the last member of his family was literally ripped from his arms.

The last sight Jay had was another shadow cat clamping its jaws over his son's face before jerking its head to the side. The small body twitched spasmodically after the neck snapped. A foul scent revealed the child had soiled his pants.

The world of the Forsaken showed the full extent of its mercy in that the father's throat was ripped out before he saw his son being eaten piece by quivering piece. As their blood spilled out on the grassy field, the last vestige of their bloodline disappeared forever.

95 breaths remaining.

Damn you, Remy thought. His fingers gripped the doorway so hard his knuckles turned white. Yet still he remained in the bunker. He couldn't help either of them, and he wouldn't waste the life left in him for nothing. He and everyone else on Earth were Forsaken, and the weak would die sooner or later. Instead, he shouted once more for the survivors to run faster.

Remy's eyes flashed upward in a particular way. His HUD phased into existence, and he examined the three bars in the upper left corner. They were the same length and were each a different color: red, blue and green. He grunted, seeing the purple corruption infesting the red line. It was what he'd expected, but it still sickened him. Breathing out, he focused on the full green and blue bars. They would have to do.

He turned his focus back to the men and women running for their lives. In the back of his mind, he reflected on the insanity of the world he was living in. Everything had changed when that "heads-up display" or "interface" had appeared in the vision of every person on Earth. It was the same moment they were all notified that their world was now connected to the Labyrinth, whatever that was.

Since then people had come to accept that if they let their eyes unfocus, they could pull up their very own video game interface. They had also figured out that it could give them information and even make them stronger. Some had gained significant powers. The "Able." That was what people had started calling the minority of the human race that had been granted an ability during the Forsaking.

8

Remy was one of those precious few. His ability was only second rank, *uncommon,* far from the nearly superhero capabilities that others had gained. Still, it had let him teach a few survivors to develop their own skills, attacks and defenses. Being "Able" had played no small part in making him the de facto leader of this group, even though that thought seemed like a cruel joke. What kind of leader lost nearly eighty percent of his people?

Dark figures continued to materialize out of the night, each a monster capable of killing a full-grown man in single combat. They gave chase while the survivors sprinted for their lives. A teenage boy was the next to fall. His screams were bloodcurdling as two of the cat monsters sliced through his Achilles. The boy's shrieks only grew in pitch and volume as he was dragged off into the night. Remy realized he didn't even remember the kid's name.

The next to go was a father who chose to spend his life to save his family. He knew what was about to happen to him, but still he bought his wife and daughter precious seconds. The little girl was peeking over her mother's shoulder, and watched her father turn to face the monsters. She reached her small hand backward and screamed "Daddy!" but her mother held on tightly to her squirming body. The woman's heart was breaking, but still she sprinted for the safety of the bunker door.

The nail-studded bat the father held glowed red for just a moment as he activated *Sweeping Blow.* The weapon moved almost on its own. The speed with which it cut through the air was far faster than the man should have been able to manage. More, it struck not one but three cat monsters all at once. The trio of monsters were knocked backward, rolling back along the ground. Sadly, the special attack was not without its price.

The man's stamina was already low from running; the special attack bottomed it out. The father fell to his hands and knees, gasping. It felt like he'd sprinted uphill in a Georgia summer. He could barely focus. The edges of his vision blackened.

Another cat approached him cautiously. It sniffed and circled his body to see if he would attack again. The man glared at it, but could do nothing more than heave labored breaths. Seconds later, it sprung onto his back and sank its fangs into his neck. A strangled *huff* mixed with his ragged breathing. More blood spilled onto the ground. A wheezing groan came out and he collapsed to the ground. Seconds later, four more cats latched on, eating him alive. In his last seconds the brave man lost all semblance of courage. His cries filled the air. He screamed for his mother as he pissed himself.

Remington just nodded at the man's passing and picked up his gun. It was almost time.

81 breaths remaining.

Remy had made a promise to get these people to safety. He wasn't a fool and wouldn't waste his life if he couldn't help, but he was no coward. It could easily be argued that he had done enough getting any of them to the bunker. God knows it hadn't been easy, and there had been sacrifices. Even though he would not waste his life on a hopeless cause, it didn't mean he wouldn't spit in Fate's eye if he found a worthy one. He saw just such a cause in the pleading eyes of the mother running toward him. Saving a woman and her child was a good thing to buy with the life he had left.

He'd left men and women to die before. Just like he'd watched Sara and Jay die, he could see the big picture and act accordingly. Making difficult decisions did not weigh him down like it did so many

10

others. That didn't mean he had no heart, contrary to what many in his life had thought. Instead, it meant that his heart was just harder and rougher than others. He was willing to bear pains that others were not. If he thought there was no hope for the people running, he would have already shut the door. Point in fact, Remy had two distinct reasons for leaving the safety of the shelter.

One, he was sure that he could help at least some of the runners make it. More accurately, he was sure he could improve their chances. That fact made it easier to focus on the task at hand. It wasn't that he couldn't feel fear or doubt. Those emotions just didn't stop him from anything he decided needed to be done. He'd learned long ago that pain was a lesser burden than regret. Remington had sworn to help these people. He would try to fulfill that promise if he could, even if it meant risking his life.

Two, he hadn't made it through the last several days unscathed. There had been a personal cost to getting his group to the bunker. A bite from a small mutated insect, like a flying ant with a scorpion's tail, had done him more damage than any monster. After everything he had lived through, before and after the Forsaking, the thought that a bug bite was going to do him in had made him chuckle more than once. Not a bullet. Not a bomb. A bug bite. He'd climbed over the bodies of his comrades, swum through rivers turned red with blood, and in the end, it was shitting on an anthill that was going to do him in.

In the past few days, the bite had grown from a small red nodule to a golf ball-sized hole in his side. The edges were black and necrotic. Tendrils of infection spread out from the wound. The contamination reached across his chest and down his leg. He'd held some hope that the bunker might have antibiotics, but in the last day he'd come to realize that a shot of penicillin was not going to kill whatever organism was eating him alive. Better to make his last days count for something.

Gripping his rifle, he took a step out of the bunker. Before he could take a second, a hand grabbed his coat sleeve. Looking back, he met his sister's eyes.

"What are you going to do?" she asked, already knowing the answer.

She asked the question in a tone that was half accusation and half begging. It held a pleading intensity that was reflected in her fevered eyes. Her face was also wan from blood loss and fever. She had lost three fingers in an attack five days ago. Now the entire limb was fire-engine red and the stumps were black. She didn't say anything else, but the plea in her rheumy eyes was obvious. Don't leave me, they said. For once, don't try and be the hero. Don't risk your life. Let them die.

The look in his own eyes was all the answer she needed. Love, apology, and steely resolve. Maybe if he was the hero she thought he was, he would have stayed. What she did not know was that he had killed more people than any of these monsters. He had sent countless more to their deaths. Again and again, he had made difficult, blood-drenched choices that men and women of conscience would balk at. He had committed atrocities for his Federation, for his people, for his government.

He was no hero.

That was why his government had always called on him. He was the one who would always look at the bigger picture and then just wash the blood from his hands when he was done. Now, however, there *was* no bigger picture. There was just a child he could help with the fading life that was still in his body. Preserving decades of potential in exchange for the few pain-filled days he had left was a good deal, plain and simple.

He didn't tell her any of that. Honesty and truth had never been major priorities. Instead, he just spoke the words that his mother instilled in them their entire lives. Words he knew that would comfort her.

"We stand."

Hearing that, something almost physical broke inside of her. She let go of him, in body, mind and heart, just as he knew she would. Tears began to form, but she didn't let them fall. If her brother could be brave, she thought, then so could she.

For his part, Remy didn't waste any more time or breath on goodbyes. Instead, he took that second step out of the bunker and raised the rifle to his shoulder. Focusing, he poured his will into the weapon and brought the stock up to his cheek. A now-familiar overlay appeared in his vision as he accessed his *Sure Shot* skill. Reticles appeared over each enemy in his view and greatly increased his accuracy.

With a second exertion of will, each bullet in the rifle was infused with gold-white light. He had no idea how it worked but, thanks to a skill, he could pour "mana" into each bullet. It made his shots hit harder. That was necessary because the monsters and invaders seemed to be able to shrug off normal bullets. In the past few days, Remy had had plenty of time to shake his head at the insanity of these new "natural laws." All he cared about in that moment though was bringing the pain.

Activating his skills took barely any time at all. In fact, it was done by the time he took his fourth step away from the bunker.

13

Despite his speed, he'd unknowingly just spent a major portion of the life he had left.

69 breaths remaining.

After triggering *Ammo of Light,* his mana had plummeted by more than half. It gave him a headache, but Remy pushed it aside. His focus was on the enemy and the innocents. The former soldier sighted through the ACOG scope and squeezed, never pulled, the trigger. Three rounds shot from the end of the barrel in a second. Each tore through the air, trailing white light. All three exploded into the body of one of the cats.

Fifty yards away the bullets entered the monster, the kinetic damage amplified by Remy's use of *Light* mana. He didn't know it, but the cat was at least partially a *Dark* creature. The opposing nature of his attack greatly magnified the damage. Three grievous wounds appeared in its body. It dropped to the ground, dead. Remy had already sighted on another and three more white tracers filled the night.

With his increased accuracy and damage, the closest members of the pack were soon dispatched, giving his people precious seconds. Even as he replaced the mag, his breath came in heavy gasps. *Sure Shot* increased the likelihood that he hit his target, something absolutely necessary with the agile cats, but it drained his stamina every second he used it. His mana had also bottomed out when he used *Ammo of Light* on the second mag. The magic depletion brought on a splitting headache that made it harder to think. When he fired again the bullets glowed, but didn't have the white tracing of magic. He just hadn't been able to put as much mana into the second round. Because of that, the bullets did considerably less damage. It didn't matter to Remy. He kept firing.

Under his cover fire, survivors made it into the bunker, including the mother and her child. The woman actually increased her pace somehow and made it to the bunker ahead of some of the others. Seeing her run past him brought a smile to his lips. The whole time he never stopped firing, advancing all the while.

When the last living member of his group finally ran by, hope surged in his breast. It was another suburban mom, Jenny. She was still wearing the ripped and filthy designer track suit she'd had on when the world ended. At some point the rhinestones on her bottom had probably spelled "PINK," but now it just read "IN."

Jenny had clearly been a Buckhead Betty, one of the young trophy wives who looked down on Publix and only shopped at Whole Foods or the farmer's market. Now though, her cheeks were sunken and her face was gaunt from weeks of near-starvation. Sweat drenched her body and made her skin shine in the fading light. She looked him in the eye as she passed, her gaze filled with both fear and gratitude. Remy just nodded, keeping his rifle trained on the cats that were coming ever closer.

"Keep going!" he shouted, while he started backing up. "I'll hold them back."

"Thank you," she cried. It was more sobbing gasp than pronounced words, but she did as she was told.

Remy kept firing as he retreated. His eyes were on a swivel, trying to keep track of the shadowy bodies of the predator cats. Not an easy task as they all but disappeared when they stepped into shadows. When his mag ran dry, the monsters slowed to an aggressive stalk. They all glared at him malevolently but didn't rush forward.

15

He kept his gun raised but didn't fire. This was his last mag, and he didn't have any mana to use his skill again. Remy had managed to kill more than ten of the monsters, but they just stepped over their fallen without a glance. The man pointed his gun at one of them, then another, hoping they were smart enough to be afraid but not smart enough to know that his stamina and mana were almost at zero.

39 breaths remaining.

For a moment, he allowed himself to think that everything would be okay. That his foolish gamble would pay off and he would make it safely back to the bunker having saved some lives. That was when he heard the scream. Risking a look behind him, he saw Jenny lying in a pool of her own blood. Two cats had circled around behind him and caught her before she could make it to safety. He looked past the duo now feasting on the woman's flesh and saw more shadow cats running toward the entrance to the fortified structure only thirty yards away.

Remy looked past Jenny's mutilated body and locked eyes with his sister. She was still standing in the doorway, her one good hand on the knob. She silently begged him to somehow run faster than the bounding cats. To make it back to safety and to not leave her. He gave her the smallest shake of his head, and his face communicated a simple request.

Close the door.

22 breaths remaining.

Her heart broke, but they had both been raised by the same strong woman. Neither was afraid to face the truth, and neither shied from difficult tasks. With a fractured cry, she slammed the heavy door shut and threw the bolt just in time. One of the shadow cats threw its body against the door so hard that it fractured its spinal column. The impact made a bone-cracking *crunch*.

The other monstrous cats immediately began scratching at the wood. Their claws gouged deep furrows in the door, but only the outer door was made of oak. The inner door was solid steel. She closed that as well, and locked it seconds after the first. The only light was the faint red from the hazard bulbs. In near darkness, she stared at the chrome metal door as if trying to see through it. Trying to let her brother know that he wasn't alone even though he was. A thick strand of spider silk drifted down and caressed her tear-streaked face. After yanking it away in shock and disgust, she noticed there were a good number of webs farther down the corridor, still thick even after everyone had walked down it.

Outside, a low-pitched growl made Remy snap his head forward again. He had only looked away for a second, but some of the cats stalking him had covered more than half the distance between them. They weren't slowing down. After having been through so many life-and-death struggles, he knew what was about to happen. He'd survived more times than he could count, but this time something inside him knew that there would be no escape. As the end of his journey raced toward him, he realized, with a slight bit of shock, that in addition to the adrenaline, pain and a wisp of fear, what he felt most was… free.

Soon, he could let go of his chained rage, his impotent fury at trying to make an ever-worsening world a better place. Soon, the clogged poison in his soul would weep, and he wouldn't have to worry about fitting into society, about being a "good" person, about keeping the monster inside him at bay. His entire life, he'd struggled against the violence and anger that always seemed to be right below the surface.

He'd joined the military to channel his impulses. He'd been recruited by the Organization to release them.

He had tried to balance out the lives he took after leaving the service. He'd gone into medicine to square his cosmic debt, though, truth be told, it was more to humor his mother than anything else. As it turned out, even in the hospital he couldn't run from what he was. He'd been drawn to blood and trauma, once again making dispassionate decisions that carried the weight of life and death. Every action and decision of his life had been aimed at "that part" of himself. Now though, he could just be what he was. Now, and forever more, he could be free.

There wasn't much time left, but with the time he had, he was going to share his anger! There was a savage smile on his face as he squeezed the trigger again and again. Cats fell, but countless more kept running toward him. Guess Uncle Yo was right, he thought with a grin, *pussy really will be the death of me.*

With the stock at his cheek, Remy squeezed the trigger and pumped rounds into the circling shadow cats. He pulled the trigger until he heard the inevitable *click, click, click.* The rifle was empty.

The pack seemed to know he was no longer a threat. They slowed down again and began to creep forward like an unstoppable black tide. The cats did not have the intelligence of a human. What they did understand, however, was pain. They also understood suffering, and they loved them both. At the end of their prey's life, they followed the instincts of their evil hearts and savored the hopelessness of the bleeding man before them. After all, surrounded and alone in the dark, what could he possibly do?

Hearing their yowls and soft screeches, the small wisp of fear Remington had felt disappeared. Anger filled the void. He had been through too many battles to delude himself that he'd survive long. He knew that these were his last minutes. That didn't bother him. He'd spent his life well. As far as he was concerned, the people he'd just saved were worth what was about to happen. He wasn't worried about his impending death. What really pissed him off was that he could feel the arrogance and scorn of the beasts. They were looking down on him. Dismissing him. Silently asking the same question that so many others had asked when they told him he wasn't good enough.

What can you possibly do?

He had the same answer he always had.

"I can do anything," he spat at them in defiance.

Reaching one hand into the diseased wound in his side, he dug out a handful of congealed blood and pus. It cost him a few health points, but that wouldn't matter soon. He reached down to his waist for the foot-long knife he'd taken from a hardware store. He liberally smeared his own filth on the blade. It wouldn't kill any more monsters before he died, but maybe, just maybe, he'd pull a few more of these bastards into the abyss with him after he was gone.

"Well," he shouted as loudly as his weakened body would allow, "let's finish this!"

The monsters could not understand him, but they agreed to his terms all the same. The rest of the pack sprang forward like a shadowy black wave. Angry yowls filled the air. He swung his weapon and scored a deep cut against the face of one of the cats. It was knocked to the ground. Before it even landed, he was already swinging at another.

This time, his knife bit deep into a monster's shoulder. His attack stopped its pounce, but his weapon caught in its flesh. It was only stuck for a second, but that was long enough. Another jumped on him at the same time, raking its Dark magic-enhanced claws down his left side. Remy cried out in pain and fury. His blood flowed fast and thick.

14 breaths remaining.

Turning awkwardly, he chopped at the head of the cat that had sunk its teeth into him. It growled deeply but didn't let go. He pulled his arm back to swing again, but a second cat pounced before the strike could land. It caught his right wrist in a bite that fractured bone.

Remy screamed in spite of himself and fell to one knee. Before he could do anything more, a third monster dove onto his back and rode him to the ground. He fell on top of the one biting his wrist. With madness-induced strength, he bit its ear and tore it free of its head. The cat screeched and Remy smiled, blood caking his teeth. A sick and cheerful laugh gurgled from his throat.

3 breaths remaining.

That was his last victory. After that, the shadow cats piled on. Then he felt only pain. The stink of his blood was heavy in the air. Lust-frenzied cries filled the night and monsters fought over the right to tear off pieces of his flesh.

2 breaths remaining.

He'd never felt pain like this before, but even as he wailed, something inside of him let go. At last, he was free. Free from expectations. Free from the selfish people who screamed arguments they didn't understand simply because they enjoyed screaming. Free from the contradiction that had made every day a confusing agony.

Free from the lesson of his father.

Free from the command of his mother.

1 breath remaining.

A cat bit into his neck, tearing into his carotid artery. His lifeblood geysered into the monster's mouth and his thoughts came to an end. The breath escaped his body with a sigh, and a final bolded prompt appeared in his vision, heavy with finality.

You have died.

CHAPTER 1

Ignorance was bliss.

Remy had always thought that death would mean everything going black. Maybe there would be a tunnel with a bright light. He'd hoped it wouldn't be a falling sensation swiftly followed by a great deal of heat and the scent of brimstone. Truth be told, he wouldn't have been overly surprised by that last one.

What happened though was that the world froze and was bleached of color. The next moment, he was outside of his body, dispassionately watching the shadow cats devour his mortal coil. He couldn't muster any emotions. Even when one of the monsters pulled his leg free from his torso, he didn't have an emotional reaction to it. Intellectually, Remy knew that he should be bothered by his own mutilation, but he felt nothing. He floated away, not higher necessarily, just "away" somehow. Everything grew darker and darker until all he could see was blackness.

Then he saw the light. Above him, a glowing white portal appeared and his astral self flew toward it. The gateway radiated an energy that made him start to feel things again. It was like the photons flying toward him were each engraved with messages of contentment, peace and love. It felt like seeing a warm glow through your house's front window after finishing a cross-country drive. It felt like he was going home.

As he floated toward the portal, he thought back on his life. He thought of the years of service when he had "protected" his country. He thought about his family, the good times and the bad, and knew beyond any doubt that there had been more "good." He thought about his sister, hiding in the bunker, and hoped that she would be alright.

With each thought that flashed through his mind, and with each moment of his life that he replayed, he let go of his mortal attachments. The reports of "one's life flashing before one's eyes" had apparently been true. It was the first part of a necessary process to truly embrace the next phase of existence. More of Remy's bonds to his old life were peeled away as he drifted closer to the shining gateway. By the time he was in front of it, he was left with a very simple conclusion.

He was ready.

It was time.

Right when he was about to pass on to the next phase of existence, however, a force grabbed his astral self and ripped him away from the welcoming light. Remy was only able to keep the portal in sight for a billionth of a second, but he thought the white luminescence had flashed an ominous, angry red. He would never be sure though, because he was pulled away so fast that everything was a blur.

As he flew away from that portal to the beyond, all his memories and thoughts slammed back into his "self." He couldn't feel actual pain, but after being in a state of near-total enlightenment, then having it ripped away from him, Remy was more than ready to cut a bitch. He would have shamed the devil with his cursing if he still had a mouth.

There had been no sounds since his death, but now what he heard was a great vortex of wind. Remy wondered if it was his imagination. Were the remnants of his consciousness adding fictitious sensory input? He felt like he was moving fast, but without a body how could he be moving at all? How could he hear the wind? Then the time for wondering was past. The feeling of movement decreased before coming to an abrupt stop. He was somehow able to cast his gaze around, and what he saw made the last vestiges of his old self feel pure terror.

He knew where he was. This was what people had come to call a Death Zone. It was a location that every human on Earth avoided. All that waited here was a brutal and painful death. That hadn't always been the case, but it'd been true ever since these words had been emblazoned across the vision of every living man, woman and child:

> Your world is now part of the Labyrinth

Remy struggled to free himself from the invisible bonds that held him, but he was helpless. His astral self continued floating forward. Humans had come to call this a Death Zone, but it had another name. It was an entrance to the Labyrinth. It was a Dungeon.

His consciousness felt the barest hint of resistance as it passed through the energy field of the Dungeon's mouth. Then, a minute later, after zipping through many turns of the Dungeon, he passed through another portal and entered the Labyrinth itself. After that his speed picked up even more, so fast that it shamed his previous movement. Even though he lacked a body, the magical force of his passage crushed his astral consciousness to the size of a grain of sand's left nut. Everything went black again.

The next thing Remy knew, he was in an open space so immense that he could not see the sides or the ceiling. What he did see when he looked around was a swirling grey… something. The environs were both wonderfully familiar and strangely disconcerting. His mind began to warp. He was old and young at the same time. His chromosomes rearranged, and he became a she. Then he was back to himself, but he had been born a twin. He was the twin. He murdered his brother. He could not remember why!

Remy's mind began to splinter until the force holding him aloft exerted a new form of pressure. It counteracted the effects of the Probability Curve and let him maintain a rudimentary sense of self. He moved through the Formless Infinite. In time a massive platform came into view and panic flared once again in his ghostly heart. There were rows, endless rows, of people strapped to tables. Some were smiling, some were screaming, but most just lay there unblinking as they stared up at the swirling grey "stuff" that was all around them.

He was afraid he would be strapped to one of those tables, but the force transporting him carried him on and he once again lost any sense of orientation or time. The next "time" he was "aware," Remy was still floating in the fathomless grey expanse, but now seven disembodied faces revolved around him. They were each the size of a house. The features of the visages flowed so quickly that they never settled on a single form. The lips of a man moved beneath the eyes of a snake all surrounded by feathers that a moment later morphed into long curls of purple hair crackling with white lightning. The other six faces shifted just as quickly and into visages even more bizarre.

~THIS IS THE CHOSEN?~ one face asked in a hissing voice.

~DANGEROUS!~ another boomed in response.

~IT MUST BE DONE!~ a third interjected.

~THIS HAS BEEN DECIDED!~ a nightmarish face thundered.

*~THIS SEED IS HEALER, FIGHTER AND MORE! IT IS THE **CHOICE**!~*

*~THIS SEED IS KILLER, TYRANT AND MORE! IT IS THE **CHOICE**!~*

*~THIS SEED IS LEADER, CONQUEROR AND MORE! IT IS THE **CHOICE**!~*

~YES! POWER IS SHIFTING ACROSS THE INFINITE FRACTALS OF THE UNIVERSE! WE MUST GROW THE INFLUENCE OF CHAOS AS WELL!~ The voice was initially the rasping of an old man, but it shifted to the innocent tones of a child.

~ITS TRUE NATURE MUST BE HIDDEN~

~THEN WE MUST BLOCK ITS TRUE FOCUS UNTIL~

~YES~, another voice interrupted, *~BUT WE MUST GIVE IT PRODIGIOUS GIFTS IF IT IS TO SURVIVE~*

~THE COST WILL BE GREAT~, for the first time, several voices spoke at once, as though united in concern.

~IT CANNOT BE AVOIDED~

~IT WILL BE NEEDED~, added a voice that Remy had not yet heard.

~SO SHALL IT BE~, all seven faces intoned together.

The disembodied heads were spinning around Remy while they spoke about his fate. Between their movement and the shifting of their faces, he could not be sure which spoke next, but he supposed it didn't matter. What did matter to him was that he did not like being discussed as if he wasn't there. For the first time in his afterlife, though by far not the first time in his existence, he impetuously spoke up when perhaps his silence would have been the better choice.

"Who are you! Why did you take me from that light? What is this place?"

Remy had wanted to speak earlier, but there had been what he could only call a "pressure" inhibiting him. Only his anger at being ignored let him force his way past it. The faces did not respond at first. When one did, he thought he heard the barest hint of approval, if not respect.

*~THE **CHOICE** IS WISE! THE SEED IS STRONGER THAN EXPECTED! THE BLOODLINE IS TRUE. IT WILL BE PREPARED!~*

All the faces began to vibrate, then they slammed into one another. The seven melded together until only one remained, and Remy's astral self started flowing toward it. The mouth yawned wide and Remy began struggling to get free again. It had as little effect as before. All he could do was project his words once more.

"What are you doing? I won't be a prisoner or a slave or whatever you're doing to those people strapped to the tables."

The face ignored him and the mouth yawned wider.

Remy continued to struggle ineffectually. But, effective or not, he was still furious. He'd spent a lifetime fighting to control his own destiny. The idea that in death he would be robbed of his choice at this point was worse than the death he'd just suffered. At least then he'd been on his feet and had died on his own terms. He would not live another life controlled by others!

What came out of his mouth next was a stream of the foulest language that the planet Earth had evolved after thousands of years of war. He let the giant faces know exactly what he thought about them, exactly what they could do with their giant mouths and exactly how long they should gargle after. The torrent of filth coming out of his mouth was so spectacular that for a moment the collective consciousness of Chaos stopped and thought, "What the hell? This guy really does give zero fucks!"

"Just kill me again!" Remy screamed after taking a deep breath. "I was already dead. I deserve to see the end of war! I will not be a slave! Not anymore! Never again!"

This time, a voice did respond. It seemingly came out of nowhere, but it was almost human.

~No. There are no slaves here, at least none that do not choose such a path. Those you saw are only being momentarily detained to improve their power and prepare them for what comes next. In either case your fate diverges from theirs, though in time they may become intertwined once more.~

"What, then?" Remy shouted. He was almost inside of the mouth, but even the idea of being eaten by some cosmic being didn't scare him. He was too angry. Most of his personality had been stripped away, but what was left was the core of who he was: a desire for freedom, a need to improve the world, and fury!

28

"What?" he spat. "What are you preparing me for?"

His astral self continued to drift into the mouth of the face, now swelled to the size of a mountain range. There was no response for the seconds or centuries that passed as Remy continued into the black hole of his destiny. Right before he was consumed, the voice spoke again, and this time there was no mistaking the pity and sorrow it held.

~Godhood.~

Then Remy entered the maw of the Lords of Chaos and his mind passed beyond thought and time.

CHAPTER 2

Welcome, creature of Chaos! You will soon enter the world of **Telos**!

This is an old world that is on the cusp of a new beginning. The Cataclysm that destroyed its civilizations, plunged it into anarchy and laid low its old gods has passed from regret, to myth, to legend, and now almost beyond any memory. Be warned; forgotten or not, the sins of the past will always haunt both the present and the future. As is always true of Labyrinth worlds, however, danger and reward are close bedfellows.

Wait, what? Remy thought to himself. He'd been eaten by the giant face and now he was here, wherever here was. All he could see was an unrelieved blackness and the words that scrolled across his vision. Did the prompt just call him a "creature of Chaos?" He had a vague memory of someone else calling him a god, but as he reached for the memory, it dissipated like smoke in the night. More words blazed across his gaze.

Ages past, the Lattice, a unique and interconnected series of worlds and realities, was consumed by the Labyrinth. For immeasurable time the mana of the Labyrinth has flooded the Lattice, sinking ever deeper into it, until finally reaching the jewel at its center. This jewel is the world of Telos.

Dungeons have now appeared across the face of the planet. Locations of magic are reawakening as the ambient mana levels of this world increase. Like water on dry sand, the first drops of magic may be quickly absorbed, but in a short time this world shall create a magic system both akin to all Labyrinth worlds and unique unto itself.

At this pivotal time, you are one of an unknown number of creatures that have been seeded with Power. Demons, monsters, gods and more shall vie for survival in this new world. Each Being of Power shall have their own strengths and weaknesses.

You are a god!

A great number of rudimentary tribes have been brought to this new and dangerous world. They call out for aid!

Your first task as a Tier 0 deity is to choose a people to worship you. As you have a Sponsor, you have been granted a short amount of time in which to prepare. Your primary senses will now be restored. You may customize this space to ease your transition into this new phase of being.

And just like that, Remy could see, hear and touch again. He took for granted that taste was back as well, but he couldn't smell anything. He stood in a featureless white room with curved walls. There were no doors or furniture. After pinching his skin and confirming that he once again physically existed, he checked the walls. Minutes later, he came to three conclusions:

One, it looked like he'd been reincarnated into the same body he'd had before.

Two, he was in an empty white room.

Three, it'd be nice to have a place to sit.

No sooner had that thought occurred to him than a short white stool appeared. It didn't slowly morph into existence. One moment the room was empty, the next, it was there.

Remy frowned at it. It was about two feet tall and had three legs. Just your average wooden stool. Not exactly comfy, he noticed. That thought triggered another change, and it became a plush recliner. It even had a console on one arm for shiatsu. Just like the stool, the entire thing was pure white. He tried to change the color with his mind, and the leather turned a rich chocolate color.

After poking it a couple times, he sat down and turned on the massage function. A slight buzz filled the air and pure ecstasy spread through his naked body. He let out a faint croon of pleasure. This was amazing.

As he lay there in his birthday suit, he thought back on how crazy everything was. He'd died and been brought back to life. Now he was in a sterile lab environment, and he could manifest his thoughts. A normal reaction would be to freak out about all of this, but Remy had never been normal. There was a reason he'd gained the nickname Zero. When most people panicked, he stayed calm. It wasn't that he had nerves of steel, it was just that he gave zero fucks.

He enjoyed the massage a bit longer before standing up and turning the chair off. Pursing his mouth, he thought about his situation. If nothing else, it was always a good idea to gather information. Testing out his new "power," he summoned a mirror and examined himself.

The most obvious thing was that he was completely naked. He'd noticed that before, but after coming back from the dead, it just hadn't seemed like a big priority. The lack of temperature, either hot or cold, had made it even easier to ignore. Looking in the mirror now though, he checked to make sure his oldest friend had made it through his reincarnation without injury. That act made him chuckle as he remembered a talk with an old ICU nurse.

She'd told him that after thirty years in the long-term recovery wing, she'd seen a great number of men and women wake up from comas. With a dismissive shake of her head, she'd then told him that every time a woman woke up, the patient would immediately ask if her husband and children were okay. A woman's first thoughts were of the well-being of their loved ones. Every single man who woke up though, the first thing they did was frantically reach down to grab their package and make sure it was still there. That was usually followed by a huge sigh of relief, asking for some water, and maybe *then* asking about their loved ones.

Remy had always thought that story was a bit ridiculous, but now, seeing that the monster was still home and hanging, he understood the profound relief those men had felt. He chuckled again but the levity quickly fled. Thinking about that old nurse had triggered another memory, this one about his favorite nephew. Other than his sister, the brilliant boy had been one of his last living family even before the Forsaking.

James had been a medical student with a bright future, but sadly he had also been one of the first victims of The Land Effect. To the government, he'd been just one of millions of lost souls. To Remy, it had been like losing a son. James had even followed in his footsteps, pursuing a career in medicine, but all of that had been lost when the boy slipped into a coma.

The only comforting thought was that his nephew's condition had kept him from experiencing the monster-infested hell that Earth had become after the Forsaking. The boy was probably dead now, but at least he'd been spared the horrors the rest of the human race had lived through. Remy shook himself free of such dark thoughts and examined the rest of his body.

He didn't look any different. He had the same dark brown skin bedecked with an unhealthy number of scars thanks to his years of military service. His eyes were what many women had thought to be a distracting shade of hazel, something he'd taken advantage of as often as he humanly could. He was only lacking the eyeglasses that he'd gained from years of studying in med school and residency.

His eyes sat above a crooked nose, broken and reset one too many times, full lips, and a strong jaw. His hair was in the simple fade style he had always sported, short cut, thick and black. He had the same six feet of height he'd had back on Earth, and even the osteochondroma in his left knee was still there.

Seeing that everything essential was where it should be, he thought about some clothes. Just like with the stool, they immediately phased into existence. Without having to move, he was suddenly wearing a perfectly snug pair of boxer briefs, some perfectly broken-in jeans and a two-hundred-wash-softened t-shirt.

The clothes weren't random. They were exactly what he'd been imagining. His favorite outfit. The shirt had originally been black, but long ago it had faded to its current dark mist-grey. A faded three-stripe Atari symbol could barely be made out on the chest. It even had the same stains and small rips. There was something comforting about being in these clothes, and another faint smile graced his face.

Clothing and shelter were taken care of and he didn't have any hunger or thirst, so he decided to sit back down in the recliner chair. The shiatsu turned back on. Oh god, he thought, shutting his eyes in bliss. This feels like heaven.

That thought made his eyes pop back open. Is this heaven? A white room where you could summon anything you thought about? Could be worse, he realized. Closing his eyes again, his fingers wandered over to the control console. Using his imagination, he created a "young Betty White" option. The sensation of the massage changed in a wonderful way. Oh god, he thought, just how I always imagined it.

He didn't know how long that went on, but after a time he heard a distinctly feminine voice greet him.

"Hello."

He opened his eyes, but didn't see anyone. A lesser man might have looked around wildly and shouted, 'Who said that?' but he was Zero. Besides, he'd always prided himself on being a bit less on the nose. He'd already been reborn in a weird white room, been given the power of transmogrification (thank you D&D vocabulary) and in the past hour had felt the wonderfully dry fingers of all four Golden Girls on his body at once. Compared to all of that, a disembodied voice was some JV stuff. A sexy voice wanted to talk to him? Sure, why not?

That was why instead of freaking out he stood up, dismissed the recliner, and summoned a table and a pair of comfy high-backed chairs. A pitcher of sweet tea and two glasses appeared as well. There were even beads of cool condensation slowly creeping down the outside of the glass jug. That done, he pulled out one of the chairs and asked, "Will you join me, please?" in a respectful tone. As his granny had always told him, 'Manners cost nothing.'

There was a pause, then a shimmer appeared in the air. It solidified into a woman garbed in diaphanous blue silk. It was so sheer that it hid nothing, but this was not what immediately captured Remy's attention. It was that her skin was the pale blue of a spring morning. That, and she was about eight feet tall.

Her body was thin with no curves to speak of and her arms and legs were overly long. Despite that, she possessed an inhuman grace as she walked. The supple giant met his gaze with her own sea-green pupils. With a smooth wave of her hand, the chair grew to accommodate her tall frame. She settled effortlessly into it, even that simple action looking like a dance.

Remy helped move her chair in and sat across from her. She looked at him and the tea inquisitively, so he poured a glass for them both. With a delicate hand, she picked it up and brought it to her mouth. Rather than drink though, a long white tongue extended past her lips, and she lapped some of the tea from the top of the glass. A look of surprised delight crossed her face. She finally raised it to her mouth and took a full drink.

A strange sound emanated from her chest, half purr and half the trill of a bird. "Thank you," her voice chimed. Her words had the faintest of echoes even though she sat right across from him. "Few Beings of Power show respect and consideration for any creature other than themselves. Such efforts do not go unnoticed. You may call me Sariel. I am an Ethereal."

Your polite invitation and welcome has impressed **Sariel** and distinguished you from other "Beings of Power." You have gained **+300 Relationship Points**. Total Relationship Points with Sariel: +300

Congratulations! Your relationship with **Sariel** has improved from **Neutral (0)** to Pleased (+250). "I am pleased to see you."

Despite his decision to just "roll with it," the appearance of an eight-foot-tall alien supermodel had definitely thrown Remy off his game. He just stared back for a few seconds before shaking himself slightly and coming back to the moment. He collected himself enough to say, "Pleasure to make your acquaintance." He leaned forward and extended his hand.

Sariel smiled faintly, amused at the quaintness of his human custom, but still extended her hand as well. As he took it in his own, he marveled at the smooth coolness of her skin, like whipped cream fresh out of the fridge. After they had both settled back into their chairs, he started to introduce himself, but she held up a hand.

"I am-"

"You should never speak your True Name again. Those with enough power and the proper magics could use that information to cause you great harm. You will need to choose a new name to be called by." She paused a moment and took another sip of tea.

She made the same trill-purr noise and closed her anime-large eyes in pleasure before speaking again, "You should know that I was not required to tell you to guard your True Name, but you, and this marvelous drink from your memory, have pleased me.

> You have been provided extra knowledge due to having reached Relationship Rank 1, **Pleased**, with Sariel.

Remy thought over what she had said. The whole "True Name" thing sounded strange, but only when you didn't take into account that you'd just been reborn and were talking to the opera singer from the 5th Element. He decided to take her advice about keeping his name close to his chest.

He also sent a silent thank you to Granny for teaching him the secret of true sweet tea. Anyone that thought you just added sugar was failing an intelligence test as far as he was concerned. He was also grateful that he'd taken the time to greet Sariel properly. In any world, knowledge was power.

He'd become familiar with the importance of "relationships" since Earth had been connected to the Labyrinth. In his opinion, this had been one of the weirdest things that had happened: being informed of when people did or did not like you. Reaching certain relationship levels also triggered certain events or behaviors. It was almost like a self-reinforcing prophecy. Having a *pleased* rank relationship with Sariel meant she was actually pleased to see him.

Of course, you couldn't follow the rankings blindly. It didn't tell you about a person's character. It was just an indication of how people felt about you. Even if you reached a "Friendship" level with someone, if that person was a no-good, untrustworthy bastard, they'd be the type of person to betray you no matter what relationship rank you reached. That phrase, "he'd sell out his own mama" was actually true for some people, so a relationship rank did not mean you were safe from treachery. Everyone had their own nature, after all.

The men and women he'd led to the bunker had reached the eighth relationship rank with him, *Trusted*. That was why they had followed his directions almost without question. His mood darkened somewhat at remembering how many of the people who had trusted him had died, but the feeling quickly passed. Those men and women were just the latest in a long line of bodies he'd left behind.

Remy turned his attention back to his new life. Namely, that his improved relationship with Sariel had already shown dividends. She had shared info that she normally wouldn't have. Information was worth more than gold.

Seeing as how sweet tea and a smile had earned him some points, he figured he might as well really pour it on. After all, you can never have too much butter on bread. At least, that was what his uncle always said.

"Thank you very much for the information, miss," he responded with a pleasant tone. "I will wait a bit before deciding on a new name if that's alright."

She gracefully nodded her head, "Of course. Part of my purpose is to tell you of your new world and to provide you with the opportunity to ask questions. I make no guarantees that I can or will answer, however. Knowing that, do you have any questions before we begin?"

CHAPTER 3

Remy did indeed. Without preamble he asked, "What is a Being of Power and why do you think I'm one?"

She nodded again, expecting the question, "Let me say first, you are no longer human. Or perhaps, it would be more accurate to say that you are no longer only human. You have been altered to occupy a higher State of Being. At the moment of your death on your home planet, your spirit was captured. After that, I do not know all that occurred, but I do know you have been implanted with a Seed of Power. This can trigger any number of possible evolutions, but it has turned you into a god."

Going to put a pin in that, he thought. Let's stay on topic. "What happened to my body?" Remy asked.

"Left to rot, I would assume," Sariel said offhandedly. This matter was obviously of no consequence insofar as she was concerned.

She might have been able to brush it off, but that simple statement made Remy's head spin. Part of him had still been thinking that maybe this was some sort of strange firing of synapses at the moment of his death. That this was just a time-dilated dream.

No.

He'd actually died, and his body had been eaten by the cats. He took a deep breath, then shrugged. He'd never understood the point of worrying. *I died, but now I'm alive again, sort of. Might as well embrace my new reality.* So he asked another question, "Who brought me here then? Who 'altered' me to a 'higher state of being'?"

"Do you not remember?" she asked carefully.

Remy furrowed his brows. *Had there been a giant face? A giant-* Even that wisp of memory faded away. "No," he replied, shaking his head. He knew that something had happened after he'd died and before he'd come here, but he couldn't recall it now for the life of him.

"Then you are not meant to have that knowledge," she told him definitively, a firm look on her aquamarine face. "Suffice it to say that you have been given another chance at life. Most importantly, you have been provided this opportunity with your consciousness intact.

"The souls of humans are only quasi-eternal. If you had not ascended, your spirit would have continued on in some fashion after your death on Earth. The specifics of 'who' you are, however, would have been lost. It is rare, especially on a mana-void world such as yours, to maintain your consciousness after death. The power that sent you here must have taken special care to preserve your personality."

Sariel looked at him pointedly, until Remy responded, "So I should be grateful to whoever brought me here?" Before she could answer he continued, "I have learned not to put my faith in hidden organizations." She started to frown, but then he added, "I have also learned to trust my instincts, however. No matter what group is behind my resurrection or whatever it is, I am grateful for your help, Sariel."

The Ethereal's face softened. She considered her words before speaking, "The unique powers and sensitivities of my race make us ideal for facilitating encounters such as this. I will not discuss such matters in detail, but I will share that I have met countless beings from millions of worlds. Few would be able to suffer the extreme trauma that death can inflict and still have the inner strength to remain true to who they are. Most beg, threaten or simply become unresponsive, unable to process their new reality." She paused, gazing at him intently, "Seeing your strength, I can understand why you were chosen."

> Your ability to bravely face the truth of your life after death has distinguished you from the masses. This has once again increased your relationship with Sariel. You have gained +**450 Relationship Points**.
>
> Total Relationship Points with Sariel: +750
>
> ---
>
> Congratulations! Your relationship with **Sariel** has improved from Pleased (+250) to Kind (+500). "It is my pleasure to help you!"

Remy was somewhat taken aback. He hadn't been trying to sway her one way or another. It was especially strange because he knew that his emotions were being artificially suppressed. Was this a coincidence, or could the beings that sent him here possibly have foreseen this?

He was about to say something, but she suddenly waved her hand. A series of glyphs appeared in the air. They looked like a mix between Chinese characters and the digital numbers that appeared on calculators. After a moment, she waved her hand again and they disappeared.

"We do not have much more time," she told him. "From what I understand, the majority of the people of your planet believe in one omnipotent and omniscient being that created the Universe. You call this being God. Though you have ascended to a higher State of Being and have evolved, you are nowhere near that state of existence. You are the lowest evolution of a godlike being, *A Spirit Made Flesh*."

He nodded for her to go on.

"All gods have a nonphysical organ called a Divine Core. It will give you great power, but will not keep you safe, especially on this new world. Unlike Earth, Telos is not mana-void."

"Mana?" he asked. "You mean magic?"

The Ethereal heard the confusion in his voice. She stopped speaking for a moment, searching for the right words to explain it in a way that he could understand. "On your world you understand the concepts of magnetism and electricity, correct?"

After he nodded, she continued, "As a loose analogy, there exists a similar relationship between mana and magic. Magnetic fields, properly manipulated, can be used to generate electricity. Mana is similarly a natural phenomenon. Through various processes, it can be converted into magic. The reason no one on your world had been able to cast spells before the Labyrinth connected to it was not because they lacked ability, but because the mana levels of your world were so low that their bodies couldn't use magic. Do you understand?"

Remy nodded slowly.

"The more mana a being can safely absorb, the stronger they become. They can increase in levels, gaining attributes and other points. They can increase in rank, something akin to what you call evolution. They can even increase in tiers, completely strengthening their State of Being."

Seeing his confused expression, she spoke in an assuring voice, "This will all become clear. For now, what you need to know is that Telos has recently connected to the Labyrinth. Which means-"

"Which means," Remy interrupted grimly, remembering Earth, "there will be monsters."

"And they will become stronger as time goes on and more mana flows from the Labyrinth into Telos. If you do not grow your strength as well, you will be consumed."

The gravity of that moment dragged out for long seconds before Remy asked, "Why did you call Earth a 'mana void'?"

Sariel coughed delicately, "There actually isn't a true classification for planets such as yours. Mana void is a commonly used term. They are also called 'Nulls' or," she coughed again, "'sad deserts.' They all refer to areas that are so starved of mana that creatures within them have their growth and development stunted."

"I was 'stunted.'" Remy repeated slowly.

"Not just you," Sariel chimed in quickly. From her tone, you could tell she was trying to help, albeit failing miserably, "Your whole race and every living thing on your planet. In fact, even the rocks and minerals of your planet were mana-retarded."

"Hmmm. Mhm. Mhmm." Remy made a few neutral noises while nodding too fast and processing her words. Sariel had basically just said that the entire Earth was so lacking in mana that they had all grown up bowlegged and nearsighted.

Seeing his distraught expression, Sariel tried to cheer him up again, "You should actually be quite proud. Mana-retarded environments typically do not allow beings to advance to your level of civilization. The low energy nearly always leads to a lack of connection to the environments such beings dwell in. That in turn leads to what is typically viewed as a deviant and self-destructive behavior. That trait can make the denizens of such environments turn on their own families, let alone society at large. The few civilizations that do manage to survive and thrive in such atmospheres are classically so wantonly cruel and vicious that they are viewed as an infectious threat to other civilizations. As such, they are typically quarantined and sterilized."

Remy blinked, trying to process what she'd just said.

"You, however, seem very nice and respectful," she concluded with a bright smile. "If you are in any way representative of humans on your planet, then it seems your people beat the odds and survived without turning horribly cruel!"

Remy stared at her incredulously. The accurate and woefully predictive description she had for human history notwithstanding, he wasn't about to admit that he was indeed from a society that fit her description. No matter how he felt about Earth, he certainly wasn't about to tell a cosmic being that his former home should be "quarantined."

"Just as on Earth," Sariel continued, "your new world will change quickly now that it has been connected to the Labyrinth. Connecting always causes an influx of mana. Monsters and beasts native to the world will rapidly absorb it. Their levels and ranks will increase. The connection will also cause cracks in the skin of reality, allowing monsters foreign to the world to force their way in. Given enough time, even higher tiered beings will appear. Your path will indeed be fraught with danger, but," she said pointedly, raising one finger into the air, "all is not lost."

"Unlike Earth, Telos is not a Null Planet. Though its mana levels have been low for millennia, it never fell to the depths of Earth. You, and the tribe you shall lead, will begin as Tier 0, Rank 0, Level 0 beings. The same shall be true of any enemies you encounter, and there shall be an even playing field, at least at first. I have not told you all of this to discourage you, but to encourage you. You must solidify your position quickly and never stop pursuing your power."

"And how do I get more power?"

"I cannot tell you specifically, but you must never forget: a god is always tied to his followers. You must advance not only your own power but that of your people. It will be a balancing act, to increase both their power and your own. For even if you master whatever lands you settle in, if you remain a Tier 0 god, any Tier 2 or 3 being could render everything you hold dear to ash with just a snap of their fingers."

Fighting on Earth had left a deep impression on Remy. He knew full well the hopelessness of struggling against a strong monster.

"Would I really be that helpless against a higher tiered monster?"

"There are no absolutes," Sariel told him with a smile. "It's the application of power that matters."

"That's something I can understand," Remy said with a nod. "Of course, applying power requires a certain amount of intelligence and common sense, two things that I've never been able to take for granted in others. I've often wondered how humanity didn't die out early. It seems like people have at best a fifty-fifty chance to make a smart decision."

"Forty-two," Sariel corrected definitively.

"What?"

"Forty-two," she repeated. "Sapient beings only have a forty-two percent chance of making the right choice at any given moment. That particular question has been definitively answered."

"Bu-. Bu-," Remy tried to speak several times, but his mind was imploding with connections. "Are you saying…"

"We don't have much more time. Heed my warning and increase your power quickly. You have leveled on Earth, so you understand the concept. You must not ignore your cultivation, however. This is how you progress your tier. Your first steps on that journey are called the Rainbow Path. It will require a great deal of time, but it must be done."

"How long?" he asked.

"It could take a year or more to progress to the first tier."

"I thought I was supposed to get strong as fast as possible. A year doesn't sound fast. Isn't there a better way?"

Sariel developed a coy smile, "It is good that you asked. I have always thought that those who do not seek the light of knowledge are doomed to die in the darkness of ignorance." Her voice carried the hint of ritual, "As the worthy seek knowledge, so shall it be shared. There is indeed a faster way. On the day you claim your Chosen, a one-time price can be paid to take the first step on the Rainbow Path."

After she finished speaking a prompt appeared.

> You have been provided extra knowledge due to having reached Relationship Rank 2, **Kind**, with Sariel.

> **You have unlocked Secret Knowledge:** A god who can inspire dedicated belief within a tenday of his arrival on Telos need only speak the words "The worthy shall know" to take the first step down the Rainbow Path.

Relationship status for the win again. He was happy it was continuing to pay off, but he didn't really understand it. Asking for clarification just earned him a mysterious smile. Changing tacks, he asked, "Are there any other shortcuts I should know about?"

She actually laughed this time, "I am positive that there are many 'shortcuts,' as you put it." Her mocking gaze made it clear she wouldn't be offering up information that easily, however, especially not after already giving him a leg up.

Remy shrugged unashamedly. Like his daddy said when he turned twelve, 'Later in life you never remembered the times you looked foolish, but you always remembered the pussy you let get away.' Put another way, shoot your shot and don't get worked up if you got a 'No.'

She waved her hand and the ubiquitous soft light in the room darkened. Between them the image of a solar system appeared. It was a yellow sun, and only one planet circled it. Except for the strange configuration of the continents, and the off-color blue of the water, it looked a great deal like Earth. White clouds floated lazily across the blue and green marble.

At first Remy thought there were countless moons circling it, but then he realized that what he was seeing looked more like motes of light. Also, while the planet was circling the sun and clouds were flowing across its surface, the motes remained in fixed points relative to the planet, like they were satellites in geosynchronous orbit.

"What are these?" Remy asked.

"These are connection points to the Lattice." Sariel waved her hand again, and Remy's breath caught, looking at the beauty of what she had just revealed.

A glistening, crystal-like web appeared around the solar system. It wasn't flat, but instead radiated out in all directions. At each of the connections points of the web hung another solar system. In each, there might have been one planet or many, but one or more of the spheres in each system had the same glistening motes of light that he'd seen on Telos. Motes that he now knew were the ends of the strands that connected each world to the next.

Remy started trying to trace the connections, but Sariel waved her hand once more. The cosmic projection disappeared and the light in the room raised to previous levels, "You are not allowed to know the specifics of the Lattice. You may be told, however, that the worlds of the Lattice are as varied as your dreams and nightmares. You may be told that each will pose different challenges, that they all possess untold power." She looked at him meaningfully in a way he had come to know meant there was more to say about that topic.

50

Sariel even cocked her head and looked at him from the corner of her eye. The message was simple: Get on with it, guy!

"Oh, right. Um, is there anything else I should know about these challenges, or, um, the Lattice?"

Sariel rolled her large beautiful blue eyes at that weak-ass attempt to learn more, but still responded with the formulaic response, "As the worthy seek knowledge, so shall it be shared. The solutions to problems on a specific world of the Lattice may not be found on that world. Do not be afraid to explore. Whoever controls the Lattice would be able to wield great and terrible power. They might just have the ability to decide the fate of us all." Her words were almost apocalyptic in gravity. The two of them shared eye contact for several intense moments. The serious vibe quickly fled when she added, "You're lucky I like you."

> You have been provided extra knowledge due to having reached
> Relationship Rank 2, **Kind**, with Sariel.

"The Lattice is the home of powerful beings, magics and items. If you wish to survive and prosper as a god, you will need to enter this realm and garner power as quickly as you can. I assure you, other gods, demons and even more exotic beings of power will be doing the same. If you do not move quickly, you will not be able to match their power."

Why was this sounding more and more like he was about to be in a battle royale... with gods and demons? Remy asked the logical question, "How do I get into the Lattice?"

"That will be made clear in time," she responded cryptically. The Ethereal had been fairly forthcoming on other topics, so Remy was fairly sure her answer had been purposeful. Trying to gain more information on this particular point would be a waste of time.

Sariel was going to speak again, but the light in their nondescript room increased momentarily before shifting back to normal. It only happened once, but it was enough to trigger the next phase of Remy's life. The Ethereal looked around, "The time of Choosing is almost upon us. Our time here is coming to an end."

The Ethereal held up one graceful blue hand like she was holding a platter. She spoke a word of power and a ring of mystic symbols encircled her fingers. In the blink of an eye, a black lacquered chest appeared on her upturned hand. It looked heavy, about the size of a large suitcase, but she bore the burden with ease. Dark grey swirls appeared and disappeared on its surface while Remy watched.

"Each new god and being of power will be sent to Telos with nothing more than a set of clothes appropriate to their new form. That has been decreed and decided by the cosmic forces. Some fortunate gods, however, have been...," she stopped, looking for the right word, "sponsored. Sponsors provide extra information and benefits. You have a sponsor and they have made two arrangements to help you, the first of which is the time we have spent together." A wry smile grew on her face. "I hope you have found it useful."

"The second," she continued, "is the contents of this chest."

Remy accepted it from her. The swirling box was slightly warm to the touch. It also felt like it weighed over a hundred pounds. He looked at Sariel's deceptively frail form and realized just how much power it must contain if she had held the chest so casually with one

52

hand. He was obviously curious about what was inside, but there was another answer he wanted more, "Who is my sponsor?"

Sariel paused as if she was listening to something he couldn't hear, "I am not allowed to share that information with you if you do not already have such knowledge."

"Why not?"

"Like every being in existence, no matter how powerful, I have laws I must abide by, and I would suffer consequences if I were to break those rules." She smiled wryly, "I like you, but not that much, young immortal."

> You have been **denied** extra knowledge due to your relationship with Sariel being of insufficient level.

Remy realized he had stumbled onto a semi-taboo subject. For a moment, he considered trying to increase his relationship with Sariel. The only problem was there wasn't much time left. The Ethereal did give him some information without any further prompting.

"What you *can* know is that a great price was paid to furnish you with the contents of this chest. Even paying for my time was a small price in comparison."

"How great a price?" he asked.

"You cannot measure such things in terms of currency. The best way for you to understand is that the energy sacrificed to provide these items would, at a minimum, be enough to destroy a sun. Whatever the contents are, I suggest you pay close attention to them, but please remember that nothing material can be taken with you into Telos. If you are found attempting to do so, the consequences will be severe."

Remy looked at her, nonplussed. What exactly did "severe" mean? He probably didn't want to find out. It couldn't be great if he was dealing with beings that could destroy a damn sun. Before he could formulate a response, she stood up.

"Part of the arrangements made by your patron were that you be provided privacy while opening the chest. I will return prior to the Choosing."

He stood as well, struggling a bit with the heavy weight of the chest. Setting it on the chair, he extended a hand. He spoke simply but with sincerity, "I don't know a lot about what's happening here, but I've been given another chance at life. Thank you for helping to make the transition easier, Sariel. I appreciate it."

She smiled at him fondly. Hesitating for just a bit, she finally asked a question. "This new world will let you be whomever you choose to be. You can be a savior, a killer, a thief, or an emperor. What are you going to do in your new world?"

Remy looked at her, not sure how to respond. His entire past life had been a struggle between wanting to save the world and needing to indulge the anger inside him. It was why he'd done such terrible things in the name of "the greater good" and why he tried to save lives afterward. He'd always sought a balance he'd never obtained.

Sariel saw his struggle to answer and let it go. With a final smile, her body became insubstantial until she faded from view completely. Forgetting her question, he found himself smiling as well.

Lady knows how to make an exit.

Remy turned his attention back to the chest. Placing his hand on the lid, the random swirls of grey energy solidified into three distinct letters: "SGS." Remy paused, his heart beating a bit faster. That message was one that had literally been beaten into him from an early age. Nodding, he pushed forward, regardless of the warning he'd just received.

Opening the chest, there were five items inside sitting on a bed of velvet fabric. The first was a simple drawing. It was scrawled on run-of-the-mill printing paper and drawn in simple black ink. It looked like a starscape with three moons in the sky. Clouds occluded part of the view. In the center of the three moons an orange comet had been drawn.

The viewpoint seemed to be that of someone staring up at a night sky. Underneath was a simple word, "Jump."

There were two more lines of text under that. The second said, "Yes, really!" Then a third line that said in all capital letters, "JUMP OR DIE, BITCH!"

Remy turned it over, but there was nothing else. He even summoned a light and held it against the glare, looking for a secret message. Nothing.

Hmmm.

Didn't really seem 'destroy a sun' worthy. Just seemed weird. Remy looked at the paper closely, turning it over in his hands, but there was nothing on the other side. He couldn't detect anything else about it. Even smelling it revealed nothing. He put the inane object to the side.

The second item was a sphere about the size of a tennis ball. It was made of a bright red metal, the color of a cardinal. The whole surface was covered in runes or some type of script. The engravings glowed a soft orange. Picking it up, a prompt appeared in his vision.

You have found a **Quest Orb**

Another prompt came right after. This time, the lettering looked as if it was handwritten.

PS – Sorry about the pain. Unavoidable side effect of smuggling this quest to you.

Pain?

Before he could do anything else, the light from the script flared and another window appeared. Right after, an ice pick stabbed into his mind with a pain so intense that he almost blacked out. It took several seconds for the sensation to pass, and until then he couldn't even think about focusing on the prompt. When he did though, he read it twice, especially the threat at the end.

WTF!

CHAPTER 4

You have been offered a Quest: **Ruined Temple**

Quest Rank: **Not Gradable (Special)**

The Cosmic Forces that have given you a new life have arranged for you to have this quest. It is always your choice whether to accept it or not. There are many hidden locations of great power in your new world of Telos. One of the most important to a god is a temple. Follow the directions that will be provided to find a ruined temple. Once there, remove any threats.

If this Quest is accepted, you shall be shown the way.

Success Conditions: Find the remains of a specific ruined temple and remove any threats.

Rewards:

A home for your new tribe.

Penalty for failure or refusal of Quest: The generation of this Quest was not *strictly* within the guidelines agreed upon by the various Cosmic Forces that conspired to seed this new Labyrinth world. If this Quest is rejected, claimed and failed, or completed by another, this *flexible* interpretation of the rules could lead to serious consequences for your sponsor.

Also, your soul will be torn into 100,000 ragged pieces and cast to drift in the formless expanse for all eternity.

There is also a possibility that if this Quest is not accepted, the Quest Orb will be discovered and you will *immediately* be torn into 100,000,000,000 ragged pieces, each possessing enough consciousness to scream.

Do you accept? Yes or No

Back on Earth, there had been a few quests picked up by people he'd met. They had usually offered experience or maybe a clue toward finding more survivors of the Forsaking. Failing those quests had also had a corresponding consequence. He had never, in his worst nightmares, imagined that there would be a consequence as bad as "torn into 100,000,000,000 ragged pieces and cast to drift in the formless expanse for all eternity." What did that even mean?

Remy obviously understood the words, but was that a literal possibility? As many difficult things as he had been through in his life, including his death, he just couldn't wrap his head around what that would actually be like. All he knew for certain was that he didn't want any part of it.

As he read it again, he was struck with another certainty. Whoever had made this Quest Orb was a dick. The prompt made a big deal about how it was his choice to accept or not, but then it said that the "soul tearing" would happen if he failed *or* said no. Not really an actual choice, now was it? That wasn't even mentioning the mind-splitting pain he'd gone through when the quest had been shoved inside his head.

He also didn't like how the penalty had been worded. The real concern seemed to be with his sponsor getting in trouble. Remy was sure that a cosmic yellow card for unsportsmanlike conduct would probably be troublesome, but not compared to his own soul being shredded.

Remy gritted his teeth. He didn't doubt that there would be advantages to having a sponsor. That didn't change a fundamental fact about his nature. If there was one thing he hated above all others, it was being forced to do something.

Whether he hated being pigeonholed or not, he wasn't a child. Of all the options of life after death, he was also 100% certain that being soul-shredded in the "formless expanse" didn't sound like a good time. That was why, still hating the fact that he'd been manipulated, he chose "Yes" on the quest prompt.

The orb in his hands flared with an intense orange light. The script began to flow from the sphere into his arm. There was no pain this time, thank god, just a strange tingling. After it had flowed up his arm, it crossed over to the center of his chest and sank into his skin. A sense of weight and obligation settled into him. It was similar to the one time he had accepted a quest on Earth, but thousands of times more profound. The orb itself crumbled to dust. Even that disappeared as it fell from his hand.

Shaking his head, Remy turned to the third and fourth items in the box. They were small leather books. The cover of the first was embossed with a picture he'd seen before on Earth. It was a man in the lotus position with a string of circles going up the middle. He wasn't fully familiar with it, Eastern philosophy having never really been his strong suit, but he was pretty sure the circles were supposed to be meridians. When he picked it up, a notification window appeared.

You have found: Basic Cultivation Technique of Gods and Clergy

Technique Rank: Common

Requirements: Divine Core or Clergy Class

This book will impart the basic cultivation technique for gods and their disciples. Practicing this technique will improve your State of Being. This will only aid you until you reach Tier 1. To progress beyond Tier 1, you will need to find another cultivation technique.

Special Benefit: This technique is ubiquitous among deities of the Labyrinth. As with all faith-based cultivation techniques, it has no bottleneck.

Do you wish to absorb this knowledge? Yes or No?

This had to be one of the ways to advance his Tier that Sariel had mentioned. Of course, this whole scenario seemed like a bad acid trip. That didn't mean he didn't want more information. Any knowledge vs none was always an easy choice. He chose "Yes."

The book slowly faded from view. Left in its place was a constellation of glowing motes of light. These twinkling stars flew into his eyes. Remy's pupils dilated as the information flew into his mind. He *knew*!

Not only did he fully understand what "cultivation" was now, he also knew how to do it. Basically, he could use the faith people had in him to grow stronger. In a very real way, the more people worshipped him, the stronger he would get. At least until he reached Tier 1.

He also now knew just what a major milestone tiers were. The warning Sariel had given him about growing as fast as possible made more sense now. He didn't know exactly how it would manifest, but he knew in his bones that gods who cultivated faster would gain major boosts in power. A Tier 1 deity would experience a qualitative and quantitative increase. If he had to fight a god with a higher tier than his own… it wouldn't be good.

As fascinating as this new knowledge was, it was useless at the moment. He didn't have any worshippers. No worshippers meant no Faith for him to use, which made the cultivation technique a nonissue for the time being.

Still, after having gained so much from the first book, he couldn't wait to gain the knowledge of the second. This one was bound in black leather as opposed to brown. It had a stylized eye on the cover.

You have found: Soul Consumption Cultivation Technique

Technique Rank: Scarce

Requirements: Divine Core or Clergy. Must follow the Soul Art.

This book will teach deities who follow the Art of the Soul how to cultivate using captured souls. Souls used in this manner will be completely consumed.

This technique will currently only progress you to Tier 1, but has the potential to be improved.

This technique has a small chance to impart special benefits depending on the souls absorbed. Do you wish to absorb this knowledge? Yes or No?

Note from your Sponsor: This technique is not exactly what you would call "street legal" so SGS protocol.

Remy shook his head again. The "note" at the end was in the same handwriting as the word "Jump" on the star picture. He chose "Yes" again and knowledge flowed into his eyes. After a short bit, he was able to fully understand the difference between the two cultivation techniques. In many ways *Soul Consumption* was superior. Unfortunately, just like *Basic Cultivation,* he didn't have the raw materials, this time captured souls, to put it into practice.

The last item was just a handwritten message in a style he was becoming familiar with.

We had to destroy a solar system to give you seven gifts, so pay attention. There is more at stake than you can possibly realize. We cannot directly affect events on your new world, we can only give you a head start on the others. For your own safety, you cannot know who "we" are. You were chosen for many reasons, not least of which is your mental aegis, though most people in your life would have called it your stubborn streak. You called it giving zero fucks. Because of this I am sure that the vagueness of this note is infuriating as hell to you. Let me just say...

Suck it up!

You died, we brought you back, and now you get to be a god. We even blew up a star to help you. Stop complaining! Appreciate the fact that we took the time to write these words to you. We had to grind a reasonably nice moon into dust just to gather the power required to write that part of the letter. The cost per word on this type of communication is insane.

Suffice it to say, the objects in this chest were determined to be innocuous enough to raise no flags among the other Cosmic Forces yet strong enough to give you a chance to rise above the pack. You can only take knowledge with you, not resources or currency. I am sure a small part of you realizes that we are cheating by giving you this advantage.

I am equally sure that a larger part of you does not care. What you need to know is that we are definitely not the only sponsor bending the rules. Other new gods will be given their own advantages. Some of these gods will be old gods from other worlds with alliances and pantheons to call upon. Do not piss off a pantheon member until you are strong enough to fight the entire group! Use the knowledge and power of these gifts well.

Our powers are vast, but we cannot influence what happens to you from this moment on. No power in the cosmos has that ability, so we cannot save you if you fuck up.

Finally, we cannot specifically tell you to break the rules of your new existence, or even bend them, but good gods, read between the lines! Do not discuss the contents of this chest with anyone. If you were to be caught cheating, ack, gwack, gak, soul dissolution, endless expanse for eternity... you get the idea.

When you are done reading this note, do what we did not tell you to do and put everything else into the chest and close the lid.

Never forget, S.G.S.

- Your Sponsor

The contents of the letter might be the craziest part of everything that was happening to him. The tone of it was even nuttier. Despite all that, whoever had penned it knew personal information about him. They knew exactly what to write to get him to fall in line. And that pissed him off more than anything. He hated being manipulated. Still, he wasn't the type to hem and haw either.

No matter what else, it seemed that his "sponsor" had done him a solid by giving him another chance at life. He was a big enough person to admit that. It didn't mean he would keep dancing to their tune if he didn't like the beat. And it didn't mean that he'd been given this chance out of the goodness of their little cosmic hearts. For now though, and for as long as their interests aligned, he would heed their advice.

Only two things gave him pause. One, there were only five items, so he had no idea where they were counting seven. Was the time with Sariel a gift? That would only be six though. He couldn't figure it out, so he put it at the back of his mind.

The other thing that gave him pause was just how personal the letter was. Even the threat at the end was custom-tailored for him. Almost no one else would understand it. If nothing else, that level of familiarity made him take their words seriously. As he set the note aside, he noticed a faint mark in the bottom right-hand corner. It was invisible looking right at the page, but it caught the light as he was putting it down. It was only a small sigil, looking like seven shining jewels. He didn't understand what it meant, but he filed it away for later.

That done, Remy put the note and the picture of the starscape back in the chest. The cultivation technique books and the Quest Orb had turned to dust, and even those small particles had disappeared. After closing the lid, the chest started vibrating wildly, shaking fast enough to leave an afterimage. A moment later, it shrank to the side of a pinpoint and disappeared. Along with it went any evidence that his sponsors had broken the rules.

Not seeing anything else useful he could be doing; he summoned his shiatsu chair again. Wondering what would happen, this time he summoned Alyson Hannigan circa Buffy years. He wasn't disappointed.

Time passed. Remy had fallen asleep, but woke when the ever-present lights began to flash. A soft chime accompanied them. Standing up, he saw that there was a disturbance in the floor. It looked like a section was bubbling. At first, he thought it might have become superheated somehow.

It turned out the floor wasn't actually boiling, it was just changing color, from milky white to crystal clear. The process picked up speed, the change occurring faster and faster until the entire surface became completely transparent. Remy felt a presence and looked up. While he'd been distracted, Sariel had reappeared and was sitting in her seat.

Remy looked askance at the Ethereal, but she remained seated calmly in her chair, regarding him with her voluminous eyes. After a moment, he decided to just accept that he was not in control and summoned a chair next to her.

Soon the entire room had turned transparent. All he saw was blackness beyond it, but then a point of light appeared. Then another, and another. He realized the lights were torches set in sconces. They not only illuminated the blackness, they also revealed a massive structure.

Remy saw what looked like an ancient coliseum. Torches of white flame dotted the circular top. In the center there was a deep dark that seemed to undulate. Remy leaned forward to get a better look.

Then he was falling.

The transparent room plunged toward the coliseum, the building growing huge in his eyes. If he didn't have such a strong mental reserve, he would have fallen out of his chair. He still cursed for good measure. The room slowed again, neither the acceleration nor the deceleration detectable. It alighted into one of the arched alcoves of the coliseum.

Remy looked around, and saw that the structure was bigger than he'd initially thought. Thousands, maybe even hundreds of thousands, of other alcoves mirrored his enclosed room. He couldn't be sure, because the structure his room rested in was so large that either end curved into darkness.

In every archway sat a sphere with a mirrored surface, at least on the lower levels of the coliseum. As he looked up, he saw that the upper levels had increasingly larger archways, all of which were empty. The ones approaching the top were so large he could not see their apexes. He could only see that there were seven of them.

Throughout the rapid descent, Sariel had stayed in her seat. Her body displayed perfect poise, and her expression was one of absolute calm. Her eyes danced merrily, however, betraying her amusement. She knew that Remy wasn't quite as composed as he appeared. The new god noticed her looking at his clenched fists. He relaxed his death grip and stared at her, daring her to make fun of him.

The amusement remained in her eyes, but she didn't rise to the bait. Instead, the Ethereal turned in her chair and gestured with a delicate hand toward the dark center of the coliseum. A light began to flicker, quickly growing into a swirling sphere that contained every color imaginable.

She spoke in a prophetic voice, "The time of Choosing has come."

CHAPTER 5

The sphere grew in size until it nearly filled the entire arena. Swaths of light flowed over its surface. Some disappeared as they were pulled closer to the center of the giant globe. Others appeared to take their place. As Remy watched, he thought he caught flashes of movement within the ribbons of color.

A human laughing.

A sharp-eared humanoid giving birth.

An asylum of loons all calmly eating.

A monster screaming as it was consumed by a larger creature.

The impressions came and went so fast that it was more like catching sight of something from the corner of your eye. By the time you focused on it, it was gone, but your mind reconstructed the image as best it could. You could never be sure of exactly what you'd seen.

A voice boomed through the coliseum.

"The Choosing will begin in 100 seconds!"

"What is this?" he asked, staring at the ever-enlarging sphere.

Sariel had expected the question, "There are many tribes in the world of Telos. Even more will be brought against their will to this world now that it has connected to the Labyrinth. This is always the way with newly linked planets. Each color on the globe in front of you is a different tribe. Are you able to discern anything about them?"

"Images," he replied after a moment.

"Good. What you are seeing are moments in time of a member of that tribe. Look closer, and see if you can feel anything else. Don't focus on any one color, but instead just try to relax your mind."

The counter dropped down to eighty. He didn't fully understand, but he tried to do as she'd asked. At first, he just kept seeing those half-captured glimpses, but after he just let them wash over him, the closest he could come to 'relaxing his mind,' he did feel something. Emotions, intentions, and personalities. His gaze somehow sunk deeper into the sphere. After a moment, he realized that the colors seemed richer and stronger the deeper he went. He delved even deeper until he felt a faint resistance. Curious, Remy pushed his mind forward. Just before he crossed the boundary, Sariel spoke with pity.

"Brace yourself," echoed her melodic voice. "There will be pain."

Before he could ponder what she meant, agony tore his mind apart. As opposed to the few images and sounds he had heard at first, his psyche was suddenly flooded with thousands... millions... of voices. Some cried out for help. Many roared in anger, asking for retribution or the strength to exact it. Some pleaded and others wailed. Even as he was nearly overwhelmed, he could still perceive that some of the voices disappeared. Some seemed to be snuffed out, but others felt as if he had just lost access to them. What that meant he had no idea. It was all he could do to even think under the sensory assault.

"Come back to me," Sariel commanded in a gentle voice. "Come back. You do not need to hear all of them. You do not need to hear them all." Her voice had the cadence of a mantra, as if she had spoken these same words to herself many times. "Focus on my voice, and on this moment."

She repeated that message over and over until Remy did indeed manage to pull his awareness back into himself. Gasping, he realized he'd fallen to his hands and knees.

"What the hell was that?" he demanded in a strangled voice. "Why didn't you warn me?"

At that moment, the fact that he was speaking to an eight-foot-tall supermodel of unknown powers didn't register. He was just an animal that had been wounded and it was all he could do not to physically lash out. The Ethereal wasn't bothered.

"What you heard were the prayers of millions of souls at once. You heard their secret desires and horrible wants."

"Those were prayers?" he spat. The impulses and desires that he'd felt made him feel dirty. Even he, who had seen and witnessed humanity at its lowest, was revolted by some of the things he had felt. The pure, unfiltered hatred and… and… *evil* of some of those thoughts made him recoil.

That was what had truly bothered him, he realized as he lay panting on the floor. The initial surge of voices had overwhelmed him, but as soon as he'd pulled his mind back, the pain had decreased to manageable levels. What was messing with him was that he'd always thought he'd seen the worst that humanity had to offer. Maybe he had, but it was clear now that he hadn't seen the worst that the Universe was capable of creating.

71

"Prayers, desires, petty wishes, it all amounts to the same thing," Sariel responded. "You reacted as all new gods do when exposed to the unfiltered demands of too many souls. It is why most gods close themselves off to such entreaties. It is simply too much, even for a higher tier being to process. The needs and wants of mortals are infinite, and no being can contain infinity."

His head was splitting, "Why did it get worse when I went deeper?"

"This sphere," she said gesturing, "is composed of the life force of every being on your new world. The deeper you went, the more concentrated the energy your mind had to swim through, which increased the pressure, and the danger. Immersing yourself more deeply, however, also gives you an increased chance of finding creatures with stronger life forces. The stronger the life force, the greater the potential and power of a race. The resistance you felt was the first major demarcation in energies. Typically, it would require at least a Tier 1 deity to withstand the mental and spiritual pressure on the other side of the boundary. That sudden increase in power is what threatened to fracture your mind."

"If you knew I couldn't handle prayers on a deeper level, then why didn't you warn me?" The counter reached forty-eight seconds.

"You may not understand, but it was a kindness. In a very short period of time, the Choosing will begin. Each alcove in this arena contains a god. They will all choose a tribe. Some tribes are more powerful than others initially, while others have greater potential. Some will perish in the first days of the new age. Others may rise to greatness."

Her expression remained sympathetic, "I imagine you were exposed to some truly horrific thoughts just now, were you not?"

Remy nodded. His jaw was still tight, but he managed to get back into his chair. "It wasn't just *what* they were thinking. It was… *how* they were thinking it. More than one prayed for the death of another, but that didn't bother me by itself. I've killed. Some men and women deserve it. I have even enjoyed killing. This… was different. The way some of the voices desired it was so intense, like a plant craving the sun, or a drowning man needing air."

As he said it, he realized *that* was the difference. While he had known men and women that had relished killing, some of the voices he'd heard almost instinctually sought it out. Like a baby for a nipple. Whoever, or whatever, those tribes were, they hungered not only for the joy of killing, but also for the pain it could bring to an individual or anyone that cared for that person. Humanity was cruel, vicious, even psychotic, but even a serial killer would think those voices needed a hug and serious therapy.

Sariel nodded her graceful blue neck in understanding, "I suspected as much. One of the reasons I wanted you to experience the thoughts of so many is that you need to know that you are not suited to every tribe.

"True good and evil do exist in the Universe, but you must also understand that some of what you term evil is simply so anathema to your existence that it feels 'evil' to you. Conversely, a god of true evil might feel the same if they examined a selfless soul that believed in placing the needs of others above their own. I understand this concept may be hard to grasp, but we simply do not have time to discuss it further."

Remy had indeed been meaning to ask her a question, but he saw that the counter had just reached thirty seconds. He wasn't one to hesitate or bemoan things that could not be changed. Instead of wasting time and energy, he just focused on what the Ethereal said next.

"At the time of Choosing, gods will be able to select one of the 'colors.' This will be your Chosen tribe. It is vitally important that you make the right choice."

Remy looked at the giant sphere. In any given moment there had to be hundreds of thousands of colors, and that was just the bit of surface he could see. How many colors were in the entire thing? Millions? Billions?

Sariel knew what he was thinking. "Once the Choosing begins, every god will begin grabbing tribes at once. It will be what your people call a 'free-for-all.' The Choosing only lasts 1,000 seconds. It is a contest that measures luck and judgement in equal measure. If you have not made a choice before time expires, you will be randomly assigned a tribe."

Sariel's voice grew deadly serious, "You must not let this happen! After what you just experienced, I believe you can imagine the consequences of being bound to the wrong type of people?"

Remy thought of the wanton hunger in some of those voices, and the joy that others had taken in suffering. He nodded, taking her warning seriously. The counter reached fifteen seconds.

"No matter which tribe you choose," she continued, "Never forget one simple truth. Followers need their god, but a god also needs their followers."

Remy nodded. That was a lesson he'd already learned in his past life. Just because people were generally unreliable didn't mean you could live your whole life without relying on anyone. Some things required other people. If you wanted to go fast, you traveled alone. If you wanted to go far, you traveled together.

"So how do I find the right tribe?" he asked.

Sariel shook her head. She turned away from him, her face serious as she stared at the sphere, "I am not allowed to give you that knowledge."

After a second though, she smirked slightly, "I imagine that a person who knows what not to choose might have an easier time making the right choice. In fact, someone who has experienced something horrible might even be able to find something wonderful. I have heard it said that wonder is the doorway to power." She looked at him meaningfully.

Remy looked at her in confusion, but then his eyes widened slightly. If he was right, then the pain he'd gone through a few seconds ago had indeed been a kindness. Hearing all of those prayers at once had almost ripped his mind apart, but if he was right, it had also been a crash course in Choosing a tribe. He reflected on the experience, and remembered that the "evil" feelings had been so strong, they overwhelmed the rest. Not every prayer had been horrible though. Some had been benign, even bland. And one had even felt... right?

He looked at the Ethereal with new understanding. She had hurt him, but he'd also learned something. All of his resentment drained away. After all, the price for growth was always love, pain, or both. She smiled at seeing understanding light up his eyes.

> You have been provided extra knowledge due to having reached Relationship Rank 2, **Kind**, with Sariel.

"Thank you, Sariel."

"There is one last thing that I have been paid to tell you. For now, the Labyrinth's connection to Telos is only strong enough to allow Tier 0 beings to enter. By the law of seven, 7,777,777 godlings will fight for survival. Once the mana levels of Telos grow strong enough, however, the connection will become stable enough for Tier 1 beings to descend, and you will have 777,777 new Tier 1 deities to contend with. Higher tiered beings that will be able to endure diving deeper into the sphere where stronger life forms reside."

She then deliberately looked at the alcoves above. He followed her gaze and saw hundreds of thousands of empty alcoves that grew larger in distinct stages. Empty alcoves that ended in seven mountain-sized arches that massively dwarfed the small recesses he and the other Tier 0 gods were in. His eyes widened as he took in the implications.

"Grow your power quickly, young godling, for time will not wait for you. I wish you well," she responded with a smile. As the counter ticked down to zero, she faded from view.

3, 2, 1...

The Time of Choosing has begun!

CHAPTER 6

The moment the counter reached zero, it was replaced by another counting down from 1,000. The coliseum exploded into ribbons of color that flew to the various alcoves. It was easy to see why Sariel had called it a race. The occupants of the many cubbies were grabbing tribes as quickly as they could, only to throw them back when they were found wanting. It was like speed dating on a cosmic level. Remy watched in astonishment. The interplay of colors was mesmerizing.

He wasn't distracted by the beauty of the Choosing, however. He was instead watching the various cubbies to gain more information. As far as he could see, most of the gods hidden in the alcoves were randomly grabbing colors as quickly as they could. Above it all, giant numbers written in orange flame counted down from 1,000.

Seeing the flurry of activity, Remy was tempted to just start grabbing colors as well. Sariel had said it was a race. As he watched, one of the formerly quiet alcoves grabbed a navy-blue ribbon. Not five seconds after that, the mirrored bubble disappeared. Remy's eyes narrowed. A tribe had been claimed.

Unlike the other alcoves though, whoever, or whatever, had been in that "room" had taken its time to choose a specific ribbon.

Once they had, they'd taken a small amount of time to confirm their choice, then they'd claimed the tribe.

Unlike the alcoves that were randomly grabbing colors as fast as possible, that one had taken its time to choose. That meant the god must have known what it was looking for before it summoned the color. The only way Remy could see to gain that kind of information though... he rolled his eyes. This was going to be awful.

Like Sariel had encouraged him to do, he reached out with his mind again. This time, he didn't just dive deep all at once. He extended his awareness gingerly. It took several seconds, but he started to hear the prayers of the tribes again. At that point he paused, not wanting to be overwhelmed. In front of him, the riot of colors continued, and more alcoves emptied. That meant more tribes were being claimed. While some of the rooms' occupants might be making bad choices, others were probably grabbing the cream of the crop. He couldn't afford to waste any more time.

Gritting his teeth, he forced his consciousness further into the sphere. He was once again bombarded with a myriad of voices. It almost overwhelmed him, but he was ready for it this time. As he searched, he kept observing the swathes of color, but none of them resonated.

Remy pushed down until he felt the resistance of the first layer again. Sariel had been clear that the deeper he went the more likely he was to find stronger tribes. His mind was being assaulted by all the various prayers, but now that he was intentionally avoiding the most abhorrent, it was much more manageable. With one eye on the countdown, he started searching for a color that felt "right."

Seconds passed and his mind sifted through the voices. He immediately rejected the prayers that were anathema to him. He never held on to any of them for more than a second, but each chipped away at his focus and sanity. It caused a constant, sharp pain, like staring into the sun, but he could manage it.

Now that his mind was able to ignore the tribes that absolutely didn't fit, he was able to pay more attention to the tribes that did. They still moved quickly, here and gone in a moment sometimes, but instead of just flashing images, he was able to gain a better sense of who and what the tribes were. This one was a set of humanoids that valued combat prowess. That one was fearful of the world around them and just wanted to hide. Another had members that only thought of amassing wealth.

Only a few of the tribes were made of humans and not all of them were even humanoid. As he continued to "read" the information, looking for a tribe he would resonate with, he became aware of something strange. There were some tribes that felt just as wrong to him as the abhorrent ones. He didn't have a disgusted or unsettled feeling when he came across them; in fact, in some ways they felt almost like the opposite of the ones he was excluding. Still, they just felt… absolute in their world views. With a slight frown on his face, he decided to exclude these as well.

The pressure on his mind increased, but the information he had to process was reduced as well. Lights continued to shoot around the coliseum. More alcoves made a choice, then disappeared. A desire to not miss out on a good tribe flared in Remy's breast again, but he forced it down. He was choosing a people to bond with in his new life, as insane as that sounded. It didn't seem like the kind of thing he'd get a second chance at or the type of choice he wanted to get wrong.

Remy kept searching through the colors until he felt what could best be called a resonance. It was the opposite of the abhorrent feeling he'd experienced before. Without hesitation, he pulled the thread toward him. It was a dark blood-orange color.

Tribe: Oomin	Race: Vampire

Characteristics
Cruel (Lvl 0): 1% Chance of causing Fear in battle (increases after winning successive battles)
Familial (Lvl 0): +1% Devotion

The Oomin are a race of living vampires. They were brought to Telos from the shadow planet Vaagur. While they will not be destroyed by direct sunlight, they will be seriously weakened by it. As such, the Oomin are nyctophiles and often live underground. The race are omnivores, but can grow much stronger by feeding on the blood of powerful creatures. Latent telepathic powers exist within the race.

Remy blinked. He didn't know what he was expecting, but it wasn't this. Sariel had hinted that he might feel an affinity for a tribe that fit his personality. As he stared at the dark orange, he still felt the same resonance, that innate sense of rightness, that had made him want to grab it initially.

He just hadn't expected to have so much in common with *Cruel* vampires. Remy had no illusions that he was a "good" man. He'd seen and done too much to think that such a person really existed. Which meant the *Cruel* part didn't bother him overly much. That was a compliment. Still, it was strange to see that he would bind well to a group of living dead.

That was only part of his reaction though. Another part, the part that had kept him alive when so many had died around him in the past, looked at the advantages of ruling over undead. Vampires that could live in the sun, albeit weakened, had serious potential. They could grow stronger by feeding on blood, but could still eat plants. It sounded like they had most of the strengths, and few of the weaknesses, vampires had in stories.

The last part of the prompt confused him. He could see it dealt with the tribe's characteristics, but what did that really mean? Focusing on it, he was awarded more information.

Characteristics – These are the traits which best typify the overall personality of a tribe. The first two Characteristics are provided, but more can be discovered or developed. It is even possible to change the fundamental nature of a tribe given enough time or a powerful event. The greater the Characteristics of a tribe are in sync with their deity, the more powerful the connection that can be established.

It seemed each tribe had unique qualities that could give them some special powers. It also seemed the reason he had resonated with the vampires was that their characteristics were in line with his own. *Cruel* and *Familial* were definitely parts of his personality. Looking at it from that perspective, it was easy to see why he'd been drawn to the tribe.

Not one to be indecisive, Remy decided to let the tribe return to the large sphere. He did feel a connection to the Oomin, but it was only a weak one. If his violent reaction to some of the tribes was any indication, then it was possible for him to feel a much stronger bond with other tribes. Sariel's hint was that the stronger the connection, the better for him. The new god continued scanning the roiling colors, the pressure on his mind increasing without stop.

Over the next several minutes, more alcoves went dark. Each empty recess meant that a color and tribe had been claimed. Despite that, the central sphere showed no signs of being diminished. With thousands, maybe tens of thousands, already claimed, it gave him some indication of just how many choices were available.

Remy grabbed another color, this one a dark green. The resonance he felt was about the same as the Oomin. This time the tribe was comprised of three-foot-tall humanoids. They looked like gnomes, or hobbits, but without the furry feet or smiling faces. Instead, the image he got was of them hiding in a forest at night, each clutching gnarled lengths of wood in one hand and a heavy rock in the other.

They weren't quivering in terror. They were eyeballing a squad of humans armed with wooden staffs or clubs. Neither group wore armor. One of the tribe hooted like a night owl. Without hesitation, every "hobbit" threw their rocks with unerring precision.

In the dark, it was almost impossible to react in time. The tribe may have been made up of shorties, but they had cannons for arms. The rocks struck arms, chests, and heads, breaking bones, freezing diaphragms or knocking their enemies unconscious. Just as silently, the small tribe rushed forward, clubs raised. It might sound ridiculous that a hobbit-sized folk would attack fully-grown human adults, but there was nothing funny about what came next. With merciless blows, the diminutive tribe bludgeoned the humans to death. Skulls were dented, skin split open and blood splashed across faces. It was easy to see why they had the Characteristics *Militaristic* and *Orderly*. The gnomes ruled the night.

Characteristics

Militaristic (Lvl 0): +5% Damage to attacks

Orderly (Lvl 0): +5% Success of Group Tactics

Despite the tribe's small stature, Remy was impressed. They had quickly overwhelmed a physically superior force. Being small wasn't always the worst thing. While they would be at a disadvantage in a stand-up fight, only a fool met an enemy head-on if they had a choice. The small tribe would have an advantage in sneak attacks.

Still, he let the color return. He decided to follow Sariel's covert advice and find a feeling that was as strong as the abhorrent ones he'd initially rejected. The only problem was that dozens of alcoves were going dark each second. If this was a race, he was losing, and so far, he'd only felt two resonances. The feeling wasn't easy to find. The colors in the sphere shifted so fast you could only react, not deliberate.

He only had a split second to grab each one after he felt a resonance. Between that, and the increasing stress on his mind, it was a difficult task that was only getting harder.

Time passed and the countdown passed the halfway mark. Five, then ten, then twenty colors came and went from Remy's alcove. With some the resonance was stronger than the first two tribes, but with others it was weaker. More alcoves darkened while he sorted through the colors. He still couldn't see the far side of the coliseum, but from what he could see, more than half the gods had chosen a tribe. He didn't let it distract him. In fact, the only time he paused was while reading the characteristics of a group of undead. The perk of *Necrophiliac* wasn't something even he could wrap his head around.

Through it all, the pressure on his mind increased. Each time he called a color to him, the pressure spiked. He came to understand that some of the alcoves probably went dark simply because the beings contained within just didn't have it in them to continue. Remy already knew that bonding with the sphere could overwhelm and incapacitate you. It was only the difficult life he had led which gave him the mental fortitude to continue.

Time continued to elapse, but he still hadn't found what he needed. There were less than one hundred seconds left on the count. With a hard sniff, he knew he was at a crossroads. He could stay where he was, or try to endure pushing past the first layer. It had nearly torn his mind apart last time, but this time he was prepared. In the last fifteen minutes, he'd learned a great deal about how to navigate the colors. His sponsors had said they'd chosen him for his high mental defenses. He had to hope this was why.

With a deeply felt *Fuck Me*, he pushed past the first layer.

The pressure on his psyche increased by more than a factor of ten in an instant. It was like he'd been walking through a forest during a heavy storm to suddenly find himself stripped of all protection. For nearly twenty seconds, he couldn't even think!

By the time he could think again, there were less than seventy-five seconds left. Nearly all the alcoves had gone dark. In his own mirrored room, his breath came hard and fast. His eyes were wide and unblinking while his mind was battered by pleas for help and wails of pain.

As fast as he could, he sifted through the different prayers. There was an immediate benefit to having crossed the threshold. The colors flowed past him much faster, increasing his chances of finding a tribe that resonated with him. It came at a cost, however, as each moment threatened to make him lose consciousness.

Before, the colors had chipped away at his consciousness. Now, it felt as if each one was like the blow of a heavy mallet. In a very real way, he felt that his resolve was a shield for his mind. One that was being deformed and knocked out of place every second. If not for his strong will, he would have succumbed. Still, it wasn't a question of if he could endure the assault, it was only a question of when he would collapse.

Remy sorted as fast as he could. Under the higher pressure, he made mistakes, grabbing prayers that were anathema to his sense of self. Each error cost him precious seconds as his mind recoiled. Each recoil threatened his focus and made it more likely for his mind to be completely overwhelmed.

It was only in the last ten seconds that he reached out for a color that resonated deep with him. He knew immediately that this was what he'd been looking for. The resonant feeling was so strong that it felt like a gravitational pull. The tribe's color was an impenetrable black. Not the black of night. The hue was richer, thicker, and had a golden sheen. As he stared at its luster, the word "sable" came to mind. As soon as he read the prompt, he knew why.

Tribe: Razin   **Race:** Pantherkin

<u>Characteristics</u>

1) **Industrious (Level 0):** +10% building speed and quality
2) **Curiosity (Level 0):** +5% to Research and chance to find interesting locations.

The Razin are a race of pantherkin, humanoids with beast-like qualities. They were brought to Telos from a lush planet, Ardendia. The Razin have a zest for life and a curiosity about the world around them that makes some consider them childlike. This could not be further from the truth, as any enemy soon finds out. In battle and war, they are ruthless to the point of sadism. Naturally agile, they make up for a slight stature with overall physical prowess.

Remy had learned a lot while browsing through the available tribes, and he'd seen many characteristics. *Warlike, Resolute, Tortured,*

Power Hungry, Fatalistic, and others. Each could apply to his personality. He'd even seen *Agrarian,* which had to be a throwback to a summer spent on a farm when he was nine, if it meant anything at all. It wasn't until he saw the razin though, that he saw the two descriptors that fit him best.

Through the several walks of his life, what had driven him was his curiosity. What would come next? What could he learn about himself if he pushed hard enough? How would he live with his choices? What new loves and enemies would tomorrow bring? It had led him to dark places, but his curiosity had also led him to some of the best moments of his first life.

Of course, those dark places might have been the end of him if not for another core component of his personality: ruthless. Whether it was an assault against an enemy or delivering tragic news to a patient's family, he had always done what needed to be done. He was not needlessly cruel. He took no joy in causing pain to innocent people. It was just that he believed when things needed to be done, it was best they were done quickly. Another, more polite way to say it might indeed be "industrious."

No other tribe had felt so right. Sariel had hinted that lifeforms past the barrier might be stronger, but he hadn't seen an appreciable difference since crossing. Maybe it was because he was at the very edge of the Tier 1 zone. Maybe there was something he just didn't understand about the tribes yet. He supposed only time would tell. Either way, he knew on a fundamental level that the razin were the tribe he had been struggling to find.

From the snapshot of life he could see, it appeared the tribe was in battle. That had been the case for most of the other tribes he had examined. Countless voices had called out for aid, but this time, Remy decided to answer.

His Choice made, and with barely any time left, the coliseum slowly began to fade from existence. The scene he could see in the swath of color grew more distinct. Remy was pulled closer to the voices he had chosen, that had chosen him. Trees, a blue sky, grass… and people. He could smell the thick scent of pines.

There were hundreds of people around him, and they were screaming. His ears filled with shouts and low-pitched roars. Cutting through the voices was a rage-filled screech. The scent of blood filled his nose and his knees bent instinctively as they landed firmly, but not roughly, on the ground.

A prompt filled his vision.

STAND AND WITNESS! An ending has come! A beginning is upon you! New powers are awake in the world of Telos. Beings of great power rise and descend. Fear the wrath of capricious gods.

This is a new Age!

The levels of all creatures on Telos have been set to zero. They will not remain so for long. Mana from the Labyrinth and a creature's own potential will rapidly increase their levels, ranks and even tiers.

In time, even the most powerful creatures of the Labyrinth may migrate to this world and come to call it home.

Grow your power quickly, godling, for the world of Telos will not wait!

THE **TIME of WARRING TRIBES** HAS ENDED!

THE **REAPING of GODS** HAS BEGUN!

A quest prompt had appeared as he traveled, a manifestation of the prayer he was answering.

You have gained a Prayer Quest: **Save Us I**

Difficulty: Common

Countless millions of souls call the world of Telos home. In this time of upheaval, nearly all of them call for aid. You have chosen to aid one tribe in particular. They can become your Chosen people! If you wish to gain their favor and worship, you must save them from the monster which seeks to destroy them!

Success Conditions: Remove the threat of the monster attacking your Chosen people and claim their allegiance before the next sunrise.

Rewards: The rewards of this quest are variable based on how many of the tribe you save. Current surviving members: **196/200**

Penalty for failure of Quest: Failing this quest will break the new connection between you and your Chosen people. The consequences of this can be far-reaching. Finding a new group to worship you is possible, but without a ready source of Faith Points, you risk dissolution of self.

This Quest cannot be refused!

Time until sunrise: 15 hours, 21 minutes, 19 seconds

His body fully materialized as he absorbed the information in the quest prompt. The moment he appeared, he was noticed by one of the razin. In a surprisingly deep voice, the pantherkin asked, "Who the hell are you?"

CHAPTER 7

Remington was about to respond, but a high-pitched screech stole his attention. The young god whipped his head to the left and got his first view of what his tribe was fighting. It had the body of a massive bear, but that was where normality ended. While its back haunches were covered in the brown fur of a grizzly, that pelt only extended halfway up its body. The front half was covered in dirty black feathers splotched with white. These extended backward from its eagle-like head. It had a yellow beak, but the color was barely visible. The monster's entire maw was covered in a thick coating of red-black blood.

A ridge of feathers outlined its forehead and two large beady black eyes glared malevolently at the tribe of pantherkin. Its hooked beak ended in a sharp point that it drove into the body of a shrieking razin. It had muscular legs, both front and back. Its extremities were shaped like a bear's, but no bear had ever had the scythe-like talons of the eaglebear. Jet black and nine inches long, they would pierce armor and flesh with ease. The eaglebear readily showed their power by using one to rip the impaled razin woman in half.

The monster was more than five feet at the shoulder, and as Remy watched it reared up on its back legs, doubling its height. The two halves of the razin woman fell to the ground in a bloody mess. The eaglebear screamed defiance at the men and women pointing crude wooden spears at it. The birdlike screech sounded strange coming from such a giant land animal. Strange or not, the menace it exuded, towering over them, was nothing short of terrifying.

That fear was almost palpable to the fighters that were engaging the beast. The pantherkin were not short; the adults looked to range between five and six feet. Even so, they truly did look like kittens attacking a doberman.

Worse, the only weapons they had were wooden spears. These weren't even formal weapons, instead looking like felled saplings, freshly carved. Basically, little better than sharpened sticks.

The god watched one warrioress jump toward the eaglebear with a bloodthirsty cry of her own. She had jumped off a small boulder to gain more altitude and put more force behind her strike. The woman, clad in simple furs, stabbed her spear down and hit the monster in the meat between its shoulder and neck. It was a perfectly executed strike. Upon feeling the weapon land, satisfaction bloomed in her heart. Her excitement lasted exactly one second. The emotions that followed in quick succession were shock, fear, horror, and then nothing.

The wooden spear penetrated the monster's body, drawing blood, but only just. The eaglebear's thick feathers served to slow the weapon down. Layered as they were, the plumes were as effective a defense as a leather jerkin. Despite her perfect strike, the monster only lost six points of health. Compared to the hundreds in its health pool, it was basically just a scratch. Even if the attack had done more damage, the makeshift spear snapped into splinters in the razin woman's hand.

The warrioress learned something in her last moments. It was a lesson that few warriors survived: never put your faith in a shoddy weapon. On impact, her spear's durability dropped to zero and threw her off balance. The feline warrior fell directly in front of the eaglebear; that was why she had felt shock. The terror followed right after.

With an angry screech, the monster raked its front claws across the woman's unarmored body. Its scythe-like natural weapons bit deep into her body and continued on horizontally. The three claws minced her into four parts. The top half of her body went flying, a pained expression on her face, while her legs dropped to the ground like the hacked and bloody stumps they were.

Her torso shot backward, and she was still screaming as her intestines unspooled in a stretchy red line. The top part of her body smacked into another cat warrior that had been preparing his own attack. The eaglebear's eyes followed the red line of viscera to its next victim.

The tribe was horrified after seeing her fate. The frozen expression of hopelessness on her dismembered corpse had a very real effect on some of the tribe. Red prompts flashed in the eyes of several of them.

*You are **Terrified**! Rational thought suspended for **2 minutes**!*

The pantherkin struck by the disembodied woman started running away in horror. Sadly, it didn't save him. Barreling forward, the beast caught up in just a few steps. It sank its cruel beak into

93

his shoulder. Red blood gushed over rich brown skin. A scream of hopeless agony issued from the man's throat as he was yanked off his feet. The eaglebear shook its head back and forth, the body flopping like a ragdoll, and it threw the man to the ground.

The monster didn't even look down as it slammed a paw into the wailing razin's ribcage. Three talons entered his chest, two piercing a lung and the third nicking the man's aorta. When the eaglebear lifted its leg, blood and flesh caked the bottom of its foot. Despite the gory mess, the horrified fighter was still not dead. He was able to take five more wet sucking breaths before his soul was ready to leave his body. Each short, panicked gasp decreased his field of vision and the light he could see. By the time darkness had fully claimed him, the monster had already reaped another life.

> **Quest Update Save Us I**: 183/200 Razin remaining

Remy watched the monster decimating his Chosen tribe. Seeing the slaughter, concern for his own safety fell away. Along with it went naïve concepts such as pity, remorse or honor. His arrival in this new world was close to the front lines, but pantherkin warriors still lay between him and the monster that threatened to wipe them from existence. For the moment, he wasn't in immediate danger.

Later, he would realize that he could have waited to act. He could have run away from the tribe and made his own way in this new world. His chances to live another day would definitely have been better if he could have let the slaughter continue. That was not who he was though, and that was not what went through his mind. There was an enemy in front of him. That enemy was going to die.

He cast about for a weapon, any weapon, and his eye landed on a softball-sized rock. As he reached for the stone, he caught sight of his hand for the first time. A shock ran through him. Instead of dark brown skin crisscrossed with faint scars, his hand was young. His skin was smooth and the color of milk chocolate. Sharp black nails tipped each of his fingers.

The surprise made him hesitate for a split-second, but only that long. A lifetime of making quick decisions, both when he took lives in battle and when he saved them in the hospital, had made him a definitive person. His hand closed around the rock and his gaze fell on the eaglebear again. In a move that was as stupid as the day was long, he raised his voice and shouted, "Hey, peckerface! This way!"

To punctuate his point, he threw the stone. As he did, he realized his new body was substantially weaker than his old human form. Still, he was able to lob the rock a good distance. It struck the large monster broadside. It caused zero damage against the eaglebear's feathers, but the message came across loud and clear.

Remy knew that there was no way the monster understood him. After his shout and paltry attack though, its head canted to one side and its beady eyes narrowed almost vindictively. A severed arm hung from its sharp beak. At its feet were two more bodies. Only one of them was still alive. That didn't make her luckier. She just made faint *burbling* sounds as each breath filled her lungs with blood. The monster paid no attention to its recent victims. Instead, the savaged limb dropped from its mouth and it screeched, rearing back on its hind legs again.

Then it landed and charged directly at him.

"Run!" he shouted to the pantherkin warriors around him.

He may never have seen something like the eaglebear before, but he had to imagine physics still worked in this new world. Standing in the path of several tons-worth of pissed off creature would only get him FUBARed. He followed his own advice and ran away.

The eaglebear's claws gouged large furrows in the ground, churning dirt and buried stones alike. Remy had spawned in a large clearing surrounded by forest. The clearing was made by a single large tree dominating the center of it. That was his destination. His only hope was to climb out of the eaglebear's reach.

Maybe some of the pantherkin tribe could escape while he had its attention. Sariel had been clear on the dire consequences of not having a tribe of followers. If all the razin were killed, he'd fail the quest. "Dissolution of self" only sounded slightly better than "cast to drift in the formless expanse for all eternity," the consequence for failing his sponsor's quest.

Remy's legs pumped like pistons. With a mental flexion, he accessed his status page, relieved that the process was the same as it had been on Earth. He pulled the information into him, becoming aware of every detail in an instant without having to read it. Hopefully something in there could save his new life.

????*	
Art: Soul	**Level:** 0
Energy: 605	**Cultivation:** Spirit Made Flesh (Tier 0/0)

STATS

Health: 90	Mana: 120 *Regen/min: 7.2*	Stamina: 99/100 *Regen/min: 6*

ATTRIBUTES

Strength: 8*	Agility: 15*	Dexterity: 15*
Constitution: 9*	Endurance: 10*	Intelligence: 12*
Wisdom: 15*	Charisma: 11*	Luck: 10*

RESISTANCES	WEAKNESSES
None	None

GOD ABILITIES

God's Eye: The sight of gods
Soul Capture: Capture the souls of defeated enemies

Most of what he saw made little or no sense. Why was his name just question marks? What was an "Art" and what was "Energy"? He knew at least what his cultivation was, thanks to his sponsor's gifts. Remy put those questions aside and focused on his attributes.

His Strength was lower than a level zero human's, but that was less important right now than his Agility and Dexterity. Higher Dexterity would be very helpful when he was dodging the hybrid creature's attacks. The truly important stat was his Agility though. It was what determined his movement speed. With a value of fifteen, he should be faster than the average human before the Forsaking.

Good Agility or not, Remy was pumping his legs as quickly as he could but still not moving nearly fast enough. The crashing sounds of the eaglebear's footfalls were coming closer, way *way* too quickly! Why aren't I moving faster, he thought desperately.

He looked down at his feet and realized something for the first time. He might have good attribute scores, but he was also short! A quick estimation looking down put his eyesight more than a foot closer to the ground than when he'd been a human. He was only four and a half feet tall!

Agility did increase movement speed, but only proportionally to a creature's baseline. Put another way, a six-foot-tall man with an Agility of twenty would run far faster than a child with the same stat. With his short stature, he was leaning way too close to the kid's table side of the spectrum.

With a curse he just tucked in and made his little legs pump faster. It helped at least that there were small claws at the tips of his toes. They seemed to work a bit like cleats. On the other hand, he was barefoot, which was already becoming a serious pain. Stepping on a small but dickishly sharp rock brought another curse to his lips.

A screech from the eaglebear forced him to do something he'd been trying to avoid. Remy looked behind him. The monster was close, barely twenty yards away! He had clearly underestimated the beast's speed. Thankfully, he had finally reached the destination of his frantic flight, the large tree that towered over the clearing. He had initially planned on having a much bigger lead on the slavering monster by the time he got to the trunk, but it was what it was.

Having nothing to lose, he jumped toward the tree, hoping against hope that maybe he could pull himself up before five tons of vicious monster slammed into him.

Remy leapt through the air and realized that he had made another miscalculation, but this time in his favor. His pantherkin legs jumped much higher and farther than he could have imagined. Rather than gaining a piddly one to two feet of height, he boom shakalaka'd four feet into the air! Put another way, he cleared his own height.

Unbidden, his claws extended out from his fingertips. During his run they'd retracted, but it was like his body knew what he needed to do. Without much difficulty, he latched onto the rough bark of the tree right before the eaglebear barreled through where he had been only a moment before. With no room to turn or stop, the monster continued forward for another four feet and slammed into the tree trunk with a hard *thock*.

The feathered behemoth had rammed its head into the hardwood and stunned itself for a few seconds. It hit hard enough to send major vibrations through the trunk. If the monster hadn't been disoriented, that would have been the end of his second life. Even with his claws, he was still a man holding onto the side of a tree with only his hands.

In any world, physics is a bitch. The pickup truck-sized monster sent more than enough force into the tree to shake him off. His loose grip failed him and he fell straight down onto the monster's back. As surreal as the entire situation was, the soldier in him wasn't one to waste an opportunity. He slammed his fist down into the back of the monster's neck, but he might as well have been punching a pillow filled with greasy feathers.

The monster's feathers effectively served the same function as armor. Even at its low level, it provided the monster with +3 to defense. With a real weapon he could have bypassed that defense, but barehanded, and with his low strength and small stature, he wasn't able to do any damage.

The eaglebear began to stir beneath him.

Ramming into the trunk hadn't caused it any real damage, and now its *Stun* debuff was wearing off. The roar of the now-aware monster showed that it took Remy's attack personally. It was starting to get back up on its feet when Remy recalled the words of an old drill sergeant, "Only losers run away... but pre-winners have no fear of a momentary tactical withdrawal."

That advice had always served him well so he promptly chose the one path that offered any hope of safety. Running in any direction meant certain death. Even if he made it to the forest, the eaglebear seemed perfectly suited to hunting him in this environment. He also already knew it was faster than him. No. Running would only result in the monster quickly changing Remy's status from *weird pantherman* to *monster snack.* That left only one option. Up!

Jumping for all he was worth, Remy landed back on the tree trunk even as the eaglebear turned to snap at him with its cruel beak. It almost got him. The beast's neck was able to twist nearly all the way around like a normal eagle's, but he cleared its back in the nick of time. His feline legs gave him extra ups again and he landed on the trunk, both his front and back claws digging into the bark.

This time he didn't satisfy himself with an unsteady perch. With his talons extended, he began to climb. He had been worried, as his Stamina was already down a quarter. During his sprint, his breath had been coming short and fast. Paradoxically, going up the tree was less physically taxing than running flat. His new body might be weaker than his human one, but it seemed perfectly suited for climbing.

As he ascended, Remy's mind jolted at the inanity of it all. He'd died and been brought back to life. He was on an alien planet. His new *clawed* body was climbing a tree to escape a hybrid bear-eagle monster. He might be the man who gave zero fucks, but this new world was trying to steal them.

An enraged screech from the monster snapped his mind back to the here and now. He could ponder over the craziness of his new reality later. Right now, he had simple goals. Namely, climbing and avoiding being turned into either crap or fewmets, depending on the physiology of the furious beast below. His body quickly ascended and he was able to reach the lowest branches of the tree, fifteen feet off the ground, in just a few seconds.

Remy pulled himself onto a branch and looked down. He was ready to climb again at a second's notice, but he figured it was worth taking a moment to reassess. The eaglebear had been confused for all of two seconds as to where he had gone, but Remy's frantic ascent hadn't exactly been stealthy.

Between the noise and the pieces of bark falling down on it the beast had found him soon enough. The eaglebear glared at its "tactically retreating" prey. It stood up on its hind legs, claws scratching furrows in the hard wood, but even at its ten-plus feet of height it couldn't get to him. The branch Remy was on was a good four to five feet higher than it could reach.

The new god's heart thudded in his chest and he couldn't help looking down at the enraged monster with a bit of smug satisfaction.

The monster might be powerful as all get out, but it didn't seem like it could jump. He'd survived. The joy of slipping past the closing gates of death filled him with life. He should be safe for at least a few moments.

There would come a time in the not-so-distant future when he would be cursing himself for tempting fate.

CHAPTER 8

The eaglebear snarled up at him for another few seconds, rage in its orange-colored eyes. Angry or not, however, it was a beast, not a man. The monster had attacked the tribe because it was hungry. When faced with the choice between continuing to chase an agile creature like Remy or pursuing other wounded prey, its bestial mind was inclined to make the easy choice.

With a slightly hissing *huff,* the monster turned its head to the left. The new god followed its gaze. When he realized what it was looking at, his smile turned into a grimace. The beast was eyeballing the escaping tribe. The pantherkin had used Remy's distraction to flee, but had not made it nearly far enough.

Nine members of the tribe had been slaughtered before Remy had led the eaglebear away, and it had injured more than a dozen. He did not know much about the group of pantherkin, but it was clear they looked after their own. They had managed to put a couple hundred yards between themselves and the monster, but it could close that distance in a matter of seconds.

The eaglebear began to lower itself back down to all fours, and in that instant, Remy was presented with a Moment of Choice. All he had to do to save himself was stay put. The eaglebear would head off and he could escape a short while later. It might not even kill all of the tribe. It might be content with taking down just a few of them. He could stay safe, and so long as any of the tribe lived, he'd fulfill the quest too.

Hadn't he already helped enough? Hell! Hadn't he already died once to help other people? He'd been torn apart by those shadow cats and had felt every bite, every tear and every shred. Now, amazingly, he'd been given a new life on a new world. True, he was some sort of midget panther-person, but he was alive! That was a lot more than he had been expecting after his terrible death.

What did he owe these people? Could he even call them people? They had tails and round panther ears! And who cared if there was some nonsense about him being a god or something. He didn't know these people and he didn't owe them a thing!

All he needed to do to enjoy this second chance at life was stay still. He just needed to look out for himself. Remy just needed to put Remy first, and he would survive to see another dawn.

And that was exactly what he would have done… if he hadn't already learned that survival was not enough.

The same drive that had forced him to lead those people out of Atlanta to safety, the drive that had made him stay outside of the bunker on the off chance of saving one more soul and for the gift of dying on his own terms, it was the reason he couldn't let the eaglebear ravage the fleeing tribe. He'd learned a simple truth long ago. Living with the regret of not doing the right thing was worse than dying because he tried. He had walked away once. He would never do it again.

In that Moment of Choice, Remy chose. He used the only weapon he had available to him. The only thing that he could think of to keep the eaglebear's attention. It had been called the first weapon, and had led to more pain and suffering than any other instrument wielded by man. A righteous anger filled him as he looked down at the eaglebear and prepared to attack.

Then, with the freedom of a man who knows he is well and truly fucked, he just let it all go… literally. Turning slightly, he aimed and let fly a stream of concentrated yellow pantherman juice. The golden liquid flew true and splashed across the eaglebear's face and into its open beak. It shut its mouth with a strangled screech, but it was too late. The juice was loose.

Time stopped. Ever so slowly, the eaglebear turned its head to fully look back at him even as the stream continued. Remy's liquid ammo ran dry quickly, and the monster just continued to look up at him, astonishment somehow playing across its avian face. Then an anger that it had never felt before swelled in its chest. All it wanted in life was to destroy this *creature* that had dared to piss on its face! In its mouth! The eaglebear let loose a bloodcurdling, high-pitched cry that was so intense, even the Universe noticed.

A prompt filled Remy's vision.

Know This! Your actions have driven the eaglebear you are facing into a state of madness. Your relationship with this creature has devolved from **Extreme Animosity** to **Soul Malice!**

You have gained a **Mortal Enemy**!

Gaining a monster as a Mortal Enemy has consequences. The eaglebear will change and evolve at a greatly increased pace to become the true bane of your existence. It will never abandon its hunt for you. The rewards from destroying such an enemy will be increased as well.

Before Remington could even react to that, another prompt filled his sight. This one was accompanied by a sound like the clarion call of a horn.

Baaa-raaaa

Know This! In the history of this planet, no other creature has gained a **Mortal Enemy** in such a short period of time! Truly, you must be one of the most infuriating beings to have ever dwelt in the cosmos.

For such an amazing feat, you have earned a **Title**!

You have gained the *Unusual* **Title**: **Infuriating Enemy** (Level 0)

When this Title is equipped, all creatures that have a negative disposition toward you will become infuriated. This can manifest in a number of ways, but aggressive creatures will most likely be filled by a primal urge to destroy you. There is a small chance that creatures with a neutral disposition may attack. Creatures with a positive disposition toward you will be unaffected.

Those who are thus affected will be driven by a need to harm you that is so powerful, it may override their ability to reason or even their instinct to protect themselves. This Title greatly increases the chances of obtaining Mortal Enemies.

Effective radius: 25 yards.

This Title can be equipped and unequipped at will.

This Title can be upgraded.

This Title will occupy **100 Energy slots**

Remington absorbed all the information at once, then blinked in disbelief. What kind of world rewarded you for giving a golden shower? Of course, a practical person would point out that someone who used a monster's mouth as a devil's punchbowl had no right to judge.

The prompts said he only got to have one Title, but it also implied he might be able to get more later. He wasn't too concerned about filling up his slot. He could definitely see the benefits of making an enemy attack blindly, so even if this Title was the only one he got, it could be worth it.

There was also the fact that this was a higher ranked title. From the numbers, he only had a one in one ten thousand chance to gain an *unusual* Title. That removed his worry that he was grabbing some basic crap. He also felt a good deal better because he wouldn't have to rock the Title all the time. It looked like he could turn it on and off at will.

The Title itself also wasn't bad at all. He hadn't gamed in years, but being able to make an opponent attack where you wanted was a primary principle of war. The fact that the attack would be coming at him was less than ideal, but the Title was still a powerful tool. In fact, it might be the key to making it out of this tree, he realized. The only thing he didn't fully understand was the Energy slot thing. His status page said he had 605 though, so he'd have plenty left even after allocating 100.

Only seconds passed as he absorbed the prompts and came to a decision. Remy chose "Yes."

Congratulations! You have chosen your first Title!

To upgrade this Title, obtain 1,000 Animosity Points.

100 Energy has been allocated to this Title. **Energy Remaining:** 505/605

Do you wish to equip the Title: **Infuriating Enemy**? Yes or No?

There were more prompts waiting to be read, but the eaglebear had overcome its shock and begun pawing at the tree trunk in renewed fury. Long strips of bark and divots of wood flew free. It was not so much driven mad with rage as its limited reason was overcome by pure, choking hatred. Seeing the hungry monster that was already eekin to freak him, he decided that making it even angrier wasn't a solid plan. The Title went unequipped.

The tribe had been afraid of the eaglebear before. Hearing the new noises coming from the crazed beast, that fear turned to pure dread. They hurried away even faster. Between the chaos and carnage of the eaglebear's initial attack, hardly any members of the tribe had even seen Remington when he'd appeared. Those few that had and realized the monster had chased after him steeled their hearts against sympathy. They appreciated his sacrifice, but their duty was to the tribe. If the life of one could save the lives of many, then they would do him the honor of remembering him in the years to come.

The new god did not begrudge them their priorities. He would have made the same call. Keeping the monster's attention had been his choice, after all. Instead, Remy looked down at the monster that was only a few scant feet below him and tried to figure out what to do next. The eaglebear was mad. Seriously mad!

Despite the fact that he had been in many battles, only an absolute fool would be unaffected looking down at death incarnate. Seeing the furious monster going crazy did have a definite effect on him. It just was not the effect that most sapient beings would call "sane." A nearly manic grin found its way onto his face as he looked down at his mortal enemy.

In a war, on a planet that might be millions of light years away now, he had learned that it was only on the edge of death that he ever truly felt alive. That fact had made it hard for him to forge close bonds when he came back from war, but at this particular moment it heightened all his senses. His heart beat with wild abandon being so close to death, so close to such a powerful killing machine. Besides, he should be safe up on his perch.

A distant corner of his mind abruptly screamed at him not to have that particular thought. He *knew* that no good came of tempting fate. That same part also said that even if he was out of the monster's immediate reach, good god, he shouldn't look down at it with the taunting grin that was currently on his face. It was a bloodthirsty monster!

It was already done though.

He'd done it.

He'd thunk it.

Fate wasn't having it.

The eaglebear looked up at the brown-skinned pantherkin in the tree above and narrowed its eyes. Its frantic screeching and manic motions paused. It glared up at Remy in such a way that the manic grin slowly vanished from the god's face. The new godling seriously started to wonder if he was underestimating the beast's intellect. What neither he nor the hybrid creature could know though was that as soon as they became mortal enemies the Labyrinth itself had started altering both him and the beast to be greater opponents for one another. As was true in all Labyrinth worlds, battle and danger paved the road to power.

The effects would take a great deal of time to fully manifest, but one of the largest discrepancies were their base intellects. After all, powerful body or not, the eaglebear's mentation was below the level of sapient beings. Due to this disparity, the core intellect of the eaglebear was already changing and new ideas were appearing in its mind. As Remy looked down at it, the eaglebear mastered its anger, something that wouldn't have been possible only minutes before. It was true that the ability to control one's emotions was a simple matter for more reasoning creatures. For the monster, it was the equivalent of an evolutionary leap.

This particular leap was about to be a serious pain in Remy's neck. The furious beast deliberately positioned its body, then threw a paw upward. Its nearly foot-long talons sank into the wood and it heaved! Its body lifted slightly off the ground and it raised its other arm up even higher. The hind claws of the hybrid beast dug into the trunk and it continued its upward progress. The eaglebear had always had the capacity to climb trees, but its new ability to coldly assess a situation was only possible due to the fact that it was now the godling's mortal enemy.

The entire time, its ochre-colored eyes never left Remy's face. They silently communicated a simple message: 'I'm going to eat you.' In the godling's mind there was also an implied follow-up to the message, 'and crap you out.'

Remy realized that his jubilation had been way, way premature. He started cursing as he prepared to ascend again. His anger was at himself as much as the situation. He was off his game. Of course he wasn't safe! Even on Earth, bears could climb trees. When you added that to the fact that eagles also lived in trees, and the fact that this thing looked like an eagle-bear hybrid... well, it was really in the name, wasn't it? Of course the accursed thing would be comfortable in trees!

CHAPTER 9

The tree was truly massive, its trunk easily twenty paces across. The good thing about that was it made it easy for Remy to keep making his way up. The bad thing was that it also supported the eaglebear's weight. The other bad thing was that the tree was so large that its roots had killed or stunted any other trees in the immediate vicinity.

Despite the fact that he was in a forest, the tree he was climbing was effectively in a large glade, so jumping to another tree to escape was an impossibility. The only way to go was up. So Remy climbed, and the monster climbed right after him. The eaglebear was slower but it was inexorable, and even before its mind had evolved it had known that once prey was chased into a tree, its victims could only go so far.

As Remy continued his ascent, he thought about how crazy his life was. Not too long ago, he'd just been a doctor at a community hospital. No real romantic relationships, but he had friends that cared about him. Then there was a flash of grey light that filled the sky and hell had come to Earth.

Dungeons, honest-to-god dungeons, had popped up all over the place like he was living in a game. With them came strange monsters, the stuff of nightmares, and semi-human invaders. So many people had died in the first few days. Of course, it was a toss-up if more had died at the hands of monsters or those of panicking humans.

Remy had needed to put aside the mantle of healer and become a soldier once again. Somehow, against all odds, he'd made it out of Atlanta. He had even managed to save some people along the way. A very small part of him had imagined that he could survive the Forsaking. Then he'd been killed by some horrendous black cats.

And now... he was a black-eared pantherman. The ridiculousness of being killed by cats then kind of becoming one hadn't escaped him. And here he was climbing a tree to get away from a giant monster bear-slash-bird. Remy shook his head. Somewhere in the universe, someone had to be laughing their ass off.

The new god risked a glance down and was confronted with the furious eyes of the eaglebear as it kept climbing after him. It screeched anew when it noticed him looking, a sure promise of pain and death. Remy sighed to himself and pushed the reflection on his life out of his mind. All that mattered now was survival, his own and the lives of the tribe he'd chosen.

He paused a moment and took stock. In a relatively short period of time, he'd climbed about fifty yards. The monster chasing him had been making a loud racket as it followed. He was outpacing it, but there really wasn't anywhere for him to hide. The lower branches, like the one he'd first pulled himself up on, were only a few yards in length. If he stopped on any one of those, the eaglebear could definitely reach him.

There were larger branches above him that extended out a much greater distance, but not far enough out to reach other trees. They were also high enough that a fall would probably mean certain death. He wasn't willing to put the 'cats always land on their feet' thing to the test just now.

Unfortunately, the ground below the massive tree was so starved for sunlight that there was barely any scrub. The only thing awaiting him down there were gnarled roots and rocks, nothing to cushion his fall. He hated to admit it, but this was starting to look like a no-win scenario. You never knew though. Besides, he thought, it's not like I have anything better to do. Another screech from the monster forced his limbs into action once again.

Remy kept climbing. In his heart he was beginning to resign himself to the fact that this new life of his was about to end as violently as his last one. The only thing that gave him some scant comfort was that his sacrifice had given the tribe a chance to escape. He wasn't some hero who would lay his life down for every sad sack he came across but, just like on Earth, if his end was coming it meant something to him that his death had meaning.

As for being afraid, well, he'd lived a lot longer than he'd ever expected the first time around. Even better, he'd gone out saving folk and with a weapon in his hand. As he climbed the tree on this new world, he supposed that every breath he'd taken since his death was a gift. Something extra. A faint grin grew on his face as he realized he was playing with house money. If that was the case, might as well try to roll the hard six. And hey, even if he was about to die again, maybe, just maybe, he could take this feathered fucker with him.

CHAPTER 10

Remy kept climbing the tree. Even though he was going up much faster than the eaglebear, the monster didn't stop pursuing him. The new god just really couldn't stress how annoying that fact was. A voice in his head told him that the beast wasn't giving up because it was his mortal enemy. Another voice, one that sounded suspiciously like his mother, pointed out that it was only his mortal enemy because he'd pissed in its mouth. Seeing as how neither point was particularly helpful, he ignored both voices. It was definitely his imagination that he heard a "Harumph" in his head.

He reached his first major branch at about one hundred yards up. While the trunk was about sixty feet across, as best he could guesstimate this first offshoot was at least twenty feet in diameter. It was easily strong enough to support his weight and he could probably even walk across the top of it without too much difficulty. The problem was, the eaglebear could probably do the same thing.

To make matters worse, the foliage had been getting thicker as he climbed. It wasn't enough to block out the light, but between the day quickly marching toward evening and the canopy, it was definitely darker than before. To Remy's surprise, the lack of light wasn't as big of a problem as he'd thought it would be. His new body seemed to be able to see in low light better than a human. No, the visibility wasn't a problem. What concerned him were the sounds.

At first, he'd thought he was just being paranoid. He'd heard a scrabbling noise, like something running across bark. Nothing had jumped out at him though, and the sound hadn't repeated, so he'd put it out of his mind. Now he was hearing it again. Whether it was because the sun was going down or because he was higher up, he no longer had any doubt; there were other things living in this tree.

It was possible the noises were coming from something as harmless as a squirrel. Then again, Remy remembered that after the Forsaking some squirrels had become deadly needle-toothed little monsters, so that didn't leave him feeling much better. The fact that some of the noises he heard were hissing sounds also did not set his mind at ease. Remy was pretty sure that, alien world or not, sweet cuddly things did not hiss!

That was why he decided not to travel down the branch. The ends of it were hidden by the thick leaves of the canopy. A chorus of what he could only describe as "warning" hoots came from those hidden recesses. More than one "something" called that branch home, and they were telling him not to come any closer. Remy took the advice. Having one bloodthirsty beast to deal with was more than enough.

As he climbed, he heard more sounds, and Remy realized that he might actually owe the eaglebear a thank you. He'd been wondering why the tree's inhabitants weren't attacking. After the eaglebear screeched at him one time though, the sounds coming from the leaves went quiet for a moment. Whatever was hiding in the canopy was afraid of his mortal enemy.

If there was one good thing about being chased by several tons of slavering monster, it was that it kept other predators away. As long as he didn't blunder into a nest, warren or whatever these tree monsters called home, he should be "safe." That thought made him snort in laughter.

"Pussies," he muttered to the hidden hissers.

Remy kept climbing.

He climbed for so long that his mind began to wander. It was a bit of a defense mechanism to avoid thinking about the pain in his arms and legs, which was steadily worsening. Suited for climbing or not, his new body was still flesh and blood. The pain and stiffness got worse as the green bar in the corner of his vision fell. Moving at a steady pace didn't overtax his stamina, so the drop was slow, but it was cumulative. There was no doubt that the ascent was getting harder.

Instead of thinking about all that, he started replaying what had happened since coming to this new world. There were probably some truly amazing things here: gorgeous vistas to behold, intricate ecosystems to discover and explore, life-changing adventures to be had. Did he go look for any of those though?

Nope! Naw! Not him! He'd decided to piss in a monster's mouth to save some people he didn't even know! What the f… Remy took a deep, slow breath, realizing that he was spiraling a bit. What had happened, had happened. He couldn't change that. He just needed to focus on the task at hand, he told himself.

After another deep breath, he spoke the words, "Zero fucks." His will firmed; he moved his aching limbs a bit faster. As if on cue, the eaglebear let out another enraged scream. Suddenly, his arms and legs didn't feel *quite* so tired. He picked up the pace.

No matter how many Zen mantras he recited though, he could not ignore the limitations of his own body. With a paltry 10 points of Endurance, he only had 100 Stamina. His Constitution was even lower at 9 points, so his green bar only regenerated at 5.4 SP/minute. While his new form wasn't exactly out of shape, his stamina had almost poured out of him while he'd been sprinting.

Also, climbing trees was an arduous activity, arguably more so than a short sprint. He was convinced that his new body had some sort of cat climbing bonus, because he should have had to stop by now. It was like he instinctually knew how to distribute his weight as he climbed. Even his tail (and he was trying not to think about *that* as much as possible) helped to balance him. He was sure that without the racial climbing bonus, the eaglebear might have already caught up with him.

Even factoring that in, he was still only level zero. His green stamina bar neared depletion several times during the climb. Each time it came close to emptying, he would get dizzy. He almost blacked out once, but as the darkness was filling his vision, he managed to cling to the trunk for dear life. That time, he'd had to wait several seconds before the world stopped spinning. Unconsciously, Remy had bared his teeth at the monster when his wits had come back to him. His pronounced canines flashed, but their sharp points did not dissuade the angry beast. Blowing out a hard and panting breath, he started climbing again, but at a slower rate.

Each time he was forced to stop, the eaglebear was able to narrow the gap between them. Thankfully, despite his burning arms and legs, and the extreme ache in the tips of his toes and fingers where his small talons met the digits, Remy was able to persevere. His new body might have been shorter and weaker than his human body in a stand-up fight, but it had its charms. After about an hour of trial and error, he found that by going at a slower, steady rate, he was able to keep his stamina from falling faster than he could regenerate it. This speed also still let him outpace the eaglebear, if just barely. The pain was horrible, but he was alive and no stranger to discomfort. He just hoped that the monster was suffering from the same fatigue, but apparently the fat bastard had nearly limitless stamina.

Even with the new pace, he had to pause periodically. After resting for a precious minute, he would regain enough energy to continue forward again, usually with the eaglebear less than ten feet away. In this manner, Remy continued to escape death by just a hairsbreadth. All around him, the noises in the tree grew louder and more numerous.

The trunk which was initially twenty paces across grew thinner and thinner. The sun, which had been close to setting when he arrived in Telos, fell behind the horizon. The loss of light made the noises coming from along the branches sound even louder. It also sounded like the creatures were venturing closer, but thankfully, they still feared the eaglebear more than they wanted to eat Remy.

His poor stamina actually saved him. If he had continued at his initial fast pace of ascent, he'd have outpaced the eaglebear enough for the tree creatures to feel safe in attacking. In a contemplative moment, it occurred to him that even his mortal enemy could serve a purpose. That made him wonder about the possible interconnectivity of all of creation. He'd been reincarnated, after all. Maybe he could somehow find a peaceful resolution to the enmity between himself and the eaglebear. In that moment of reflection, a jutting piece of bark scratched his face real hard. After that he just started cursing the feathered fucker chasing him again.

As he neared the top, the trunk started swaying to a greater and greater degree. The tree's movement slowed the ascent of both the eaglebear and himself. At one point, Remy stopped and held completely still. It wasn't just to replenish his stamina. He was hoping that the pitch-black canopy might make the eaglebear lose sight of him. He even closed his eyes. A minute later though, the monster caught up again. When he snuck a peek, he saw that its gleaming, hate-filled eyes were zeroed in on him. Nope, he thought sourly, this bastard can definitely see in the dark. The screech it let out further cemented that conclusion.

With a heavy sigh, Remy started climbing again.

Two hundred yards.

Four hundred.

Finally, after what felt like an eternity, he crested five hundred yards above the ground and had basically reached the top. The trunk's diameter was now only four feet across. When a powerful wind blew past the tree, it made the treetop sway at least five yards in any direction. With how tired he was, if there had been a storm or even strong gusts, he might have been thrown from the trunk. Thankfully, the night was calm.

At this height, the branches and leaves had also thinned considerably. Remy wasn't at the top, but he was close. He was resting on the last small branch there was before the tip. This afforded him a large view of the surrounding countryside, but the vista was lost on him. He only had eyes for the furious, persimmon-colored gaze below him.

The eaglebear had managed to ascend almost the entire length of the tree. Remy had kept hoping that it would give up or fall, but the hybrid seemed just as suited to climbing as he was. Its giant claws were dug into the bark and it stared up at him with undiminished rage. The new godling didn't know if that was a function of it being his mortal enemy or just the natural reaction to his having given it a Tijuana mojito, but the eaglebear showed absolutely zero signs of giving up the chase.

The only thing keeping him alive right now was that his nemesis' own powerful body was working against it. It was partially resting its large form on a thick branch about forty feet down from where he was recovering. Powerful or not, physics was still a bitch. The trunk of the massive tree narrowed rapidly near the top. Beyond where it was resting, the tree was too thin to support the thing's weight. So now the two of them were just glaring daggers at one another.

About a minute into the stare down, Remy huffed, shook his head and did the only productive thing he could think to do. He gave it the finger, then leaned his face against the tree and closed his eyes. His arms and legs still ached, but after half an hour his green bar was fully refilled.

Once he was feeling better he didn't bother to check on the monster. It had shrieked at him periodically while his stamina was refilling. He knew it was still there, and if it was going to act like a needy bitch, then he saw no reason to give it more attention. What he did do was take stock of his surroundings. As he did, he realized why it was so much easier to think now. His low stamina hadn't been the only consequence of his long climb. He'd also been struck with debuffs.

*You are **Weary**. Stamina regeneration decreased by 10%.*

That debuff had struck him when he was halfway up the tree. It had evolved into something worse in that last one hundred yards.

*You are **Worn Out**. Stamina regeneration decreased by 25%. Cognition decreased by 20%.*

It explained why it had taken so much longer for him to recover, and also why the last part of the climb was so much slower and more painful. The *Worn Out* debuff hadn't faded until he'd had a full half hour of rest. The debuff disappearing did nothing to remove the ache in his extremities, but at least he could think again.

The first thing he thought about was how his balls were freezing. He was wearing the same outfit as the male members of the tribe had on: a pair of rough brown pants and a prickly woven shirt. The material was thin, poorly made and uncomfortable. Now that he was up so high, the windchill was substantial. Worse, his shirt was now badly torn. He didn't even have a belt. The cold wasn't anywhere near unbearable, but as his family had often said, he was descended from "tropical people." Basically, he wasn't a huge fan of the cold.

There wasn't anything he could do about that, so he continued to look around. Now that he wasn't exhausted, he was more inclined to appreciate his surroundings. His high vantage point gave him quite a view. Though night had long since fallen, he was able to make out a few things by the light of two moons. One moon was pale white with faint blue rings encircling it on two different planes. It looked slightly smaller than the moon on Earth. The second was an angry red. It was much larger than the other one.

The two moons were only crescents and did not spare much light. To make it worse, the cloud cover was thick. As the clouds moved though, a third moon was revealed that he hadn't been able to see before. This one was half full and was twice the size of the white one. It glowed a soft lavender. There were also countless stars in the sky, forming unknown constellations.

The strangest thing was that at one point he saw white lines connecting a few of the stars. It was like the stylized drawings of constellations, but only three stars were connected. Remy studied that part of the sky in fascination until the drifting clouds obscured it again.

As the moons were the only sources of light, the surrounding countryside remained almost completely dark so he couldn't make out much. To the left of Remy's view, there was a shining ribbon lightly reflecting the moons' light. He could just make out the sounds of the river as it flowed dispassionately through the forest. The only other thing he could make out was a sea of trees that were weakly illuminated in the moons' halflight.

With not much else to look at, he decided to learn what he could from his interface. It only took a thought to pull up his status page.

????*			
Art: Soul		**Level:** 0	
Energy: 505/605		**Cultivation:** Spirit Made Flesh (0/7)	
STATS			
Health: 87/90	**Mana:** 120 *Regen/min: 7.2*		**Stamina:** 98/100 *Regen/min: 6*
ATTRIBUTES			
Strength: 8*	**Agility:** 15*		**Dexterity:** 15*
Constitution: 9*	**Endurance:** 10*		**Intelligence:** 12*
Wisdom: 15*	**Charisma:** 11*		**Luck:** 10*
RESISTANCES		WEAKNESSES	
None		None	
GOD ABILITIES			
God's Eye: The sight of gods **Soul Capture:** Capture souls			

Focusing on the words one at a time gave him more information.

The first one he looked at involved his name.

> **Name** – A Cosmic Force has bound your True Name. Knowing it could give enemies great power over you. It must remain secret. As such, you will need to decide upon a new moniker.

What? he thought to himself incredulously. His name was "bound?" Wasting no time, he opened his mouth to try and say "Remy," but to his astonishment nothing came out. He knew his name was Remington. He knew that everyone called him Remy, but he just couldn't make his lips form the words. He even tried to trick himself: "Hennesy, Grand Marnier, Blamy Martin." Gah, he thought in frustration.

This didn't seem to affect his thought process. He could still think of himself as Remy, but he couldn't say the word or the longer version. He tried saying his last name, but that didn't work either. It wasn't like he had lost his sense of self; it was just that he couldn't make verbal use of the information.

As a man who liked to call his own shots, it was extremely irritating. His mind still reeled a bit, but after a few breaths, he found calm. The truth was, the fact that he couldn't speak his own name would have been noteworthy on any other day. Today though, it just didn't rank high enough on the weird-o-meter.

Compared to the realities that he had recently died, been reincarnated into the body of a cat man, and was currently stuck in a gigantic tree because a monster that was half eagle and half bear was trying to eat him… Well, compared to that, the fact that he couldn't say his own name was kind of par for the course.

Also, Sariel had warned him about using his real name. At her prompting, he'd already come up with a new name to go by. It was a mixture of a moniker he'd earned in his past life along with the craziness of his new one. As he thought it, the blanks morphed into his choice.

The next tile raised another question. What was an "Art" and why was his the "Soul?"

Soul Art – Your power is most in tune with the Art of the Soul. The consequences of this will grow vastly over time. At your current State of Being, it has the following effects:

1) *Soul Deep*: As the soul transcends the flesh, so too do your attacks move beyond the material. Ignore either 10% of physical armor or 5 points of Defense, whichever is greater.

2) *Spiritual Foe*: Focusing on the Soul allows you to perform extra damage against beings that lack a physical body. +50% damage against beings that lack physical form and are comprised of only spiritual energy.

He still didn't know what an "Art" was, but the effects were not bad. Not bad at all. It meant he was good at fighting ghosts and he could bring some pain against armored enemies. After seeing a spirit literally rip the life out of five people on Earth, he did not underestimate the dead. The ghost had been immune to any physical attack, and had killed them without hesitation.

The armor penetration effect was also great. The only question he had was if it applied to just enemies wearing leather or chainmail, or monsters that had thick skin as well. In fact, he wondered if he could apply it to monsters with thick armored feathers? Time would tell.

The next line showed his "Energy."

Energy – The latent potential and power of a being.

This line was a bit different than before. Instead of just showing "605," now it showed "505/605." The reduction was easy enough to explain; it was because of his Title. He read the prompt again and the concept of "Energy" started making sense. It looked like Energy would limit the number of powers he could hold at one time. He still thought the Title was a good ability to have, but he'd have to be careful about accruing other powers in the future. Focusing further, he discovered his total Energy value of 605 stemmed from his attributes, which contributed 105, and something called a Divine Core, which supplied the last 500.

He couldn't find any more info about the Divine Core, so he moved on to the next line. It showed his current cultivation. Without souls or Faith Points, there was still nothing he could do about that at the moment. His eyes kept traveling.

The next line showed his Stats. Those seemed to be pretty straightforward and the same as on Earth. His Health, or HP, was how much total damage his body could take before death or serious injury. He'd lost a couple points on some scrapes while climbing, but it was overall full.

That was a good thing. Losing HPs caused pain in an increasing amount and also decreased his physical abilities. Making it down to 10% health was pure agony, and would limit his attack and defense. It was still strange thinking about how real life could be broken down into a mathematical formula, but then again, physicists had been saying all life could be deconstructed into 1's and 0's for decades back on Earth.

The blue line showed his mana, which determined the amount of Magic Points, or MPs, a person had. The few people who had learned to cast spells back on Earth had used MPs to power their incantations. Some people had also found other ways to use mana. Remy's own skill, *Ammo of Light*, had let him imbue his mana into his bullets. That had increased their damage and vastly increased their attack against creatures of darkness.

Stamina basically determined how much you had "in the tank." It determined how far you could walk, run, or fight before passing out from exhaustion. In the days after the apocalypse found Earth, the smart people had invested points into Endurance. It wasn't as sexy as the other attributes, but it increased stamina. If you couldn't last more than a minute in a fight or run away for at least five, you just weren't prepared to survive in the new world.

The next rows dealt with something he was more familiar with, his attributes. He just didn't know why the asterisks were there. Focusing on the symbol brought another explanation, but one that again raised more questions.

> Know This! The Attributes of all new gods shall be heavily influenced by their actions. Until you perform a **Profound Act**, your attributes will be that of a Level 0 creature who is a perfect specimen of your Chosen tribe. Due to your Divine Core and cultivation, at each level you will gain points as if you were a *limited* soul, the peak of the mortal ranks.
>
> Each level will provide **+2 Agility**, **+2 Dexterity**, and **+2 Free Attribute Points**

It looked like his attributes were as close to genetic perfection as the razin tribe could get. Still, he didn't understand the *Profound Act* part. He'd have to hope that that would reveal itself in time. He also didn't get the importance of a *limited* soul or the "mortal ranks."

What mattered more to him was that two thirds of his points were going to go into Agility and Dexterity. He didn't like that. It meant most of his progression was being pigeon-holed. It still sounded like the most bizarre dream ever, but putting points into attributes triggered real-world consequences for his body. Back on Earth, everyone had started at level zero after the Forsaking, but not with the same stats. Talking with other survivors, it had quickly become clear that some people had higher or lower starting stats.

Some bodybuilders had higher Strength, for instance, though if they were too muscle- bound most of them had lower Agility and Dexterity. That also came to make logical sense, seeing as how Agility determined movement speed, and Dexterity had something to do with dodging attacks. Anyone that had seen roided-out guys walking around the gym would understand that they weren't exactly Cirque du Soleil material.

There had been exceptions. Remy had met a well-built man who had trained in martial arts for years. The guy'd had a higher Constitution, Endurance, Strength, Agility and Dexterity than other people who had survived the initial days of the Forsaking. Even his Wisdom was high, which he had attributed to meditation. That fighter hadn't been the only example of a person with higher stats.

Years of schooling or having pursued various types of higher education apparently had an effect on Intelligence. A college professor told him that her Intelligence score had started at fourteen, several points higher than most other people he had met.

The highest initial stat he had heard of was the Wisdom of an Imam who had led a local mosque. The man was ninety years old and had apparently spent his life in service to his community. The Imam had had a Wisdom of seventeen at the moment of the Forsaking. Unfortunately, despite having survived the first day of the apocalypse, the religious leader had died soon afterward trying to save a child.

After speaking with enough survivors, something had become clear. Humans had a common baseline. All their stats seemed to naturally hover around a value of ten. What this meant varied per statistic. A Strength of ten, for instance, meant that the average human could lift a maximum of one hundred kilos, though not for very long.

Another example was having a Charisma of ten. That meant you looked average. He had taken a perverse pleasure in finding out that breast implants did not increase Charisma, no matter how much silicone had been used.

Once he had discovered humanity's baseline, other things had started making a good deal of sense. He had been able to extrapolate how certain attributes were affected by life choices. Smokers, for instance, usually had a Constitution that was two to five points below the baseline. A lack of physical exercise had also seemed to be one of the biggest dividing lines. He had met a morbidly obese man whose Endurance was only three. The majority of people who had lower-than-normal stats had died quickly after the Forsaking.

Chronic medical problems had claimed as many lives as monsters in the days immediately following the Forsaking. Diabetics went into shock without their insulin. Patients needing dialysis had all died within a month when the machines that kept them alive stopped working. Even diseases like the common cold had become deadly if the infection mutated due to rising mana levels. He'd lost several good people after they started sneezing blood.

Remy shook himself free from those dark remembrances. He had to focus on his present. He couldn't save them, but he could save himself. That meant understanding his new body and how it was different from being a human on Earth; namely, how he could get points and survive his current situation.

Back on Earth, every level provided four free points at once, which could be placed in any of the nine attributes. Investing wisely could vastly improve a person's chance at survival. That was why he wasn't super-excited that most of the points he could gain each level were being auto-assigned.

Agility was helpful; it let you dodge attacks. It basically let you feel like you were more settled in your body. But he had little use for Dexterity right now. On Earth, he'd discovered it let you punch or swing faster. That could be useful down the road, but if he'd had his choice, the points from leveling would have gone into Constitution or Endurance.

He couldn't do anything about that now though, and he hadn't even gained a level yet. He turned his attention back to his status page. "Resistances" and "Weaknesses" seemed pretty self-explanatory. He didn't have either of those. It was the last line that held any hope of saving his life.

> **God Abilities** – These are abilities associated with your godhood. As your State of Being improves, these powers will increase as well. These abilities do not consume Energy slots.

So free powers, basically. Or at least, powers that didn't use up any of his potential. He examined the first ability.

> **God's Eye** – The ubiquitous God Ability that all godlings share. Merely gaze upon something or someone with the appropriate intent to gain information about them.

He just had to look at something? The god stared downward at his mortal enemy. He'd done that before, but this time he thought about getting information about it. A table popped up and almost made him lose his grip in shock.

CHAPTER 11

For the first time, he was able to gain information about his enemy!

EAGLEBEAR (MORTAL ENEMY)		
Level: 5	**Monster Rank:** Common	
Energy: 228	**Soul Rank:** Common	
STATS		
Health: 307/310	**Mana:** 30	**Stamina:** 205/370
DESCRIPTION		
Eaglebears are a hybrid creature, a mix between avian and ursine species. It is unknown if they were the product of fell experiments in a forgotten age or were warped by the magic of the Labyrinth, but these predators are extremely suited to hunting in both cave and forest environments. While the males of the species roam alone, the females care for their cubs until adulthood.		

He was able to see an enemy's status page. He was able to see an enemy's status page! In a game this wouldn't have been impressive, but after having lived through hell on Earth, this was a godsend. Literally!

The number of times he'd had to make judgements about monsters or mutated beasts based on physical observation alone made him shudder. How the hell was he supposed to know if he could beat a slime, or even what level it was? This kind of information would have made the difference between life and death for a lot of people. Rather than just rolling the dice with your life, you could know if an enemy was too much for you or easy pickings. Despite his bad situation, he couldn't help but smile at how useful this was.

Of course, that excitement faded fairly quickly. The news he was getting wasn't exactly good. The eaglebear, correct name apparently, was five levels higher than he was. That didn't necessarily spell doom for Remy. In old games back on Earth, it was literally impossible for lower level creatures to defeat higher level enemies if the disparity was too great. The damage the lower level fighter inflicted was heavily penalized to the point of it being negligible.

An attack that would normally do 100 damage might be reduced by 90%, causing only 10 HP damage to the target. When you added in the fact that higher level creatures almost always had hundreds or thousands of Health Points, it was easy to see why such battles would be futile.

Thankfully, the godling's experiences on Earth had shown him that such disparities did not hold true in Labyrinth worlds. Higher level people had more Attribute Points to distribute and so were tougher, but they bled the same as anyone else. Of course, that didn't help him much now. Even at level 0, the eaglebear would probably have been able to rip his arms and legs off. No matter what its level, it was a multi-ton beast with nearly foot-long claws. So, while the godling wasn't hopelessly discouraged by its level, he wasn't feeling too great about it either.

It was also officially his mortal enemy. He already knew that, of course, but seeing it in grey and red really drove the point home. Honestly, it seemed a bit of an overreaction in his opinion. Pissing in someone's mouth was never nice, but way to hold a grudge!

Its Energy was lower than his, but so far Energy only seemed to indicate potential, not actual power, so that didn't help. It might also mean something completely different for monsters. The right column talked about its monster rank and soul rank, both of which were *common*. Focusing on each gave more information.

Monster Ranks – As a monster's rank increases, they can gain amazing powers and become more powerful versions of themselves. *Common* is the lowest rank.

Soul Ranks –More powerful souls will be of greater use to you. *Common* is the lowest rank.

This thing was the lowest rank of monster? Remy shook his head. The eaglebear was more than a thousand pounds of big bad nasty boy. How tough would it be if it had been a rank higher?

The next lines showed its stats. Sadly, it had more than three times as much health as he did. Its stamina was massive as well. No surprise that it hadn't gotten tired while it chased him. In fact, the climb had basically just slightly winded the monster.

There wasn't any more info, and none of it helped him out of his FUBAR situation. He hadn't found anything to help him, and the eaglebear continued to growl only yards away. Thankfully, there were more prompts to read. While he was running and climbing for his life he hadn't had the time to check, but ever since arriving in Telos there had been blinking notifications to read. He opened the first one and absorbed the info. The grin that came after showed sharp canines.

Know This! Gods and mortals alike can claim numerous powers, but not without limit. The potential of all beings is determined by their Energy.

Know This! Each new god of Telos is awarded **2 Divine Powers** that align with your Art. Skills that align with your Art require less Energy slots.

The next prompts were preceded by a sound that he could only describe as an angelic whistle.

AUULAAA!

You have gained the Divine Power: **Soul Strike**. Causes a maximum 20 Damage with a melee strike. Must be powered up to achieve full effect. Max charge rate: 5 damage/second. 20 points of damage will deplete a full charge from your State of Being.

Art: Soul

Energy Slots Required: 50 (Base Cost 100 decreased by 50% due to this power coinciding with your Art)

Requirement to Reach Level 1: 50 Divine Points

Do you wish to accept this Power?

AUULAAA!

You have gained the Divine Power: **Soul Heal**. Restores a maximum of 20 Health upon touch. Must be powered up to achieve full effect. Max charge rate: 5 healing/second. 20 points of healing will deplete a full charge from your State of Being.

Art: Soul

Energy Slots Required: 50 (Base Cost 100 decreased by 50% due to this power coinciding with your Art)

Requirement to Reach Level 1: 50 Divine Points

Do you wish to accept this Power?

With no hesitation he accepted them both. He felt knowledge and power flow into him, like cool water down a parched throat. It just felt right. These new powers resonated with him on a deep level. It was like they'd been tailor-made for him!

Total Energy Remaining: 405/605

He couldn't keep a chuckle from leaving his throat. He had an attack and a healing ability! His odds of survival were looking up. It looked like these Divine Powers had taken another 100 Energy slots, but that was money well spent as far as he was concerned. He didn't have any better use for his Energy right now, after all. He'd even gotten a discount since apparently his Art matched these Divine Powers. There even seemed to be a way to level the powers up. Excitement filled his chest.

> Know This! The Arts of Gods each have their own strengths and weaknesses. Divine Powers are fueled by your Energy and State of Being. As you follow the Soul Art, however, your Divine Powers can also be powered by captured souls. Channeling a Divine Power through a soul will provide extra charges and can even augment your powers.

Remy read the prompt several times. Basically, it looked like there were a finite number of times he could use his Divine Powers, but any souls he captured could work like batteries. Unfortunately, there was no indication of how many times he could use his new abilities. He'd have to figure it out by trial and error. It was time to get to work.

With a serious expression on his face, he assessed his situation the way he had been trained to do. He was a level zero man... pantherman... whatever. He wasn't human anymore. He was a razin. His new body was smaller and weaker than a human's, but also more agile. Oh, and he was stuck in a gigantic tree.

And sadly, the only way to the ground was down. Sadder, there was a carnivorous eaglebear between him and the exit. And since Remy's name wasn't Gandalf, he had no reasonable expectation that eagles would come to save him at the last minute.

Remy also had god abilities that, though powerful, didn't seem to have any offensive capabilities. *God's Eye* was incredibly useful, but seemed to be only an informational tool. His second ability, *Soul Capture,* could lead to greater power according to the Divine Power prompts. It only worked on an "untethered" soul, however. He was pretty sure that was just fancy-speak for after a soul left a body. That meant he had to kill something. The problem was that the only creatures near him were the eaglebear and...

Remy stopped his musings. The seed of an idea was starting to sprout.

For the first time in a long time, a cold, but long-cherished, feeling started to grow in Remy's heart. It was a feeling that had led his fellow soldiers to give him the name "Fell." Maybe there *was* something he could do. It was definitely dangerous, and possibly suicidal, but it was a plan. A devilish smile grew beneath his rounded black ears.

He looked at the eaglebear resting on the large branch farther down the tree and hoped he was eyeballing this correctly. Then he accessed his interface.

You are about to equip the Title **Infuriating Enemy**

All Enemies within **25 yards** will be driven to attack you. Enemies with weaker willpower will be driven mad by this compulsion. This Title may be deactivated and reactivated at any time.

Are you sure you wish to equip this Title? Yes or No?

With a deep breath, he chose "Yes." Within moments, the soft chittering and growling sounds that were coming from the nearby branches grew into mad shrieks of fury. The closest leaves quivered furiously before a pair of screaming animals shot out of the foliage. Remy just managed to identify them with *God's Eye* before they bounded up the tree toward him.

SNAPTOOTH SIMIAN	
Level: 3	Monster Rank: Common
Energy: 93	Soul Rank: Common
STATS	
Health: 83/83	Mana: 21/21 — Stamina: 140/140
DESCRIPTION	
Extremely agile, these monkey-like creatures normally reside in large trees and consume creatures in the surrounding forest. Snaptooth Simians are not afraid to attack larger creatures, often swarming them with superior numbers. Their serrated teeth inflict wounds that cause a *Bleeding* status.	

It's a monkey.

Remy barely had time to process that thought before they reached him. Their speed was intense, especially the way they shot straight up the trunk to where he was waiting. They both had coarse grey hair covering their bodies. The hair around their faces was orange with green tips. Neither was any larger than a chimpanzee back on Earth, but anyone who had ever seen an angry monkey would know that was scary enough. Both hooted savagely as they practically sprinted up the trunk. With a final bound, they attacked.

The godling was ready. Before activating his Title, he had triggered *Soul Strike*. A pale blue aura had immediately surrounded one hand. As he'd poured more energy into the skill, the aura had grown thicker and easier to see. He found he was able to moderate the flow of power, giving him a +1 to damage all the way up to +20. It had taken four seconds to fully power it up.

As the energy grew more concentrated, Remy had been able to make out sharp edges in the pale blue light, like his hand was sheathed in a sapphire gauntlet. He'd been a bit cautious using the skill for the first time. The last thing he needed was to overtax himself in this situation. While he powered it up though, he didn't feel any drain on himself. That was why he was able to absolutely devastate the first simian.

It dove at him, both arms outstretched, its mouth fixed in a shrieking snarl. Remy smiled back and punched out. The monkey twisted its hands slightly to grab the god. With its agile body, that should have been easy, which was why it was completely shocked by Remy's fist rocketing into it. One hit obliterated its ribs, heart and part of a lung.

The god's mouth dropped open. He'd been wondering what a +20 attack would do to an unarmored body. As it turned out, it was pretty much the same thing that happened when someone is hit point-blank with a shotgun blast. A spray of blood washed over the god, and the simian fell to its death, bouncing off tree limbs as it fell fifty stories.

The other beast didn't slow, unbothered by the death of its fellow. Whether the creatures had zero sense of camaraderie, or whether Remy's Title had driven it mad with hate, it didn't matter. What mattered was that Remy finally understood the cost of using his skills. The price wasn't paid while he was powering them up. It was after they'd been used.

Even as he shifted to attack the second monkey, two things happened: the razor-sharp sheath of blue energy disappeared, and he felt something drain out of him. Not expecting it, the feeling caught him off guard. It was a mixture of dizziness and emptiness. If he'd been prepared he could have ignored it, but as it was, he staggered. That left him ill-prepared for the simian's savage assault.

It barreled into him, almost knocking him off the branch. Only the fact that he had one arm on the trunk kept him alive. Still, his left foot flew free as the creature clambered up his body. He was struggling to right himself when it sank its fangs into his arm. He could feel its sharp teeth ripping through his biceps.

Remy screamed in anger. He wasn't new to pain, but the agony of having something bite a piece out of you was just not something you "took like a man." Only people who'd never experienced real pain would think that was possible. It twisted its head, trying to tear the piece of meat free.

The god gritted his teeth and glared down at the simian. The pain was intense, but it didn't burn as hot as his anger. He found his footing and let go of the trunk. With his newly free hand, he swung downward. Already a bit lightheaded, he didn't dare use *Soul Strike* again after so few seconds had passed. If the effects were exponential, there was a good chance he'd fall off the tree limb. That would mean almost certain death. But even without his Divine Power, he had other weapons. The talons at the ends of his fingers sank into the monkey's body. All five gouged their way into its neck.

The attack wasn't enough to be life-threatening, but it made the beast's mouth pop open in pain. It was its turn to scream. The creature's eyes darted wildly, crazed and bloodshot. Foam flecked out of its shrieking mouth. It didn't stop attacking.

The snaptooth simian grabbed his arm in both of its hands. With freakish strength, it pulled on him to bring its mouth close enough to bite his neck. Even though it was much smaller than he was, its strength was the same. It also was able to use all its appendages, while one of his arms was bleeding and wounded.

Remy tried slamming its head into the tree trunk. Keeping it at arm's length, he pivoted his body. He managed to lightly ring its bell. Its struggles only increased in strength and ferocity. After slamming it the first time, he tried to smash it against the trunk several more times. Only the first two connected solidly. For the rest, the agile beast contorted its body to avoid any real damage.

The creature writhed in his grasp, and only the fact that his talons were literally piercing its neck kept it from breaking free. Blood flowed from the puncture wounds, but only at a trickle. He hadn't managed to nick any critical vessels; his talons were too short. The whole time, it kept trying to sink its teeth into his neck.

It quickly became clear that he couldn't overpower it. Not with only one good arm. What made it worse was that he was basically holding it aloft while they were fighting. In less than a minute, his stamina had decreased by half. It was getting harder to fight.

The grey monkey's stamina didn't seem affected at all. Like it was demon-possessed, its mouth gnashed open and shut. Flecks of spittle and foul breath washed over him. The monkey's grip was so tight that it carved furrows in his arms until both were bloody. Scarlet flowed freely. Pain shot through the god, and his health bar continued to fall due to a weak *Bleeding effect.*

Fuck. Fuck!

Remy's breath whistled through his bared teeth. He was straining as hard as he could, but he was losing ground. His tongue ran across the inside of his mouth, and he noticed something he hadn't picked up on before. An idea bloomed, and he didn't hesitate. There was only one thing that had kept him alive so far on this world, and it was time to rely on it again. Physics was a bitch, but it was his bitch!

Remy reversed the pressure he was applying to the monkey. He pulled it close before it knew what was happening. The distance between them vanished in a blink. While he did, he pulled his arm in and up. Its snapping jaws clacked less than half an inch from his ear.

Before it could do anything else, he sank his own newly discovered fangs into its neck. They weren't nearly as long as the simian's, but they were a great deal sharper and more dangerous than human canines. The bristly grey hair on the monkey's neck was no armor at all, and Remy's sharp teeth tore into its skin. The coarse dark strands scratched the roof of his mouth right before its blood gushed into his mouth like a river of salt.

It bucked in his grip with a pained shriek. The risk to its life finally overcame the effect of Remy's Title. It tried to escape, but Remy held it close and repeated his earlier movement, shaking his head back and forth to deepen the bite.

Liquid hot iron spilled down his chin and splashed down his throat. He had to swallow to keep from choking. The simian beat against the top of his head, hands curled into fists. The attack worsened the headache from using his Divine Power, but he still didn't let go. He just tightened his grip on the beast and sank his teeth deeper. Pure panic flooded the monster and all thoughts of attack fled its small mind. With a strength fueled by a fundamental need for survival, it finally yanked its body free from his cruel bite.

The damage was already done. A new god had tasted his first blood.

When Remy had sunk his fangs into the simian, he had bitten through skin, flesh and tendon. His incisors had initially missed the large vessels in its neck, but when the snaptooth simian pulled free, one of its major arteries was severed. Its life was measured in seconds. A geyser of blood shot into the night like a broken water main. The liquid remained in a perfect column for a couple seconds, so high was the pressure behind it. Then the beast stopped fighting. It just looked at Remy's face, drenched with its own vitality, and it felt confused. It knew something horrible had happened, but it couldn't understand what.

The next beat of its heart caused another column of blood to be ejected, though it was more sluggish than the last. A look of sorrow crossed the simian's face as it instinctively realized it was dying. It struck at Remy again, but the blows held only a ghost of its earlier strength.

The god maintained his grip on its neck, watching it die. Each pump of blood was weaker. Every hit landed softer. Each frantic beat of its heart hastened its own death. The simian's life essence splattered across the godling, anointing both him and the tree as it fell down through the branches. Some of it even splattered across the eaglebear's face. The large predator screeched in hunger.

Within seconds, the simian weakened to the point that its struggles were pathetic, no stronger than rain on Remy's face. The strong spurts of blood turned into a trickle. His own heart thudding hard in his chest, Remy gazed deeply at the dying snaptooth simian. Looking into its eyes, he could almost see the flickering spark of life sputtering out. He had always enjoyed these moments. They had always felt so intimate and pure. Hundreds of feet above the ground, while his mortal enemy screeched beneath him, he watched his latest vanquished foe take its last breaths. Despite the pain he felt, he smiled faintly as its arms and legs went limp. That fond expression in the face of horror was what had earned him his second moniker in his past life, Fell.

A prompt appeared.

For killing **2** *common* **rank** enemies with the Title **Infuriating Enemy** equipped, you have gained **20 Animosity Points**. 20/1,000 obtained to upgrade your Title.

You have gained: **374 XP**. 374/2500 XP to reach Level 1

The level difference between him and the monkeys gave copious XP. He still immediately dismissed the prompts because something much more interesting was happening. Looking at the corpse hanging from his hand, he saw more than just meat. There was something inside it. Something that was reacting with something deep inside him. He reached out with this new feeling and *pulled*!

Wisps of energy floated free of the body. It coalesced into a sphere of rainbow-colored light that only the godling could see. With hot blood coating his face, chest and mouth, he looked at it in surprise and amazement. Even the howling of the eaglebear couldn't distract him. Time seemed to stand still, but it couldn't have taken more than a few seconds for the energy to coalesce. Without being told, he knew what it was. He was looking at a soul.

Once formed, the soul floated in midair, the lights within pulsing slightly. After a few moments, it began to float away, presumably to begin the next phase of its journey. Remy watched it slowly glide away, a kaleidoscope of colors playing across its surface. As it moved farther away, it also began to fade from view as it transitioned to another phase of existence.

With a frown, Remy realized something inside him didn't want it to go. That part of him wanted to hold it, to possess it… to consume it! As soon as he had that thought, a deep hunger awoke in the god. A growl sounded from deep in his throat and he reached out, not with his hand, but with his Soul Art. Like flexing a muscle he had never known he'd always had, he pulled the soul to him.

For the first time since being formed, the soul showed agitation. It stopped gliding away, caught in the power of his Art. It quivered, struggling to break free. To Remy, it felt no different than a small child trying to wrench his arm away. The godling had only gently reached out at first, but with his hunger raging, he pulled harder. Remy watched the lights within it flash in panic as it desperately tried to escape. With an inaudible cry he felt rather than heard, it flew toward him. His mouth opened wide and a pale blue light could be seen in the depths of his throat. He consumed the soul and the world of Telos was changed forever.

A warm feeling bloomed in his chest, and another prompt appeared.

Congratulations, godling! You have captured a **soul!**

146

CHAPTER 12

A series of prompts appeared in his vision. He ignored them for a second, lost in the wonderful sensation that claiming a soul had brought. It was like drinking warm whisky on a cold winter day. It was like feeling just a bit too full after Thanksgiving dinner, but still having room for pie. It felt like a completion, like something that he'd never known was empty was finally filled. For a few moments, he lost himself in that wonderful sensation.

Right after that though, his Zen feeling was interrupted by a harsh reality. In the corner of his vision, his health bar was flashing at a dangerous tempo. Worse, he noticed that it was continuing to fall at a noticeable rate.

*You are **Bleeding!** You are losing 4 HP/sec*

It was too fast! He only had 90 health at his peak and he'd already lost 17 HP when the snaptooth simian clawed and bit him. He must have gotten a *Bleeding* status at that point because, without even noticing it, he'd lost another 44 HP since. Now he had less than half his life left. If he didn't stop the bleeding, he'd be dead in seconds. Even worse, there was no time limit to the debuff which meant he must have an ongoing injury. He had to find it and fix the issue, now!

Remy frantically let go of the body of the grey monkey. Its body crashed through the branches of the tree as it fell through the canopy before finally hitting the ground. He didn't give it a second thought. Instead of thinking about the dead, he was desperately checking himself. He first looked at the gouges in his arm, but the red furrows weren't that deep, definitely not deep enough to explain his brisk bleeding status. That was when he noticed that a wound on the underside of his arm had something in it. Cursing at the pain, he dug his fingers in, quickly finding something hard.

Even though the initial bite had hurt like hell, after that there hadn't been much pain. That was why Remy hadn't given the wound much thought. Now his searching fingers found two fangs embedded in the meat of his arm. Blood was flowing out of both at a steady rate. Eyes wide, he realized the teeth were hollow. They were letting his blood pour out like water through a spigot. With a curse, he pulled both teeth out. The debuff changed.

*You are **Bleeding!** You are losing 2 HP/5sec for the next 45 seconds.*

A big improvement, especially since the debuff was time-limited now. Still not good enough though. It had taken him 4 seconds to find and remove the teeth. That had cost him another sixteen HP, leaving only 13 health. He was feeling woozy now, and he'd be dead before even his improved *Bleeding* status elapsed. He ripped off a piece of his blood-sodden shirt and pressed the wadded cloth to the injury. A moment later, the debuff changed again.

*You are **Bleeding!** You are losing 1 HP/5sec for the next 10 seconds.*

Removing the teeth had ameliorated the blood loss to a great extent. The makeshift bandage did the rest. Unfortunately, the damage was already done. He had less than 10 health left. The drop in vitality not only made him dizzy, it spread a diffuse pain through his body, making it harder to think. It was like an infected toothache, if his whole body was made of teeth. Remy took a deep breath to steady himself. He knew what he had to do now. He just wasn't sure he'd survive it.

Remy slowly climbed back up to his previous perch. It was a short ascent, but he might not have made it without the claws of his new pantherkin body. Once he was back in place, he straddled the branch. Both of his hands reached around the trunk and his claws dug into the bark. If he'd had enough cloth he would have tied himself to the trunk, but this was as secure as he could be. Reaching into himself, he called on his Divine Power again, this time to heal.

He felt something drain out of him again. As expected, it was accompanied by another bout of dizziness. Thankfully, it wasn't as bad as the first time. Now that he was prepared, it wasn't nearly as disorienting. A warm feeling spread through him and diffuse blue light surrounded his whole body.

You have restored 20 HP. Total HP 23/90.

The pain lessened considerably. The *Bleeding* status disappeared as well. From gauging the feeling inside him, he could use his power one more time. This time, he didn't use it all at once. Instead, he tried focusing on exactly what he wanted healed and slowly dribbled his Divine Power into his mangled arm. To his delight, he was able to control his healing ability. His HP only rose by one point a second, but he was able to focus it completely on the arm that the monkey had savaged. By visualizing what he wanted, rather than just flooding his body with energy, he was able to bring both arms back to full operation with some power to spare. The slow approach also barely took a toll on him.

*You have restored **20 HP**. Total HP 43/90.*

Whatever Divine Power he'd been drawing on was now completely empty. The power was more versatile than he'd originally thought, being able to fuel both healing and offense, but three tries were all he had in him, no matter how he used it. The good news was, now that he'd emptied the tank, he could feel that it was slowly refilling. The power lacked any kind of points total unlike his health or stamina so he had no idea how fast it would happen, but at least he knew that it would refill. Remy decided to wait on his high perch to see how long it would take.

Resting would also let him replenish his stamina. It hadn't taken nearly as hard a hit as his health, but the green bar was still half depleted. Anyone that had been in a fight knew how quickly exhaustion could come.

Absently, he disabled *Infuriating Enemy,* unsure how many monkeys' uncles, nephews, cousins, nieces, grand-aunts and side pieces were eyeing him as he bled to death. While he waited, he examined his spoils of war and the prompts that came from capturing his first soul.

CHAPTER 13

"Spoils of war" might be a bit grandiose, he thought, looking at the monkey's teeth. They were each three inches long and hollow. Seeing that, he realized the snaptooth simian's name had been a hint. It was clear now that when the creatures bit their prey, the teeth snapped off. Then they would basically operate like syringes with the stoppers removed. As such, the *Bleeding* effect was far worse than what would have resulted from a simple bite. The monkey might have been much smaller than him, but it still almost killed him.

If the beast had hit an artery, he might have bled out in seconds. Even just sticking out of his arm, the teeth had created a bleeding channel that would have killed him in under a minute. Looking at the simple ivory sticks that had nearly been the death of him, Remy realized he needed to realign his perceptions. This world was dangerous, and nothing could be underestimated.

He placed the teeth between his fingers, wondering if they could be used like brass knuckles. Sadly, they were heavily curved. Without a way to secure them, they'd slip after his first punch. They might even stab him if he wasn't careful. Instead, he tore a strip off his ruined shirt and wrapped them up. Another strip of cloth tied them securely to his arm. They might come in handy later.

Despite his near-death experience, he was in a good mood. He was alive and his enemies were dead. Was there a better feeling in any world? He had encountered three animals in this new world. Two had been hacked to death, and he'd pissed on the third. If he wasn't careful, someone was going to call PETA. He chuckled to himself while he leaned against the tree trunk.

For a couple minutes, he just rested his head against the bark, tired and dizzy. As soon as his head cleared a bit, he turned his attention inward. There were notifications waiting to be read. He had captured a soul!

You have captured a soul: **Snaptooth Simian.** Soul Rank:

Common

A *common* soul consumes 25 Energy slots until used.

Energy Slots Remaining: 380/605

Know This! *Common* souls are the lowest and most ubiquitous type of soul. Even the lowest soul can offer immeasurable power, however.

At present, you have **3 Open Soul Slots**:

1) Soul Strike

2) Soul Heal

3) State of Existence

In addition to fueling your Divine Powers, a soul can be added to your State of Existence and provide a bonus consistent with its nature.

You may assign this soul to any of the 3 slots, but be warned, possessing a soul is not without **risk**!

Remington did not like the ominously vague nature of that last prompt, but he would cross that bridge when he came to it. There were other things to take care of first. Number one was replenishing his health. If this soul could empower *Soul Heal* then that was the right place to start. The spirit was a warm feeling nestled in his chest. He willed it to bond with his Divine Power.

The warm feeling inside him grew hot. Not painfully so, but like the burn after a perfectly spiced meal. He also felt it adhere to his Divine Power.

Your Divine Power, *Soul Heal*, has been augmented by a *common* soul. *Soul Heal* now has an additional charge. When your Divine Power has been used up, this soul can fuel your power one more time.

> This charge will be refilled at the same rate as other charges and will be determined by your State of Being.
>
> Current recharge rate: 1 charge every 10 minutes

It turned out letting the soul fill the slot gave him another charge for his Divine Power. It wasn't as good as he'd been hoping for. He'd hoped it would make his *Soul Heal* stronger, but maybe the reason it hadn't was because it was only a *common* soul. Who knew what stronger souls might do? Still, it was something. Another heal might mean the difference between life and death for him. He also now knew how quickly his Divine Power refilled.

Remy wasted no time and triggered his power again. This time, he allowed it to just diffuse through his body. The healing energy flowed out of the bound soul. The warmth localized on the spots of his injuries, but also pervaded his entire self.

Relief spread through his body. There was more damage to be healed, but the difference was remarkable. He was able to stand straight, and his breathing was no longer beleaguered. Checking, he saw that there were only a few small tears in his skin rather than open wounds.

He also examined the bound soul in greater detail. While it had been somewhat depleted by his skill usage, he also somehow knew that it hadn't been harmed or permanently weakened. It just felt like a warmth inside of his chest. A warmth that belonged there.

After resting for ten minutes, Remy found that his power had indeed refilled enough to use *Soul Heal* again. He knew instinctually that it would only recover while he was at rest. He couldn't rely on his power recharging while he was in combat.

He also made another discovery. After healing, instead of having 68 HP like he'd expected, he had 69. Focusing on his internal log, he saw that he was able to regenerate his health! It was abysmally slow, only 1 HP every 10 minutes, but it was something. He didn't yet know it, but it was a function of his Energy and divinity. The higher they rose, the faster his natural healing would become.

Forty minutes later, all his stats, his Divine Power, and even the slotted souls were filled again. Though there was a cost, he couldn't help but marvel at what he had just done. He'd engaged in hand-to-hand, unarmed combat with two higher level beasts, killed them, and in less than an hour was back to full strength. After the Forsaking, he'd met several people with powers, but no one had had the power to heal. Now he could do it on a whim. Before his very eyes, the bleeding furrows and deep bites filled with new pink tissue and then turned into unbroken skin.

Remy stretched his body on the branch. Dried blood cracked on his skin. He would've loved to get clean as well since he was sure he looked like the bad guy in a horror movie, but stuck up in this massive tree there was nothing he could do about that. For now, he had an immediate goal: he needed more souls. One to power his *Soul Strike* and the other to augment his State of Being, whatever that meant. He had to assume it'd be a good thing, despite his lack of information.

He got ready to climb down and pull more grey-haired simians. He knew there were more monkeys hidden down in the branches. As long as he moved slowly, the AoE of *Infuriating Enemy* shouldn't attract too many enemies at once. At least, that's what he hoped.

Luck was on his side. After going only a few feet down a branch, a single simian rushed at him. Remy quickly backed up, coming once more to rest against the trunk of the tree for support. This time he didn't use *Soul Strike.* Despite that, this fight went much smoother than the last. He was more willing to take damage in return for hurting the monkey. Less than a minute later, Remy dropped another body through the darkness of the tree. His body was covered in scratches and bites, but he had avoided any major injuries. Another ten minutes and he was hale again.

While he'd been healing himself, he'd stared at the soul trying to escape his Art. He didn't immediately consume it this time despite having an almost instinctual need to do so. Like the first one, it was a sphere of rainbow light shooting around. It was a bit mesmerizing to watch, honestly. Remy wasn't just there for the light show, however. He was deciding if he should use this soul for *Soul Strike* or to bind it to his State of Being.

He ultimately went with the attack power. He still didn't understand this State of Being thing. What he knew was that having an extra attack was a sure bet. He consumed the soul and linked it to *Soul Strike.* There was just one soul slot left to fill. Not seeing any reason to wait, he started edging down the branch again. The eaglebear continued to screech periodically below him, but the god was still well beyond its reach.

Things didn't go as he'd hoped this time around. Even though he moved slowly, there must have been a cluster of beasts hidden in the foliage. Six furious monkeys rushed at him all at once.

"Damn it," he muttered as he turned and ran back to the trunk. Something wet splattered against his bare back. A second later, the smell made it clear that one of the monkeys had chucked its poo! What kind of low-level primate would do something like that? There was no time for disgust though. The battle was joined.

Remy wasted no time powering *Soul Strike.* The effect was even greater than when he'd used it on the first simian. He threw a punch at a monkey that leaped at him. The creature's mouth was open wide, four fangs flying toward the god's throat. His fist plowed straight though the beast's body, making blood and organs splatter against his chest. It died in midair. He didn't let the soul go to waste though, pulling at it while it was still in the body. It floated free even as he readied his next attack. It didn't even require conscious effort for him to keep it trapped on this plane. Without realizing it, he'd already become a stronger soul hunter.

As fast as he could, he spammed *Soul Strike.* A head flew free, a heart imploded and one more monkey fell shrieking as its entrails tangled in its own feet. His Divine Power made him a dealer of death, but the last two simians did not hesitate and were not impressed. They were driven mad by Remy's Title. One sunk its fangs into his thigh, and the other leaped high, landing on his shoulders.

The god backhanded the monkey ravaging his thigh. He didn't have any charges left for *Soul Strike*, but his claws punctured one of its eyes. He'd already planned for being outnumbered. The greatest threat the snaptooths posed was their teeth, which needed to be dealt with immediately. The most vulnerable spot on the head was the eyes, so that was what he went for.

Its mouth popped open as it screamed. Holding its eye socket, vitreous fluid flowing between its fingers, it fell backward onto the branch. It left two fangs in his leg, and he gained another *Bleeding* status.

Before Remy could remove the ivory syringes, the other monkey sank its teeth into his neck. The god screamed in pain.

Bleeding status worsened! You are losing 14 HP/sec

He was seconds away from death.

Remy reached up and shoved a taloned thumb into the second monkey's eye. Just like the first, it screamed in agony. There were a couple things you couldn't ignore no matter how mad you were. Tits full of rock salt or a talon in the eye, they'd both gentle you down some. Screaming opened its mouth, but its teeth remained in his neck. The god threw its small body off the branch. He frantically dug in his own flesh, causing a bit more damage but successfully yanking all four teeth out.

The beast he'd just thrown fell about sixty feet but grabbed a thin limb and stopped its descent. It righted itself and began to come at him again. He'd only bought himself seconds, but he didn't waste them. He formed his hand into a knife blade, fingers slightly curled, claws extended, and turned to the first monkey. It had gotten back on its feet and was readying itself to attack him again. He got to it first. His hand swept out and across, his claws opening a faint red smile on its throat. The cut wasn't deep, but the simian staggered backward, both hands holding its neck.

The darkness inside him laughed at how human the creature looked in that moment. He'd seen more than one man, and quite a few women, stagger backward in the exact same way back on Earth. It made the mistake of taking one too many steps because the last one hit only empty space. A second later it was falling. From the crashes he heard, it saved itself just like the first, but not before hitting several limbs. Hopefully, that would buy him some more time. Every second was precious to him, now.

Remy used one of his bound souls to trigger *Soul Heal.* He'd have focused the healing energy, but the monkey he'd thrown was back. Warmth spread through him as battle was joined once again.

The monkey didn't come straight at him this time. Instead, it bounded around him almost too fast to follow. Remy's mobility was greatly reduced from having to balance on the tree limb with his back against the trunk. When it finally attacked, it came at him from an odd angle. That let it get close before he could knock it away. Just like his first fight with the beasts, this one's unnaturally strong arms matched his own strength. It obviously held a grudge because its rough nails were reaching for his eyes in retaliation. Remy bared his teeth, only just managing to keep it at bay. Sorry, One-Eyed Jack, I'm pretty enough without your help.

The beast howled, driven mad by his Title. Its frenzied status added strength to its attacks, and Remy could hear the other one only seconds away. The godling didn't try to throw the agile monster away again. He had learned his lesson. He needed it close for this.

Remy had been using both arms to keep the simian from biting him, but he freed one. His position was precarious, and only leaning against the trunk kept him upright. He still almost fell several times. With only one arm fighting it, the simian teeth immediately got closer to his unprotected skin. The ones it had left in him earlier had already been magically replaced. As he watched, they even seemed to grow longer.

Flecks of monkey spittle fell on Remy's face. The simian gibbered excitedly. Being so close to its hated enemy had driven it crazy. Remy wasn't just a god though, he was a man who had long ago learned to do whatever was necessary to survive.

With his free hand he reached out, talons extended. A moment later, he yanked downward for all he was worth. A look of profound sorrow crossed the simian's face. Its bellowing cry transformed into a high-pitched scream. He hadn't gone for its eyes this time. He'd gone for orbs even more precious.

Blood fell in a hot gush from its ruined crotch. Remy didn't exactly take pleasure in using talons on the thin skin of its wrinkle-purse. Still, he didn't hesitate to remove its manhood. And he was all about a bit of psychological warfare as he slapped it with its own severed penis.

He threw the shredded remains of its junk aside. While it shed tears of ultimate sadness, he looked down at its groin and thought: *Now* that's *a bleeding status.* He was reflecting on that when the other monkey sneak-attacked him.

The cut against its throat truly hadn't been that deep. After it recovered from the momentary shock, the agile beast had arrested its fall. While he'd been feminizing the other one, it had climbed back up. If not for its maddened gibbering, he wouldn't have noticed it was coming before it reached him.

When it dove at his back Remy spun, blocking the monster's attack with the body of the castrated beast he still held. All fight had gone out of the gelded simian. It just limply batted at its own groin, desperately trying to reassure itself that Remy hadn't actually ripped off its sex nose. It failed miserably.

The attacking simian was trying to climb over the body of its fellow to get to the godling. At this point, Remy was supporting the weight of both their bodies. It made his arms strain, but it also gave him control. He continued his spin until he was facing the trunk. Yelling, Remy slammed both monkeys against the tree. Sandwiching the monkeys between himself and the wood, he was chest to chest with the first, its cries barely audible as it bled out.

He grabbed one of the back monkey's arms to restrain it. His Strength might not be high, but it was enough to keep that one limb from attacking. His talons sunk in. It didn't cause much damage, but it secured his grip.

The monkey in the back screamed in anger. Its eyes were bloodshot and crazed. The beast's free hand swiped at Remy with sharp, broken nails. It dug gashes in his left side, but Remy forced himself to ignore the pain. Even if their strengths were equal, his larger body mass was enough to keep them pinned for a moment. That was all he needed.

With a cold grin, Remy grabbed the scalp hair of the gelded simian in a tight grip. Barely any life was left in it, but there was enough for it to look at him in dread. The god bared his teeth in battle-fueled anger and snapped the castrato's head backward into the face of the other.

The first hit seemed to puzzle the still-struggling simian more than anything else. It blinked in confusion, but then started trying to snap at him again. The second time he slammed their heads together, the beast seemed a bit dazed. The next time he used the dying simian's head as a weapon, the other monster's eyes unfocused. After the fourth *thud*, both beasts had stopped making any noise and their arms had fallen limp.

Remy didn't stop. He smashed their heads together again, then again, and then again. Remy could feel the crumpling of bone on the sixth blow. It was a familiar feeling. He knew it meant that the bones in the back simian's snout were fracturing. There was always an almost delicate "crumpling paper" feeling when the interlocking bones of the face were destroyed.

After two more strikes, the monkey closest to him was dead, and the one in the back was in a world of hell. Its snout had fully caved in, leaving a small round bloody hole. Teeth festooned the enlarged orifice, but they were no longer in orderly rows. There were also several missing. Some had fallen free, some were at the back of its throat and more than a few were embedded in the skull of the dead simian.

After the tenth hit, a small mist of blood appeared on each impact. He heard the monkey's teeth rattling together, like tic-tacs on hard plastic. On the eleventh strike, the *thud* became a wet *thwack*. The face of the one in back began to resemble raw meat.

With a cold and impassive countenance, the godling continued to beat it to death with his bare hands. When blood splattered across his face after a particularly juicy collision, he just blinked before continuing his grisly work. After the twentieth hit, its face was not recognizable.

Seeing that, Remy pried open the mouth of the dead monkey. Yanking sharply, he was able to snap the fangs off. Exhausted, he stood on the branch, his chest heaving from his exertions. He used *Soul Heal,* replenishing twenty health. He'd need to use the skill several more times and didn't see a reason to wait.

It was time to finish the fight. One at a time, he shoved the fangs into the neck of the battered simian. It was so injured that it didn't respond when its blood started to trickle out. Red blood flowed thick and dark out of the fangs. In seconds, it breathed its last and another sphere of rainbow light began to dance frantically around him. Exhaustion may have filled his body, but victory and bloody joy filled his heart.

CHAPTER 14

He pulled the fangs out of the simian's throat. They went into his impromptu arm pouch. After they were put away, it occurred to him that the bodies might be useful as well. Looking down, he dropped them one at a time on the eaglebear. The beast snarled at him, batting the first body away. It caught the second in its beak though, and started eating. The baleful look it gave him was almost haughty, thanking its mortal enemy for a good meal.

Remy just glared with a faint smile. Laugh it up, fuzzball. After climbing back up to the higher limb, he sat down and leaned wearily against the trunk. Now that he was relatively safe again, he called up his interface. A blinking icon in the corner showed that he had prompts

Congratulations! You have met the qualifications for the **Warrior** Class! Warriors specialize in physical combat, gaining bonuses to attack, damage and more.

Qualification: Defeat five enemies in martial combat

163

Warriors are a *common* Class and require **50 Energy Slots**. Progressing in this Class and unlocking its Skills will consume more energy slots.

Adopting this Class will:

Unlock some combat-focused Skills

Give immediate bonuses to melee damage

Do you wish to become a **Warrior**?

A warning came along with the question.

Be warned! A **Class** cannot be easily cast aside once adopted. Each Class will also increase the Energy Cost of future Classes. Allocate your Energy wisely.

The topic of Energy had come up again. He remembered the first prompt describing it. It had said it was a measure of potential. At the time, that description had seemed obtuse, but now he got it. Becoming a Warrior would let him become a better fighter, but it would use up some of his Energy slots. The prompt also seemed to imply that the more Warrior powers he obtained the more Energy slots it would take up as well.

If he kept accepting Classes, he might get to a point where all his Energy slots were filled up. At the very least it would mean he couldn't learn any more Divine Skills, like *Soul Strike* or *Soul*

Heal. With Energy as a limitation, he'd need to carefully plan what he wanted to become.

Remy considered the choice before him. Using up twenty-five slots wasn't that big of a deal for him. His Divine Core provided him with five hundred Energy Points. And while planning ahead was great, he was sure there would be more killing in the future. Becoming a Warrior was a good idea.

Congratulations! You have adopted the **Warrior Class**!

+5% to melee and ranged damage

Warrior skills are now unlocked, but you must still meet the criteria to gain each skill.

You are now a **Level 0 Brawler**, the lowest rank of Warrior

---

As soon as he got that prompt, another appeared.

You have qualified for the *common* Warrior skill **Unarmed Combat**

Qualification: Defeat 5 enemies in unarmed combat

Adopting this skill will increase the damage you deal with unarmed strikes.

This skill costs **5 Energy** Slots.

Do you wish to learn this skill?

Remy didn't hesitate.

Congratulations! You are now a Copper Novice in **Unarmed Combat.**

+5% speed unarmed strikes. +5% unarmed damage.

Total Energy Remaining: 391/605

He immediately wondered what a "copper novice" was. Thankfully, the next prompts supplied the answer.

Know This! Mundane Skills are separated into ranks: **Novice, Initiate, Apprentice, Journeyman, Adept, Master** and **Grandmaster**.

Know This! Each rank is subdivided into **Copper, Silver** and **Gold**.

Know This! Skills can be advanced through understanding and experience as well as practice. You have been found to have a proficiency in Unarmed Combat greater than that of your current rank of **Copper Novice**.

Your true proficiency is that of a **Silver Journeyman**.

+100% speed to skill progress until your rank matches your proficiency.

No rank tests will be required until you reach your true proficiency.

Remy hadn't seen a prompt like this before. He read it several times to make sure he wasn't missing anything. It looked like his punches would hit 5% harder now that he had qualified for the skill. It also looked like the years of training on Earth had not gone to waste. He'd be able to advance the skill twice as fast as normal. The prompt did make him wonder just how much of a damage boost his fists could get and what bonuses could come from reaching another rank.

The next thing he did was look at the souls he'd captured. Of the six enemies he'd just slain, he was only able to claim four of the souls. Two of the bodies had fallen to the ground before he could claim their spirits. There just hadn't been enough time in the heat of battle, not even with his new instincts. Those souls gave him new options, however. With no hesitation, he filled his last soul slot.

Congratulations! You have powered your State of Existence with the soul of a **Snaptooth Simian**.

Know This! In addition to powering Divine Powers of the Soul Art, a bound soul can offer specific benefits to a follower of the Soul Art.

Bound Soul: Snaptooth Simian	**Class:** Common
POWERS	
Profound Balance – Binding this soul has greatly increased your Secondary Attribute, Balance. +50% to Balance. +100% to Balance while in a tree.	

Remy's eyes widened after he read the description. Back on Earth, there had been plenty of time to talk. Without the internet, people had been forced to converse with one another again for entertainment. That had triggered a good deal of speculation, and one of the popular topics had been if there were more Attributes than the nine you could see on your status page. Many believed there were hidden Attributes. He'd thought so as well, but he'd never met anyone who could confirm it. It seemed he now had proof that Secondary Attributes existed. Another prompt described Balance in detail.

Know This! You have discovered a Secondary Attribute: **Balance**.

Secondary Attributes can be governed by any number of factors, including but not limited to: Primary Attributes such as Strength and Dexterity, skills, bloodlines, and abilities. No one has ever fully quantified the number of Secondary Attributes which exist.

Balance is the ability to remain upright and steady. The higher its value, the less likely you are to lose your footing. A higher Balance also makes certain physical actions more efficient and lowers stamina consumption.

Most adult humanoids have a baseline Balance of +0.9-1.1. The Razin have a +25% boost to Balance compared to other races and have a base Balance of +1.1-1.4

Your Balance is +1.33

After binding the Snaptooth Simian soul, your total Balance is +2 or +2.66 while in a tree

---

The prompt actually explained a lot. For one, it cleared up how Remy himself had been able to climb the tree so easily. When he'd been making his ascent, not only had his stamina fallen slowly, but he'd instinctually seemed to know how to distribute his weight. He'd thought the razin might be particularly well-suited to climbing. It turned out it was the bonus to Balance that explained it. What confused him though was that he didn't feel any different now. Maybe it was because he was still suffering from blood loss, but when he looked at his hands…

That was when he realized that he was no longer bracing himself against the trunk. The realization made his heart race. For a moment, his waking mind threatened to disrupt the equilibrium he had unconsciously found. His arms pinwheeled a bit, but then he found his center again. His eyes widened as he grasped the enormity of what was happening. As he gingerly got to his feet he came to a conclusion. This was amazing!

The branch he was standing on was only a foot in diameter. Before, he might have fallen off if he'd lost his concentration. Now he felt like he could dance a jig, if he were a jig dancer. Which he wasn't. He was seriously impressed though. The soul of the snaptooth simian was only *common*, but it had increased his Balance so much that the limbs of the tree felt like the middle of a wide street.

Despite the pain he was still feeling, a sharp-toothed grin found its way onto Remy's face. If this low-level monkey let him get such an advantage, then he could not *wait* until he captured stronger souls. For now, his gaze found its way to the eaglebear that was looking up at him. Just you wait, you feathery fucker. I'll be grabbing your soul soon enough!

CHAPTER 15

With all his soul slots filled, he was certainly more formidable than he had been before. With his Balance doubled, he might even be able to sneak by the eaglebear. If he was able to go around it, he might be able to make it to the ground first. The whole time he'd been in the tree, he had been dreading the first blush of sunrise.

He only had until daybreak to finish the *Save Us I* quest. He hadn't gotten any more quest updates about tribe members dying, but he still had to find them and claim their allegiance. If he didn't, he'd lose his connection to his Chosen tribe. When the possible consequences included "dissolution of self," he wasn't really eager to have that happen.

He couldn't ignore the fact that the eaglebear wasn't the only monster in this tree though. Even if he snuck by it, he might get swarmed by the monkeys. The only thing keeping them at bay was the feathered fucker below him. Then, even if he did make it to the ground, it might follow him back to the tribe. That would defeat the purpose of all of this. He wasn't sure where that left him. Basically holding a crapsack of bad options, he thought sourly.

The truth was, he just didn't see a way around it. He had to kill the eaglebear. Somehow. If he was going to do that though, he needed to maximize his chances. That meant gaining a level. He'd already covered half the distance to level one. The requirements might be much higher than on Earth but, according to his status log, the level 3 monkeys were giving nearly two hundred XP each thanks to the level difference. He needed to keep farming.

A pained groan came out of his mouth as he sat back down against the tree trunk again. He was still covered in wounds, and needed to recover his charges as well as heal. He definitely needed to farm more monkeys. Just as soon as that "I'm going to throw up on myself" feeling went away.

The good news was he still had three more captured souls. The bad news was he wasn't sure what to do with them. His first thought was to replace the souls in his soul slots. With a ready supply of souls, he could theoretically have an unlimited supply of charges for his Divine Powers. Trying that though, he got a warning prompt.

Do you wish to remove the **Snaptooth Simian** soul from your *Soul Heal* slot?

This will destroy the soul.

It will also be impossible to replace it with a soul of the same rarity for 1 full day.

He honestly wasn't too bothered by the idea of destroying the soul. If he was bothered by ethical concerns, which he made it a policy not to be, he'd have already crossed that line by basically enslaving it. His plan for unlimited charges wouldn't work though, not with all the souls being *common* rank. That left him only one thing to do while he waited.

For the first time, the new god began to cultivate.

He still didn't fully understand what cultivation would do, but he took Sariel's warning about not ignoring it to heart. If cultivation was a way to increase his strength, then he couldn't ignore it, not with an unseen clock counting down until more powerful beings came to Telos. He had two methods right now, the *Basic Cultivation Technique of Gods and Clergy* and the *Soul Consumption Cultivation Technique*. Those were both mouthfuls so he shortened them to the basic and soul techniques in his mind.

The basic method needed Faith Points, of which he still had zero, so that was out. The soul method was what he tried now. The knowledge of what to do had been poured into his mind by his sponsor's gift. He knew it so well it felt as if he'd been doing it his whole life. Sitting as comfortably as he could on the branch, he let his Divine Powers recharge and started to cultivate.

After closing his eyes, he split his attention. Part of him listened to the world around him while the greater part focused its attention inward. Reaching out without moving, he focused on his Divine Core. Without the cultivation techniques he might have never known it was there, but now it was easy to visualize it.

After a few seconds of focus, he saw a stylized version of himself floating in a sea of black. In front of the figure, a white three-sided pyramid slowly rotated. Each of the four faces of the tetrahedron were equal in size. The edges were a glowing metallic gold, and the inner white structure was translucent. It exuded a profound stillness, but also an expectant feeling that it desired to be more.

After visualizing both his body and the core successfully, now came the harder part. Into that "other" space that held his Divine Core, he pulled one of the captured souls. It still struggled against his control, but it was almost completely suppressed now that he had consumed it. Focusing, he moved the soul into the pyramid. It hovered in the exact center. This was when his cultivation began.

Rays of light formed at each of the vertices and grew at the same speed, reaching inward. After several breaths, they reached the soul simultaneously. Then, like electrical cables, they began to siphon the soul's energy.

As soon as that happened, the soul began to struggle even harder. If it could be said that spirits had a survival instinct, then it knew it was in danger. This made it harder for Remy because the soul technique was both simple and strict in its requirements. The four rays had to siphon energy from the soul at equal rates. If the draw became unbalanced, the soul would be destroyed, the power would be lost and it was possible for him to suffer harm. With it struggling, its perfectly centered position was threatened.

One of the reasons Remy had been chosen, however, was his high mental strength. Focusing, he kept the soul in place. As its energy was siphoned, the golden lines of the core grew brighter. In an inverse relationship, the kaleidoscope of colors on the soul slowed and grew dimmer.

Several times Remy had to focus to keep the soul centered and ensure the rays drew equal amounts of power. Each time it slowed the process, but he never lost control. In fact, as time went on the process grew easier, due to both him getting more comfortable with it and the soul growing weaker. What Remy did not know was that this cultivation technique was perfectly suited both for his personality and his Art. If it had been another technique, he most likely would have failed several times until he learned enough about it. Thanks to his sponsor, however, after nearly fifty minutes he successfully cultivated on his first attempt!

Congratulations! You have cultivated for the first time! While levels will grow your power and ranks will improve your limitations, only tier ascension will remove them altogether.

You have created **1 Divine Point!**

Create 99 more to take the first step on the Rainbow Path.

The soul had vanished and the golden rays retracted. Above the white pyramid a mote of red light appeared. It floated down until it touched the nearest vertex, and then bled into the white interior of the pyramid. The milky color gained the faintest hint of pink.

Remy opened his eyes. He felt a sense of satisfaction from what he'd just done, like finishing a home improvement project, but he didn't feel any stronger. He guessed he'd have to wait until he finished the first step of the path before he felt an actual change. Still, it was good to know that he could actually use this method to improve his power. Even though he had the information downloaded into his mind, it had still seemed a bit too mystical to be true, even for a reincarnated man. He'd seen magic and he knew how leveling worked. Cultivation though was something new.

The god used *Soul Heal* three times, bringing his health back to full. That left him only the charges from his bound souls. He decided to wait another thirty minutes, bringing his charges back to full. With the time it took, he also decided to use one of the two remaining souls to cultivate again. This time it went more smoothly.

An hour later, he'd consumed another soul and made another Divine Point. Just like last time, the soul had created a mote of red light that bled into the pyramid. The pink hue deepened in a barely perceptible way. After he opened his eyes, he turned his Title back on and went to lure more monkeys.

This time, luck played in his favor. He never lured more than three at a time. To save charges, he used *Soul Strike* until only one was left. Thanks to his newly improved Balance, he was able to fight without bracing against the trunk. That made it much easier to overpower the last monkey. That was why, less than two hours later, he gained more prompts.

For killing **12 *common* rank** enemies with the Title **Infuriating Enemy** equipped, you have gained **240 Animosity Points**. 260/1,000 obtained to upgrade your Title.

You have gained: **2,312 XP**. 2,686/2,500 XP to reach Level 1

He'd captured another 12 *common* souls, but more importantly, he'd gained enough experience to level up! For the first time on this new world, he heard the sweetest of sounds!

TRING!	
You have reached level **1**! The power of a god is potentially without limit, but it must be grown. Your soul rank is the equivalent of **Limited**. Never forget, there are many forms of power and this is only one.	
Attribute Points	+2 to Agility and Dexterity +2 Free Attribute Points
Bonus Energy Slots	+10
Class Points	+30

The amount of experience he'd needed to level up was substantially more than he'd required on Earth. It had only taken 1,000 XP to reach level one back then. The fact that he needed 2.5 times as much experience meant that levels were both more difficult to come by and more valuable in this world. He needed to be very careful about how he allocated his points.

Four of the points were beyond his control. Both his Agility and Dexterity had gained +2. He could immediately feel that his body was a bit looser. Those two points had increased each attribute by more than 10%. He already felt a bit more limber. Even though he was still wounded, he could tell that twisting and bending over was easier. His footing on the branch also felt surer. While he still didn't like that his points were being auto-assigned, he couldn't deny the benefit to having a higher Dex and Agility.

The question now was what to do with his two free points. Magic wasn't really an issue for him right now. He didn't have any skills or spells that would use up his mana. That made Intelligence and Wisdom lower priority. The biggest lacks he'd had so far were his Strength, health and Endurance.

He wanted to put more points into his Strength, but he'd been too close to death too many times already. His high Agility and Dexterity should let him avoid hits, but with a low health, one or two hard ones might be the end of him. Hoping he was making the right choice, he put both points into Constitution. His shoulders widened slightly and his body mass increased almost imperceptibly. The outward changes were far less important than the extra twenty Health Points he now had.

Remy brought his new status window up to see the changes.

#### ####		
Art: Soul	**Level:** 1	
Energy: 391/621	**Cultivation:** Spirit Made Flesh (Tier 0/0) Progress: 2/100	
STATS		
Health: 98/110	**Mana:** 120 *Regen/min: 7.2*	**Stamina:** 83/100 *Regen/min: 6*
ATTRIBUTES		
Strength: 8*	**Agility:** 17*	**Dexterity:** 17*
Constitution: 11*	**Endurance:** 10*	**Intelligence:** 12*
Wisdom: 15*	**Charisma:** 11*	**Luck:** 10*
RESISTANCES		**WEAKNESSES**
None		None
GOD ABILITIES		
God's Eye: The sight of gods **Soul Capture:** Capture the souls of defeated enemies		
CLASSES and SKILLS		
Warrior: Level 0 - **Unarmed Combat:** Copper Novice		

His name was still masked, for some reason. His attributes though had adjusted, just like his health. His Energy had increased. But what really drew his eye were the two new lines at the bottom. It showed his Warrior Class and Unarmed Combat Skill. It also reminded him he had Class Points to spend. He had no idea what those were for exactly, but focusing brought up a new prompt.

Congratulations! You have taken your first step toward improving your **Class**! Classes can be improved in a number of ways, but the most direct is by spending Class Points.

NAME	COST	DESCRIPTION
Advance Level	10	Advance to Level 1 of your Warrior Class **+5% >> +10%** to melee and ranged damage May unlock further Class upgrades +5 Energy
Fast Hands (0/5)	10	+10% Attack Speed Requires 5 Energy Slots

Bell Ringer (Requires Unarmed Combat Novice)	10	Head Strike to *Stun* Enemy for **3 seconds** **Cost:** 10 Stamina Points **Cooldown**: 2 minutes Requires 5 Energy Slots
Advance Rank	100	Advance the rank of your Warrior Class Brawler (Rank 0) >> Fighter (Rank 1) LOCKED until Level 5

Remy had 30 Class Points to distribute. After looking over the options, he spent thirty of them on *Level 1 Warrior*, *Fast Hands* and *Bell Ringer*. He absolutely wanted the boost to the damage he could deliver. Being able to hit faster was also great, and *Bell Ringer* gave him a trump card.

Total Energy Remaining: 386/626

His Energy had fallen by another five after his upgrades. It looked like progressing a Class was a way for him to increase his max Energy which was good to know. As he'd already seen though, it probably wouldn't be enough to keep up with the upgrades the Class offered. Remy realized he needed to find other ways to increase his Energy as well.

For now, upgrading to a Level 1 Warrior had increased the bonus damage he delivered by +10%. It also unlocked another upgrade called *Dodge*. Purchasing it would increase his chance to evade an attack by 10%, but it would cost him 25 Class Points. He could upgrade his other two choices as well at a cost of 20 CPs each. Either way, any further purchases would have to wait until he earned more points.

Remy looked down. Sometime in the past two hours, the eaglebear had gone to sleep. With his newly gained level and capabilities, he was as ready as he was ever going to be. He climbed back up to the highest branch again and waited for his charges to refill. Once they were, there wasn't going to be any more time to waste. It was time to bring the fight to his mortal enemy. More than half the night was gone, and the tribe was getting further away by the moment.

The clouds had partially cleared while his Divine Power refilled. It afforded him a panoramic view of the sky and a sea of new stars. It was beautiful. Countless points of light festooned the dark sky. The three moons hung like lamps and swaths of color crisscrossed the night. In two other places now, he was able to see the rays of light partially forming unknown constellations.

Looking up, he realized this might be his last chance to enjoy the peaceful vista. It was entirely possible he'd be meeting death for the second time soon. Thanks to his bound soul, the swaying of the tree didn't bother him at all anymore. Remy lay on his back on a tree limb, easily balanced even while lying down. Scant clouds continued to blow across the sky. Right before his last bound soul was recharged, he saw it.

A flash of orange caught his eye. Right in the center of three moons was what he thought was a star at first. Focusing, he saw it had a tail behind it. Not a star at all. A comet. Looking at the entire sky, Remy's mouth fell open.

He'd seen this particular configuration of celestial bodies before. Not in his first life, but at the very beginning of his second. The sky was an exact copy of the picture his sponsor had left for him. It defied credulity. How the hell had his sponsor known he'd be in this exact spot at this exact time to see this?

Even crazier, Remy heard a voice. What he didn't know is that the ink used to draw the picture had contained a psychic residue. Triggered by his seeing the same image, the words written on the page sounded in his ears in a very real, and very gruff, voice.

"Jump!"

Remy shook his head vigorously. Was this really happening?

"Yes, really!"

The godling scoffed. He was no stranger to danger, but if his sponsors really thought he was going to jump out of a giant tree and fall hundreds of yards to the ground, they must be smoking crack. Now that he had the souls and had leveled up, he had a better chance fighting the eaglebear. Even without his new bonuses, a fight made more sense than jumping out of a skyscraper-sized tree! Why the hell would he-

A soft hoot made him look down. Staring up at him were dozens upon dozens of gleaming lights. It was hard to make out, but suddenly his brain made the connection. While he'd been waiting for the eaglebear to get the 'itis, dozens of the monkeys had been sneaking up on him. Apparently, once the eaglebear had fallen asleep, they'd lost their fear. Remy was just too tasty of a snack to ignore.

For a long moment neither side moved, but then the monkeys abandoned all attempts at stealth. With loud howls, they surged the last dozen yards toward his position. There was no way he could fight his way through all of them, even with his new Balance. At that very moment, he heard the last line of text that had been written on the paper.

"JUMP OR DIE, BITCH!"

Faced with the attack of nearly fifty snaptooth simians, the words had the very effect his sponsor had known they would. Gritting his teeth, he quickly clambered to the top of the tree and, without hesitation, leapt off. He didn't know how Spider-Man made it look so easy. When gravity caught hold of his body, the air filled with what might be his last request.

"Fuck meeeeeeeeee!"

CHAPTER 16

For a split second, Remy's upward momentum perfectly matched the pull of gravity and he hung motionless in the air. Then that moment shattered and he started to fall. Faster than seemed right, he was pulled to the ground. In less than a second, he was past the attacking monkeys. Right after that, he was in sight of the eaglebear. If it had been asleep before, the hoots of the snaptooths had woken it up. He was falling directly toward it. The eaglebear squawked in surprise. It tried to lift an arm to swat at him, but it was too slow.

Remy's body bulldozed into it. The feathers cushioned the impact by a miniscule amount, but his body easily knocked it from the branch it had been resting on. As they both launched out into space, the godling grabbed a handful of the eaglebear's feathers. It roared in protest and swung a heavy paw at him as their plummet began. Locked in battle, the two Mortal Enemies fought as they fell.

Using *Bellringer*, he punched the squarely eaglebear between the eyes. A faint red aura surrounded his fist as it landed squarely on the beast's head. His stamina dropped by twenty points, but he learned something in that moment. There was something insanely satisfying about seeing a cross-eyed eagle. The massive creature was only stunned for a single second, but it let the godling adopt a cocky smile.

Gandalf ain't got nothing on me!

The two continued to fall.

Remy braced his feet against the eaglebear, preparing to kick free. Thanks to *Profound Balance,* if he got away from it, he might be able to grab a branch and stop his fall. At the very least, he could slow his descent and let it crash into the ground. Problem solved.

Unfortunately, the two of them hit a branch before Remy could jump free. It struck the eaglebear in the middle of the back. The beast took the brunt of the blow, but the hit slammed Remy against its chest. The two of them were pressed against each other like lovers. That was the only thing that saved him. The beast snapped at him with its cruel beak, trying to fracture his skull. He was too close for it. Still, the tip of its beak tore a strip out of his scalp.

Remy ducked his head, avoiding further damage. With its arms around him, he couldn't keep the eaglebear from raking his back with its sharp claws. The godling's back arched and he cried out in pain. That one errant blow was enough to drop his health back down into the 80s.

The eaglebear's other paw landed on his back again, cutting even deeper. The attack also pushed him into the monster's rank feathers again. The beast smelled like must and rotten meat. Between the pain and the foul odor, it was too much. When the next branch hit the eaglebear, Remy vomited over them both. Disgustingly, gravity made a good deal of it fly back into his face.

Blood arced off the eaglebear's claws, and it screeched in triumph even as it fell. It wasn't bothered at all by its foe's vomit.

All it cared about was hurting its mortal enemy. Remy tried raking his small claws against the beast, but the feathers were too thick. He couldn't penetrate its defense. He might as well have been massaging the eaglebear's armored feathers. He needed a change in tactics, something that was extremely difficult to pull off while he was doing his best plinko ball impression with several tons of pissed off eaglebear.

Remy triggered *Soul Heal,* restoring 20 HP. He hadn't wanted to waste his skill during the fall. Not when the landing was still to come. That was also why he wasn't using *Soul Strike.* The godling was pretty sure he'd need all the health he could get when they reached the bottom. That meant if he was going to use his special attack, he only had the charge from his bound soul. He needed it to count.

They continued to fall, branches striking them as they did. Struggle as he might, the eaglebear kept Remy in its embrace. If he laid flat against its chest, it couldn't get a solid hit on him. If he moved though, its cruel claws were waiting. In this position, he couldn't even throw an effective punch. He could use *Soul Strike,* but it wouldn't be any different than holding a dagger flat against an enemy's skin. It just wouldn't do very much.

They tumbled through the air, flipping end over end. They hit tree limbs, both large and small. The larger ones slowed their descent, but never enough to actually stop them. The smaller ones snapped right in half. More than a few monkeys started falling with them after their homes were suddenly destroyed by an eaglebear-shaped meteor.

By the time they were halfway to the ground, both the eaglebear and Remy were bruised all to hell. If it wasn't for the limbs that kept slowing them, they would have already landed. Thankfully, even though they were spinning as they fell, the beast's larger bulk took the majority of the beating. The awful racket they made was punctuated by the eaglebear's pain-filled screeches and Remy's muffled curses. The truth was, by hugging the damn beast, he was able to avoid the worst of both the drop and its claws. Still, he had to use *Soul Heal* two more times to keep his health near the halfway mark.

In the last moments of their fall, their bodies were nearly aligned the ground. Remy saw it rushing up to meet them, fast as fate. They continued to spin, however, which is why neither the godling nor the beast saw the last large branch that they struck. While there had been many glancing blows as they fell the five hundred yards from the top, this time Remy heard a solid *CRUNCH*! The force of the hit was several times stronger than anything else they'd experienced during the fall.

Everything went black.

A flashing red light brought him back to consciousness. His health bar was almost empty. Only a faint sliver of red remained. Agony wracked his body, both as a result of his low HP and the massive toll he'd suffered from falling out of a goddamn tree. He'd never been more relieved than when he groggily realized he had one more *Soul Heal* charge. His health shot up by twenty, and the agony throbbing inside him lessened just a bit.

With a long and agonized groan, he picked up his head and looked around. At least he tried to do that. As soon as he started craning his neck, he blacked out. Coming to again, he decided to ponder his situation in a reclined position.

What the hell had just happened? He remembered the fall. Then it felt like a truck had hit him full speed. But the truck had been made out of... funky-ass pillows? Wait! His mind started clearing a bit. Where the hell was the eaglebear? And why was that red light still in his face!

It was only then that his addled mind realized that the red warning light hadn't just been because of his low health. He also had debuff prompts.

You have suffered a **Mild Concussion**.

Mentation, coordination, and reasoning are decreased by 30% for the next 10 minutes. Greatly improved chance of spell miscast and/or backfire.

You have suffered a **Serious Head Trauma**.

You will experience Profound Confusion for the next 5 minutes. Moderate Confusion for 5 minutes after that. Mild Confusion for 5 minutes after that.

There were more debuffs dealing with internal bleeding, a broken nose, two dislocated fingers, and a bruised kidney. None of them seemed life-threatening though, especially now that he had started circulating healing energy. He was sure there would have been more if he hadn't already used *Soul Heal.*

The *Serious Head Trauma* and *Concussion* explained why he couldn't move. All he could do was lay there and hope neither the eaglebear nor the monkeys would finish him off. Any attempted movement made his vision darken again. It was the longest five minutes of his new life. The *Confusion* debuff was horrible. It felt like the worst drunk since… no, it was too hard to figure out when, but it sucked.

He knew that he *could* think at a higher level; he just couldn't manage it.

By the time his *Profound Confusion* had improved to *Moderate Confusion* he had recovered a Divine Power charge. He must have been unconscious for at least five minutes after impact. Using it again, he focused the energy around his head this time. The *Mild Concussion* debuff disappeared and his *Moderate Confusion* improved to *Mild.* At last, he could sit up again. Pain spread like chain lightning inside him and made him curse.

Pain-filled or not, he was alive. Grunting softly, he grabbed the fourth finger on his right hand. The dislocation was at his DIP. Wrapping his left hand around it, he tried to bend at the same time. His eyes watered and a hot needle of agony shot up his arm, but then there was a soft pop. The pain disappeared all of a sudden, one of those strange facts about dislocations. Repeating the process with his third finger almost drew a full tear. It definitely drew some colorful words from his mouth.

He'd have loved to heal again, but his Divine Power needed ten minutes to recharge. After being on the ground so long, he wasn't willing to let his mortal enemy have any more time to rally. The fact that he was still alive made it likely the eaglebear was hurt worse than he was, but it might be recovering as well. He couldn't let that happen. It was time to end this.

Remy stood up. Unfortunately, the sky and the ground decided to switch positions. By the time he knew what had happened, he'd fallen, vomited again, and was struggling to stay on all fours. Staring at his spew, he wondered how there could possibly still be anything inside him. He'd never actually eaten before, depending on how you looked at it. It made no sense for him to keep throwing up. His new body didn't agree and continued to expel bile.

Once he recovered again, he realized he'd been dumb. Just because some of his debuffs had worn off didn't mean that he was back in top shape. The world might operate by video game principles, but real-world consequences still existed. And in the real world, you didn't bounce back fifteen minutes after major head trauma.

Soul Heal, for instance, had removed the pain of having a depleted health bar, but his body was still sore and battered from the fall. It felt like he'd been worked over in a boxing ring and had only had a night's sleep to recover. Not sharp pain, but horrible soreness and dull aches. His ability didn't fix that.

Similarly, the duration of his *Concussion* debuff might be fifteen minutes, but as a doctor he knew that the sequelae of an actual concussion could last days, or even weeks. It was just that the specific consequences listed in the debuff were no longer artificially being imposed on him. Basic point being, he had just fallen out of a tree the size of a skyscraper and *somehow* had managed to survive. He needed to go slow.

Standing up more gingerly this time, Remy wished he had some water to rinse the foul taste from his mouth. He'd vomited twice in the past thirty minutes. The taste was vile. A part of him realized the irony in that complaint. This had all started because he'd pissed in a monster's mouth. Perhaps this was just a little bit of karma coming back at him. He decided not to bemoan his situation any further. He was still alive. He was doing pretty good. Looking around, he took stock.

He'd made it back to the ground. He was still under the massive tree, but couldn't see the eaglebear. That didn't mean too much though, as the ambient light of the moons barely illuminated the area under the tree. Looking up, he was just able to make out that the end of the lowest branch above him had been snapped off.

It was fifteen feet off the ground. Thinking back, the last thing he could remember was a crunching noise. He realized that must have been when he and the eaglebear had struck the branch. Seeing as how his little body wasn't a sticky mess right now, the monster must have taken the brunt of the hit.

Looking down again, he was able to detect a line of crushed grass. That must be how my body rolled after it hit the ground, he thought. If I fell on one side of the branch and rolled, he reasoned, maybe the eaglebear fell on the other side. Casting about, his eyes fell on a rock about the size of a volleyball. Truly not an ideal weapon, but it was better than nothing. Hefting it with a pained groan, he walked around the trunk, ready to kill or be killed.

What met his gaze was a pathetic sight. The eaglebear had indeed hit the tree limb, at over a hundred miles an hour. The branch had snapped its spine. It was lying on the ground, back twisted at an unnatural angle. Ironically, it was the monster's own death grip on Remy that had saved him. Its large feathered body had absorbed almost all the impact. Even so, the small portion of the hit that had transmitted through to the godling had almost depleted his ninety points of health.

The monster's injuries were not limited to blunt force trauma. Whether on the initial impact with the branch or during the fall, the eaglebear had been impaled. A length of wood as thick as his wrist was sticking out of the beast. Remy could only see the foot of blood-covered branch that was jutting out of the eaglebear, but from the way the creature was gurgling as it breathed there was a fair chance its lung had been punctured. He looked at it with his God's Eye.

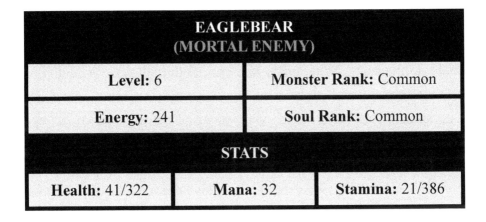

EAGLEBEAR (MORTAL ENEMY)		
Level: 6	**Monster Rank:** Common	
Energy: 241	**Soul Rank:** Common	
STATS		
Health: 41/322	**Mana:** 32	**Stamina:** 21/386

It had gained a level. Remy took that as proof that the mana leaking into Telos was strengthening the world's monsters. That level hadn't saved it, as its health and mana were too severely depleted. Remy couldn't see any of its active effects, like debuffs, but he was sure there were plenty. As he watched, it lost another point of health. It was dying, but dying slowly. He took a step closer and it noticed his presence. The pitiful noises it made were a tragic shadow of its earlier proud cries. The beast locked eyes with its mortal enemy for a moment. It could not even summon rage. It just looked at him with resignation before laying its head back on the ground and crooning in agony.

Remy studied it objectively. Seeing it defeated, he didn't feel hate or mercy. As a soldier, he had always been able to compartmentalize. To do what needed to be done. That was why he had been able to savagely beat the simians to death. He'd taken no joy in their pain, though he quite enjoyed the feeling of victory.

The savagery itself, however, had simply been... necessary. Unlike normal people who worried, fretted and avoided violence, something shifted inside him when there were distasteful things to be done. His consciousness occupied a mental and emotional space that simply didn't allow for distractions like morality and conscience.

During his days of service, he'd met other men and women who could do the same. What made him special though was his ability to turn his empathy and compassion back on when the time for brutality had passed. That combination was what had actually drawn the eye of the Organization. His ability to laugh in polite company mere hours after having his hands drenched red with blood had made him a "versatile asset." Of course, he'd ultimately committed acts so heinous that even he couldn't compartmentalize or rationalize it away...

Remy took a deep breath to steady himself. There was no benefit in picking at old wounds. He had done what he had done. He was what he was. All he could do was continue moving forward. Besides, he thought, looking at the gravely wounded beast, there was work to be done.

He had continued to watch its health bar and it had only lost one point every thirty seconds or so. It was dying, but slowly and in pain. The rock he'd been holding thumped down near his feet.

The godling circled around to the head of the eaglebear, well wide of its claws. Despite the fact that it was gravely injured and near death, Remy did not want to make the mistake of underestimating it. Wounded animals could still kill. He planned his approach carefully. The monster was lying on its back. Its right front leg was snapped in two. Neither of its back legs were moving, thanks to its severed spine. He was careful as he walked around it.

He reached a hand toward his waist. Before his dive out of the tree, he had twisted his shirt like a wet towel and tied it around his waist. In the center of that cloth belt were several of the snaptooth simian fangs, each three inches long. With care, he unwrapped them. Miraculously, only half of them had been destroyed in the fall. Taking them in his hand, he approached the head of the eaglebear.

It oriented on him again, drunk with pain. It did not lift its head again though. It was too weak. The beast just looked at him upside down. Remy knelt by it and placed one hand on the side of its face, well away from the beak. He was ready to snatch his hand back in a flash if need be, but it just continued to lie there, crooning in pain.

Nodding to himself that the fight had left it, he dug his fingers into the overlapping layers of feathers and lifted them, exposing the vulnerable flesh beneath. The godling looked at the eaglebear and spoke simply in a voice of true intention, "I am sorry for the disrespect I showed you, and that you have come to this end." There was no pity or regret in his tone. He merely spoke, one honored enemy to another.

With no further delay, he forcefully plunged the simian fangs into the hybrid monster's neck, one after the other. Blood that looked black in the night flowed out of each hollow bone tube. The eaglebear's health dropped to zero in seconds. Its burbling, wet cries faded as it was finally freed from pain. Its chest inflated one last time before it exhaled and let loose its mortal coil.

The forest was quiet in benediction of one of its fallen giants. Remy remained kneeling, one hand holding its feathers, and the other drenched in its blood. His brown skin was coated in the blood of his fallen foes and his own sick. The coppery scent of the eaglebear's spent life mixed with its foul odor, both filling his nose. Exhausted and filthy as he was, he no longer cared. He just gazed out at the blackness of the night... right before it exploded with colors.

CHAPTER 17

Notifications chimed in his ears, but he kept them minimized. In front of him was a kaleidoscope of wonder. Bright ribbons of rainbow light were being siphoned from the eaglebear's body. The soul light was much more vivid than the spirits he'd collected from the snaptooth simians. The sphere being created was also much larger. The time it took for the monkey souls to coalesce had only been about a second or two; it took over half a minute for the eaglebear's soul.

When it was finally done, it was easy to see that the sphere was half again as large as the monkeys'. The colors it contained were also twice as complex; as opposed to just a morass of bright hues, Remy felt like he was able to see a pattern in the chaos. The biggest difference though was the fact that the soul didn't try to escape. Instead, it floated up into the air and came to hover before him. With a flash, another notification appeared. It was accompanied by a sound like monks singing a benediction.

You have uncovered a true **Prayer** by meeting the following Secret Conditions:

1) Personally deliver a death blow to a **Mortal Enemy**.

2) Bathe your skin in the lifeblood of a **Mortal Enemy.**

3) Speak words of **True** respect and honor your foe.

Congratulations! You have discovered your first Prayer: **Honored Foe's Panegyric**. Your heartfelt words can potentially remove any anger a soul may feel toward you. This Prayer might be effective against undead and other Death creatures.

To deliver this prayer in the future simply touch a dead or dying foe and speak the words, "**Final Rest.**"

This Prayer can be upgraded by performing it over 100 Enemies. **Current Count:** 1/100

Future usages of this Prayer must be powered by Faith Points.

The actions of the eaglebear's soul started to make sense. If its anger had been removed, then that might be why it wasn't trying to flee. It would also explain why it had coalesced without any intervention from him.

Remy examined the hovering soul. To his surprise, he got more information now than when he'd examined the monkeys' souls. It was as if using his Art had unlocked more abilities. It also explained why this soul was so much bigger than the ones he'd seen before.

> Know This! You have ensnared the soul of a Mortal Enemy.
>
> While such a foe is dangerous, there are benefits to defeating such an adversary. Danger and Power are close bedfellows. A Mortal Enemy experiences a depth of emotion that most beings never reach.
>
> Slain Mortal Enemies will have their souls upgraded by **1 rank**.

It looked like killing a mortal enemy was a way for him to collect stronger souls. He'd just checked the eaglebear's status page a few minutes ago and was sure its soul had been *common,* but now a quick glance showed it had changed to *uncommon.* This prompt explained why it had gotten an upgrade. The question now was, how did that help him?

Looking at the soul, he was able to instinctively feel what would happen if he assigned it to one of his Divine Powers. Instead of the single charge *common* souls gave, it would give two. There was also the chance of adding a special effect to his powers.

While that sounded great, what was more interesting is what would happen if he assigned it to his State of Being.

UNTETHERED SOUL: Eaglebear (Mortal Enemy)	**Class:** Uncommon
POWERS	
1) Eyes of the Eaglebear– Capturing this soul will greatly increase your vision. You will be able to see extremely well in the dark. Additionally, your sight will gain a "zoom" effect, providing you the ability to increase the maximum distance of your vision by up to 100%. This will narrow your field of vision proportionally. **2) *Unknown* (LOCKED!)** – Provide 100 Soul Points of nourishment to unlock.	

Not only would assigning the eaglebear soul give a very useful power, it would give two. At present though, it looked like the second one was locked. As he stared at the word "Unknown," another prompt appeared.

Know This! Some of the powers of higher ranked souls will be locked until specific conditions are met. To unlock the 2nd Power of the Eaglebear, supply it with captured souls equivalent to 100 Soul Points.

There was nothing else in the message. He had no idea how much 100 Soul Points equated to. Did that mean one hundred souls? He hoped not, but he'd figure it out as time went on.

What he had to decide now was if the eaglebear's higher ranked soul would serve him better than the snaptooth simian's. The increase in Balance from the simian soul had probably saved his life during the fall. He'd instinctively tucked and curled his body at certain times, shifting both his and the eaglebear's position so it was always on the bottom. While a high Balance sounded trivial, it already had demonstrated its value. On the other hand, the bonus was halved now that he was out of the tree.

Conversely, the eaglebear's soul would let him actually see in the dark. That had great appeal to him as he could barely see thirty feet in front of him right now, and then only vague shapes. The Razin race might have a bit of night vision, but not enough to trek through unfamiliar, monster-infested terrain.

Being able to see in the dark might be the difference between being eaten or making it to sunrise. For that matter, it might be the difference between failing the quest or finding the tribe before sunrise. Hours had passed while he was in the tree and the razin were long gone.

It looked like the soul also provided a binocular effect. That could be very helpful, especially when coupled with his *God's Eye* ability. He'd be able to scope out enemies before they got close, and decide whether to engage or flee. It was true that he'd killed several beasts thanks to his powers, but he did not overestimate his abilities.

Slaying the eaglebear had been a matter of luck as much as anything else. If not for that weirdly cryptic drawing, he never would have tried something so foolhardy as throwing himself out of a perfectly good tree. Based on the accompanying note, sending him that particular piece of advice had cost his sponsor the equivalent of a moon. Remy didn't think he'd be getting help like that again.

In future battles, he'd have to rely on himself. Truth be told, even if his sponsor did give him more help, the godling had zero desire to go up against another giant monster anytime soon. The eaglebear had been a truly daunting mass of flesh and talons. Even in death it looked like a small boulder in the night. Without a boost to his night vision, Remy might walk right up to something just like it if the monster didn't move beforehand. That realization as much as anything made night vision insanely attractive right now. The only downside was he had to give up the simian's soul.

Remy stopped for a second, then shook his head at the inanity of his mental deliberations. There was a monster's soul *inside* his chest! It was the height of lunacy that such realities had become his new normal. A couple months ago he'd just been a regular human. A few weeks before the Calamity, he'd spent three *days* researching the next iphone.

Now he was a pantherman, a razin, on a new world where eaglebears existed and screaming monkeys could regenerate fangs in seconds. He dragged both hands over his dirty face, inhaling deeply before expelling the air in a quiet huff. His mind firmed. Crazy or not, it was time to get to work.

Nodding to himself, he released the monkey's soul. Its spirit flew free from his chest and quickly disappeared from sight. It looked like once he released a soul he couldn't reclaim it. Meanwhile, he watched the eaglebear's soul continue to hover in front of him.

It occurred to him that he could just let the eaglebear's soul go free. He could have let all the beasts' souls go free. He had no reason to think that any of them were evil. Despite their magical natures, they were just animals doing what animals do. A lion wasn't evil for hunting a gazelle, after all. He only entertained that idea for a few seconds before chuckling in sarcastic laughter.

He would never ignore something so valuable. Let it go? That was nothing more than a vestigial thought left over from his tender youth, like believing in Santa or checking for herpes. His years as a state-sponsored killer had instilled in him a pragmatism much stronger than childhood frailties. Even if the soul hadn't seemed to be willing, he still would have captured it. He would take it, use it, then move on. Rectitude was not one of his virtues.

Remy opened his mouth and inhaled. The soul flew into the pale blue furnace of his throat. Rainbow energy phased into his body, and he realized there was a countdown icon in the corner of his vision. While the monkeys' souls had been assimilated almost immediately, it would take a full minute to bind the eaglebear's. Remy wondered if this was because it was a higher rank, *uncommon* rather than *common*. Only time would tell.

The point was, killing a Mortal Enemy gave extra benefits. Namely, it had increased the rank of the soul. He'd have to weigh the costs and benefits of using the souls of Mortal Enemies in the future. He'd also have to be careful when using his Title. *Infuriating Enemy* made it more likely for him to make a Mortal Enemy. If something deadlier than the eaglebear made it its life mission to kill him… "Danger and Power," he reflected.

About sixty seconds later, his senses expanded dramatically. He looked around in wonder. The night no longer held any secrets. Remy might as well have been standing in a field at noon. The shadows that had hidden everything just a moment before were gone. Looking up into the tree he could now see countless simian eyes looking back at him. The intensity of their gazes was actually a bit unnerving.

The monkeys were currently intimidated by the fact that he had slain the eaglebear. It was instinctual. Anything that could kill a large predator must be even more dangerous. Now that he could see clearly though, the godling saw that a large number of their eyes were actually fixated on the corpse and not him. With such an abundant feast right beneath them, who knew how long they would restrain themselves?

Looking around again, he felt a great deal better now that his eyes could pierce the gloom. Nothing seemed to be threatening him at the moment, so he allowed himself a bit of self-reflection. He'd done the impossible. He had survived. The body of his mortal enemy lay cooling at his feet and he remained standing. He was awesome!

The Universe seemed to agree with him. He was awesome... awesomely stupid!

No sooner had he been praising himself when angry red words flashed across his vision.

You have bound the soul of a Mortal Enemy! Performing the **Honored Foe's Panegyric** has removed some of the soul's anger, but was not successful in removing its status as your Mortal Enemy.

As you have bound it to your State of Being, this soul will grow stronger as you do.

At any time, it may attempt to resist you or even revolt. If the second eventuality occurs, you may suffer negative effects such as: **Soul Damage, Soul Dissolution** or **Possession**.

> If you do not come to terms with the soul of your Mortal Enemy, such a confrontation is inevitable!

"Shit!" Remy spat.

CHAPTER 18

He immediately tried to let go of the soul, only to receive more red lettering.

> The soul of a Mortal Enemy cannot be unbound unless both parties agree.

"Damn it!" he cursed again. A hooting from up in the tree reminded him this was not the time to worry about a future problem. The hooting spread until dozens of monkeys were letting him know that it was time to move on. They were hungry, and the eaglebear looked delicious.

As quickly as he could, Remy retrieved the snaptooth fangs from the eaglebear's neck, rolling them in the remains of his ruined shirt once again. He wasn't sure when they would be useful in the future, but they were the only real tool he had.

His next task was more distasteful, but definitely necessary. He grabbed a fistful of the eaglebear's feathers and, pulling as hard as he could, ripped several free. The scent of blood was all over him. If he could smell himself, then the beasts and monsters of the forest could as well. There was no way he could get rid of the smell here and now. His only choice was to coat himself with another scent that might not be so appealing.

Remy rubbed the foul-smelling feathers over his body. Even though he was already covered in blood and vomit, the funk on the feathers still made him retch. The eaglebear carcass also chose that moment to relieve itself. With an abnormally long hissing fart, its bowels let loose on the ground. The stench increased by a factor of ten. Only years of dealing with death on battlefields and disease in hospitals kept him from vomiting immediately. Still, he worked faster to conceal his scent. While pain hadn't made him weep, the noxious smell made tears stream freely down his face. As soon as he'd rubbed himself from head to toe, he left the body at a quick march.

As he walked away, he picked up a solid stick about two and a half feet long. It must have snapped free during his fall. One end was relatively sharp from the break, while the other was more rounded. Slightly thinner than his wrist, the makeshift weapon was better than nothing.

With his new nightvision, he started after the tribe. He hadn't gone more than fifty yards when shrieks sounded behind him. Looking back, he saw a living mound of fur and fangs tearing pieces off the eaglebear. The simians were fighting over each gobbet of bloody flesh. The godling stared at the feeding frenzy and realized just how close he'd come to being on the menu. Shrugging, he turned his back on the pandemonium. Short spear in hand, Remy faded into the night.

The godling jogged in the direction the tribe had escaped. He had to find them before daybreak and claim their allegiance.

While he ran he kept a watch out for more enemies and went over the prompts still awaiting him. Apparently, there was another benefit from defeating a mortal enemy.

> For killing a Level 6 Eaglebear, you have gained: **323 XP**
>
> Know This! XP is doubled for slaying a Mortal Enemy.
>
> **Final XP:** 646 XP

The extra XP didn't hurt. He'd also apparently gotten credit for a few more simian kills. He remembered knocking them out of the tree while he fell. It made him wonder if he'd split the experience with the eaglebear. Focusing on the soul inside him didn't elicit any answers.

> For killing 7 Snaptooth Simians of various levels, you have gained: **2,312 XP**. 3,547/7,500 XP to reach Level 2

Checking his status log, he saw that he got a bit less for the kills than he had when he was level 0. It looked like he'd get less experience from enemies the more his level rose. Which meant he'd ultimately have to hunt higher level creatures. As it was, he was halfway to level two, so that was yet one more problem for later.

Besides, while the bump to his XP was definitely useful, it was nothing compared to what awaited him next. He absorbed the information from the next windows and his eyes widened in shock. The asterisks next to his Primary Attributes were about to be removed, and he learned what a Profound Act was.

Know This! The initial Attributes of new gods of Telos are heavily determined by their first actions. In your short time on this world, you have performed **2 Profound Actions**. Normally only the first occurrence would be considered and your attributes would be adjusted accordingly. The impact of Profound Actions are only calculated upon their resolution, however.

In your case, your second Profound Action resolved the first.

As such, you shall be given a Choice!

Know This! A Profound Act can impact your State of Being to various degrees. The specific change will vary depending upon the facet of yourself that is being changed, but the loose order of changes in ascending order is: **Minor, Moderate, Major, Meaningful, Life-Defining, Soul-Defining, World-Shaking**

With this knowledge, Choose which Profound Act shall define your Characteristics!

DEATH OF A MORTAL ENEMY

You have made and defeated a **Mortal Enemy at least 5 levels stronger** than you. This has the potential to impact three of your Primary Attributes: *Strength*, *Charisma* and *Wisdom.*

***

Strength – To defeat a wild beast that is 5 levels stronger than you shows you have great internal power.

MAJOR adjustment to Strength: +10

Charisma – Impacting the attitudes of those around you is a reflection of your force of personality. Making a negative impact can be just as powerful as a positive one.

MODERATE adjustment to Charisma: +5

Wisdom – Making an enemy that is solely dedicated to your destruction so shortly after arriving on a new world does not show good judgement. Making an enemy out of a creature that outweighs you by several tons and has several levels on you is something only a profound idiot would do.

MINOR Adjustment to Wisdom: -3

Remy carefully read the effects of the first Profound Act. He couldn't argue with the reasoning. He'd physically beaten a monster stronger than he should have been able to, so his Strength got a large bump. The fact that he'd been able to enrage it also reflected on his Charisma, but to a lesser extent. Finally, "pissing" off the eaglebear to the point that it considered him a Mortal Enemy had just been dumb. The fact that its spirit might possess him or destroy his soul pretty much underlined that fact.

As such, his Wisdom would take a hit. There was no part of the last assessment that Remy disagreed with. It had been egregiously stupid to challenge such a dangerous monster, especially with no armor or weapons.

Just looking at the numeric changes to his attributes, the net yield was positive for this Profound Act though. He pulled up the definition of the various attributes to get a better idea of just what the effects would be.

Strength	Improves damage with melee weapons. Each point increases carrying capacity by 10 kg.
Agility	Determines movement speed. Each point increases walking speed by 0.1 mph. Determines dodge. Improves attack with melee weapons.
Dexterity	Determines attack speed. Improves damage with ranged weapons. Improves Dodge. Improves Attack with ranged weapons.

Constitution	Determines Health. Each point increases Health by 10 points. Affects resistance to poison, illness, extreme temp, etc. Affects stamina regeneration.
Endurance	Determines stamina. Each point increases Stamina by 10 points.
Intelligence	Determines mana. Each point increases Mana by 10 points. Affects resistance to mental attacks. Affects effectiveness of certain skills.
Wisdom	Determines mana regeneration. Affects magical resistance.
Charisma	Determines the likelihood others will like you or want to interact with you. A higher charisma may open certain quests that would otherwise be locked.
Luck	It will affect you in a million different ways… or not. But as the man said, "I'd rather be lucky than dead."

He could definitely use more Strength, especially since his body was smaller and weaker than a human's. Being able to hit something really hard was just one of those universally useful skills. The boost to Charisma could also come in handy. He had a quest pending to get a tribe of people to call him their god. Who the hell knew how that was supposed to go? All he knew was that if he didn't somehow manage it by daybreak he was screwed. A little sex appeal couldn't hurt.

The obvious issue with choosing this Profound Act was the drop in Wisdom. After the Calamity on Earth, it had quickly become clear that Wisdom influenced mana regeneration. The higher it was, the faster your magic would be restored. That obviously had been useful for anyone who gained a mana-dependent skill. In his last fight with the shadow cats, he'd had to stop enchanting his bullets because his MPs had run dry. A higher Wisdom would have meant he could bring the pain for a longer period of time.

In this life, he didn't know any spell or skills that used mana yet. The fact was, however, that Wisdom wasn't only useful for mana regeneration. As the prompt said, it also affected magical resistance. That meant he could lessen the damage an enemy's spell caused or fight off the effect altogether. When a spell could make you fall asleep, rendering you utterly defenseless, resistance was important.

Back on Earth, some of the people he'd fled with had been gamers. They'd told him that the prompts everyone was seeing looked like information windows from video games. Specifically, the prompts from a VRMMORPG called The Land.

There had been countless arguments among the refugees about the importance of the right "build" in the new world. It had honestly sounded like serious nerd talk to Remy, but he'd still paid attention in case there were any pearls of wisdom hidden amongst the mind-numbing dross that comprised most of the random conversations he overheard.

One of the things that had stood out was that Wisdom was important in magical resistance. Put another way, a high value in the attribute would reduce the damage enemy spells would do to you. It might also make it easier to shake off debuffs like *Confusion* or *Weakened.*

There hadn't been any real way to test it though. After the Forsaking, they had spent every day in a state of heightened fear, worrying about monster attacks. There hadn't been anyone actually throwing spells at them though. Also, almost no one was going to spend any precious points gained from leveling on something like Wisdom. Not when Endurance could make you run farther, Agility could make you run faster, and Constitution literally gave you more life.

There had been a pair of brothers that had planned on becoming wizards, and so had invested in Intelligence and Wisdom. The last time he'd seen them, they were getting eaten ass-inward by something that had looked like a scorpion with a snake's head. The brothers hadn't made a strong argument for investing in Wisdom, but they had convinced everyone of the importance of being able to run just a bit faster than the slowest guy in the group.

To Remy, Strength was much more important than Wisdom. He also recognized that there might be some serious consequences to having an abnormally low Attribute though. Back on Earth, the obese guys with an Endurance of three hadn't just run out of breath faster. They'd barely been able to exert themselves at all. He didn't want the equivalent happening to him because of a low Wisdom.

He wasn't discounting the option, but he definitely wanted to see what the second Profound Act offered. He pulled up the window and absorbed the information. While the first set of options had made his eyes widen, the next made his mouth drop open just a bit.

LEAP OF FAITH

There is perhaps no more soul-defining expression of faith than to leap into the abyss and accept your fate, come what may. Though your action was tempered by the acquisition of a soul that increased your Balance, you also accepted that there was at least an equal chance for your action to result in your death. In the worlds of the Labyrinth, danger and fortune are close bedfellows.

***

Luck – Had your Leap of Faith failed, even if you had survived, your Luck would have been proven to be abysmal and your sense of self would have been irrevocably shaken. The bonuses you are about to receive would have been reversed, crippling your Attributes. That, however, was not your fate. You succeeded! As such, your benefits will be equally profound.

SOUL-DEFINING Adjustment to Luck: +20 to Luck, +100% to Luck

Mental Aegis — An unaligned deity's faith is only in himself. This fact, coupled with your nearly unshakeable confidence in yourself, has shown that you have a strong sense of self. As such, your Leap of Faith has also increased a Secondary Attribute: **Mental Aegis**.

Know This! Nearly all beings have a degree of mental defense. This can serve to protect their minds from threats ranging from the banal stresses of mundane daily life to magical attacks against one's psyche.

The Secondary Attribute **Mental Aegis** measures mental fortitude. The base Mental Aegis of most sapient creatures on Telos is +1. The difficulties you have overcome in your past life have hardened your mind. Your base Mental Aegis is +1.5

LIFE-DEFINING Adjustment to your Secondary Attribute:

Mental Aegis: +0.5 to MA. +50% to MA.

You may choose either Profound Act, but the choice is irrevocable. If no choice is made within the next **7 minutes**, it will be made for you!

Remy considered everything he had just read. The term "Leap of Faith" easily tied into his new status as a "god," as ridiculous as that still was. Religious overtones or not, he had a decision to make. The truth was, he was tempted by the benefits of the first option, even with the loss of Wisdom. He only got 2 free Attribute points per level. 10 points of Strength was the equivalent of five levels dedicated to just that one Attribute. It was something he couldn't disregard.

He also couldn't deny the much larger impact of the *Soul-Defining* adjustment to his Luck. He still wasn't sure what the real point of the Attribute was, but the numbers didn't lie. The *Major* boost to strength was worth ten points, while his Luck would be increased by twenty.

Even more important, a *Major* boost was just a one-time increase. *Soul-Defining* and *Life-Defining* improvements apparently gave a modifier. His Luck would also be increased by 100%. The second option also increased one of his Secondary Attributes. After experiencing the boost to his Balance, he knew just how powerful these hidden Attributes could be.

The second option would increase his mental defenses, his Mental Aegis, by 50%. Remy may not have fully believed in Secondary Attributes until recently, but he'd always known the importance of mental strength. After the Calamity, suicide was one of the leading causes of death. Some people just could not go on. Even in the caravan he was leading in his final days, there had been a married couple who had made the decision to shoot themselves one night rather than face another day.

Both his time as a soldier and his work as a physician had helped him understand the vital importance of mental strength. Also, it seemed like the bonus could help him survive if he came up against a higher-level monster. As powerful as the eaglebear had been, it was still just a physical threat. The fact that it was dead while he was still standing showed that he could prevail against opponents of the material realm.

214

If he was attacked by something that specialized in psychic attacks, however, he might be as unprepared as a man attacked with biological weapons. Didn't matter how much of a badass you were, you were still just meat if someone hit you with one. From what he was reading, a higher Mental Aegis, or MA, might be like having a suit of armor for his mind. It also gave a permanent percentage bonus that could help him long-term.

He once again recalled the strange words from the note given to him by his sponsors. His high MA was one of the reasons his mysterious benefactors had chosen him in the first place. After a lifetime of hard decisions, of being the one to face realities others couldn't deal with, he'd trained his mind to be resilient. The bonus from the second option was in line with his nature, and so it appealed to him on an unconscious level.

A final consideration was perhaps the most important: the Leap of Faith had only happened because of the picture his sponsor had given him. It was one of the trump cards that he'd been given to give him a leg up in this new world. He'd originally thought the purpose of the photo was to help him survive the initial encounter with the eaglebear, but now it seemed much more likely that it had been to trigger his Leap of Faith. No one in their right mind would just jump off something high and hope for the best. This wasn't Assassin's Creed.

He had though, and only because of the note he'd been given. Otherwise, fighting off the simians, even outnumbered, would have made more sense at the time than leaping a hundred stories to a likely death. It also hadn't escaped his notice that while the prompt had mentioned the fact that his Balance had been increased, it had made no mention of his foreknowledge.

His sponsors had made it clear that if their cheating ways were found out the consequences would be dire, but thankfully, it looked like they were good cheaters. It would be the height of idiocy on his part if he ignored the bonus they'd arranged for him. Especially if he could get away with it. Because of their advice, he'd discovered and increased another Secondary Attribute, the same attribute that had been specifically mentioned in the note from his sponsor. That was obviously not a coincidence.

The choice was obvious. He selected the second option, *Leap of Faith.*

Congratulations, godling! Your Attributes have been adjusted. View your status page for full changes.

He continued to trek through the night and pulled up his status sheet. The asterisks had disappeared and his values had changed.

PRIMARY ATTRIBUTES Name: Total (Base)		
Strength: 8	Agility: 15	Dexterity: 15
Constitution: 11	Endurance: 10	Intelligence: 12
Wisdom: 12	Charisma: 11	Luck: 60 (30) (Leap of Faith: +100%)
IDENTIFIED SECONDARY ATTRIBUTES Name: Total (Base)		
Balance: 1.33	Mental Aegis: 3.0 (2.0) (Leap of Faith: +50%)	

His mental defenses were strong and his Luck had shot through the roof. He didn't really feel any different initially, aside from perhaps having a firmer focus on what was happening. As he continued to search his feelings though, he realized that he was able to focus on the "now" extremely easily, thoughts and concerns falling away. Remy wondered if that was an effect of his improved mental defenses but had no way to know.

There was one more series of prompts that appeared after his Luck shot up.

Know This! One of your Primary Attributes has reached **25**!

You may make this your **Main Attribute** if you wish. Main Attributes provide extra bonuses, but you may only select one.

Do you wish to make **Luck** your **Main Attribute**? Yes or No?

To be honest, Remy really didn't like the idea of relying on Luck. Still, he knew he'd choose "Yes." One reason was that if his sponsor had somehow planned for him to survive the Leap of Faith, that meant they knew his Luck would go up. It wasn't hard to read between the lines. It meant they had known he would have this choice.

The other reason was Remy was extremely enamored with the idea of breathing, even if only for a few more days. He wasn't going to turn his back on long-term planning, but short-term survival was way more important right now. He didn't know what bonuses he'd get from having a Main Attribute, but even the smallest edge might mean the difference between life and death. He was alone in an alien and hostile world. He needed all the help he could get.

If twenty-five points was the threshold, it would take three more levels before he gained that many in another attribute. And that was only if he invested his free points into Dexterity or Agility. It would take six levels if he chose one of the other attributes. If having a Main Attribute could give him more power, than Luck would have to do.

Remy chose "Yes."

Congratulations! **Luck** is now your **Main Attribute** and by having a value of 25 it has reached its **1st Threshold**! You will randomly be awarded your 1st Benefit.

There are a number of Benefits associated with attributes, and two beings with the same Main Attribute have no guarantee of obtaining the same one.

The rank of 1st Threshold Benefits for a soul in the Mortal ranks ranges between *common* and *limited.*

Your Divine Core has increased the range by +2: *limited* to *rare*!

Remy smiled. His Divine Core has just provided another hidden benefit. For seven seconds the sound of dice rattling in a cup echoed through Remy's mind. Then a plum-colored prompt appeared, showing he'd gained a rank four benefit!

> You have been awarded the *scarce* Secret Benefit:
>
> ### Golden Sight
>
> **Golden Sight** is a passive benefit that scales with your Luck stat. People, items and terrain that possess a greater potential for a fortuitous encounter or event may randomly light up golden in your vision. Such occurrences indicate the potential for a positive turn of events.

It looked like Golden Sight could sometimes give him hints about which path to take. Remy didn't mind the bonus. He believed in making his own luck anyway. A hint, now and again, could only be considered a positive. Luck might be his Main Attribute now, but he'd rely on his judgement and planning to guide him. Any lucky turn would just be a bonus. That was his personality.

The next prompt showed that his choice of Main Attribute affected his future followers as well.

> Know This! Gods and their worshippers are irrevocably bound. By choosing Luck as your Main Attribute, any followers who offer true prayers have a chance to have their Luck temporarily increased.

% to increase Luck = 1% for every 10 points of their god's Luck * personal Devotion

Increase in Luck = 1 point for every 10 points of their god's Luck * personal Devotion

Duration = 1 hour for every 10 points of their god's Luck * personal Devotion

It looked like his people would have a specific reason to pray to him, as insane as that sounded. From what he could tell of the convoluted system on the prompt, the more devoted his people were and the higher his Luck, the more likely his people would get a bonus. He guessed that checked out.

The benefits weren't done. His Leap of Faith had catapulted him to the second grade of his Main Attribute as well.

For reaching a value of **50**, you have reached your Main Attribute's 2nd Threshold!

The rank of 2nd Threshold Benefits for a soul in the Mortal ranks ranges from *uncommon* to *scarce*.

Your Divine Core has increased the range by +2: *scarce* to *epic*!

This time he gained a fifth rank benefit!

Tough Luck

Tough Luck is an active benefit that scales with your Luck stat. Your Luck is so high that any attacks land at the worst angle, robbing them of strength. This makes you nearly impossible to kill!

Natural Defense Bonus: Random amount ranging from +1 to your total Luck

Duration of Defense: 1 minute to (total Luck/10) minutes

Cooldown: 10 hours

This benefit was more like it! If he was reading it right, it could give him a natural armor equal to the number of points in his Luck attribute. That meant +60 defense! Of course, the bonus might be only +1, but he supposed that was the nature of luck, and any bonus was better than nothing.

Tough Luck wouldn't protect him from everything, but it just might make him invulnerable to lower level attacks. It might also only last a minute, but a lot of fights lasted even less time. This could be a game changer; he just had to use it at the right moment and hope for the best. His decision to have Luck be his main attribute seemed like the right one.

There was one last notification, and in some ways, it was the most important.

> You fulfilled some of the Success Conditions for a Quest: **Save Us I**
>
> You have killed the monster that threatened the Razin tribe. Reconnect with the tribe to claim your reward!
>
> **Time until sunrise and Quest Failure:** 4 hours, 7 minutes, 51 seconds

A sharp cry split the silence, sounding like the call of a hawk, only much louder. Remy froze, hiding in the shadow of a tall tree. The moonlight bathed the ground around the tree in silver-blue. Beneath the thick boughs, it was as dark as midnight. Still, the godling's enhanced vision pierced the gloom easily. Scanning again for enemies, the coast looked clear.

He knew the overall topography thanks to having climbed so high previously. The massive tree he'd been in was at the blind end of a closed valley. When he'd been up in the tree, he'd seen the tribe moving to the open end of a large gorge. They probably hadn't known that, of course. It was more likely that they had only been following the path of least resistance, and the open end of the valley was lower in elevation. Incidentally, that was also the direction that his *Ruined Temple* quest seemed to be leading him.

That was something else he'd noticed while he was up in the tree. When he focused on the quest his sponsors had given him, there was a strange "pulling" sensation inside his chest. The feeling was faint, not strong enough to give a true heading but enough that he knew his goal lay somewhere in "that" direction. It had been extremely strange to feel something "pulling" him forward. He realized that was only if you didn't also take into account the fact that he now had captured souls inside him, so he put it out of his mind.

CHAPTER 19

He continued moving at a light jog. If it wasn't for the eaglebear's soul, his speed would have been barely better than a crawl. The moons provided some light, but in the forest, they provided just as much shadow. If he had been relying solely on his natural sight, hidden branches would have taken out an eye or a fallen limb would have thrown him into a briar.

With his new night vision, however, it was easy.

It wasn't that the darkness was completely gone, but more that it was no longer impenetrable. The best way he could describe it was that if a red light bulb tinted everything in a room that color, you could still see fine. With his eaglebear vision it was like everything was tinted black, but was still just as easy to see through. The tribe had several hours' head start, but his bound soul made the trail easy to follow. Remy was fairly certain he was moving faster than they would be, especially with their wounded.

The entire time he pursued the razin, he kept his head on a swivel. He stayed to the shadows as much as possible and avoided open patches of moonlight. The sounds of the forest were all around him. Hoots, screeches, growls and even cries of pain echoed out, proof that there were predators making kills. They all stayed away from him though. Either because the eaglebear was an apex predator for this valley or because his new Luck was manifesting, he traveled unmolested.

While he moved, he scanned his surroundings for signs of the tribe. His training in his previous life served him well. Remy found blades of bent grass, snapped branches and even stray tufts of hair. Hours passed as he trailed them. The entire time, he kept his eye on his quest counter. He began to feel uneasy as the time ticked down.

3 hours, 24 minutes, 8 seconds remaining

2 hours, 17 minutes, 37 seconds remaining

1 hour, 8 minutes, 3 seconds remaining

Less than an hour was left and the sky was beginning to lighten when he climbed a final hill and exited the valley. What lay before him was a gently sloping plain. It was covered with waist-high grass that looked purple in his sight. Seeing the gently waving violet stalks really drove home that he was on an alien planet.

In the far distance, he saw the twinkle of a large body of water. The fact that he could detect the scent of salt on the air led him to think it was an ocean. Out on the plain, the trees only appeared sporadically, leaving his field of view unobstructed. Tightening his binocular vision, he was able to see the tribe resting on the plain less than a mile away. They looked haggard and exhausted. Many were injured.

His binocular vision showed something else though. Just beyond the area the tribe was camped, there were disturbances in the tall grass. He could only see it because he was higher up than the razin. If he'd been where they were, the grass would have hidden everything. Remy enhanced his vision as best he could and was able to make out a group of short but powerfully built figures moving stealthily toward the encampment.

His Chosen tribe was about to be attacked… again! Cursing, Remy immediately started running full-out. Once he was off the hill, he lost sight of both the stealthy attackers and his tribe. He just had to hope that he would reach the razin before this latest batch of assholes threatening his quest reward.

Hope wasn't enough. Before Remy had covered half the distance, a blade flashed in the night. At the last second, a razin sentry noticed the small encroaching army, but it was far too late.

The pantherkin man was only able to let out a warning shout before the sword fell. His yell transformed into a gurgling cry. The tribe was alerted at the cost of his life. The attacker yanked his blade out, releasing a spray of blood. Other figures rushed into the camp, and the exhausted razin desperately tried to defend themselves. Remy cursed anew as quest updates started flashing in his vision again.

Quest Update **Save Us I**:

182/200 Razin remaining

175/200 Razin remaining

167/200 Razin remaining

In the first moments of battle, the attackers had killed more than fifteen of the people he needed to save! Remy pumped his legs faster. The camp came fully into view. What he saw was pandemonium. The injured razin were barely able to stay on their feet while the rest of the tribe defended against the invaders. Sadly, the sharpened sticks the pantherkin were using as spears were once again inadequate against the weapons of their foes.

Remy watched a metal axe fall, reaping the life of another of his Chosen. More attackers came into the light, and even without using his God's Eye he knew who and what the invaders were. He couldn't believe what he was seeing, but there was no mistaking the short, bulky stature of the people killing the tribe.

Dwarves. His tribe was being attacked by dwarves!

A notification appeared while Remy sprinted the final distance separating him from the razin.

Prayer Quest Update: **Save Us I**

Most of the tribe do not know who saved them from the eaglebear, but they are thankful nonetheless. They cry out again for someone to save them from yet another unprovoked attack. Disperse or destroy the attackers to gain more favor with the tribe.

Success Conditions: Save the Razin from their attackers.

Rewards: Drastic increase in the rewards from the Quest: *Save Us I*

Failure Conditions: The tribe's population drops below 100.

Penalty for failure of Quest: Dissolution of the bond between you and your Chosen tribe.

This Quest cannot be refused!

He swiped the quest alert away in annoyance. He was already going to help the tribe. If being a god meant being bombarded with prayers every time his people needed something though, this was going to be incredibly aggravating. Another scream split the night and one more razin died. Remy put his irritation aside and tried to move faster. The clash of battle filled the air as the razin attempted to survive this latest threat. As he grew closer to his enemies, his heart grew cold.

The tribe of pantherkin were clearly not cowards, but they had no real weaponry. All they had were a few sharpened sticks masquerading as spears. The dwarf attackers had what looked like copper swords and axes. There was nothing elegant about the weapons, but they were more than good enough to reap the razin like wheat.

Also, based on the bulging muscles in the dwarves' arms, their Strength attribute was most likely much higher than that of the lithe razin. As Remy drew nearer, he used his God's Eye. A blue light sparked in his eyes as he gathered information about the attacker closest to him.

KINDRADE		
Level: 1	**Race:** Murk Dwarf	
Energy: 134	**Soul Rank:** Common	**Deity:** Vúr
STATS		
Health: 118/120	v	**Stamina:** 126/130 *Regen/min:* 6

RACIAL DESCRIPTION

Dwarves have several subclasses that determine their specific powers. Murk Dwarves are known to be one of the evil dwarven races. Adept at stealth and with a proclivity toward Dark and Death magic, they are not foes to be taken lightly. Murk Dwarves are as strong and adept at forging and crafting as their other dwarven brethren. *Common*-souled Murk Dwarves are allotted +1 to Constitution and +1 to Endurance per level. They also gain 2 Free Attribute Points per level.

TRIBAL DESCRIPTION

The **Chosen** people of the god **Vúr**
Tribal Qualities
1) *Metallurgist* – Forge 25% stronger arms and armor
2) *Stealthy* – +25% to Concealment
Free Tech: Copper Working

Another prompt accompanied his inspection.

Know This! The group attacking your Chosen tribe worships another deity. The Razin have not accepted any being as their god and so are considered **Faithless**. As such, they are more susceptible to the powers and persuasion of other gods. Save them before they are all slain or converted!

Know This! You have used your **God's Eye** on a creature that possesses an unknown language. You have now learned their language.

Remy bared his sharp teeth, absorbing the information in an instant. Not only did the dwarves have higher health and stamina than his Chosen, but they also started off with better weaponry. To make it worse, they were also a full level higher than the razin. In every aspect except one, the pantherkin were outclassed by the dwarves. The only saving grace was that the thirty attackers were outnumbered, but that margin was decreasing by the second. The godling dismissed the status window and kept sprinting forward. His stamina was falling fast, but he couldn't be stopped by that right now.

As he closed the distance, he considered the fact that these dwarves worshipped a deity. It meant he was about to go up against another god, or at least another god's followers. Whether he bought into his own holiness or not, there was no denying his own Divine Powers had let him overcome the several tons of evolved killing machine that was the eaglebear. Who knew what other powers this enemy god could unleash?

There wasn't anything to be done about it though. The razin were dying. Even if they weren't his quote unquote Chosen people, he couldn't just let them be slaughtered. Not while he still needed them for his quest, and not after all the energy he'd already invested in keeping them alive. Remy ran into the fight.

The razin were fighting the murk dwarves in a haphazard manner. There was no battle line, only pockets of fighters doing their best to kill each other. The razin were nimbler and so had an easier time dodging the dwarves' strikes, but their weapons were pathetic, even compared to the crude copper blades of the enemy. A successful blow from the razin might only cause single or double digits worth of damage. The dwarves, on the other hand, could maim or kill with almost every blow.

Even with the razin's superior numbers, it was clear that the dwarves had the upper hand. The bodies of the razin lying dead on the ground were proof of that. In contrast, only one of the dwarves had been seriously injured, and the enemy had suffered no fatalities.

Remy bared his teeth in a feral grin. He was about to change that.

The godling drew stares as he rushed past the razin that had been injured by the eaglebear, but none of them could do more than look at the stranger rushing through their midst. As he ran by, he scooped up a short length of wood a razin had been in the process of sharpening.

Remy dashed toward a dwarf who was about to deliver a coup de grace. The bearded murker raised his blade high over a fallen foe. His ash-colored skin was partially hidden behind a full and unkempt beard, yet Remy could clearly see the glee in his eyes, matched by a sadistic grin. The razin had one hand raised toward his attacker in a vain attempt to stave off the blow that would savage his body. Blood ran down one side of his face.

Remy knew he wouldn't make it in time, so he activated his Title. *Infuriating Enemy* immediately created an aura of antagonism twenty-five meters around him. The effect was different than it had been on mindless beasts. Rather than driving the dwarf into an immediate rage, the murker just cast about with an aggrieved expression. When his eyes landed on the god though, he was overcome with intense anger and a profound burning desire to harm the black-eared pantherkin running toward him.

The difference in the Title's effect was not in its strength, but in the fact that the sapient mind of the dwarf was better able to reason. When overcome with a directionless anger, the murker had realized that something was wrong. It was only when he finally saw Remy that all reason fled his mind. Upon laying eyes on his new attacker, all he wanted in the world was to wipe the god's existence from the face of Telos. His previous target forgotten, he turned to strike at Remy.

The blow never fell.

Remy sprang forward. A moment before they met in battle, he triggered *Soul Strike*. The length of wood in his hand became a +10 weapon. Sheathed in pale blue light, it stabbed into the dwarf's face.

The murker's sneer disappeared along with his jaw. Remy's broken branch blasted right through it and the force shot up into the skull. The dwarf's flesh was ravaged and one eye burst under the assault. The other eye flew free of the skull, two inches of optic nerve still somehow attached. The left side of the dwarf's mouth was ripped free and the mandible was left hanging by only a few strips of stretchy flesh on the right. The branch exploded, not able to handle the Divine Power, even at half charge. That was fine. Remy had an upgrade now.

The dwarf fell to his knees, shortsword dropped and forgotten. He tried to scream. Only a muted bleating emerged as he no longer had a working chin. In the distant, cold place Remy always lived in during a battle, he had no reaction to the horror he'd created out of the dwarf's flesh. He picked up the copper blade and shoved it into the dwarf's desecrated face. The screams stopped. A sharp pull on the blade and the dwarf dropped to the ground, dead.

The razin on the ground stared at Remy in horrified confusion. He knew he was looking at another pantherkin, but he had never seen this man before. He'd also never seen any brown skinned tribe members, especially not with midnight-black fur covering his ears and tail.

The man had also never seen a piece of wood glow blue and then make someone's head explode. A minute before, he'd never even imagined such efficient brutality. Looking back and forth between the slain dwarf and his gore-covered savior, he wasn't sure which was more deserving of his fear.

Remy didn't give him time to work it out. Leaning down, he grabbed the front of the man's fur shirt and pulled him up, "Go! There is more fighting to be done and I can't do it all by myself." Seeing that the razin was still in a bit of a daze, he slapped the man hard across the face. "Move!"

The tribesman finally got over his shock and nodded. Grabbing his fallen spear, he ran toward another knot of fighting. Meanwhile, Remy turned his attention to the body. Reaching out with his Soul Art, he summoned a rainbow-colored sphere that only he could see. It was the same size as the simian souls, but the colors were far more complex. While he examined it, a prompt appeared.

UNTETHERED SOUL: Murk Dwarf	Rank: Common (Refined)
POWERS	
Your Soul Art is not powerful enough to access the special powers of Refined souls. As such, they cannot be assigned to any soul slots.	

What was a "refined" soul? Did it mean the soul of a person? Someone sentient or sapient? He had no idea. He could still capture it though. The ramifications of capturing the soul of a person didn't affect him in the slightest. He might not be able to gain any special perks from it, but there were other ways he could use the ball of energy.

Remy reached out a hand and focused. The murk dwarf's spirit tried to resist, but it was helpless. The godling pulled the spirit to him and a second later pure, unadulterated power flowed into the soul of the eaglebear. He had enjoyed the warm, calm feeling of having souls inside him before, but this time it felt like he'd grabbed a wire with electricity flowing through it. If electricity was made out of orgasms and candy, that is.

While the experience was profound and powerful, the sensation lasted all of an instant. The razin he had sent to fight had barely taken three steps by the time the soul energy was coursing through him.

> Your bound Eaglebear soul has consumed **+4 Soul Points**. 96 more Soul Points required to unlock its second Power.

> Know This! *Common* souls will provide **1-5 Soul Points**.

Siphoning energy from a refined soul for the first time increased his understanding of his Soul Art.

> Know This! You have absorbed energy from the faithful of another deity. Your **Soul Art** allows you to gather information and resources from **refined** spirits. The acquisition is random, but will be influenced by various factors.

Stronger connections with other deities will make acquisition more difficult, but also more rewarding.

For absorbing energy from a faithful of Vúr, you have gained **+3 Faith Points!**

Know This! At baseline, the number of Faith Points you can absorb is less than or equal to the number of Faith Points a creature can generate for their god in a given tenday.

He still had no idea why Faith Points were important, but for the first time he had some. He'd figure out what to do with them after the battle. What mattered now was that he'd taken a step toward unlocking his eaglebear's second power.

Despite gaining both Soul and Faith Points, what truly distracted Remy was how it had felt to harness the power of a refined soul. Despite his many battles, he still made the mistake of losing focus for a moment. It was unavoidable. The feeling of absorbing the dwarf's soul was so much more intense than the simian's or eaglebear's. It felt like…

He was at loss for words trying to describe it. It felt like there was a profound truth that had been shouted, but the person proclaiming it was on a mountaintop thousands of miles away. As if a wind had spoken secret knowledge, but then blew past him before he'd begun to truly listen. Enough to tantalize him, enough to even plant the seed of obsession inside him, but not enough to give actual information. It tickled his mind. Remy didn't know it, but something pivotal had happened. He'd tasted the power of a *refined* soul for the first time and, like many gods before him, he'd awakened a hunger that could never be sated. He didn't know what it meant, he just knew he wanted more!

A scream of pain drew his attention back to the battle. He'd only been distracted for moments, but he still castigated himself. Losing focus during a battle was unacceptable. The truth was, less than ten seconds had passed since he'd killed the murk dwarf, and if not for the intense feeling of absorbing the murk dwarf's spiritual energy he never would have let himself get so distracted. But none of that mattered. The reasons for failure never did. There was still a battle happening. There were people dying. There were enemies for him to kill.

His next opponent was not caught unawares. Red blood stained the dwarf woman's blade and a body lay behind her. The razin's chest was hacked open and his mouth was frozen in a silent scream. The murker bellowed at Remy in her guttural language. He ignored it, thinking it would just come out as gibberish, but to his surprise, he understood.

"Come to me, kitty! My sword is still thirsty!"

His God's Eye had translated the words! Despite his surprise, he didn't let himself be distracted again. Even if he hadn't understood her language, her challenge would have been clear. Hefting his new short sword, he gave her a grim nod and rushed to bring her death.

The dwarf woman swung her axe in a powerful chest-level swipe. Not losing momentum, Remy used his superior agility and lowered his center of gravity. His tail lashed, subconsciously improving his balance. He went into a three-point stance, his rough feet and hand sliding in the pre-morning dew. Almost without thinking, talons extended from his toes, giving him traction. The godling skated past her, the axe missing his head by mere inches. Remy could feel the air whip past his scalp. The murk dwarf immediately tried to correct her swing, but her momentum carried her forward for a critical second.

As soon as he had ducked under the axe, Remy was already turning, blade in hand. The short sword was larger than the knives he'd trained with during his days in the Organization, but not so different that it felt unwieldy. Spinning, he ended up behind her but facing the same direction. With no hesitation or mercy, he swung the sword across her unprotected ankles.

She was wearing black cloth clothing similar to what the razin had on. Her skirt didn't cover her legs and wouldn't have offered any real protection if it had. Even if the dwarfess had real defenses, the armor negation from his Soul Art would have made it as effective as tissue paper. The blade Remy swung was unbalanced and of poor quality, but it was still sharp enough to slice through tendons. The fibrous strands connecting her feet to her calf muscles were severed as he swung his blade. The dwarfess collapsed to the ground with a cry of anguish. Her pain meant nothing to the Remy.

The vengeful godling rose smoothly. Taking one step forward, he buried the copper weapon in the base of her neck. Putting both hands on the hilt, he wrenched the blade first one way, then violently to the other side. The copper edge severed bone, spine and muscle. Her legs were still kicking spasmodically even as he searched for his next target. He left that soul in the body. It'd be good to know how long spirits remained in a body after death. Besides, there was plenty more meat to butcher.

After killing two of the attackers, the entire battlefield was aware of his presence. His presence and the death of two of the murkers galvanized and heartened the razin. The beastkin fought back with greater ferocity and managed to bring down a few of the dwarves on their own. The attackers redoubled their efforts in response. The battle reached a more fevered pitch. More lives were reaped on both sides.

With Remy present, however, the battle's balance had shifted. Each downed dwarf made the razin tribe stronger as weapons were claimed. The razin clearly had little experience wielding metal weapons, but they fought with passion and ferocity. Between their greater numbers, claiming real weapons and Remy's *Soul Strike,* more dwarves fell to the ground, choking on their own blood.

With so many slain dwarves, he had no shortage of spirits to consume. Each time he did so, he gained Faith Points as well. A smile grew on his face, more than just battle lust. He was riding a high. Each drained soul was a small injection of pure pleasure and power. None were quite as powerful as the first, but it still felt amazing.

Time passed, and a quarter of the attackers fell. Minutes later, nearly half the dwarves lay dead or dying. The battle looked like it would soon come to an end. The godling had received several small wounds, but judicious use of *Soul Heal* kept him in the fight. He got more comfortable with it, using just the right amount of power to keep him battle-ready. It let him spread out the use of a charge. He slew a club-wielding dwarf and was looking around for his next victim when the tide of battle turned again.

A murker, slightly larger than the others, raised his copper axe high in the air. He spat words heavy with portent, "May the Dark powers of Vúr send you to eternal torment!"

During the battle, the sky had been brightening. Dawn could not be far off, but with that chant everything within a hundred yards darkened. Streams of pure gloom flew to the copper axehead and a moment later it was black as onyx. The dwarf wasted no time and swung it sideways in a devastating chop. The bodies of three razin were flung through the air. One blow had cut through both wooden spears and the bodies that held them. All three were dead before they hit the ground. Dark energy continued to play across their wounds. Their tissues quickly decayed into a black glop, leaving only ribcages and steaming goo behind.

Remy looked at the results of the attack in shock. The strength to cut three people in half was startling. The effects of whatever dark power the dwarf was using though, were horrifying. Even as he rushed to meet the dwarf in combat, he used *God's Eye,* focusing on the relevant information. Something about this dwarf was different.

CHAPTER 20

BRANINON (Acolyte of the Deity Vúr)		
Level: 2	**Class: Cleric** *Rank:* **Acolyte**	**Race:** Murk Dwarf
Energy: 184	**Soul Rank:** Uncommon	**Deity:** Vúr
STATS		
Health: 117/150	**Mana:** 110	**Stamina:** 84/140 · **Faith:** 50/100

The dwarf's Energy value was much higher than the other attackers. What jumped out at Remy though was the top line. The dwarf wasn't just a follower of another god, he had some special status. He was some kind of priest!

While the status window shed some light on what he was facing, it didn't help the god in terms of knowing how to defeat this new enemy. It certainly didn't help the next two razin the acolyte killed, turning the pantherkin into festering pools of necrotic glop. Remy pushed himself to close the distance faster.

While Remy raced to destroy this latest threat, the cat tribe's morale had plummeted. Seeing the acolyte's devastating attack, the battle fervor of the razin was immediately quenched. What could they do against such fearsome magic? The murkers, on the other hand, rushed forward again, bloodlust rekindling in their hearts. The dwarf holding the wicked axe lifted it to strike a third time.

Blood caked the acolyte's black beard. His eyes and smile were bright against the backdrop. He loved his newly granted power! All hail lord Vúr! With that thought in his mind, he started to swing his axe at a female razin when something made him pause. An irrational anger filled him. It was a fury so strong that it overrode even his bloodlust. Looking around for what was making him feel so strange and full of rage, his eyes fell on a black-eared pantherkin rushing toward him.

With grim appreciation, the godling noted that his Title even worked against enemy clergy. He rushed to close the final yards between himself and the Darkness-wielding dwarf. Remy knew he had to end this quickly. Affected by *Infuriating Enemy*, the murker abandoned his previous victim and eagerly accepted the god's challenge.

In those final moments, Remy coldly assessed what he'd learned from watching the murker butcher his Chosen people. The dwarf swung the axe in a more sure manner than the other dwarves Remy had faced. In addition to the enspelled weapon, it was obvious the man had a higher level of combat skill than the rest of the attackers. None of this slowed the godling down. Remy raised his sword to meet the blow, and the two weapons collided with a powerful *clang*!

Remy was immediately overcome. Not only was his Strength pathetically inferior to the dwarf's, but the magically augmented axe was a far superior weapon to his own stolen copper sword. Coupled with the fact that the dwarf had swung with both arms on the haft, there was never any real contest. The short sword was knocked from Remy's hand. The weapon was deformed by the blow and the godling's shoulder was nearly dislocated for good measure.

None of this was a surprise to Remy. Even as agony shot through his body, his mind remained cold and clinical. He'd never believed he could overpower the dwarf. The razin weren't built for strength. He'd only needed to deflect the axe wielder's attack by the smallest of margins. The god had intentionally extended his blade so that it collided with the axe before the dwarf's swing could reach full power.

His enemy's half-moon copper weapon slid down his shortsword for just a moment before he let go. The blow missed him by mere inches. He felt the Dark power singe his skin even though it didn't make contact. His health dropped by five points. If the dwarf were to attack again, the axe would cleave Remy's body in two. The god would die for a second time.

While Remy battled his acolyte, the Dark god Vúr watched from a safe distance. The immortal's heart thrilled. As far as he was concerned, this was a time of triumph. His acolyte was about to slay an untethered god! The power he would receive from Remy's death would catapult his own. The god might even be able to convert some of the beastkin tribe once their god was dead. All he needed was for his acolyte Braninon to make one more swing.

That swing would never fall. Remy might not have been aware of the watching god, but he was laser-focused on his dwarven enemy. His real attack had never been the copper sword he'd swung in his left hand. It was the *Soul Strike* he'd conjured with his right.

241

Remy's hand flattened into a knife strike. Pale blue energy surrounded it, turning his unarmed strike into a +20 one-use weapon. The ebon axe-wielder was wearing the same black cloth as the rest of the dwarf tribe. It offered the same paltry protection. Either way, it didn't cover the dwarf's head.

At the same time Remy's copper short sword was flying off to the side, he shot his hand forward. With his talons leading, the godling's strike caught the acolyte under the chin. It continued unabated through the dwarf's meaty neck and came out the other side. Vúr was still gloating when Braninon's head flew into the air, a look of shock on the bearded murker's face.

Just a second before, the dwarf had been reveling in triumph. Now his brain didn't even have the blood flow needed to understand how he had died. For the split second before the neurons of his brain stopped firing, he felt nothing but confusion. The bearded killer, who had glorified in causing pain, learned the true meaning of anguish. Too late he learned the axiom: never defy a merciless god.

Remy watched blood spurt from the dwarf's neck stump in satisfaction. There was something hilarious about seeing Braninon's confused expression. It almost let him ignore the pain ratcheting through him. His shoulder was in agony. Worse, even though the axe of his vanquished foe hadn't made contact with him, the dark energy it held took a toll nonetheless.

When the two weapons had met, magical power had flowed down the copper shortsword and into his arm. Even now he could feel the decaying energy of the attack eating at his muscles. Remy's health began to plummet. He'd already lost nineteen points of health during the initial clash. His health bar emptied like a bottle turned on its side.

Sure enough, the power of gods was not to be trifled with. The gloom-imbued axe was worse than any poison, and would kill anything it touched. If it had been any other creature so afflicted, they would have spent their last moments in cursed agony. Remy was no mere mortal, however. He too had the power of a god.

Almost instinctually, Remy cast *Soul Heal*. As soon as his Divine Power flowed through him, relief spread. The decay debuff disappeared immediately. He looked at his interface in relief. If his Divine Power hadn't countered the axe's energy, he'd have died in seconds. Luckily, it looked like the two energies had canceled one another out. Twenty points of health wasn't enough to bring him back to peak condition, but it was enough to keep him on his feet.

With cold and brutal eyes, he looked at the remaining dwarves.

The acolyte's blood had bathed him, and the severed head lay staring on the ground. Spurts of red continued to shoot up from the murker's body, which perversely had stayed on its feet. The squirts grew weaker as the heart died. Seconds after that, the body of Remy's decapitated foe joined its head on the ground.

The entire time, Remy stared death at the eight dwarves lucky enough to still draw breath. They gaped at the pantherkin god in horror, reacting instinctively to the killing intent he exuded. They had all seen Remy rip their leader's head off with his bare hands. That wasn't power they could resist. To add to the fear in their hearts, Remy's entire body was coated in blood, both dried and fresh. The murk dwarves weren't even sure their enemy was alive and not some undead horror that had come to punish them for their sins.

Still, the dwarves were no strangers to blood and gore, and they were not cowards. If all that confronted them was a bloody warrior, they still might have attacked. The worst part though was the god's eyes. How could eyes the color of a golden sunset be so frigid, delivering both judgment and the promise of death? They took involuntary steps backward under the pressure of that fell gaze.

Quiet had replaced the sounds of battle. The stink of blood hung heavy on the air and the two sides looked at each other across only a few yards of space. The entire tribe of razin stood behind the being that would soon become their god. Hands gripped weapons and they stared stonily at the dwarves. Any kindness that may have dwelt within their hearts was cast aside. Like Remington, only death filled their eyes.

Before anything else could happen, a wall of sheer darkness appeared between the murkers and the razin. It was like looking into a barrier made of reflective obsidian. Remy and the tribe took a step back in shock and alarm. What new attack did this portend?

The wall started fading seconds later. Suspicion replacing caution, the godling stepped toward the wall and swung a captured bronze club through the barrier. It traveled through the barrier without meeting any resistance. The wall faded in its entirety as the god stepped forward and through it.

Without the illusory barrier in his way, Remy could see the surviving dwarves running for their lives. They might not have been fast, but their legs pumped like tireless pistons. They were already a hundred yards away and showed no signs of slowing. Part of Remy wanted to chase after them. If they escaped today, then they could be a threat tomorrow.

Remy also knew there would be a high cost to finishing the fight. The battle had not been long, but it had been brutal. They had killed most of the dwarves, but dozens of razin lay unmoving on the ground. Several times that number were screaming or moaning from open wounds. On top of that, Remy's stamina was on its last legs, the green bar in the corner of his vision almost empty. His breath came heavy and haggard.

Even if he wanted to chase the dwarves, he wouldn't have been able to keep up. Looking at the tribe of razin, he saw the same was true for those that were lucky enough to still be standing. None of the wounds of the injured looked that serious, but that was only because the murk dwarves had finished their kills. Most of the wounded had been double-tapped.

There was also the unknown factor. Someone or something had conjured that black wall at the end. If there was another acolyte, or the god Vúr himself was out there, then the risk of chasing the dwarves was too high. His own Divine Powers were strong but he'd already used three charges. If he was faced with five or six enemies at the same time, he'd be overwhelmed. His second and most likely last life would come to a swift end. Remy did follow them with his eyes, however, silently promising one thing. If they ever came back, he'd be waiting.

***

The pantherkin god didn't see it, but the immortal watcher still observed him from the shadow of a distant tree. His eyes were pure matte black and filled with an anger that matched the fury in Remington's heart. The deity lusted for blood and violence, but had also learned patience during his long life. He marked the black-eared god as an enemy, but now was not the time to finish this.

Vúr stared at Remy for another long second before fleeing into the forest with the few dwarves that had survived. He was furious. He'd almost reaped hundreds of lives! The energy from their deaths would have skyrocketed his cultivation. Not only that, but losing the battle meant that he'd failed a quest! He'd lost out on the Faith Points the quest would have given, and the penalty for failure had dropped his people's Devotion.

He had only arrived in the world of Telos hours before. He had quickly claimed his Chosen people and used them to power level. A small tribe of peaceful gnome-like creatures had been the first group his tribe had slaughtered. It had let him reach level one.

They'd butchered other random beasts as they'd traveled. Unfortunately, they hadn't come across any other settlements, which was why he'd been so excited when they'd spotted the pantherkin. When he had ordered his strike team to attack the beastkin, he'd thought it would be an easy battle. The Grey Thorn tribe were ideally suited to be his worshippers; they craved power and loved violence. Best of all, they obeyed his commands without a hint of morality or conscience. Vúr gritted his teeth. If not for the enemy god, he would have succeeded!

If he'd had the full force of his tribe, they would have been able to wipe out the cat men even with the other god's interference. Because he only had thirty fighters though, with the rest searching for a settlement site, he'd lost more than three-quarters of his strike squad. The god wanted to scream in anger. He did not actually care about the lost lives; they were only mortals, after all. That did not change the fact that they belonged to him. They were *his* property!

If not for one of his Divine Powers, *Deep Shadow*, he'd have lost the entire team. It was not useful for attack at its current level, but it could summon a wall of pure darkness. It was excellent for stealth and evasion. That Power, coupled with the murk dwarves' propensity for stealth, had let them sneak up on the razin tribe. Vúr had never imagined he would need to use it to flee. The indignity of it burned inside his cold, cold heart.

That was why, as Vúr glared at Remy from the shadows, he made a silent promise. The beastkin god would pay. He would make his enemy's Chosen people turn against their god. The men would be killed. The women would be tortured morning and night. Every female child would be sacrificed and the male children would be kept in pens. They would not be fed, left to starve until they began to eat each other. When only a single male child was left, and the boy had been driven mad by the sights it had beheld and the pains Vúr had inflicted on it, Vúr would have him slaughter the women one by one. The last sight they would see before death took them was the corruption of what they held most dear.

Such was the anger of a god!

***

Remy was unaware of Vúr's wrathful promise. Even if he had been, his answer would have probably been something along the lines of, "Try it, cocksucker."

All the god felt at that moment was a wave of exhaustion washing through him. His Divine Powers made him deadly, but he was still flesh and blood. His stamina had nearly bottomed out even though the battle had only taken minutes. Now was not the time to show any weakness though. Instead, he turned to formally address the tribe that were all staring at him in wonder, horror and worship. While he regarded them, one young female walked up and asked him a simple question, "Who are you?"

Her words triggered a notification to appear.

> **Quest Update for: Save Us I**
>
> Your Chosen people have been saved, but need a name to call you in worship. Your first name has been bound by a Cosmic Force and cannot be spoken. Therefore, you will have to give your people another by which to address you. In so doing, you will bestow upon them the words required to gain their devotion.
>
> **Time until sunrise and Quest Failure:** 0 hours, 0 minute, 7 seconds

Remy still didn't like the idea of people worshipping him, but he hated the idea of failing his quest. The penalties were severe. His real name had been locked away by his sponsor for whatever reason, so he couldn't tell them that. Instead, he told them the name he'd decided on when he was with Sariel. Two words that encompassed his mentality and would remind him of who he had been on Earth.

Seconds after he spoke it aloud, the first rays of sunlight blessed the land. After the din of battle, the morning seemed abnormally quiet. Even the wounded had stilled their groans to hear his answer. The godling cast his gaze about as the sun rose behind him. To the tribe, his figure looked like a dark silhouette with the heavens itself giving him a crown of light. Every member of his new Chosen people remembered the first simple words their god spoke.

"Call me Zero Fell."

CHAPTER 21

Several opened their mouths to ask questions, but Fell held up a hand. "There are wounded we need to tend to before we do anything else." His *Soul Heal* skill would only replenish 20 HP per charge, but he was still a doctor. If he targeted that healing to the most dire injuries and spread out the energy, he could hopefully keep the greatest number of people alive. He also had more than magical healing at his disposal.

A few quick orders set up a rudimentary triage. He split them into groups. Everyone not injured moved to one side. That was his green group. Everyone injured that could still move moved to a second spot. Everyone that couldn't move was placed together by the green group. Those were his reds and the most critical patients. After that, he took stock of the resources they had.

In addition to the scant clothing they wore, all the razin had small satchels made out of the same brown material. When he asked what they held, he found each tribe member was carrying rations and a waterskin. According to the tribe, when they'd been brought to this world, they'd all had these bags. Other than the clothes and moccasins they were wearing, they had no other belongings. Remy had hoped they would have pots to boil water in or, at the very least, bandages, but he quickly found out that technologically speaking, the tribe was barely out of the stone age.

Shrugging, he gave orders to pile the water skins near the red and yellow wounded. He then ordered the uninjured members of the tribe to set up a perimeter. With the sun up it was much less likely they would be ambushed again, but he wasn't taking any chances.

The tribe looked at him for a moment upon hearing his commands, but only for a moment. One and all flew into motion. They experienced a deep-seated compulsion to follow the instructions of this powerful figure. It did not override their free will, exactly; it was more that they all felt like they "should" do as he asked. Neither side knew it, but the connection between a god and his Chosen was already manifesting itself in all their lives.

Remy himself was somewhat surprised by how readily these strangers followed his orders. There would be time to consider that later, however. For now, there were lives to save. He began to pour his healing energy into the most gravely injured razin. Unfortunately, he didn't have the power to fix the most grievous wounds, not with only one charge left. With a discontented sigh, he moved on to the less critical red patients, giving orders to make the dying as comfortable as possible.

That didn't mean he couldn't help others. A man with a severed hand was close to bleeding out. After using *Soul Heal,* the blood loss stopped. The wound still looked fresh, and it still oozed blood, but it was no longer gushing. Sadly, his power wasn't strong enough to regrow limbs. Maybe when he enhanced it that would be possible, but for now it was beyond him.

The amputee lay on the ground, glassy-eyed but stabilized. Before moving on to the next patient, Fell gave an order to heat one of the copper weapons until just before it glowed and then to sear the stump with intermittent pressure. He took the time to teach his people that if the blade was too hot or applied too long, the flesh would stick to the side of the blade and tear when it was removed.

His words snapped the injured pantherkin out of his shock. The man looked up at his new god in fear and disbelief, but Zero had already moved on to the next patient. While he continued to judiciously use his Divine Powers, the other razin followed his orders. A few minutes later, a sizzling sound accompanied the scent of cooking meat. Right after came a scream of agony.

Fell didn't stop what he was doing. He merely noted happily that he was with people that would follow distasteful orders. While he continued healing the tribe, he started going through the prompts he'd earned in battle. The first showed the bonuses from choosing a name and finishing his quest.

Congratulations! You have completed the Prayer Quest: **Save Us I**

The rewards of this quest have been magnified due to increased difficulty.

Saving the Razin not once, but twice, has forged a strong connection between you and the tribe. The Prayer you answered was not from just one member of your people, but was a collective prayer from the entire race!

By telling them your name, they can now bind their belief to you. This has forged an indelible mark upon their souls, and until the end of this world and beyond, every member of your Chosen has received a Mark. This shall be a channel for their Faith and your Power.

Your Chosen people are now the **Razin**!

Rewards: (All rewards increased by 200% due to increased difficulty)

7,500 Faith Points (base 2,500)

3,000 Experience Points (base 1,000)

600 Devotion Points (base 200) for the Razin tribe

A Chosen people: **The Razin**

The god known as Zero Fell felt Faith Points flowing into him for the first time. To his surprise, it was a cool, smooth feeling, like drinking frosty lemonade on a hot day. It felt like he'd been missing something that his body needed, like he'd been parched, but on a level deeper than the physical. He realized he'd been missing something that his soul needed. What he was feeling was the instinctual craving of a god to be worshipped. There had been a faint hint of this sensation after absorbing energy from the dwarf souls, but getting such an influx was on another level entirely.

The relief he felt was like seeing the sun for the first time at the age of twenty. His head cleared and the pain left his body. The new god sighed heavily in reprieve. The power of faith coursed through his body and made him feel like he could do anything. Fell looked at the small sea of faces gazing at him in adoration and knew one fact beyond a shadow of a doubt: he needed these people.

More prompts were waiting to be read.

> Know This! **Prayer Quests** can be generated in response to individual prayers made in your name, but will usually be due to a subconscious collective prayer from your Chosen people. Such Quests will always provide Faith Points as a reward, though other prizes may also be provided upon completion.

Zero read through the quest prompt carefully while the razin stared at him with rapt attention. A piece of themselves, a piece they had never known they were even missing, had been found. It allowed them to feel a connection and a sense of purpose that even the oldest among them had never experienced. The god himself felt a connection to them that he could barely describe. While they murmured to one another, he examined his next prompt.

> You have been offered a Prayer Quest: **Save Us II**
>
> **Quest Rank:** *Common*

You have saved your Chosen tribe and they have formed a bond with you. They require guidance in this new world. Specifically, you must find them a new home to settle in.

Choose well the site of the tribe's new home, for it may one day be your Holy Land!

Success Conditions: Find a location that is suitable to your people's needs and growth.

Rewards: The rewards of this quest are variable based on the appropriateness of the location selected.

Penalty for failure of Quest: Failing this quest will break the connection between you and your Chosen people.

This Quest cannot be refused!

It looked like the penalty was the same as the earlier links in the quest chain. He needed to find a place for them to settle. He was pretty sure he already had that covered thanks to his *Ruined Temple I* quest. It looked like his cheating sponsors had found a way to double-dip, not that he was complaining.

The next window showed that worshipping him had a direct benefit to his worshippers.

All worshippers of Zero Fell gain:

+1% of your Main Attribute: **+1 to Luck**

Increasing your power will increase these benefits, thereby securing the devotion of your followers and gathering more.

+1 to Luck, Fell thought. Not quite as good as a boost to Strength or Constitution. He might have a hard time getting followers in the future if this was all he had to offer. And now that he'd made the connection, he knew beyond a shadow of a doubt that he did want more followers. He needed more followers!

At least I'll be popular with gamblers, he thought wryly.

The next windows showed that he'd made headway on evolving his *Infuriating Enemy* Title.

For killing **14 *common* rank** enemies with the Title **Infuriating Enemy** equipped, you have gained **280 Animosity Points**.
540/1,000 obtained to upgrade your Title.

You have gained: **1,276 XP** from combat.

You have gained: **3,000 XP** from finishing the Quest: Save Us I

7,823/7,500 XP to reach Level 2

Remy had killed nearly half the attackers. That was because he followed the words of his first sergeant.

"I won't teach you how to fight. I'll teach you how to kill. That way, when your enemy tries to fight, you'll send them straight to hell."

The kills he'd gotten were mostly assists. He'd backstabbed, hamstrung and sucker-punched every dwarf he could. Fell had always preferred a coup de grace to a stand-up fight.

His Warrior Class had come into play as well. *Fast Hands* let him swing his weapons faster than the dwarves had expected. Coupled with his higher Dexterity, the murkers just hadn't been able to keep up. Being a Level 1 Warrior also added 10% damage to any of his strikes. As he had a tendency to only aim for critical areas, that bonus was compounded.

He also used *Bell Ringer* twice. After his enemies were stunned, a quick stab to the throat put them on the ground. Following that, their own frantic heartbeats bled them out. If not for his low stamina and the move's cooldown he would have used it more, but doing it twice consumed nearly half his green bar.

He'd gained plenty of XP from his kills. Examining his status log, he saw that this time there were no level modifiers. They'd all been level one, just like him. In the heat of battle, he hadn't stopped to think about it, but now it made him wonder. How was that possible?

If they'd arrived yesterday and had been level zero like him and the razin, just how many victims had the murk dwarves preyed upon to level up before attacking his Chosen? He'd probably never know, but it just underscored the importance of advancing and doing it quickly.

The dwarves had held a decided advantage over the pantherkin, both in weapons and levels. If their numbers had been the same, Fell had no doubt his tribe would have been wiped out. His people needed to get stronger, and they needed to do it now. While it was possible he would meet a race of high leveled people that were actually benevolent, everything he'd learned in both of his lives argued that the chances for that were zilch.

For a second, he paused. His people? When had he started thinking like that and not just seeing them as a means to an end? Fell had just met them, and yet he couldn't shake the "rightness" of that feeling. These were "his" people. *His* worshippers. Again, the connection to his Chosen was making itself manifest. Even his resistance to thinking of himself as a god was fading by the minute. He couldn't doubt it anymore, not with the bond he could now feel.

He turned back to his prompts and a smile came to his bruised and bloody lips. It was accompanied by the most wonderful of sounds.

TRING!	
You have reached level **2**! The power of a God is potentially without limit, but it must be grown. Your soul rank is the equivalent of **Limited**. Never forget, there are many forms of power and this is only one.	
Attribute Points	+2 to Agility and Dexterity +2 Free Attribute Points
Bonus Energy Slots	+10
Class Points	+30

His Agility and Dexterity both increased to nineteen. He could feel his body getting looser again, but to a slightly lesser extent. The returns from adding two points per level would decrease as the overall numbers got higher. With his two new Attribute Points, he was heavily tempted to put them into Constitution again. He was racking up a good deal of abilities and powers, but it didn't matter if an enemy could one-shot him.

What stopped him was the modifier he'd gained for his Luck. He still didn't like the idea of placing his hopes on something so... impractical, but he couldn't deny that the bonus basically doubled the free Attribute Points he gained. Even that might not be enough to convince him, but the bonuses of his Main Attribute were enough to make him take a chance. He'd gotten a boost at 25 points and another at 50. He'd be shocked if he didn't get one at 75.

He also had thirty Class Points now. Remy decided to invest those in advancing his Warrior level again. It cost him 20 CPs, but his melee and ranged damage bonuses both increased from 10% to 15%. He had ten more points, but he decided to save them. Remy had a feeling that advancing the rank of his Class could have strong bonuses. It also earned him another 10 Energy Points.

More exciting was that he'd gained his second skill!

You have qualified for the *common* Warrior skill: **Short Blades**

Qualification: Defeat 5 enemies with a dagger or short sword

Adopting this skill will increase the damage you deal with short blades

This skill costs **5 Energy** Slots

Do you wish to learn this skill?

Remy grabbed it quickly and felt a cool feeling flow through his arms.

Congratulations! You are now a Copper Novice in **Short Blades**

+5% attack speed with short blades. +5% damage with short blades.

Your true proficiency is that of a **Gold Apprentice**!

+100% to speed of skill progress until your rank matches your proficiency. No rank tests will be required until you reach your true proficiency.

Total Energy Remaining: 381/626

The other thing that stood out was that he'd made serious strides toward unlocking the second perk of the eaglebear's soul. While he walked around, he inspected the fallen dwarves with his Soul Art. To his delight, even the ones he hadn't killed were available for harvest. The battle had lasted about a quarter of an hour. If a spirit did flee the body after death, it took longer than that. Walking around the battlefield, he ended up collecting another twenty-two *common* souls.

It was quite a harvest, but for the first time, his Energy wasn't up to consuming all the souls at once. Each *common* soul he consumed temporarily took up 25 slots. As he continued to consume them, he received a red prompt.

> You have reached your **Energy** limit!

Of course, the answer to that was simple. He currently had two uses for the *common* souls: cultivation or feeding the eaglebear. He hadn't forgotten he needed to get on the spirit's good side, so he gave it a feast!

> Your bound eaglebear soul has consumed **+2 Soul Points**…

> Your bound eaglebear soul has consumed **+5 Soul Points**…

> Your bound eaglebear soul has consumed **+1 Soul Points**…

After feeding on all of them, the eaglebear spirit only needed another 17 Soul Points before its 2nd power could be unlocked. He considered using the souls of the razin, despite the fact that it felt wrong somehow. A red warning prompt told him that was not possible.

> Warning! No god can use their Art against their own Chosen.!

That came as a surprise. He'd had no issue using *Soul Heal* on the razin, but apparently he couldn't do something that was seen as harmful. Honestly, Fell didn't have a problem with that. Again, it had felt wrong on a deep level. Unlocking the eaglebear's second power would just have to wait.

Consuming the souls of the regular murk dwarves had also earned him Faith Points.

> For absorbing energy from a **Faithful of Vúr**, you have gained +3 **Faith Points**!

A few of the dwarves he'd killed hadn't given him anything, but the dwarf that had been wielding the darkness-imbued axe gave much more. Killing enemy clergy turned out to be good for business.

> For absorbing energy from an **Acolyte of Vúr**, you have gained
>
> **+500 Faith Points**!
>
> **Total Faith Points:** 8,074

The acolyte had given a hundred times as many Faith Points as a basic worshipper. Remy didn't know how to use Faith Points yet, but he knew they would come in handy somehow and he wanted as many as he could get. Braninon's spirit was the only *uncommon,* higher ranked soul. He didn't feed that one to his eaglebear, keeping it for his own experimentation later.

Realizing that the last dwarf he'd killed was an acolyte brought his mind to the men and women of the razin tribe. They were apparently his "Chosen" people now. Assuming the murk dwarves had been the Chosen of the god Vúr, the deity had been able to give his acolyte a powerful spell. If another god could do that, why couldn't he?

The next prompts answered that exact question.

CHAPTER 22

Congratulations! You have found your Chosen people, **the Razin**.

Their race is called **pantherkin**, a branch of beastkin. Just as you have been brought from another world, so too were your Chosen. They are an intelligent and curious people. You will find they are capable in many different areas. The Razin have less strength than your previous race of human, but are also more agile and dexterous.

This is a race of great potential, and you will only express their true power by nourishing them.

Know This! Each tribe on Telos starts with **2 Tribal Characteristics**. The Characteristics of the Razin are:

1) **Industrious (Level 0)**: +10% building speed and quality
2) **Curiosity (Level 0)**: +5% to Research and chances to find interesting locations.

Honor these two Qualities to progress them and open up new potential!

Fell wasn't sure how he "honored" qualities, but he'd figure it out. The next prompt was a bit more straightforward.

Know This! Each new tribe of Telos is awarded **1 Free Technology**. The Technology of the Razin is **Construction I**.

There was a description of what the tech *Construction I* did, but it had a lot of information so Fell just skimmed it before minimizing it for later. Basically, it provided the blueprints for a few simple buildings. It was interesting but wasn't useful for the moment. The next prompts were far more germane to the here and now. They showed just how valuable Sariel's advice about searching for resonance had been.

In addition to the **Qualities** of the tribe, their innate compatibility with their god shall greatly affect their daily lives and communal fate.

This intrinsic connection is quantified by the **Soul Resonance (SR)** between yourself and your Chosen people.

Soul Resonance is the innate similarity between a Chosen people and the deity they would worship. Each being in the Universe has an innate nature that can grow and manifest in many different ways, but can rarely be broken without also breaking the soul. A tree may be cultivated to grow tall or short, but when exposed to fire, all wood will burn. So too would a Fire deity have a low Soul Resonance with a tribe highly in tune with the properties of water.

A high SR can lead your people to much greater heights. Having a high Soul Resonance greatly increases the ability of a deity to convert new worshipers, allows for deeper bonds of Faith, and increases the Devotion of worshipers, to name just a few of its effects.

Conversely, a low Soul Resonance can make the formation of a strong religion a near impossibility. It can cause **Breaks of Faith**, **Schisms**, and **Perversion** of your doctrine, and many other negative effects!

This is not your fate, however, Zero Fell. You have bonded with the Razin people and your Soul Resonance is **97%**!

As such, you are in the 7th and highest tier of SR, and will be awarded accordingly.

Award for reaching Tier 1

SR > 25%

Your people's Max Devotion can reach the 1st 2 positive ranks

Each additional Tier increases this by 2 ranks

Award for reaching Tier 2

SR > 50%

+5% Faith Points from your Chosen

Each additional Tier increases this by an additional 5% (max 25%)

Award for reaching Tier 3

SR > 75%

+5% Devotion Points from your Chosen

Each additional Tier increases this by an additional 5% (max 25%)

Award for reaching Tier 4

SR > 80%

+5% Reduction in Summoning costs for your Chosen people

Each additional Tier increases this by an additional 5% (max 20%)

Award for reaching Tier 5

SR > 85%

1 Free Building or 1 Free Repair of an existing Building

This must be used within a tenday of founding your settlement

Award for reaching Tier 6

SR > 90%

1 Free Technology

This must be used within a tenday of founding your settlement

Award for reaching Tier 7
SR > 95%
1 Free Resource on Starting Hex
Resource can only be awarded upon creation of settlement
Resource rank ranges from *common* to *rare*

Fell understood basically none of that, but from the tone of the text it sounded really good. Basically, he and the razin were innately simpatico. It looked like the pain he'd gone through during the Choosing had paid off.

The next notifications told him more about the tribe and the importance of Devotion.

Your actions have bonded you to your Chosen People. While **Soul Resonance** can be said to measure the potential for that bond, the actual strength of your connection to your faithful is measured by **Devotion**. Each tribe, group or population you interact with can have varying levels of Devotion toward any number of deities.

Your actions have led your people to not only worship you, but also be Devoted. Your quests have earned you 600 Devotion Points

Total Devotion: +750 Devotion Points (base 600 x +25% for Tier 7 Soul Resonance)

Fell heard a sound like a small cymbal ringing together twice.

CLING! CLING!

The Devotion of your Chosen people has increased from rank 0, **Casual Understanding (+0)** to rank 3, **Dedicated Believer (+500)**. "We are dedicated to following your teachings."

Devotion Rank 3 Rewards

1) Faith Points generated increased from 0 to **+10** FP/worshipper/tenday (Faith Points are awarded based on average Devotion for a people, not individual levels of Devotion. They are awarded every tenday to the deity toward whom a worshipper has the greatest Devotion)
2) 3 FREE Clergy creation Tokens (Single-use items)
3) 3 Clergy Slots

Fell still didn't fully understand everything, but that darkness-wielding dwarf had been a member of Vúr's clergy. Now it looked like he'd be able to make three of his own! If the enemy acolyte was any indication, his clergy would be strong fighters.

The next prompts gave him more information about his clergy.

Know This! Acolytes are the lowest rank of the **Cleric** Class, i.e., faithful that can utilize their god's power. Their powers will be fueled by their Faith Points rather than their State of Being. Their powers will also be a weaker imitation of your own. Even one acolyte can turn the tide of battle.

Deities create clergy by investing their followers with a piece of their Divine Power. Unless special circumstances are met, each created clergy occupies a deity's Energy slots. The specific number of slots is determined by the rank of the clergy and the State of Being of their god.

To create an Acolyte Token, invest **50 Divine Points** into your altar.

Having his people be devoted was already paying off. He could make three acolytes. Having three fighters that could use magic like the dwarf with the dark axe was a game changer!

Fell read the rest of the prompts.

Know This! Due to the specifics of your Focus: **Soul Art**, your clergy will all be awarded the **Soul Capture** ability. They will also be able to capture souls to fuel their powers.

He moved on to the next prompt that told him more about making an acolyte.

> A follower must fulfill 2 requirements to become an Acolyte of Zero Fell
>
> 1) A personal Devotion of rank 1, **Acknowledge Divinity**, or higher.
> 2) Be a Chosen of the god Zero Fell

That shouldn't be too hard, he thought. The tribe as a whole had reached the third rank of Devotion, and he was benefitting from that fact. To Fell, it was obvious that this system was set up for gods and their worshippers to be codependent. It made him think back to something he'd heard years before.

Back on Earth, there had been countless theories about religion. He'd never paid too close attention, but one thing he'd heard had stuck with him. It boiled down to the idea that people needed their god, but their god also needed them. He'd always liked that. It just seemed fair in some way.

An amused smile graced his face. Maybe this new life as a god was punishment for having blasphemous thoughts in his last one. As a new god, was he even capable of blasphemy now? Was *that* thought blasphemous? Fell shook his head. A rabbit hole with no bottom.

What he needed to focus on now was making his clergy. This world was dangerous, and the faster he had powerful helpers, the better.

> Do you wish to create an **Acolyte**? Yes or No?

Fell would definitely be making clergy, but he only had three slots. He couldn't dole out power haphazardly. It was important that he chose the right people. As his old boss had once told him, "When you're choosing employees, don't worry about hiring an asshole. That's inevitable. Just make sure they're your kind of asshole."

He chose "No," for the moment.

There were two more prompts left to review. It was almost like the Universe was saving the best for last.

> You have met the **Secret Conditions** to advance your State of Being. Speak the words to claim your prize.

At first he was confused, then he remembered Sariel's words. With a faint smile, not quite sure it would work, he intoned, "The worthy shall know."

With those words, he heard a sound that reverberated throughout his entire body. It was so deep that he felt the entire planet must be vibrating.

> **DIRRNNN!**
>
> Congratulations! Your **State of Being** has advanced!
>
> Awarding **98 Divine Points** to your State of Being.
>
> By fulfilling a set of Secret criteria, you have taken the first step on the Holy Path of Immortality. You are now a Tier 0, Rank 1, **Weak Spirit Made Flesh.**

The Secret conditions were:

1) Bond with your Chosen people.

2) Reach a Devotion Rank of 3 or greater within one tenday.

3) Speak the phrase of power.

0/200 Divine Points earned to take the next step on the Rainbow Path.

+100 Energy Points!

To everyone's shock, red flames enveloped Fell's body. They didn't burn, but they did invigorate! The razin stared at their new god in awe and fear. A bellow echoed out from Zero's throat and power flooded his body.

The godling's eyes widened in shock as everything about himself felt like it improved all at once. He felt stronger and lighter on his feet. He had greater clarity of thought, and the weariness that had been plaguing him decreased. As he looked around, he realized that colors seemed sharper. His hearing was more acute. It was as if the entirety of his being got an instant upgrade. With a startled realization, he realized that was probably exactly what had happened.

He pulled up his status page, expecting his attributes to have increased. To his surprise, his health, mana and stamina had improved, but the attributes were the same. Whatever increasing his State of Being did, it didn't increase his Primary Attributes. Still, he could *feel* that he'd changed. Frowning slightly, he focused on just one, Strength. A description appeared like before.

> **Strength** – Improves damage with melee weapons. Each point increases carrying capacity by 11 kg.

He read it carefully and quickly realized that the definition had a crucial difference. Before his State of Being had improved, each point of Strength had only let him carry 10 kg. Now, it was 11. His heart started thudding in excitement. If he was right, this was way better than when he got points from leveling. He checked his health, mana and stamina again.

Just like he thought, the increase in each was due to every point in his Primary Attributes being more valuable now. Each point of Constitution now gave him 11 HP. The same was true for his Intelligence and Endurance increasing his mana and stamina. The improvement to his State of Being made everything about him more powerful!

He now fully understood why Sariel had told him not to ignore his cultivation. Just this first step on the Rainbow Path had increased the value of his Primary Attributes by 10%. Judging by his increased hearing, vision and overall awareness of his surroundings, it also had some hidden benefits beyond that. His hidden Secondary Attributes must have been modified as well. He suddenly realized just how vitally important cultivating truly was.

Fell bounced on his feet and threw a couple quick jabs in the air. The red flames had faded, leaving the rich black fur on his ears and tail with just a bit more luster. His cocoa skin radiated an improved vitality, and some of the tribe could swear he was a bit taller now.

The tribe looked at their new god curiously, watching a miracle come to life who was now… shadow-boxing. Remy just ignored them, lost in this new sensation. His improved body was amazing! While he tested his outer changes, he also turned his gaze inward.

A changed awaited him there as well. The white pyramid of his cultivation Divine Core had turned fully red. There was not a drop of white to be seen. The edges of the pyramid remained the same shining gold as before. The figure behind it was no longer empty. Now a red sphere of circulating energy had appeared in the groin.

He knew without being told that further cultivation would yield orange energy, changing the color of the pyramid until it was a deep ochre. That would awaken another… he searched for the word before arriving on "chakra." Before another chakra was created. Seeing the color pattern now, he exclaimed aloud, "Oh! Rainbow Path." Not as stupid a name as he'd thought.

He got back to healing his people and reading his prompts.

As a reward for growing your power, you are awarded a FREE advancement of one of your Divine Powers by 1 level.

Choose well, godling!

1) Soul Strike
2) Soul Heal

Another unexpected benefit. Both skills had kept him alive up to this point. The problem was, there were no descriptions of what would happen when either leveled up. He'd be choosing blind. He was sure upgrading *Soul Strike* would let him deliver more damage, and improving *Soul Heal* would give more healing points. He just didn't know by how much.

He was tempted to upgrade *Soul Strike*, but he was already doing some good damage. He also had a few weapons to choose from now. With so many of the tribe needing healing, he went with the second option.

You have progressed the Divine Power **Soul Heal** to level 1. Restores a maximum of 40 Health upon touch. Can heal more severe wounds. Healing speed increased from 5 HP/sec to 7 HP/sec

Energy Cost increased: 50 >> 55

He was satisfied with his choice. The Divine Power had doubled in strength. It would be effective against more dire wounds now. The extra five points of Energy was nothing, especially as walking down the Rainbow Path had given him another one hundred.

Fell walked back over to the "red" zone, where the most injured razin lay. Several had already died from their wounds, but there were three that were still desperately clinging to life. He held his hands over a man that had been stabbed in the gut. The blood loss was substantial, and a loop of intestine hung outside of his body. Even with two pantherkin applying pressure, the bleeding hadn't stopped.

From the looks on everyone's faces, the entire tribe knew he was not long for this world. In fact, everyone had backed away from the dying man. Everyone except for a woman holding his hand. No one spoke, but they all knew the truth: there were only minutes left. The tribe came to an unspoken agreement to give the two siblings as much privacy as possible at the end.

A moment ago, the tribe would have been right. The man would have been beyond all help. Even with his medical knowledge, there was no way Fell could have saved the man in time, lacking anything but the most rudimentary of tools. Now though, there might be a chance.

Fell knelt down next to the man, examining his wound. Emotions warred on the sister's face, wondering if her new god could actually save the only family she had left in this world. Surely he would have done so before if possible, but still, was he not a god?

Zero paid her no attention, his gaze lasered in on his new patient. Palpating the wound, he checked for any large foreign objects. It would be impossible to remove all dirt or particulates, but if any small rocks had entered the wound, he wanted them out. His follower hissed through his teeth before bellowing out loud.

Satisfied, the god visualized what he needed to do. He had seen plenty of gut wounds back on Earth. Some he had caused; others he had fixed. He knew what needed to be done. Fell visualized the filth that had spilled from perforated intestines, and then imagined it gone. He thought about the torn tissues of the bowels knitting back together, of the man's body being restored: tissue, nerves and vessels. Then he thought about the muscles strengthening and the skin repairing. After manually pushing the man's intestines back into his abdomen, Fell closed his eyes. With his hands bloody and soiled, he released his power.

He felt an immediate difference. The sensation of his energy entering the razin was more tactile. Leveling the divine skill had given him markedly improved control. A blue glow surrounded his hand as usual, but now there was a faint haze above it, like heat over the desert. It was also accompanied by the faintest of sounds.

If anyone were able to listen to it again, they might have heard the faint cry of a monkey. It only took a few moments for the man's breathing to ease. Astonished, the formerly gravely injured patient checked his own stomach and found the wound gone. His sister stared, tears streaking the fine hair on her face. As Remy stood, she grabbed her god's hand and kissed it fervently.

Fell was rewarded with a prompt.

For saving the life of her brother, the Devotion of the Razin, **Autumn Ghost**, has increased by +5,000 (base 4,000 +25% for Tier 7 Soul Resonance). Her personal Devotion rank has increased from rank 3, **Dedicated Believer**, to rank 6, **Fully Committed to the Faith**.

Fell received a similar prompt for her brother. The increase in the man's personal Devotion was only a tenth of what Autumn Ghost's had been, but it was still something. More importantly, it gave him a clue on how to increase the Devotion of his followers. Just telling them to believe "harder" wouldn't work. That made sense, of course. You couldn't just decide to believe in something. He'd have to do meaningful acts to improve his people's opinion of him.

As she clung to him, he looked at her name again: Autumn Ghost. It seemed strange, especially because looking at her brother's status sheet, he found his patient was called Sleek Fawn. Using God's Eye on the other razin, he found they all had Native American-sounding names.

Asking Autumn about it, he discovered her name was actually a bit more poetic. It appeared the razin were named for a phrase that was meant to describe their nature. Her name was actually, "Soft steps over fallen leaves without leaving a trace." The razin weren't crazy though. No one had the time to say a phrase every time they called their kids for dinner, so they also shortened everyone's names. Hers became Autumn Ghost.

After he healed Autumn Ghost's brother, Fell's charges were depleted again. He continued doing what he could with his medical skills, but in the middle of nowhere without medicine or tools, his impact was limited. The others in the red triage section died before he could use *Soul Heal* again. After that, however, by using targeted healing he only lost one more patient before everyone was stabilized.

The increases in Devotion trickled in as he continued healing. He realized that the only reason he probably got such a strong increase from Autumn Ghost was because he saved her brother and it was the first time the tribe had seen him heal someone so gravely ill. Now that the initial shock over his powers was wearing off, he wasn't getting the same response. Put simply, his powers seemed like less of a "miracle." He'd hoped that healing them would be an easy way to regularly increase Devotion. It appeared it wouldn't be that easy.

As he healed his Chosen, he looked at his last notification. There was one final prompt waiting to be read, and it was a new quest.

CHAPTER 23

The frequency with which he was gaining quests was surprising to the new god. They certainly hadn't been common on Earth. Here he was averaging more than one a day. As he thought about it, he realized he would never have gotten this new quest if he hadn't had the old ones. Was this a ripple effect from his sponsors?

He didn't know, but ripple or not, he was shocked by the source of the quest.

You have been offered a Quest by your bound soul: **Last Wish I**

Quest Rank: Common

You have captured the soul of a **Mortal Enemy**. The level of enmity it felt for you is embedded in its soul. Though it still wishes you harm, it has a greater desire. Its primary thoughts are for its offspring.

Now that it has died, its den is left without a protector. While its scent might keep away other monsters for a short time, once that fades, its young will be eaten. They will be protected for another day at most.

Your Mortal Enemy charges you with finding its progeny and ensuring they are not in any immediate danger.

If you agree, it will guide you to its den and let go of its enmity toward you. You may then release it or continue to keep it bound, but without the threat of inevitable battle between the two of you.

If you refuse, it will continue to fight you until you are harmed or possessed.

Success Conditions: Find the eaglebear's cave so that it can see its young.

Rewards: Ability to release the eaglebear's soul. Removal of Mortal Enemy status with your bound soul.

Penalty for failure or refusal of Quest: Faster degradation of your control over the eaglebear's soul. This will decrease the time until possible possession.

Do you accept? Yes or No

Fell gritted his teeth. He hated being told what to do. This quest was technically his choice, but it was a choice made with a gun to his head. It seemed obvious now that he shouldn't have absorbed the soul of a Mortal Enemy. He could definitely feel that his hold on its soul was not as strong as on the simian souls.

Maybe it was because its hate lived beyond the grave, or maybe it was because the eaglebear's soul had been a higher rank. He didn't know. He did take the threat of it fighting against him seriously though. What if it tried to get away while he was in the middle of battle? What would that do to him? Whatever it was, it wouldn't be good.

He forced his irritation aside. He'd known it was a bit crazy to possess the soul of a Mortal Enemy. How could there not be consequences, after all? It had been a bit like sticking a bomb in his chest. There was no denying the power it had given him though. He most likely wouldn't have been able to see the murk dwarf ambush if not for the eaglebear's soul.

Still, he'd never forgotten the red warning he got when he bound the soul.

> "... soul damage, soul dissolution or possession"

If he could avoid any of those consequences, or all of them ideally, then it was worth a detour. He'd hoped feeding other souls to the eaglebear would improve their relationship, but so far as Fell could tell, it hadn't moved the needle. Besides, when he'd spoken the prayer over the eaglebear's still cooling corpse he had meant every word of the apology, so if he could save its offspring it was the least he could

281

do. He didn't care about much, but his word, that mattered. Irritation nearly completely gone; he accepted the quest.

As soon as he did, images started to flash through his mind. It confused him at first, but then he realized he was reliving the eaglebear's last day. He watched it leave its cave to hunt. He could see it walking through thick trees, and then out into an open patch of grassland. A strange mountain loomed in the distance, the top curving over like a question mark.

It was then he realized that the open patch of grass was the very plain he was standing on now. Turning, Fell saw the very same mountain in the distance. The rest of the images showed the eaglebear following a similar path to the one he had just taken to reach the tribe, but in reverse. It would be easy enough to flip what he'd just seen and find the eaglebear's lair. He had already traveled most of the way actually, just by leaving the valley. Getting to the den was doable, but it would take several hours. The quest had said he only had a day to complete it. There wasn't time to waste.

This wasn't his first rodeo though, and he knew he couldn't go off half-cocked. The first order of business was figuring out what he had to work with. That meant getting to know the tribe and deciding which of them would become clergy.

Fell started thinking. It made no sense to try to drag the whole tribe with him. He would be better off taking a few of the best fighters to find the cave. A small force could move quickly and quietly, hopefully avoiding any other monsters or hostile tribes. He had to make sure that the rest of the tribe was safe until he got back though. Some of the wounded weren't ready to be moved yet. There was also the matter of scavenging the bodies, both dwarf and pantherkin, for whatever might be useful.

The razin didn't have much, but they had a few simple tools and food. Thankfully, it looked like most of the supplies had survived the dwarf attack more or less intact. That was probably because one of the reasons for the assault was to steal resources.

If all the tribes had been dropped onto Telos like the razin, then everyone was short on supplies. The razin had found that each man and woman had enough food for a week. Now that so many had died the rations would stretch longer, but still, basic needs would be a deadly concern very soon.

Remy had seen firsthand what people would do when they were desperate. He'd seen it in war and he'd seen it after the Forsaking. Soccer moms and pilates instructors had murdered and tortured other people to stay alive after the monsters appeared. Remy knew that the question wasn't *if* his tribe would be attacked again, but when.

That was a worry for tomorrow though. Now was the time to act. He put his God's Eye to good use. It was relatively simple to get information about each and every member of the tribe. There were small variations, but the adults more or less had the same attributes. They looked a lot like his own had when he'd first examined his status page, but a point or two lower in places. What grabbed his attention was that of the one hundred and forty-two members of the tribe still alive, five of them had abilities.

The first he discovered was a brown-haired razin male named Sharp Leaf. He was a quiet person with a square jaw. The pantherkin stood an inch taller than the others and had a more defined musculature. He was still level zero, but had an ability called *Shrewd Fighter*.

> **Shrewd Fighter** – Able to perceive an enemy's weakness on a subconscious level.

When Remy asked him about it, the man shrugged and said he was generally able to read an opponent's body language to see what they were going to do next. He had never put too much stock into it, thinking it was just a "knack." He had been able to kill two of the murk dwarves in the recent attack using "the skills his pa had taught him."

Another two men also had abilities, though only one was combat-related.

> **Keen Eye** – Increased Perception of one's surroundings
>
> **Comedic Light** – Others will find your words and manner amusing

The first belonged to a razin with pale white skin and black fur on his ears and tail. His name was Midnight Dust. The second was a razin with a ruddy complexion, orange-red fur and eyes the same color. Of all the tribe, he seemed the most at ease with his new god, though he was still respectful. His name was Heart Ripple.

The remaining abilities belonged to two females of the tribe.

> **Shrewd Negotiator** – You have an instinctual understanding of deals
>
> **Fierce Heart** – Your emotions are strong and not easily manipulated by outside forces

Shrewd Negotiator was the ability of a more matronly razin. Her ears and tail were striped with beige and brown. Her face was a bit pinched and she had reddish skin. When she gave orders to the children, there was a snap in her voice that made them obey quickly. Fell observed though that after the kids had run off, her face would soften with affection.

The last ability belonged to Autumn Ghost, the woman whose brother he'd saved. Her hair was blond, her fur a light pink, almost white. She was a striking beauty, with green eyes and bronze-colored skin.

As he thought about her ability, Remy started to see why her Devotion had spiked so much. She wasn't easy to sway, but when she felt something, she felt it hard. It would make her the kind of person who would be difficult to convince, but once she was, she was all in. Fell approved of that. It reminded him of his own family.

Something interesting was that everyone with an ability had a soul rank higher than *common*. Four of them were *uncommon* and Autumn Ghost was actually rank three, *limited*. There were two other *uncommon* souls among the survivors, but they didn't have abilities. It made him wonder. Was a higher ranked soul required to have an ability? A requirement, but not a guarantee?

In addition to finding his five followers with abilities, the god also got a basic breakdown of the tribe's demographics. Of the one hundred and forty-two members of the tribe still living, there were sixty-eight men and seventy-four women. Everyone had been in reasonably good health when they arrived on Telos. If not for the attacks of the eaglebear and murk dwarves, there would be two hundred of them. After losing more than a quarter of their number, there were many tear-streaked faces. No one was shutting down though, and everyone met Fell's eyes. These people were strong.

Talking to the tribe also revealed information about their origins. The razin had come from a world that sounded not unlike Earth, with trees, mountains and oceans, albeit with a green sky. Their level of technology was rudimentary though. They seemed to be at the beginning of the hunter-gatherer stage.

Their lives had changed drastically within the past few weeks when fierce beasts had started appearing. From what they said, it sounded very similar to what had happened on Earth. They gave reports of entire villages being destroyed overnight. A survivor from a neighboring tribe had warned them to leave their home.

That was why they had packed up what they could and started walking, carrying their few possessions. They had only been walking for half a day when the sky changed. Fell got slightly varying reports from all of them, but it came down to "things had gotten strange" and everyone had been disoriented.

The sky seemed to flash, and then they were in the valley where he'd met them. They hadn't even had time to realize they were on a new world before the eaglebear attacked them. It was that night, looking up at stars they had never seen before, that they knew beyond a shadow of a doubt that they had traveled far from home.

That was the entire story. There hadn't been any time lag during transport that they could appreciate. They'd been there, the sky had flashed, and then they were here. After listening, Remy was able to fill in a few gaps for them. It was pretty obvious that their world had connected to the Labyrinth just like Earth, though it had been a more gradual and calm transition. A few admitted to seeing flashes in their vision in the weeks prior to leaving their village, but no one admitted to an interface. Now, however, they all had access to their individual status pages. Most hadn't realized it, but at Fell's prompting, they began examining the information in amazement.

Fell was seriously impressed with how calm and put together they were, all things considered. When the Forsaking had hit Earth, it had been pure panic and bedlam. People had literally lost their minds. Suicides were a daily occurrence. These people, though they were from a much earlier era technologically speaking, were just dealing with what was happening. Even their choice to leave their homes in the face of danger spoke to their matter-of-fact approach to life. That was something he respected. A universal truth was SSDD. Bellyaching about it didn't help a thing.

He was starting to see why the Universe, or Labyrinth, or whatever the hell was responsible for the interface, had said he had such a high Soul Resonance with these people. He'd always been one to tell it like it is and to not run from harsh truths. If a thing didn't have a use, he didn't have time for it. That was doubly true for people and emotions. He wasn't a robot, and he didn't consider himself an evil man. He'd met evil men. He'd killed evil men. It was just that he was able to compartmentalize extremely well, especially in battle.

When there was something hard that needed to be done, he'd separate himself from emotions, morality, all of it. Then he'd take care of business. There might be a price to pay later, but by then the mission was complete. From what he'd seen and heard, the razin were his kind of people.

After he took stock of the tribe, he got a quick list of what supplies they had. There were some simple stone tools, more rocks with a sharpened edge than anything else. He had them bind a few to stout sticks and make rudimentary axes.

There was also enough food to feed the tribe for the next week and a half. There was more to go around now that a full quarter of the tribe was dead. Their water jugs were also mostly full, enough for the next three days.

That was the end of the list. It was enough for them to survive for today, but they needed to start making serious plans for the future. Pragmatic the tribe might be, but the truth was, their spirits were low. When enemies seemed to be jumping out of every hole in the ground, Fell didn't blame them for their solemn faces. The future must look grim indeed.

Since they arrived the day before, they had only been moving to stay alive. Looking for somewhere, anywhere, to hole up and get their bearings. There was no real plan. Now that Remy had appeared, the tribe latched onto him like a life preserver. They were all looking to him for guidance. The feeling was subconsciously strengthened by the connection they'd formed with their new god.

Back on Earth, Fell had felt the same way they did. All he could do was survive from day to day. If not for his training and luck, he'd have died the first day, as so many had. Those first weeks had just been a daily life-and-death struggle. A struggle you were more likely to lose than win. It wasn't until he'd found the location of the bunker, solely by luck again, that he and his group had gained a direction. Except for one thing, the razin would be in exactly the same position now, having no idea where to go and just praying for another day of life. Luckily for them, Fell's sponsors liked to cheat.

He still had the *Ruined Temple* quest. The reward, "a new home," had sounded a bit vague and underwhelming before. Now that he knew how deadly this world was and had a hundred-plus people to care for, it was just what the doctor ordered.

Only problem was that the quest didn't give any details about this new home. He had no idea if it would have access to fresh water, natural resources, etc. So far, his sponsors' advice had panned out, so he just had to assume this would as well.

His sponsors had triggered his Leap of Faith. They'd given him the soul cultivation method. So far as he knew, this quest was the last bit of help he'd get from his sponsors. He couldn't deny that their help had been crucial so far. They clearly had some way to predict events, so he would just have to trust them one more time. Also, the reward fit too perfectly to be a coincidence. Whoever his sponsors were, they had known things would work out like this.

Focusing on the *Ruined Temple* quest, he gained a basic heading again. It was telling him to continue west. Specifically, it was telling him to continue in the direction of the rising sun, which he was deciding to call west. This was good news, because the quest to find the eaglebear's offspring was leading him in roughly the same direction.

From what he could make out from the images the eaglebear's soul had shown him, its den was to the northwest. The tribe was tired, but they were also emboldened by their faith in their new god. It was a level of belief that shouldn't exist, at least not in the short amount of time they had known each other. In this new world of gods and monsters, however, for a Chosen people, it did.

CHAPTER 24

Before moving out, Fell chose his clergy. Sharp Leaf, Midnight Dust and Autumn Ghost became his acolytes. All three razin were solid choices for clergy, but Ghost had a gravitas that was easy to see. The two men showed her deference immediately. Fell wasn't surprised. She was a natural leader. In fact, she reminded him of the women from his family: strong, loyal and physically incapable of taking anyone else's bullshit. She was a perfect fit to be his clergywoman.

He converted Midnight Dust first. As he did, he was given a choice on what power to bestow.

Choose the Chant to bestow upon your acolyte	
	+ 5 Soul Damage
Soul Strike	Ignores 10% of a target's defense
(Level 0)	**Duration:** 10 seconds
(Active)	**Activation Cost:** 50 Faith Points
	Upkeep: 25 FP/10 sec

Soul Heal (Level 0) (Active)	Heals 5 HP/sec **Duration:** 10 seconds **Activation Cost:** 50 Faith Points **Upkeep:** 25 FP/10 sec

Remy decided they would all receive *Soul Heal.* Being able to survive a battle was more important than ending one quickly. A blue light kindled in Midnight's eyes as he received his power.

***

MIDNIGHT DUST		
Level: 0 (139/2,500 XP until Level 1)	**State of Being:** Mortal (0/7)	**Class:** Cleric Acolyte of Zero Fell
Ability: Keen Eye	**Energy:** 23/98	**Soul Rank:** Uncommon
STATS		
Health: 90	**Mana:** 110 *Regen/min: 7.2*	**Stamina:** 110 *Regen/min: 5.4*	**Faith:** 100/100 *Regen/hour: 10*
PRIMARY ATTRIBUTES		
Strength: 8	**Agility:** 12	**Dexterity:** 16
Constitution: 9	**Endurance:** 11	**Intelligence:** 11
Wisdom: 12	**Charisma:** 10	**Luck:** 10

Dust's eyes widened in shock and wonder. He felt power flowing through him, and new status windows appeared in his vision.

Congratulations! You have adopted the **Cleric Class!**

Clerics are an *uncommon* Class and require 75 Energy Slots.

Cleric skills are now unlocked, but you must still meet the criteria to gain each skill.

You are now a **Cleric, Level 0**

You now have access to a new form of power: **Faith**

The two Cultivation techniques known by your god are now accessible to you:

- **Basic Cultivation Technique of Gods and Clergy**
- **Soul Consumption Cultivation Technique**

You have gained a Soul Slot: **State of Being**

That wasn't the only prompt. Midnight Dust also learned about a new power he'd gained.

You may now also call upon your god's power through **Chants.**

Congratulations! You have learned a new Chant:		
SOUL HEAL		
Speak the words, "Through the grace of Zero Fell be Healed!" to activate your power Heals 5 HP/sec		
Chant Level: 0 *Duration:* 10 sec	*Initial Cost:* 50 Faith *Upkeep:* 25 Faith/10 sec	*Range:* Touch

Midnight Dust's Devotion increased at his god's clear show of divine power. It was not enough to increase his overall Devotion rank, but he was much closer now.

Dust described the prompts he'd received to his deity, who nodded in thought. As he did so, Dust cast more than one surreptitious glance at Autumn, hoping she would finally be impressed and notice him.

***

Dust's power was similar to Fell's own, but weaker. Weaker, but more versatile, as it seemed they could keep their powers going for a longer period of time. They also had to chant to invoke them, meaning it was not instantaneous.

Another difference was that their chants were fueled by Faith Points. Dust's status page said they only regenerated 10 FPs an hour. That meant they could only use their chants a few times a day.

Weaker or not, having more healers would be invaluable. Fell ordered his new acolyte to heal one of the tribe. As Dust ran off, the godling reflected on the topic of Energy. His own was rather high because of his Divine Core, but most of the tribe had less than one hundred points. Midnight Dust and Sharp Leaf both had a value ten to twelve points higher than the rest of the tribe members, while Autumn Ghost had an Energy an additional ten points higher than that. She was the only one whose max Energy was one hundred.

Fell already knew that gaining levels added Energy, but if a *common* Class took up fifty energy slots, which was more than half the average razin's total amount, then it would be nearly impossible for them to have two Classes. That wasn't even taking into account that Class-related skills also took up Energy slots. Unless he found a way to increase his people's Energy, they would be stuck with a single Class at most.

While he considered that, he repeated the acolyte creation process with Sharp Leaf and Autumn Ghost. Fell laid his hands on each of them and felt power flow from his body into theirs. The faintest of rainbow lights kindled in each of their eyes before disappearing. The power transfer from Fell to the acolytes took a couple minutes each, and each time he was informed that he'd used one of his three tokens to create an acolyte.

Creating his first cleric made him feel a bit weary, but making all three downright took it out of him. He imagined there was an acclimation process to achieving the deeper connection he now felt with all of them. Fell sat down heavily on the grass afterward. Autumn Ghost reached toward him in concern, but he covered his moment of weakness by saying he needed to meditate. The clergy took it as gospel, shooing away the rest of the curious tribe.

One thing had been different after he'd invested his power into Autumn. Another prompt had appeared.

You have created an acolyte whose personal Devotion is high enough to warrant a *Unique* Class: **Head Acolyte of Zero Fell**

If you choose to bestow this Class, it will cost **1,000** Faith Points

The recipient will gain another FREE Chant and a +25% points increase to their max Faith pool.

Do you wish to make Autumn Ghost your **Head Acolyte**? Yes or No?

Fell didn't even have to stop and think about it. Having Autumn Ghost be able to use both of his Divine Powers would be a game changer. He chose "Yes."

Total Faith Points: 7,074

Autumn Ghost's eyes widened as the knowledge of a second Chant poured into her. Fell was well and truly knackered after that. The three acolytes put their new powers to good use and finished healing the tribe.

Next, he turned his God's Eye on the dead dwarves' loot. The invaders didn't have much. They each had clothes and copper weapons, and some had grey stone beads woven into their beards. There were copper short swords, axes and clubs. More than half also had a backup dagger. The weapons were crude, barely holding an edge. Despite that, the loot was far superior to the razins.'

You have found: **Makeshift Wooden Spear**	**Attack:** 1-3 **Durability:** 1/4 **Item Class:** Common **Quality:** Trash **Weight:** 1.1 kg
You have found: **Copper Axe**	**Attack:** 6-11 **Durability:** 12/12 **Item Class:** Common **Quality:** Poor **Weight:** 2.4 kg
You have found: **Copper Short Sword**	**Attack:** 5-9 **Durability:** 11/13 **Item Class:** Common **Quality:** Poor **Weight:** 2.2 kg
You have found: **Copper Club**	**Attack:** 6-11 **Durability:** 12/13 **Item Class:** Common **Quality:** Poor **Weight:** 2.3 kg

You have found: **Copper Dagger**	**Attack:** 4-7 **Durability:** 10/11 **Item Class:** Common **Quality:** Poor **Weight:** 0.9 kg
You have found: **Stone Hand Axe**	**Attack:** 2-3 **Durability:** 4/4 **Item Class:** Common **Quality:** Trash **Weight:** 3.2 kg

It was no wonder the razin had been so thoroughly dominated. The murk dwarves' weapons were vastly more powerful than the simple spears the pantherkin were using. Not only was the damage much greater, but the quality was also better. The durability of most of the razins' spears was down to one, if the weapons hadn't snapped in half already. In contrast, the dwarves' weapons were still ready to rock. If the battle had gone on any longer, the razin would have been fighting barehanded.

The dwarves' clothes, on the other hand, were nothing to write home about. They were made of the same material as the razins' and offered no protection. Zero would still have scavenged it, but when they stripped the murkers his nose caught the sickly-sweet scent of disease on more than one of the corpses. Not willing to risk a pandemic, he ordered it all burned along with the bodies.

Fell examined the gear while waiting for the dizziness to pass. It took several minutes. It had felt like a mix of exhaustion and the strain of a stressful day. Had his soul or spirit been overtaxed? Was there even a real soul, the way he'd always thought about it? What the hell was he capturing after his enemies were killed? All these questions just joined the long line of "no damn idea."

Once he was feeling better, Zero stood up and started giving orders. Thanks to the healing spells of his clergy, all members of the tribe were back on their feet. The bodies of the fallen had been piled up and set on fire. He handed out the weapons left behind to the most able-bodied razin. He was able to arm nearly forty of them. Remy made sure that each of his acolytes had a dagger and a larger weapon. They would be the ones accompanying him to the eaglebear's den.

After seeing how awkwardly the tribe held their weapons, he resolved to wait a bit longer and give them some basic combat tips. His training hadn't taught him much about medieval warfare, but he knew hand-to-hand combat, and he knew knives. He taught them how to hold the weapons and to strike in short controlled motions. The most common mistake most people make when using a close-combat weapon for the first time is to swing as hard as they can.

If your goal is to kill another man, you really don't need much. A knee can be buckled with less than five pounds of pressure; a blade can pierce a heart with less than two. They took to his instruction quickly. None of them were battle-hardened, but they were determined.

That done, he ordered the caravan to continue moving west. After two hours, four figures broke off in another direction. A god and his clergy went to fulfill a quest. Fell looked at each of the pantherkin while they traveled. From what he could see, all three

298

of them looked calm, with no doubt on their faces. He'd seen that look before, on the visages of men and women he'd led into battles on another world. Fell couldn't help but wonder if all three of them would live to see another sunrise.

CHAPTER 25

Fell led his clergy at an easy clip. They jogged for about a hundred yards before slowing to a walk for the same distance. The process was repeated over and over. It allowed their stamina to stay more than half full, but still let them cover ground quickly. That did nothing for the pain they were all feeling in their sides after twenty minutes.

It was the faith they had in their god kept them going without complaint. Seeing their deity performing the same exertions without wincing made them want to do the same. They had no idea that Fell was suffering as much as they were. Zero had learned a lesson long ago that came into play now: never vomit in front of the men.

He checked their status pages periodically to monitor their stamina. As he did, he also watched their Faith Points slowly refill. They had emptied their Faith to finish healing the rest of the tribe. That meant it would be five hours before they could use a Chant again. Autumn Ghost had started to apologize to him for being so limited, especially as the head acolyte, but Fell just patted her shoulder and told her not to worry.

After making the motion once though, the god did it again. He'd felt something strange when he'd touched her. Like she was depleted in some way. When he laid his hand back on her, he'd gotten a prompt.

> Your head acolyte is Faith-depleted. Would you like to invest her with your own Faith? For Acolytes, the conversion rate is **10:1**.
>
> Yes or No?

Curious, he chose "Yes." With the conversion ratio, he only did a single point. To his surprise and delight, his own FPs did indeed flow into her, though it cost him ten times as much. It was a useful trick to know, even with the cost. Even more curious now, he tried it the other way. Unfortunately, he got a red prompt.

> You cannot absorb **Faith Points** from your clergy.

Hmpf. It was a one-way street. For a moment, he'd been hoping his acolytes could be Faith Point batteries. It would have been a great loophole. He knew he needed Faith Points to cultivate, and now he knew they could augment his clergy's powers. There wasn't a doubt in his mind that he'd find more uses as time went on. Fell was starting to get a clearer understanding about how important Faith truly was.

They kept moving roughly north and west. While they did, Fell kept his eyes peeled for landmarks, searching for images from the eaglebear's shared vision. The quartet left the grassy plains and were back in thick woods before long. The god never forgot as they traveled that his clergy needed souls of their own. Upon gaining their Cleric Class, they also gained a State of Being soul slot. The grassland hadn't offered any creatures to hunt. Now that they were back in the forest, however, he was more hopeful.

That hope started to wither after thirty minutes had gone by. They came across several forest creatures, large and small, but none that were interested in attacking them. Even when he reactivated his Title, the party remained unmolested. It reminded him of one weakness of *Infuriating Enemy*. It could stoke the anger and animosity that was already in someone's heart, but it could not fabricate it in creatures that only wanted to live in peace. Fell even chucked a rock at a deer they saw, but the animal merely bounded away. Without a bow and arrow, there was just no way the party could keep up.

Zero kept leading them by the eaglebear's memories. When they moved past a lichen-covered boulder next to a flowering tree, he knew they were getting close. There were only two more memories after that one. The process was somewhat frustrating as the memories weren't like following a map, but after only a few hours they found the last marker. They were close to their destination. He was about to share that knowledge with his people when Midnight Dust shouted a warning.

Less than a second later, a scaled creature about the size of a Great Dane tackled Fell from above. Before the god could even register the attack, his health bar flashed. Pain bloomed in his back and he received a damage notification:

*You have lost **27 Health Points!***

Years of battle drove Zero to roll with the hit even as a scream tore itself from his mouth. His acolytes rushed to help him with their copper weapons. Zero felt large talons exit his back, doing more damage as they did. He didn't dwell on that. The point was, he was free. Fell pulled on the power of one of his bound souls and triggered *Soul Heal.*

Energy flooded him, the ruined tissue of his back knitting together in less than a second. Even as he used the Divine Power, he kept rolling. Whatever had hit him hissed in anger that he had momentarily escaped death. Fell could hear its heavy footfalls behind him. There was no time to draw his short sword, but his dagger was another matter.

The god's momentum elapsed, leaving him lying on his back. Before stopping he'd drawn his dagger, and he managed to get it pointing up just before he was attacked again. All he could see was a mouth filled with pointed teeth, an avalanche of green scales, and long hooked talons. As his attacker lunged at him, he pushed his dagger upward and drew on his other bound soul. Blue crystalline energy surrounded the blade, and he stabbed into the creature's chest.

It screamed in anger, but the weapon hadn't penetrated far. He'd only had a second to channel *Soul Strike*. The dagger had only +5 added to the damage it could inflict. After penetrating through the beast's thick scales, it lost momentum when it struck a bone, stopping the thrust completely. The creature shrieked and jumped back, and his dagger tore its way free of his attacker's body. Blood sprayed, but little damage was actually done. Without his Soul Art, he might not have done any damage at all. Thankfully, he wasn't alone.

Sharp Leaf was the first to catch up. He swung his axe down at the beast, bellowing the whole time. The copper axehead bit into the creature's side. Blood flowed down its scales, but the attack was not strong enough to cause serious harm.

The beast lashed out with a three-clawed hand, leaving deep furrows in Leaf's chest. The acolyte fell back with an agonized cry. It might have finished Leaf off, but Fell activated *Infuriating Enemy.*

With a sharp intake of air, its reptilian gaze swung back to the god, madness filling its eyes. Zero was still scrambling to his feet. If not for Autumn Ghost and Midnight Dust, he would have been mauled. Midnight had opted to carry a short sword like his god, while Autumn carried a copper club. They attacked from both sides.

Each blow they landed did damage, but not enough to distract the lizard from the one it hated most. They had bought Fell enough time to regain his feet, but the god still wasn't able to defend against its next attack. Ignoring the two acolytes, the scaled beast lunged forward. It sank four-inch teeth into the space between Zero's shoulder and his neck. The bite was deep, and the godling's clavicle was shattered in an instant. His subclavian artery was shredded in even less time. A bellow of true pain issued from the Fell's mouth and hot red blood jetted from his ruined artery.

Ghost and Dust's attacks hadn't done much initially. The high-level monster's hide was just too strong and their weapons too weak. Neither were fools, however. Rather than continue to beat ineffectually at the monster's back, they changed strategies. Dust took careful aim and plunged his short sword into the gash that Sharp Leaf's axe strike had left.

An entire foot of the copper short sword sunk into the monster's side. Two of its organs were pierced, and it finally suffered an attack that it could not ignore. It tore its mouth free from Fell's neck, taking a tennis ball-sized chunk of muscle and bone with it. The beast's face was smeared with dark red blood, looking garish as it screamed. The pain only distracted it for a moment.

It was not only driven mad by Fell's Title, it also hungered for the god's blood more than anything it had ever experienced in its life. Taking the first step along the rainbow path had imbued Fell's blood with power. The beast craved more! It twisted its body to snap at Midnight Dust, eager to kill the man so it could get back to its true meal. It might have been injured, but it was still deadly in the extreme.

It turned so fast that Dust lost his grip on his short sword. Only quick reflexes let him dodge out of the way of its counterstrike. A bare inch of air separated his neck and its teeth. The copper weapon remained sticking out of its side, but the lizard paid it no heed. Crouching slightly, it prepared to pounce on the god again, and this time it would rip Fell's throat out. Before it could spring, Autumn Ghost swung her copper club.

This attack was far different from the first. This time the beast was hit with a club invested with a god's wrath! Autumn Ghost had used one of her new Chants, *Soul Strike,* and increased the damage on her club by +5. After seeing how useless her first blow had been, she had cursed herself for being so stupid. Her god was suffering, and in her panic, she had forgotten her new power! With anger and shame in her heart, she had chanted the words:

"In the name of Zero Fell, know my wrath!"

Light-blue soul energy surrounded her club, begging to be used. When the weapon hit the scaled monster this time, the result was spectacular. Ghost's club stuck its back leg, crumpling the limb at the joint. The creature fell to one side, its tail lashing the ground savagely and more animal screams filling the air.

Autumn clubbed it again, knocking it fully to the ground. She would have kept bludgeoning it, but a shouted "Master needs healing!" shifted her focus. Midnight Dust was already pouring his healing power into Fell. The god had activated his own healing as well, but it still wasn't enough. The wound was deep and blood kept flowing.

Autumn Ghost ran to her god. Zero's hands were pressed to his own neck in a desperate attempt to staunch the bleeding. Blood also outlined his teeth, which were bared in a rictus of pain. His health was in the thirties. Fell used another charge, and his HPs started to tick up, but he'd be vulnerable for another few seconds. Ghost fell to her knees and used *Soul Heal* to aid her god.

With his acolytes' help, Fell was able to remove his *Bleeding* status. His health started to rise and his vision started to clear. Throughout this desperate attempt to save Fell's life, the god heard a strangely wet *thunkush* sound being repeated over and over.

The two clergymen helped Fell struggle to his feet. Stumbling up, his eyes desperately searched for the deadly creature. The blood loss made him dizzy, even with the healing, but he still feared that the sound he was hearing was the monster tearing Sharp Leaf apart. He could not have been more wrong.

The acolyte had immediately healed himself after being mauled by the scaled beast. After retrieving his axe, he was ready when Autumn destroyed its knee. With its mobility sharply decreased, the creature could not defend against the razin and his battle-focused ability.

Sharp Leaf had no pity for the crippled monster. After several blows aimed at its arms, he had savaged those limbs as well. Now truly helpless, the beast could not avoid his coup de grace. The axe was raised high above his head and, as Fell looked on in pride and amazement, Leaf brought his weapon down on the beast's neck with all his strength. The razin tribe might have been much weaker than the dwarves, but the force he brought the copper axe down with would have been enough to split a log in two. It was more than enough to bite deep into the soft skin under the monster's chin.

Blood sprayed over the forest floor. Sharp Leaf didn't stop with one swing. He pulled his axe out of its neck with a wet *shlurp* and swung it down again. The weapon fell five more times. As his god and fellow clergymen watched, the weapon finally bit clean through the monster's neck. Its chest fell for the last time and its health dropped to zero. Only its tail kept flicking back and forth spastically. A few seconds later, even that death reflex ceased.

The four of them stood back to back, looking for any other attackers. They all panted heavily. The battle had not lasted long, but it had been intense. After a minute had passed, the clergy let out a collective sigh of relief. They had been reminded yet again how dangerous this new world was, but they'd survived.

What came next took their breath away. For the first time, panting and bloodied, the clergy saw the awe-inspiring power of a soul leaving a body. They watched in wonder as the rainbow lights leached from the body before coalescing into a sphere. They did not get to see it try to escape, however, as their god immediately latched onto it and pulled its power to him. If they had doubted his divinity in any way after seeing him injured, those doubts fled at seeing his command over the afterlife itself.

Fell held the soul immobilized in midair. Then he locked eyes with Autumn Ghost and spoke in a voice that would allow for no refusal, "Claim the soul."

In the face of her god's power she took a step forward, unsure of what to do but unwilling to refuse. As she focused on the sphere of rainbow light, she felt an instinctual drive to reach out to it. Not with her hands, but with something inside her. She was so startled when she connected with the soul that she nearly broke the link. Her will firmed, however, and she called it to her exactly as Fell stopped using his Art.

Her mouth opened and a light blue furnace sprang to life in her throat. She inhaled, and the unwilling rainbow sphere flew into her mouth. Seeing it from the outside for the first time, Fell couldn't help but think it looked insanely cool. Dust and Leaf thought the same thing, staring at her in envy.

As the soul settled into Autumn's body, a warm feeling bloomed within her. She felt complete in a way she had never before experienced, and her Devotion rose again by one hundred points. More prompts appeared, but her reverie was interrupted by loud screeches echoing all around them. The four of them looked at each other, and realized they were standing in the middle of a gruesome slaughter. All of them were bloodied and breathing heavily. Meanwhile, the calls of other forest predators reverberated off the surrounding trees. Blood had been spilled, and more monsters were coming to share in the feast.

CHAPTER 26

Hearing the cacophony around them, Fell looked at his clergy and said, "We have to move. Now!"

He knew he owed his life to these three, but this wasn't the time for claps on the back. They had to move. Animals weren't intelligent, but predators weren't stupid either. Beasts might not rush headlong into a recent battle, but they also wouldn't let fresh meat go to waste. In a very short amount of time, other creatures of the forest would be coming to investigate. If they thought they were tougher than other contenders, they would lay claim to this "treasure" and kill anything nearby.

Fell turned his Title off and Midnight Dust retrieved his weapon. Less than a minute after the beast was slain, they were off. The godling only spared a moment to look at the creature that had almost killed him. It was a large lizard, about seven feet tip to tail. Its spine was curved so much that it would only stand four feet when up on its hind legs. Long talons tipped the fingers of each three-digit hand. A dark swath of green ran down its back, the color of evergreen needles. The rest of it was covered in grass-green scales.

GREENBACKED SKINK	
Level: 7	**Monster Rank:** Common
Energy: 149	**Soul Rank:** Common
STATS	
Health: 0/236	**Mana:** 0/15 **Stamina:** 0/263
DESCRIPTION	
Greenbacked skinks are common forest predators. Belonging to the reptile family, they are cold-blooded. While the females are communal creatures, living in packs of five or more, the males are smaller and solitary. Their coloring offers natural camouflage in their preferred hunting environment.	

The god's party fled. Behind them, the ground hungrily drank in the god's essence. One small and unassuming flower had been crushed during the fight. Despite the destruction of its stem, its roots were all intact. These drank in the divine energy of the god's divine blood. The chance for mutation was less than a percent of a percent of a percent, but the flower's nature was indeed changed.

It was originally only an unremarkable orange forest flower. It had never been named. While the god and his clergy fled, the crushed flower stalk straightened and a new bud appeared. The plant was small, no more than a few inches in height, and looked innocuous. As a faint wind made it sway, however, it left an afterimage in its wake. A ghostly copy of the flower remained in its original position, evidence that even a small flower could one day grow a soul.

The drops of divine blood in the skink's stomach remained mostly unabsorbed, an unexpected treasure for whichever predator consumed it.

Zero Fell was unaware of any of this as they fled. His mind was focused on the dead monster's status page. The thing had just been a common forest animal. Not a dragon, not some mythical creature from legend, just a regular beast of the forest. The god seethed. The damn thing was a glorified iguana, and he'd nearly been killed by it! Even Dust had barely detected it before it had struck, despite his *Keen Eye* ability. It all came down to one thing. He and his acolytes were horribly outclassed.

He was level two and they were still only level zero. The skink had been level seven. Put another way, the creature's level was over three times his own. That was a big Attribute Point swing. It was also two levels higher than the eaglebear had been. It seemed that the mana flow from the Labyrinth was still advancing the levels and powers of this world's beasts and monsters. It hadn't escaped his notice that the first time he'd scanned the eaglebear it had been level five. Only a few short hours later, it had been level six.

Now he'd come across this so-called "common" forest predator that was level seven. It had almost taken him out, and his highfalutin had just barely kept him alive. It had been a deadly adversary. Even worse, according to the description, the females were bigger and travelled in packs. He most definitely did not want to run into the missus.

Fell pushed the pain and anger to the back of his mind while he used *Soul Heal* again. He only had one charge left now, but he had to be at his best in preparation for the next attack. As he did, his mind firmed upon what he held as an indisputable fact. He and his people *had* to get stronger. And they had to do it fast. He had no idea if there was a ceiling on how quickly or how far the monsters of this world would progress before things stabilized. For all he knew, they were running through a level fifty zone, or maybe even a level one hundred.

This whole damn planet might be level one hundred for all he knew.

Just two hits from the skink had nearly finished him off. The only reason he was still alive was because his clergy had healed him. If he didn't increase their power along with his own, they wouldn't be able to help him in future fights. He and these people truly were dependent on one another.

While they ran from the battle site, he thought back to the words Dust had chanted, "In the name of Zero Fell, be healed!"

It was strange-and-a-half being healed in your own name, but he certainly wasn't complaining. He was just delighted that he'd given them all *Soul Heal* instead of *Soul Strike*. That decision had already saved his life. Thinking of the chant usage reminded him that he needed to top off their Faith pools. His own bank dropped again by more than 3,000 points, but he considered it money well spent. He needed them to be powerful.

Total Faith Points: 3,856

It was now painfully obvious just how quickly he could burn through Faith Points. He'd used nearly half of his bank just to make sure his acolytes were fully charged. Fell was tempted to only bring their FP pool back up to 90% and let their own regen handle the rest, but that would be foolish. If another attack occurred, being able to use their Chants twice instead of once might mean the difference between life and death. He'd just have to find a way to get more faith.

The four of them ran as fast as their stamina permitted them. They only slowed to a walk when one of them was close to bottoming out. While they got closer to the eaglebear's den, he checked the prompts he'd gained in the fight.

For killing **1** *common* **rank** enemy with the Title **Infuriating Enemy** equipped, you have gained **20 Animosity Points**.

560/1,000 obtained to upgrade your Title.

You have gained: **377 XP** from combat.

8,200/15,000 XP to reach Level 3

Fell used God's Eye to check how much experience his clergy had gained. Each of them had received the same amount, four hundred points. It was easy to see that they gained a bit more than him because he was level two, whereas they were all still level zero.

He paid special attention to Autumn Ghost's status page, wanting to examine the perks of the monster's soul.

AUTUMN GHOST		
Level: 0 (517/2,500 XP until Level 1)	**State of Being:** Mortal (0/7)	**Class:** Cleric **Rank:** Acolyte
Ability: Fierce Heart	**Energy:** 34/109	**Soul Rank:** Limited
STATS		
Health: 90	**Mana:** 120 *Regen/min: 9*	**Stamina:** 43/110 *Regen/min: 5.4*	**Faith:** 125/125 *Regen/hour: 10*
PRIMARY ATTRIBUTES		
Strength: 9	**Agility:** 13	**Dexterity:** 16
Constitution: 9	**Endurance:** 11	**Intelligence:** 12

Wisdom: 15	Charisma: 11	Luck: 11
BOUND SOUL		
Name: Greenbacked Skink	**Soul Rank:** Common	**Soul Slot:** State of Being
Hidden Scales – +10% Camouflage, affects physical body and all held equipment		

It looked like she'd gained a kind of stealth ability. Fell's near death experience was firsthand proof of the threat an unseen enemy could pose. He was guessing that 10% meant she could match her surroundings, but to a limited degree. Could come in handy. As he thought about it, he realized this soul would probably complement Midnight Dust and the man's Keen Eye ability more. With increased Perception and also increased stealth, the acolyte would be a great scout. Fell resolved to see if souls could be transferred when they had accumulated enough for everyone. For the moment, he let Autumn hold on to it.

Another thing Fell was curious about was if she could accumulate more souls. He had three soul slots, one for each of his Divine Powers and a third for his State of Being. Ghost's bound soul was connected to her State of Being.

One question he'd had was if more souls could strengthen an acolyte's chants. Sadly, it appeared the answer was no. Their chants didn't have soul slots. That was somewhat disappointing, but they were only level 0, both in class and personal level. Maybe things would change once they leveled up or cultivated.

As they trekked deeper into the forest Fell worried they were going in the wrong direction, but after searching he found the last marker from the eaglebear's memories: a small stream with purple stones lining the bottom. The group slaked their thirst and washed the worst of the blood and gore off. Fell was doubly happy about that. He'd used some water from the tribe's waterskins to bathe before, but he'd still been crusted with old blood: his own, dwarf, eaglebear and skink. The entire time they'd traveled, Fell had worried about the scent of blood attracting beasts and monsters.

Sadly, his fear was the appropriate response.

High above, two silent predators looked down on them. Their multifaceted eyes recorded everything. The monsters had been following them through the forest for more than an hour. No one in Fell's group had noticed the silent stalkers jumping from tree to tree above their heads. Not even Midnight Dust could detect them. As the party cleaned themselves, the spiders split up. One continued to follow, while the other scuttled back home to report. Both trailed strands of webbing so fine they were almost impossible to see and yet were strong enough to strangle.

While a hidden storm built on the horizon, Fell and his acolytes were all just relieved to be clean. The blood and gore from battling the skink had already been dried into a paste on their skin. Their fur had been even worse, just a matted mess. The godling had decided that having ears on top of his head was just a pain in the ass. He didn't think it let him hear any better. Thankfully, his tail seemed to avoid trouble on its own. For the most part he forgot he had it, but then he'd catch a glimpse of it out of the corner of his eye, whipping about randomly behind him. *Fucking weird*, he thought, each and every time.

The quick bath didn't help their clothes much. Everything they were wearing was irrevocably stained, but bathing was at least an improvement. Minutes later, the group felt much refreshed. They had left the main group only a little over three hours before, but the fight with the greenbacked skink had set them all on edge. That, coupled with their forced pace, had also wearied them.

Fell slowed the pace now that they were near the den. Not only so he didn't miss the cave, but also to let them catch their breath before venturing in. He hoped to avoid a fight, but only a dummy entered a monster's lair expecting tea and cookies.

Ten minutes later, the four of them stood in front of a moss-covered cave opening. It was also half covered in vines, and indeed would have been easy to miss if he didn't already know it was there. Before they went in, Fell checked to see how the party was doing.

Their faith, health and mana were completely full. Only their stamina remained a bit low due to the flight through the forest. Cleaning up by the stream had let them recover some, but with their low Constitutions they were only able to regen about five points a minute. Seeing their lowered stamina, mirrored by their sweaty faces and lightly heaving chests, he considered letting them recover further, but decided against it. Every minute they were in the forest risked another attack by a higher-level creature.

Fell stepped into the darkness of the cave.

CHAPTER 27

A spider the size of a small dog crawled silently through the trees in the forest. Its destination was a web that was several stories tall. Bundled sacks clung to the strands in odd places. Some were small like a ball, but others were oblong and large enough to hold a person. A few of the web bundles had red splotches where the creatures inside had been fed upon. Others still struggled. None broke free.

More spiders ran across the web, strengthening and enlarging it. Most were the same size as the ones that had spied on Fell, but a few were several times larger. They all scuttled around the web, dedicated to a common task. More perched on the limbs of nearby trees, keeping watch for prey and potential enemies. In the center of the web was a humanoid figure. The nude creature had the body of a man and sported impressive musculature. His eyes were bulbous and multifaceted like his followers, and two small mandibles jutted out of his large mouth. Other than that, he looked human. Tightly woven webs hung down from his body like a tunic.

He was currently feasting on the body of a horned buck. His face was buried in its neck, and warm blood flowed down his throat.

The spider that had spied upon Fell came closer and began to chitter at him. The figure didn't stop drinking, but he listened closely.

After hearing the report about strong prey, he finally lifted his head. A clicking language issued from his mouth. Despite being alien, anyone could have identified the tone of command it held. In response, a horrifying creature descended from the tree limbs above.

The bottom half of her body was that of a dinner table-sized spider, but the top half was a lithe woman with light-grey skin. Like her god, mandibles jutted from her mouth. She was still adjusting to both her recently increased intelligence and new humanoid form. Other spiders had been altered by their new god, but only she had been granted a body similar to their deity. Only she had been blessed with the ability to reason. She alone had been given the honor of being the acolyte of the Most High.

"Strong prey have been discovered," her god softly informed her. His voice was like the whisper of webs in the wind. "Take twenty of your brothers and sisters and bring their bodies back to me. I wish to feast upon their strength."

"Yessh, masster," she hissed in response. Her body shivered and her dusky grey nipples hardened in excitement. Like all Chosen, she was bonded on the deepest level to her god, the tie limited only by her Devotion. Even without that connection, however, she would have been loyal. Her increased intelligence had allowed her to experience something amazing: the joy of inflicting pain. When she smelled the fear of a suffering creature, it could nearly bring her to climax. Sadism and savagery were precious gifts given to her by her beloved god. In return, he had her undying fidelity.

She quickly gathered a small army of spiders, careful to take only the twenty allotted. Their god had charged them all with building something called a "temple." His Most Divine Malevolence had made it clear that he needed to focus on creating a thing called an "altar." It was a task of the utmost importance, and he could not be bothered with lesser affairs like safety or food. That was the role of the tribe.

That was why she could take only twenty spiders, and that was still a significant portion of the web's strength. Other than those dedicated to spinning silk for the structure, most of the remaining members of the cluster were already out hunting for more sacrificial creatures or patrolling the forest for enemy intruders. Besides, twenty would be more than enough. It was unfathomable that any creature would be able to resist her new power, a power provided by The Most High himself!

Less than a minute later, she was bounding through the trees, her army hopping behind her. Glee bloomed in her bile-filled hearts at the thought of serving her master and causing pain.

All would be sacrificed to the fangs of Neith!

CHAPTER 28

Fell made eye contact with his acolytes. They each nodded, ready to follow him into hell. Their eyes quickly acclimated to the darkness of the cave thanks to their racial bonus. What had been an oppressive gloom turned into just a low-light area. Thanks to Fell's eaglebear soul, to him it was bright as noon.

The entrance led to a steep ramp of stone. After descending ten feet, it hooked to the right. They made their way carefully forward. Bones and shed feathers littered the stone floor. The entire place was musky, but not overpoweringly so. Zero recognized the scent of his Mortal Enemy. Thankfully, a current of air kept the cave from becoming too rank.

Fell wondered if that had been something the eaglebear had been aware of while it was alive. Just how smart had the beast been? It was intelligent now, but was that a function of becoming his Mortal Enemy? He'd tried to talk to it while traveling but it never responded, so there was no way to know.

They continued forward for about one hundred yards, following the twisting cave until they saw the end. At times it was too dark for the acolytes to see, but they trusted and followed their god. When they turned a final corner, they saw the end of their quest. It was not what Fell had been expecting.

Huh, Fell thought. The eaglebear was a hybrid, half ursine and half avian. He supposed that meant it could have lived in a den or a nest. Turned out, it lived in both. The eaglebear's home was a cave that held a nest large enough to accommodate its massive body. The entire thing was made out of two-inch-wide branches that were interwoven. Fell could only see one side of it, but it had to be five feet high and at least twenty feet deep.

The party could hear scratching sounds coming from inside the nest. It was sitting on a shelf of stone five feet off the cave floor. Between its placement and the fact that the sides of the nest were so high, they couldn't see anything inside.

Fell motioned for his people to spread out. They approached the nest and, as one, looked over the rim with weapons raised. Twenty-four golden eyes stared back at them, each belonging to a cub. One of the baby eaglebears pissed in fear and they all screeched as they pushed themselves as far away from the razin as possible. Their mother had been gone too long and they were all afraid. Seeing the small cubs, the god and his clergy realized there was no threat. Before he could lower his weapon though, the eaglebear's bound soul began to rage inside his chest.

Fell cursed! Was this what he'd been warned of? Was it going to try and take control of him? He shifted all of his focus inward, to the dark place that held the soul, and prepared for a battle. After examining the hybrid's spirit though, he realized it wasn't trying to break free and it wasn't trying to attack him. It was just more agitated than he had ever felt it.

Fell lowered his weapon and sent calming feelings to the soul. It didn't stop raging completely until he handed his copper blade to Autumn. Once that was done, however, a quest prompt appeared.

Quest Completed: **Last Wish I**

You have found the Eaglebear's nest and 12 of its Cubs. They are not in any danger, therefore you have fulfilled the dictates of your quest!

Rewards:

2,000 XP

Unlocking the Quest: **Last Wish II**

The two thousand experience catapulted his acolytes past their level threshold. While Fell went through the rest of the prompts, the acolytes dealt with their own.

***

Autumn Ghost heard a wonderful sound for the first time.

TRING!

You have reached level **1**! By following the teachings of your god, Zero Fell, you have advanced in power! You are a **Limited** soul and will be awarded accordingly. The following points are yours to distribute:

Attribute Points	+2 to Agility and Dexterity
	+2 Free Attribute Points
Bonus Energy Slots	+20
Class Points	+30

She now had two free Attribute Points to distribute. Ghost considered asking her god his advice, but she saw he was deep in thought. Gazing upon him, a sense of joy and satisfaction filled her. To be so truly connected with a deity… it was a contentment she had never known. Her god had not only saved the entire tribe, but had also invested her with power. If she'd had these abilities before, her brother would never have been so injured. If Ghost had one wish, it was showing her beloved Zero Fell that she was worthy of his trust.

When she thought about where to place the extra points, the only thing on her mind was how best to serve her beloved deity. She wanted to walk beside him all the days of his immortal life. That would be impossible if she died. After some deliberation, she placed the points into Constitution, gaining another twenty points of health.

That left the question of what Class Points were. There was a new icon on what Zero Fell had called her "HUD." It looked like a four-pointed white star, and it was blinking. Focusing on it brought up another window.

Congratulations! You have taken your first step toward improving your **Class**! Classes can be improved in a number of ways, but the most direct is by spending Class Points.

NAME	COST	DESCRIPTION
Advance Level	10	Advance to Level 1 of your Cleric Class +25 Faith Points May unlock further Class upgrades +5 Energy
Inc Max Faith (0/4)	25	Increase Faith Pool by +25% (Current: 100 FP) Requires 10 Energy Slots
Inc Faith Pool Regen (0/4)	10	Increase Faith Regen by 25% (Current: 10 FP/hr) Requires 5 Energy Slots

		Advance the rank of your Cleric Class
Advance Rank	100	Acolyte (Rank 0) >> Priest (Rank 1) LOCKED until Level 5!
Learn a Chant	50	No Chants Available!

Autumn Ghost's eyes widened in understanding. Her Class Points let her grow the gift from her god! A light flared behind her eyes, and the corners crinkled in joy. This would let her honor him to an even greater extent! The pleasure she felt was a reflection of her Rank 6 Devotion, *Fully Committed to the Faith.*

She considered her options. Becoming a level 1 Cleric seemed like the best option. It not only increased her maximum faith, but also opened new options. If she could have, she would have chosen to become a Priest and deepen her connection with her beloved god, but that required too many points and was locked until she reached Level 5 in her Class.

After advancing a level, she saw that it only cost 20 CPs to get to level 2. It gave another +25 faith and improved her Energy by another +10. With her Head Acolyte modifier, her Faith Point total reached one hundred and eighty-eight. That would let her chant three separate times or maintain one chant for five minutes. Neither level unlocked more upgrades.

No sooner had she thought that than something amazing happened in the cave. Watching the interplay of light and magic, Autumn could not help but stare at her god, marveling at his beneficence.

Fell was oblivious to the look of love and adoration Autumn was sending his way, just as he missed the same look on Midnight's face directed at her. If he had known about either, he probably would have been fifty-fifty about them. Workplace romances were always a problem. On the other hand... hot chick. Luckily, he didn't need to worry about such existential dilemmas. He was focused on the next link in the quest chain.

Congratulations! You have unlocked the Quest: **Last Wish II**

Quest Rank: Common

You have found the Eaglebear's nest and 12 of its cubs. You have fulfilled the dictates of your quest. The **Mortal Enemy** status of your bound soul has been removed. You may now release the Eaglebear's soul if you wish.

Seeing its young has moved the bound spirit, however. It wishes to aid its offspring. It cannot do so without help.

The Eaglebear wishes to manifest to its cubs and give them its Energy. This requires a strength far beyond its capabilities; it will require Divine Power.

As such, it makes a request of you. If you agree, it promises another quest that will offer great personal rewards as well as a special reward that will benefit your tribe as a whole.

You are now presented with **3 choices**. Only the third signifies accepting this quest. The first two will end this quest chain. Your options are:

1) Continue to hold the Eaglebear's soul and it will remain in its current state, but the threat of spiritual battle will have been removed.

2) Release the soul of the Eaglebear and it will be drawn into the firmament, and will leave this plane of existence.

3) Release the soul of the Eaglebear and imbue it with your Divine Power. As you have taken the first step on the Rainbow Path, you have garnered just enough Divine Power to manifest the Eaglebear's soul in the physical realm.

Know This! Using your power in this manner is not without consequence. It will require you to forcibly burn your cultivation. The specific repercussions cannot be known, but at a minimum you will be returned to your earlier State of Being. Other consequences may occur as well.

Choose carefully. If you pursue this course of action, the Eaglebear's soul promises you help afterwards, but the reward has not been specified. To be clear, it cannot lie and the reward will benefit your tribe, but you cannot know in what way. You will also not be able to bind it again after investing it with your Divine Power.

What do you choose?

There was a lot to digest. While he considered his options, Fell sent Dust and Sharp Leaf back to the cave mouth to ensure that nothing would sneak up on them. He kept Autumn Ghost with him. The eaglebear cubs were pretty much the size of brown bear cubs back on Earth and none of them were acting hostile, but he wasn't about to underestimate wild animals. There were also a dozen of them. If they suddenly decided to attack, it'd be good to have an ally by his side. Immediate security concerns taken care of, he considered his options.

He had already fulfilled the tenets of the first quest. If he wanted to, he could just leave. The eaglebear's soul was one of the strongest he'd seen. It was a *common* soul that had been bumped up a rank to *uncommon* thanks to its Mortal Enemy status. It provided two soul perks, twice as many as a *common* soul. He was only 17 Soul Points away from unlocking the next one. Whatever it was could be a serious boon. Did he want to give that up?

The greenbacked skink was an example of just how dangerous monsters with *common* souls could be. Even capturing one of those required risking his life. He had the enemy acolyte's spirit but it was refined, whatever that meant, so he couldn't bind it to a soul slot. If he let the eaglebear's soul go, he might not find another soul of the same strength for a long time. Even if he did, there was no guarantee he would be strong enough to slay such a powerful opponent.

He had learned long ago that if you had a head start in life, it was vastly easier to continue winning. If you started from behind, even simple tasks could be difficult. If you had little or nothing, it was nearly impossible to move forward. He'd been given a leg up in this new life, and that included having the eaglebear's soul. That wasn't an advantage he would give up lightly. The head start he had now might be what saved his life in future.

The eaglebear's soul had even let go of its Mortal Enemy status. It was easy to check the veracity of that... the angry red words were indeed gone. He could also feel that whatever resistance it had before had now dissipated. If Fell chose to, he could keep the soul and even slaughter the cubs.

If his whole party attacked at once, they could probably kill the babes with little difficulty. It would earn them experience and his acolytes would harvest a good number of souls with little risk. Of course, it was possible that the eaglebear might become his Mortal Enemy again if he did that. Still, that wasn't why Fell decided not to do it. He just wasn't one to start a slaughter without a very good reason. And, if he was going to kill the cubs, it might be best to fatten them up first.

His mind raced through those thoughts in scant seconds. Just thinking of himself, the best choice was option one. Basically, take the soul and run. He'd honored his word to the eaglebear. His conscience was clear.

As pragmatic as Fell was, he did indeed have a moral compass. Oh, he could turn it off like a switch, but it existed. It was just that his morality was governed by his own beliefs. For whatever reason, his thoughts and mainstream society's had never been closely aligned. From his standpoint, that was society's problem.

The point being, when he gave his word, that meant something. It was why he'd left the safety of the bunker back on Earth, and it was why he cared about honoring his enemy's last wish. He'd done his duty now though. Option one was looking pretty good.

As far as the other two options, the second one was a nonstarter. No way he'd give up the eaglebear's soul without reason. He'd won. It'd lost.

Life was tough, and it would serve him now.

That left option three and the nebulous reward. Something that could help his tribe as a whole was a serious carrot to dangle in front of his face… so to speak.

Ever since his State of Being was increased he'd felt wonderful. It was like he'd never been so alert, clearheaded, and alive. During the hike through the forest, he'd really gotten to appreciate the bonus to his stats. Not only did he have more stamina, but how he used it had improved as well. He was surer of foot, his breathing was automatically more stable and he seemed to pick the right spots to step without even trying. Everything about him was improved. Not by a massive amount, but by a noticeable one. Giving that up was no small thing.

On the other hand, he had cultivation techniques. With that knowledge, he should be able to reach this State of Being again in a week or so. It was just a matter of time. The unknown reward also said it would help his entire tribe. If he knew one thing now, he knew he needed his Chosen. If they didn't get stronger, and soon, they'd be wiped out. If that happened, his fate would be that same. That meant anything that could help his Chosen as a whole was invaluable. If all this quest cost him was a cultivation delay, wasn't that worth it?

Finally, there was a selfish reason to choose option three. It was the only choice that kept this quest chain alive. That meant more experience and more rewards, especially if the next link in the chain was triggered. That would make him and his acolytes stronger now. They might even level up again. Losing his cultivation progress meant momentarily becoming a bit more vulnerable, but if you wanted to win, you had to roll the dice.

The god thought it over for another few moments before deciding he was in the mood for a show. With a grunt that meant "why the hell not" he chose option three. He immediately regretted it when red fire enveloped his body.

If advancing his Cultivation had cleaned and improved his cells, this felt like someone had attached hot wires directly to his nerve endings. It wasn't just that there was pain, it was that every sensation got ratcheted up past the red line. The veins in his neck and forehead stood out while he struggled to contain the power unleashed inside him. His Divine Core drained of all color, leaving a pure white pyramid again. Once the color had totally drained the pain vanished as well, but he was left with an unmistakable sense of loss. He was… less, and the world seemed dimmer because of it.

The red blaze was leached away from his body. It coalesced in front of him, forming a framework. Over the next five seconds, the pattern grew more complex and the outline of the eaglebear formed in the cave.

The cubs were fearful at first but, one after another, they recognized the form and feel of their mother's soul. The sound of their mewling filled the cave. The spirit looked at Fell for several long moments. The god rubbed his sore chest with his fist, ready for whatever came next. She just turned her head to stare into the eyes of her brood.

The cubs stopped crying all at once, as all sound disappeared from the world. Instead, their eyes began to twinkle with rainbow lights. The spirit raised her head and let loose a baleful scream, a sound she never could have made in life, then her body began to break apart. Dual streams of red energy flowed out of her disappearing form and into the eyes of her young. Seconds later, all that was left of her body was a single floating sphere.

Fell and his acolytes all watched this, but only he understood. Each stream of light was part of the divine energy he had donated. The eaglebear had harnessed his gift and was investing it in her children. She did what any mother would do. She gave her children a chance at a better life.

The sphere of energy shifted from brilliant red to the roiling rainbow of a soul sphere. To the god's surprise, the newly freed spirit didn't flee. Instead, it floated up right next to him. The soul had saved a bit of Divine Power, because it only had one desire left. Autumn Ghost was extremely alarmed at seeing the spirit approach her deity and prepared to attack it with *Soul Strike,* but Fell stopped her with a raised hand.

Zero didn't know exactly what was happening, but he didn't feel any malevolent intent coming from the sphere. That was why, when a wisp of soul light extended out from the rainbow globe to slowly caress his face, he didn't pull away. The tendril grazed his cheek and a new prompt appeared.

Quest Completed: **Last Wish II**

You have shown mercy to a Mortal Enemy. The Eaglebear has been able to use the divine energy you gave her to strengthen and teach her children. Each has had their bodies and souls altered. The cubs have changed into a new species, Divine Eaglebears, creatures that have never been seen in Telos before. Despite their young age, they are now much better equipped to survive in the wild.

> *Rewards:*
>
> 3,000 XP
>
> Unlocking the Quest: **Last Wish III**
>
> *Special Reward:* Unknown, but guaranteed if the Quest **Last Wish III** is accepted.

CHAPTER 29

The two acolytes on guard duty gained the same notifications. They shared a grin. The experience they'd just gotten moved them more than half the way to their next level. Both had *uncommon* souls, so they'd only gotten 25 Class Points instead of Autumn's 30. Once they reached level two, they'd be able to buy the attack chant.

After that they kept their eyes peeled, chatting infrequently until Dust's body tensed. Sharp Leaf immediately raised his axe, but he couldn't see what had put his friend on edge. Dust's *Keen Eyes* ability gave him a Perception that Leaf just couldn't match. A few seconds later though, he did see. His heart started thudding in response. Seconds after that, the two were running back into the cave as fast as they could.

***

Inside the cave, Fell was examining the third link in the quest chain.

Congratulations! You have unlocked the Quest: **Last Wish III**

Quest Rank: Limited

You are once again offered a choice:

Option 1: You may leave the cave now without accepting this quest. The soul of the Eaglebear will move into the firmament and the next phase of existence.

Option 2: You may bind the soul of the Eaglebear again. She will serve you willingly as an ally rather than as a slave. She will become your Spirit Animal. This will provide all the benefits of binding her to your State of Being in addition to other far-reaching bonuses. Growing her power will augment your own. The Soul Slot of your State of Being will remain free to bind another soul.

Your formerly bound soul was prepared to move on to the next phase of existence, but connecting with its progeny has sparked a new desire.

She is willing to do this for only two reasons:

1) To ensure the safety of her progeny
2) To be able to watch them grow.

That is why there is an additional requirement if you choose Option 2. You must establish a secure settlement, and at least half of her offspring must reach this location and be allowed to live there.

Know This! The Eaglebear's soul is motivated by seeing her progeny prosper. If you agree to this quest, in addition to other rewards you will be guaranteed the allegiance of her offspring and their lineage. The loyalty of these divine beasts will inspire your tribe!

What is your choice?

Rewards for accepting this Quest:

1) You and all of your Chosen will receive a Mark: **Soul Tame** Everyone with this Mark will have the chance to claim a spirit animal if they encounter an unbound soul that resonates with their own

2) Willing submission of the Divine Eaglebear's Soul (Uncommon Rank)

3) 12 Tamed Divine Eaglebear Cubs

Rewards for completing this quest:

1) XP

Penalty for failure or refusal of Quest:

1) Loss of allegiance of Divine Eaglebears

2) Loss of Eaglebear soul

3) Loss of the Soul Tame Mark

Zero Fell blinked. The rewards for this link in the quest chain were extensive. Just accepting it would get him twelve tamed monsters to command. They were babies, but they'd grow. He also hadn't been expecting a chance to rebind the eaglebear's soul. That was a definite plus. The benefits of accepting were pretty great.

Perhaps most important was this... Mark? He hadn't heard of something like that before. He also didn't understand what a spirit animal was, but one thing he did grasp was how much power souls could give him. Now it looked like his entire tribe could harness that power! That might skyrocket his tribe's chances to survive in this hostile world.

Not only that, he'd get the benefits of having the eaglebear tied to his State of Being without filling the soul slot. Wasn't that the same as having two soul slots? Without the simian's soul he probably never would have survived the Leap of Faith. Without the eaglebear's soul, he wouldn't have seen the murk dwarf ambush in time to save the tribe. The power of a bound soul couldn't be denied, and now he'd have two!

Fell was about to accept the quest when he had a thought that brought a smirk to his face. He'd been on this world for only one day, and it seemed like he was constantly being confronted with life-and-death decisions. Maybe the cubs would want him to refuse. Whatever else was going on, there was no doubt that the eaglebear was being a bit clingy. He certainly wouldn't want *his* mom haunting him after death.

Or maybe it was him the eaglebear couldn't let go of. It just didn't seem to be able to get enough of him. The monster had been a mortal enemy at one point, but now it was like an ex that wouldn't stop calling. Those inane thoughts helped reset his mind, relieving the constant stress of the past day.

Considering the quest again, he still felt the pros outweighed the cons. For one, he would be able to take all twelve cubs with him. That might have seemed daunting, guiding young creatures through dangerous terrain, but after the rainbow energy flew into their eyes, the cubs were obviously changed. They all stood quietly on their short legs and stared directly at him. They were clearly not just younglings anymore.

The personal gain for him would be great too. He was already missing the enhanced vision the eaglebear's soul had provided. As soon as it had left his body, his vision had decreased markedly. The area around him was dark as dusk. The unbound spirit had previously lit up the space, but after investing the cubs with Divine Power the soul barely gave off the glow of a candle.

Fell was about to accept the quest, but at that moment Sharp Leaf and Midnight Dust ran panting into the cavern. The smaller razin shouted, "Spiders!"

Boiling behind them came three arachnids as large as manhole covers. One ran along the ceiling, another clung to the wall and the third skittered along the ground. Fifteen more spiders spilled into the cavern behind the vanguard. Fell grabbed his short sword back from Autumn Ghost.

There wasn't time to deliberate any longer. He accepted the quest and a cascade of notifications flooded his vision.

The soul of the Eaglebear has evolved into a **Spirit Animal**! This only occurs when a soul resonates with you and willingly chooses to serve you for all eternity. Your **State of Being** soul slot is no longer occupied, and can be used to bind a new soul!

As this Spirit Animal willingly chooses to follow you it consumes no Energy.

Congratulations! **Luck** has surely smiled down upon you.

Your Spirit Animal has been altered by your Divine Power and has bonus capabilities that others of its kind lack. It can manifest its previous form in the material world and fight alongside you!

As a spirit creature, it will have a **50% reduction to physical damage** it receives but will suffer an **extra 100% damage from spiritual sources**.

Know This! Such an ally does not come without cost. Every tenday it can only manifest for as long as its Energy allows. After being altered by Divine Power, its Energy has increased to 350!

As such you can manifest it in the material world for **7 minutes** every tenday.

Feed it more souls to increase its power!

> Know This! Your Spirit Animal shares the same bonuses with you as when it was bound to your State of Being.
>
> 1) **Eyes of the Eaglebear**
>
> 2) *Unknown* **(LOCKED!)** – 83/100 Soul Points to unlock

> Know This! Thanks to your Soul Art, your Spirit Animal will ignore 10% of a target's defense.

The eaglebear's soul shot into his chest. As soon as it did, the darkness of the cave receded as if lamps lit every nook and cranny. Now wasn't the time to celebrate though. Not with a wave of spiders bearing down on them.

Instead, he considered summoning the eaglebear. The fact that he could manifest it in the physical realm was fascinating, but he could only do it for seven minutes. It sounded like the ability reset every "tenday" which he was guessing meant every ten days, but that wasn't much. It sounded badass with its physical damage reduction, especially if it really did have all the power that it did in life, but if he used it now, he might be screwed if he needed it later. In this dangerous world he couldn't squander resources.

If the upcoming battle went the wrong way he'd summon it, but otherwise, he needed to save it. Using it now might mean dying tomorrow. Still, it was good to know he'd have a hidden trump card to play in the future. Of course, to have a future, he'd have to survive the next battle.

Zero Fell and Autumn Ghost jumped out of the giant nest but kept it at their backs. His other two acolytes joined them. More spiders poured into the cavern, but they didn't attack. To everyone's surprise, the insects just waited while their numbers built. Sharp Leaf's hand shook slightly with adrenaline and excitement.

Without taking his eyes off the spiders, Leaf asked, "Most Holy, what do we do?"

"We stand," Fell replied.

The deity used God's Eye on the attacking monsters. Information washed over him, and he grimly pronounced, "We kill'em all."

CHAPTER 30

As more dog-sized spiders poured into the cavern, Fell seriously reconsidered summoning the eaglebear. Only years of battle helped him stay calm. He just absorbed information about his latest enemy.

ORBWEAVER DRONE		
Level: 0		**Monster Rank:** Common
Energy: 61	**Soul Rank:** Common	**Deity:** Neith
STATS		
Health: 70	**Mana:** 40	**Stamina:** 99/100
RACIAL DESCRIPTION		
These monsters are the **Chosen** creatures of the god **Neith.** The most basic members of the Orbweaver race are drones, creatures without their own personality. They are driven by basic instincts, though their intellect has increased since bonding to their god. Stronger members of the race have additional capabilities.		

The spiders were true monsters, far larger than any arachnids on Earth. Most of the creature's body was in its legs, with a thorax only about eight inches wide and a spindly abdomen. Unfortunately, their mouths were filled with needle sharp teeth.

Their Energy was much lower than his or his acolytes', for whatever that was worth. His people were also armed and higher leveled. Head-to-head, he was pretty sure his group could emerge victorious, even outnumbered as they were.

What bothered Fell was that these spiders were somehow bound to another deity. He hadn't seen any monsters during the Choosing, but that didn't mean much. He'd actively avoided any colors that had a negative resonance, and he'd probably gone through less than 1% of the total options. Monster or not though, the spiders had a god backing them up. Memories of the darkness-wielding murk dwarf came back to him. Who knew what powers this Neith douche had given to his Chosen? Which raised another point. Was every single god he came across going to start shit?

As if in answer to his question, two larger spiders skittered into the cavern. They were twice the size of the drones. They stayed in the back, hulking over the smaller spiders. Fell sucked his teeth as seeing those two, but the duo was nothing compared to the final monstrosity that stalked in. With slow, delicate steps, a creature that was half woman and half Volvo-sized spider entered Fell's view.

Seeing the four pantherkin, she spat words in a language that sounded like a high-pitched chittering. The twenty or so smaller spiders had been bobbing up and down while they stood in place. At her words, they froze. That was somehow more eerie than their rhythmic movement. The two hulking spiders froze as well. Fell used *God's Eye* on the larger spiders and the hybrid, only focusing on the relevant info.

ORBWEAVER SOLDIER		
Level: 1	**Monster Rank:** Common	
Energy: 105	**Soul Rank:** Common	**Deity:** Neith
STATS		
Health: 120	**Mana:** 40	**Stamina:** 140
RACIAL DESCRIPTION		
The foot soldiers of the orbweaver race. They cannot spin webs like drones, but are stronger and more resilient. They are smarter than drones, but still lack the intellect to form anything more than the most rudimentary of personalities.		

Neither of the larger spiders had names. They were both just identified as soldiers. It was easy to see why. Their energy and stats were substantially higher than the drones. The values were pretty close to that of his Chosen. They were also a level higher than the smaller spiders. That meant an unknown boost to their base attributes. Fell was still confident of overcoming the soldiers, but he knew they weren't the real danger.

Using God's Eye a final time confirmed Fell's suspicion. As he absorbed the information, he had to resist the urge to curse. The hybrid was an acolyte!

CRUEL THORN		
Level: 2	**Class:** Cleric *Rank:* Acolyte	**Race:** Orbweaver Spider
Energy: 184	**Soul Rank:** Uncommon	**Deity:** Neith
STATS		
Health: 110	**Mana:** 140	**Stamina:** 120 / **Faith:** 125/125
RACIAL DESCRIPTION		
An acolyte of the god Neith. Originally a drone, she evolved when touched with her god's Divine Power. Cruel Thorn lived up to her name, becoming a transformed monster of terrible will and appetites. She now levels like any other sapient creature. Her newly emerged personality is capricious and sadistic.		

Unlike the drones and soldiers, she had a name. That minor detail couldn't compare with the shock Fell received after using God's Eye. In the fight with the murk dwarves, Fell had been able to learn their language after scanning one of them. That had been a wonderful discovery, but it hadn't blown his mind as the dwarves were humanoid. He now knew his language discovery power didn't discriminate. The fierce clicking noises coming from Cruel Thorn's barbed mouth were now easy to understand.

He hadn't learned how to talk to the greenbacked skink, but maybe the spiders were different because they were Chosen. Or maybe it was because the skink didn't have a language. It didn't matter. What mattered was that he was able to understand Cruel Thorn as she called out her battle plans.

The tunnel was narrow, but the cave with the eaglebear nest was much larger. Rather than have the spiders attack in a long stream, she had ordered them to file into the cavern and amass their numbers. Now that they were all out of the tunnel, she was telling the spider drones to get ready to swarm over their prey. The soldiers were to hold back at first, then move in for the kill once the drones had worn them down.

Zero Fell was about to speak his own plan of attack when another voice beat him to it. Autumn Ghost's voice held a fury he'd never heard before.

"You really must be a dumb bitch if you think you can defeat our god with a couple spiders!"

What shocked Fell wasn't Ghost's tone or her words. He already knew she was tough enough to chew nails. What stunned him was that she was speaking in the chittering language of the spiders. A language he'd just learned himself!

Later, he would read a minimized prompt that explained it.

Know This! The clergy of a god can speak in any language he himself knows. All the better to spread the word of the one true Faith!

For now, he just gave Autumn a nod of amused approval. He couldn't have said it better himself.

Cruel Thorn had been shocked at hearing her language spoken, but that was quickly replaced by a wrathful screech. She had only recently gained the ability to reason at a higher level. This was her first time being exposed to mockery. Thorn found she didn't care for it. Also, seeing another woman for the first time just infuriated her for some unknown reason. Raising one hand, she pointed at Autumn and screamed, "Bring me her body!"

With no hesitation, the spiders surged forward. Fell responded by giving a quick, but calm, order of his own, "Get into the nest."

Despite Autumn Ghost's anger and provocative words, she and the other acolytes didn't hesitate to follow their god's instructions. They turned and leaped over the edge of the wooden barrier.

Seeing them flee, Cruel Thorn mocked the group, "There is nowhere you can go that my spiders cannot follow. They fear nothing and will never stop! We shall drain your corpses slowly, and it will take you days to die!" Especially that blond one, she thought vehemently.

Indeed, the spiders had already crossed half the distance separating them by the time the party had jumped back into the nest. The drones climbed over the short barricade, barely slowing down, with the spider acolyte and soldiers following close behind. Cruel Thorn's mouth salivated at the thought of sinking her mandibles into her prey. Seeing them run had sent a sexual thrill through her. This was her first battle against other beings that could speak. Her hearts thudded in frantic excitement.

She gazed upon her army in pride. Her spiders were fearless! They would not stop even if they were stabbed and were near death. Their last act would be to kill their attacker. That was the power of her god. That was the power of Neith! How could anything ever deny his divine will? How could anything deny her, his chosen vessel? Whoever these people were, they would soon be only blood sacs! Only the latest in a never-ending line of sacrifices to the glory of her god! Only-

Cruel Thorn's exultant inner monologue came to a screeching halt as she crested the wall of the nest. What she saw wasn't the four humanoids being buried under her army of spider drones. Instead, the four creatures had gathered at the far end of the nest, more than a dozen yards away. The spiders were still surging toward them, but twelve eaglebear cubs stood in a line between her minions and their targets.

The spark of divine inside Cruel Thorn could faintly sense god-power inside each of the small hybrid creatures. She did not know that was what she was feeling, but it made her uneasy. She shouted for the drones to stop their headlong charge, but received her second painful surprise. For the first time, the spiders did not respond to her commands. They were under the thrall of another god!

When Zero Fell had seen the spider soldiers and acolyte enter the cavern, he'd known his party might not beat them in a straight-up fight. At the very least, there would be casualties. When he told Sharp Leaf that they would kill them all though, it hadn't been an idle boast. After accepting the last link in the quest chain, he'd gained control of the divine cubs.

Know This! For accepting the Quest, **Last Wish III**, all descendants of the Eaglebear's Bloodline are automatically **Tamed**. They will follow simple instructions from you and any you designate in your Chosen tribe. Further training and time with them will be required to fine-tune the commands they will follow.

A list of verbal commands appeared in Fell's mind. They were indeed basic, i.e. *Move, Attack, Stay*. He checked to see if they would fetch and roll over, but those weren't options yet. There was one command that was in bold on the prompt though: **Sonic Screech**.

While the spiders were massing at the cavern entrance, he'd used God's Eye on one of the cubs. Initially, he'd planned on staying outside of the nest. Having it at their backs would limit the directions from which they could be attacked. After reading the cub's prompt though, Fell's face had broken into a savage smile. His newly Tamed pets had a special ability! With his acolytes by his side, he'd been confident that they could deal with spiders; now he was sure of it.

DIVINE EAGLEBEAR CUB	
Level: 0	**Monster Rank:** Uncommon
Energy: 135	**Soul Rank:** Uncommon

STATS		
Health: 30	**Mana:** 40	**Stamina:** 50

DESCRIPTION

These Eaglebear Cubs are the progeny of your onetime Mortal Enemy. They have been instilled with some of your Divine Power. Like the soul of their mother, they are able to evolve by consuming the untethered spirits of the fallen.

The Divine Power that has been instilled within them has also created a new attack! Increasing their level will increase the power of this attack and possibly unlock further powers.

Known Attacks

Sonic Screech – A cone-shaped auditory attack that causes minimal damage but can *Stun* enemies for 1-5 seconds. Range: 20 feet. Cost: 30 mana. Cooldown: 30 minutes.

349

The cubs weren't helpless noncombatants. They were another twelve soldiers for the battle to come. Some people might have found it distasteful to use young creatures in a fight. Fell, however, had learned long ago that children died even easier than adults in war. There was not a doubt in his mind that the spiders would eat the cubs if he and his party died. They were all in this together.

He also immediately saw the potential of *Sonic Screech*. Used correctly it could be a powerful weapon. The problem was that the range was so short, only seven yards. To maximize the effect, he needed the spiders to rush them en masse. Even his own Title, *Infuriating Enemy,* only worked on creatures within twenty-five yards. The cavern was more than a hundred yards deep and fifty yards wide, so he couldn't blanket the space with it. Fell had been about to taunt the spider acolyte to try and goad her into an all-out attack when Autumn Ghost had done it for him. You had to love a woman with a sailor's mouth.

After the enemy acolyte lost her cool and ordered an attack, all that remained was forming the cubs into a line. The wall of the nest might not have slowed the spiders down, but it blocked his pets from view. The drones and soldiers weren't smart enough to fear a trap, and by the time Cruel Thorn arrived the drones were all within range of his Title.

By the time Cruel Thorn tried to stop the drones from rushing into a trap, it was too late. Zero Fell was the bait and the eaglebears were the jaws, waiting to snap shut. *Infuriating Enemy* filled the spiders with rage and made them ignore Thorn's commands. The drones were fearless, just as Cruel had boasted. What she failed to understand was that sometimes, fear was the appropriate response.

With a willpower that had been forged in battle, the god waited until the last possible moment before commanding in a general's tone, "Screech."

The eaglebear cubs let loose their new special attack *Sonic Screech* all at once. It was like a row of twelve sonic cannons firing simultaneously. The range and effect of their ability were extremely limited due to the cubs' young age, but lining up and releasing it in a confined space magnified the effect and wreaked damage on the spider army.

Every single spider drone lost a small amount of health. The physical damage was small, and if only a single cub had attacked, it might have been negligible. So close, however, each spider was struck by three to five cones. They each suffered damage of ten to twenty HPs. Yet the true power of the attack was the *Stun* effect. The cub's divine screech overwhelmed the spiders. Every monster collapsed to the ground, helpless.

Fell wasted no time giving his second order, "Kill."

The eaglebear cubs rushed at the invaders of their home, their ferocity no less than their mother's had been in life. The small creatures would not have been able to accomplish much against a prepared opponent. Against the soft bodies of the stunned spiders, however, their claws and fangs were more than enough.

Along with the twelve cubs, Zero's party attacked as well. Blade, club and axe rose and fell. They did not even need to use *Soul Strike*. Spider guts spilled across the floor of the nest, and a gross stink filled the air. The *Stun* effect would normally only last a few seconds, but the overlapping effects from each cub had at least doubled the effect. By the time the soldiers and Cruel Thorn closed in, most of the drones were already dead or maimed.

For her part, Cruel Thorn did not take this lightly. She ordered the orbweaver soldiers to form up in front of her. Together, they would attack the pantherkin that were slaughtering her brothers and sisters. To her dismay and anger, her minions ignored her commands.

While she and the soldiers had been beyond the range of the eaglebears' screech attack, they were not immune to Fell's Title. As soon as the larger spiders entered the AoE of *Infuriating Enemy,* they lost all reason.

The soldiers' mandibles clacked together manically and spittle fell from between their sharp teeth. Their eight legs almost blurred as they rushed at the godling. The only thought in their rudimentary brains was to kill the hated god in front of them.

A moment later, Cruel Thorn felt it herself. She nearly gave in to the desire to mindlessly rush toward Zero as well, but the spark her own god had placed in her provided the strength to resist. She might have been new to strategy, but the acolyte was no fool. This prey was powerful. To defeat it she would need the power of her god!

While the orbweaver soldiers rushed to kill Fell, and the enemy acolytes killed her drones, she chanted words of Power.

"By the hunger of Lord Neith, be bound!"

Her faith pool dropped in response to her Chant, but the deed was done. Her mouth opened wider than it should have been able to and a softball-sized sphere of webbing shot out. All she needed to do was bind the enemies of her god, then she could destroy them one at a time. They would pay for their sacrilege!

The sphere of webbing flew through the air, tendrils of rich purple energy dancing across its grey-and-gold strands. Cruel Thorn watched expectantly, her evil hearts already quivering at the slaughter that was to come. In moments the ball would detonate, shooting powerful webs in every direction. Every enemy within fifty yards would be bound and helpless. The death of some drones would be a small price to pay to ensnare such powerful prey!

The sphere tumbled through the air toward her enemies. The purple energy danced even faster. Thorn's eyes widened in anticipation before widening even further in shock and dismay.

A split second before it was going to explode, Autumn Ghost swung her club directly at it. Pale blue soul energy surrounded the weapon. She hadn't known what the spider-woman was going to do, but when she saw Cruel Thorn perform a Chant, Ghost had responded in kind.

While the spider acolyte had called upon her god, Autumn had done the same.

"In the name of Zero Fell, know my wrath!"

Crystalline blue energy had turned her club into a mace. When the power surrounding her weapon connected with the web ball, they both disappeared in a shower of blue, purple and gold sparks. The Chants of the two gods neutralized one another. Fell's priestess smiled when she saw the shock in Cruel Thorn's eyes. The web sphere was gone, but the copper club remained in Autumn's hand, albeit without the blue aura. She punctuated that fact when, still staring Cruel Thorn in the eye, she crushed the head of one of the drones.

After gaining the aggro of the soldiers, Zero kept moving backward. His plan was to kite them, allowing more time for the cubs to winnow down the drones' numbers before the *Stun* wore off. He focused only on defense, swinging his short sword at the soldiers' questing legs and biting mouths. With the larger spiders' attention on him, his acolytes were able to attack from the side.

A heavy swing of his copper axe let Sharp Leaf sever two legs from one of the soldiers. It collapsed to the ground, scrabbling to keep itself upright. Both Dust and Leaf scored hits against its abdomen. Spurts of green blood shot out from the wounds. A hard stab into its head made its remaining six legs curled inward in death.

The male acolytes readied their weapons to kill the other soldier. They needn't have bothered. A swing of Fell's sword caused it to rear back, and when it leaped forward to attack again, he didn't dodge this time. Pale blue energy had been building on his copper blade for the last several seconds. He swung his arm forward with a fully empowered *Soul Strike*.

The large spider's body was more resilient than the drones, but it was nothing compared to a god's Art. Fell's blade had an extra +20 of soul damage and ignored 10% of his enemy's defense. The spider's body was cut completely in twain by his blade and its own momentum. Light purple viscera fell to the ground with wet *smacks*. The monster's life was extinguished in an instant. The two halves fell to either side of Zero who stood tall, weapon outstretched, cerulean power wrapping his blade.

His clergy shared a look of pride before turning all their attention to the drones. The *Stun* effect had worn off, and the living spiders were fighting the cubs. They had wasted no time retaliating. Though damaged, they fearlessly bit the eaglebear cubs. As venom pumped into the bodies of the young beasts, they screamed. They all had the heart of their mother, however, and kept fighting. It helped that the drones still wanted to harm Fell more than anyone else. Thanks to that, none of the cubs were killed outright. Several had dropped to the ground though, limbs kicking spastically in response to the poison.

The battle was almost done, and the power of Fell's Title was clearly shown. If he had faced the swarm of spiders alone, he would have been overcome in seconds. With every spider remaining already injured though, his party and his tamed beasts were sickles reaping wheat. The drones might be more agile than cubs, but the beasts' talons and beaks were sharp. Against the god and his acolytes, the drones were no match. With the soldiers dead, the smaller spiders were destroyed in quick succession. That left only Cruel Thorn.

Sharp Leaf delivered a final blow to a drone. His axe sheared through its head, leaving only a mandible and one eye attached to the body. Fell ordered his acolytes to heal the poisoned cubs. Leaf and Dust had been shocked that the beasts were fighting on their side, but they didn't hesitate to follow their god's orders.

Autumn Ghost had something else in mind. She pointed her club, like the great bambino aiming at the outfield, and spat, "I want *her*, my lord."

Cruel Thorn had backed up to the entrance of the cavern. After Ghost had destroyed her web attack, she'd experienced a new emotion: terror. All animals can understand fear, even the dumb drone she'd once been. It took imagination and intellect to feel terror, however.

Seeing the power given by her god destroyed so casually, with only the swing of a club, had shaken the foundations of her belief. While the soldiers kept Fell and his acolytes busy, she'd eased away from the battle. The savagery of the pantherkin and their beast allies had fed her terror until it felt like cold claws gripping her hearts.

Seeing Ghost point a weapon at her, a weapon slick with the pulped flesh of her brothers and sisters, Cruel Thorn lost all reason. She had been able to resist the effect of Fell's Title, but she was powerless against the horror Autumn Ghost's blood drunk face instilled in her. Without another word, Cruel Thorn ran from the cavern.

Ghost bared her sharp canines and hissed in anger. Her blond hair was streaked with ichor and several strands stuck to her face. Something about the spider-woman filled her with rage. After being attacked multiple times since coming to this new world and nearly losing her brother, her god had given her the power to strike back at anyone that tried to hurt her. After this battle, she knew there was nothing she enjoyed more.

The spider-woman had attacked her, had attacked her god, and now had the audacity to flee? Rage filled Ghost, and she started to give chase. It was only a sharp command from Zero Fell that stopped her. Even so, she turned back to her god with a furious expression. He just stared back stoically, no stranger to the emotions she was experiencing, then pointed to the few drones still twitching and her fellow acolytes that were healing their new pets. The fires of her anger were banked by shame when she realized she'd ignored her god's command. Bowing her head in acquiescence and apology, she walked up to a wounded drone and delivered a death blow. As her club fell, she imagined it caving in Cruel Thorn's face.

CHAPTER 31

The spider acolyte ran from the cave and into the trees. As she fled, Autumn Ghost's fierce visage appeared in her mind. Her legs started moving faster. As soon as she left the cave, she jumped onto a trunk and scurried up into the larger branches. She didn't pause for several minutes.

She might have kept running farther, but even in her fear she didn't lose her devotion to Neith. Thorn paused to make sure that she wasn't being followed before moving off again at a more careful pace. The acolyte would rather die than lead enemies to the home web.

Half an hour later, she made it back to her god. Neith was in the same place, hanging in the middle of the giant web. He was fully enjoying a meal, the first humanoid his minions had brought him, a creature with long hair and pointed ears. Cruel Thorn barely noticed. Instead, she scuttled along the strands until she was only ten feet away from her deity. Her body quivered in fear, anger and shame.

Neith noticed his acolyte quickly. He immediately dropped the body he was feasting upon and beckoned her closer. The elf was not dead yet, but was too drained of blood to do more than struggle weakly. The man's body rolled several feet along the web before catching on a sticky strand. Drones began cocooning the elf for their god to consume later.

Terror, an emotion that Cruel Thorn might now recognize, shot through the condemned man while he was being enveloped. First the elf's eyes were covered, blocking out the light, then his ears, and then his nose and mouth. Even at that point, his nightmare didn't end. The webbing was loose enough to breathe through but too tight to swallow, so he could not choke himself to death. All the man could do was issue muted screams inside his white cocoon and wait for the pain to begin again.

Neith did not pay attention to any of this. Even if he had, he would not have cared about the elf's suffering. All life existed to feed him. His attention was on Cruel Thorn. "Report!" His voice cracked in her ears and the acolyte flinched in fear. It did not stop her from truthfully relaying everything that had happened. It never occurred to her to lie. Who could defy a god?

He had her repeat the story multiple times, teasing out details that she'd initially omitted. It wasn't until the fourth telling that she spoke of the insults the cat woman had hurled at her. She had left it out previously, not wanting to appear even weaker to her god. She would not lie, but her shame had compelled her initial silence.

That final piece of information confirmed what Neith suspected. When he had heard about the power of the pantherkins' attacks, he had reasoned that the cat people might have enchanted weapons. After hearing that the woman could communicate in spider-speak, a language that probably hadn't even existed until recently, he knew what his acolyte had found. She had gone up against another god.

Worse, the god had had several clergy members with him. Neith was only able to make a single acolyte at this point until his altar was completed. That meant the pantherkin god could call upon more strength than he could, at least for the moment. It also sounded like the pantherkin god could command beasts to fight alongside him.

A critical and cold intelligence dwelt behind Neith's multifaceted eyes; an intellect matched only by his voracious hunger. He clicked his mandibles together absently while considering his options. The enemy god had defeated nearly two dozen of his drones. Neith could summon several times that number to hunt them down, but two of his soldiers had also been slain, and he had only three of those left. Once his altar was completed that would no longer be the case, but for now his resources were severely limited.

A small group of elves had already attacked his nest. They had driven them off and even managed to capture one, but he was not safe. He needed his creatures to defend against strong monsters and enemy tribes. Orbweaver soldiers were his strongest servants at this point and he couldn't afford to lose another. Also, the pantherkin god and his people were probably already gone from the cave by now, and his spiders were not skilled at tracking. Without a web trail, it would be very difficult to find the escaped prey.

The spider god decided to leave this pantherkin tribe alone for now. Soon his shrine would be completed and his altar would be consecrated. After that, his power would rise dramatically. Once his spider army had grown in size he would take his revenge, but for now he would bide his time. After all, spiders were always patient.

His gaze shifted to Cruel Thorn. Patient he might be, but he was not forgiving. Reaching out a hand, he beckoned her with a gentle voice, "Come here, child. You have done well to bring me this information."

Relief crossed his acolyte's face. An indescribable and foolish joy bloomed in her heart, seeing that her god was not angry with her. Her eight legs moved easily on the web. Her hand fell into his, and he pulled her even closer. Neith's hand slowly lifted her chin, and he laid a kiss on her lips. Thorn's mind dissolved in bliss.

To feel the love of her god was the greatest wish of her soul. To actually know his touch was a pleasure that caused her hideous spirit to quiver in ecstasy. When Neith's hands moved to hold her arms in a vice-like grip, she mistook the strength of his grasp for passion. When he spat thick digestive fluid down her throat, only then did she realize her life had come to an end.

Cruel Thorn's throat melted and was slurped greedily by her heartless god. While he fed, Neith placed a taloned hand on her left dusky breast. Digging his fingers into the mound, he then ripped the tissue away. While Zero Fell had performed a Leap of Faith, Neith's own Profound Act had been to lure a powerful forest creature into a trap before ripping out its throat.

Destroying the ghaburdin, a monster with a musculature similar to a bull, had greatly increased his Strength attribute. In comparison, tearing off pieces of a disappointing disciple's body was child's play. The god shuddered in sexual pleasure as his acolyte's agony reached an even higher level. The bloody hunk of mutilated flesh fell from his hand. It dropped through the holes in the web, already forgotten by the spider god. Cruel Thorn's former subordinates fought over the right to consume the bleeding meat. Neith continued his pattern of dissolving and consuming her, while Thorn's body arched in pain.

The acolyte would not believe it, but Neith had actually meant what he had said when he complimented her. Returning and reporting had been the correct decision. He did not even fault her for losing to another god. The deity and his clergy sounded strong. It was likely that only he, in his divine magnificence, would be able to destroy the god, and for now that was impossible. He was bound to this location. The fact that the cat god could roam freely was actually a very important piece of information.

The divine being that had killed his followers had not yet claimed a domain. As such, he was a fool! The time required to consecrate an altar could not be rushed. While the pantherkin god was running around the land, he, the all-knowing Neith, would finish his altar. His power would spread and his webs would stretch across this new world. His influence would grow and, inevitably, the entire Lattice and all its residents, including the cat god, would fall under his dominion.

Neith paused his thoughts for a moment, savoring the wonderful meal his former acolyte had afforded him. A feeling that distantly orbited affection stirred in his chest. It was more for Cruel Thorn's taste than any pleasant remembrance of her short life, but the spider god congratulated himself on his own magnanimity.

The deity pushed his self-indulgence aside and turned his thoughts back to the pantherkin. Fantasies of revenge swirled behind his bulbous eyes. His rival would not be shown the mercy of a quick death. Not like his acolyte. That brought his attention back to Cruel Thorn's pathetic, mewling form.

The spider god congratulated himself again for his own generous spirit. He truly was magnanimous, allowing his acolyte to serve him even after she had failed. As he drank more of her liquefied insides, he reflected that Cruel Thorn's real sin hadn't been losing to the pantherkin god.

Her true sin had been failing *her* god. No other factors mattered. Failure was an unforgivable sacrilege. With renewed passion and excitement, he buried his face deeper into Cruel Thorn's carcass. As he drank the dissolved viscera of his acolyte, the spider god exulted in his own magnificence. His new monster body converted life into Faith Points, and every swallow made him stronger. All would be consumed by Neith!

CHAPTER 32

In the aftermath of the battle, a cascade of alerts appeared in Zero's vision. To his surprise, a heavenly sound filled his ears.

AUULAAA!
Congratulations! Your Chosen tribe has gained a Mark: **Soul Tame** Soul Tame is a rank 5, *Rare*, Mark!
Monsters and beasts are now yours to command! By using the power of the Soul, your Chosen tribe can ally with the spirits of beasts and monsters.
To use this new racial ability, your people must slay a beast or monster. While its soul is still on this plane of existence, those with this Mark can attempt to use **Soul Tame**. By using 100 MP, you can attempt to attract an untethered soul. If the attempt fails, the spirit will be forcefully ejected from this plane to continue its journey.

> Discrepancies between Energy, Levels and States of Being will heavily affect the chances of Taming.
>
> Soul Tame can only Tame monsters with souls equal to or lower than the Marked (i.e. a Marked razin with an *uncommon* soul can Tame an *uncommon* or *common* souled beast)

The new ability was amazing. Were his people about to become necromancers? His clergy all received the same prompt. All four of them felt an itching on the back of their left hand. Fell looked down and saw a tattoo glowing blue diamond. It wasn't hard to figure out that was his Mark. In the center, was a picture of the eaglebear, mouth opened in a screech. It was his spirit animal.

When he checked, the acolytes had a blue diamond as well, but there's was dull and empty. At Fell's urging, the acolytes tried out their new Marks on the spiders. Autumn chose one of the orbweaver soldiers while Dust and Leaf fought over the other one.

Pale blue light surrounded the hands of all three acolytes. A circle of light appeared around their wrists, floating like the rings of Saturn, and filled with glyphs none of them could read. A beam of blue light shot down onto their targets. When it struck, it splashed over the corpses like water. A moment later the blue beams winked out and all three gained red prompts.

> You have failed to **Soul Tame** your target.

There was no physical change in the bodies, but Zero reached out with his Soul Art. Just as he'd thought, the souls were gone, the bodies no more than empty husks now. Hmpf. It won't be as easy as I'd hoped, he thought. Only trial and error would show the exact chances of *Soul Tame* being successful, but for all three to have failed, the odds couldn't be great.

The three of them were all holding their heads in one hand, wincing. It was their first time suffering from mana depletion. The 100 MP cost wiped out their pools completely for the most part. It would be great for them to try again, but with their low Wisdom, they just couldn't afford the twenty minutes it would take to refill their mana. Also, there were plenty of other uses for the souls. Like unlocking his eaglebear's second power, fueling his cultivation, or assigning them to his soul slots. He started to realize how finite resources could be a problem in this new world.

Fell siphoned a soul from one of the drone's bodies and examined it.

UNBOUND SOUL: Orbweaver Drone	Class: Common
POWERS	
Soft Steps – +10% lighter steps, decreases noise while moving and decreases the tracks that are left behind	
This is the soul of a **Chosen** creature! +10% Attack vs faithful of the God Neith +10% Conversion ability vs faithful of the God Neith	

Soft Steps seemed to mimic the eerily quiet way that the spiders had moved. It wasn't exactly a combat ability but would definitely make it easier for them to move stealthily. What surprised him was the fact that binding the soul of a Chosen had an extra effect. A 10% increase in strength could mean the difference between life and death.

The soul prompt also introduced a new concept, "conversion." Fell had no idea how you would convert bugs to worship you, but then again, how did the first god do it? Things making sense was a luxury in his new life. As he thought about it, he realized logic and sense had been a luxury back on Earth as well, so what had really changed?

What mattered was that all three of his clergy had souls to augment their powers now. The souls were only *common* rank, but they all granted extra powers. Sharp Leaf bound one of the drones and Midnight Dust bound another.

The drones had only been level zero. Between that and the fact that Fell's party was higher leveled, the XP gained from each kill was modest. That didn't mean it didn't add up. Each gave about forty experience. As there had been nearly two dozen, that meant more than seven hundred points of XP. Fell had been worried that the experience would be decreased due to the eaglebear cubs fighting on their side, but it turned out that wasn't the case.

The cubs hadn't been counted as party members. The next prompt he read told him they were considered pets. The cubs didn't take away from the experience the party had gained, but they didn't benefit from the cumulative effect either. Instead, they gained experience based on their own actions. They were all still level zero.

Fell scanned them in curiosity. He'd always wondered, if beasts and monsters couldn't reason, how did they assign points? Now that they were tamed, his God's Eye gave him more information. It turned out that as beasts leveled, their attributes progressed in a unique way according to their nature.

The eaglebear cubs, for instance, would each gain a point in Constitution upon reaching level one. That attribute would apparently increase every level. Their Luck, on the other hand, would only increase every five levels. Each of their attributes had a pattern of progression and it varied based on the type of beast.

There was also a notation at the bottom of the prompt that the cub was getting fewer points than it would have if it had been an adult. It wasn't a surprise that juveniles wouldn't gain as many points as a full-grown beast. What was a good surprise was that upon reaching adulthood, all the points they had banked would be supplied all at once. If he did manage to nurture the younglings, they'd get a serious boost in power after they were grown.

With the entire party healed, including the cubs, that left only one matter to attend to. Fell started feeding souls to his new spirit animal.

Your Spirit Animal has consumed **+3 Soul Points**

Your Spirit Animal has consumed **+4 Soul Points**

Your Spirit Animal has consumed **+3 Soul Points**

After supplying the fifth soul, his spirit animal was only 1 point away from unlocking her second power. Fell could feel her growling happily as she consumed the energy of the drone souls. He himself felt a sense of contentment, like he was feeding a pet. The god was about to consume one more, when he heard a strange sucking sound. Before he could even turn, the sound multiplied.

What he saw when he did turn around made Fell's eyes widen in shock. Each of the cubs had their mouths open, and blue soul light emanated from their throats. They were the source of the sucking sounds. Before he could get over his astonishment, struggling drone souls were being pulled into their mouths, like golf balls down a garden hose.

Once consumed, the eaglebear cubs' mouths snapped shut. To Fell's growing rage, the greedy little bastards started making yummy in my tummy noises. A few even licked their lips, something that looked weird and disconcerting, seeing as how their "lips" were actually cruelly hooked beaks.

Just like that, twelve of the souls were consumed. A prompt appeared in the god's vision.

Know This! The celestial power that infused the eaglebear cubs was altered by your Soul Art. These beasts can now grow by absorbing Soul Points. Provide **100 Soul Points** to each divine eaglebear cub to advance them to adulthood.

It looked like he wouldn't have to wait years for the cubs to mature. Each *common* soul provided 1-5 Soul Points. That meant twenty of them might have gotten his new spirit animal to level one. That didn't mean he wasn't irritated at seeing them gobbling down his spoils of war like they were hungry hungry hippos. He'd found one more use for souls. It looked like they'd be a valuable and way too finite resource.

He wasn't going to be able to gather 1200 SPs any time soon. The cubs growing stronger was a longer-term investment. Being able to unlock his spirit animal's second power was something he could do now. That was why when he saw one of the cubs amble toward the last soul, a hungry glint in its eye, he shouted, "No! No!" If he'd had a rolled-up newspaper, he would have whacked it across the nose.

The cubs glared at him in reproach, but he just stared back until they hung their heads. Fell nodded in satisfaction. There's one Alpha here, and ya'll gonna know it's me! He quickly consumed the last soul. The cubs whined a bit, but a sharp "Hey!" from Autumn Ghost got them under control. She just had that kind of voice.

After feeding it the soul, the eaglebear's powers were finally unlocked!

Congratulations! You have unlocked all the powers of your Spirit Animal!

1) **Eyes of the Eaglebear**

2) **Vitality of the Eaglebear** – +50 Health +50 Stamina

Fell's health and stamina soared! Both stats rose by nearly 50%. He could feel his body swell slightly in response to the boost. He'd been wondering what the second power could be. It turned out it was a taste of what had made the eaglebear such a tough SOB to take down. With this, he didn't need to worry so much about being one shotted in a fight. There were definite benefits to being a pantherkin, but lacking in strength and health was a real dick punch.

With all the souls gone, Fell and his clergy checked the cave quickly to see if there was anything that could be helpful, but all they found were the remains of dead creatures. The group left the lair, the eaglebear cubs in tow. It was only minutes after Cruel Thorn had escaped, but in Fell's opinion they had already tarried too long. The last thing they needed was for the spider acolyte to return with reinforcements.

While they moved out, Autumn Ghost brought up that they were all close to reaching level two. They asked him where they should allocate their points once they reached that point. What he ended up saying defied their expectations.

"If you are going to work with me, you will need to be able to make your own decisions. I don't want slaves. I want powerful people who know their own mind. Do you understand?"

The three clergy shared a look before nodding hesitantly. Zero sighed, realizing that the bond to his Chosen was stronger than he'd thought. Their loyalty wasn't absolute, but it was as ingrained as a mantra they might have repeated since childhood. That kind of blind faith and loyalty might be useful for the grunts of an army, but Fell already knew that his clergy would need to operate at a higher level.

He needed his people to think for themselves and to act independently. As useful as the bond between them was, he'd have to pay attention that he didn't end up with an army of sheep.

Fell was still unsure about his role as a god, but he realized that relating to his faithful wasn't too different from raising children. Making a child's life easy all the time was not a kindness. It could actually be crippling. His followers, especially his clergy, would need to be pushed and forged into something stronger than they already were. As he looked at their expectant faces, however, he reminded himself that change was a gradual process.

"Think for yourselves, but you can always ask me for help. Just realize I may not always know the answer or even be able help, so you'll need to rely on yourselves as well." They seemed a bit more at ease with that answer.

The party continued to travel, the eaglebear cubs moving in a cluster between the four of them. Fell kept his eyes peeled. If they encountered another greenbacked skink or something worse, it was unlikely that he could save all the cubs. He knew from his previous life that there was no crappier task than escort.

The god's luck was with them. They were able to make it out of the forest in the next couple hours, and they avoided any other attacks. After they reached the grassland, their speed picked up. About six hours had passed since they'd left the caravan. The sun was high overhead. The detour had taken longer than Fell had hoped, but it also had been much faster than he'd feared. Time-consuming or not, he and his party had gained some serious dividends on this trip. The remaining post battle prompts proved that.

Congratulations! You and your Chosen have defeated the followers of another god! They cannot help but be impressed with your Divine Power!

+28 (base 22) Devotion Points with all of your Chosen. Devotion Rank: Dedicated Believer (+3)

+11 Devotion Points with the orbweaver spiders (base +22 - 50% Chosen resistance to Conversion). Devotion Rank: Adversary of the Faith (-4).

It looked like winning battles was a way to make people believe in his divinity. Another parallel to life on Earth, he realized. It was a bit surprising that even the spiders believed in him a bit after the battle. It looked like the difference was marginal, seeing as how they started off viewing him as the enemy. The effect had also been decreased due to the orbweavers being another god's Chosen tribe. Still, it was interesting to note.

His Title had also progressed a great deal.

For killing **20 *common* rank** enemies with the Title **Infuriating Enemy** equipped, you have gained **240 Animosity Points**.

800/10,000 obtained to upgrade your Title.

You have gained: **738 XP** from combat.

13,938/15,000 XP to reach Level 3

One of the prompts Fell was most excited by was the reaping of Faith Points they'd gained for killing the spiders.

> For absorbing energy from a **Faithful of Neith**, you have gained
>
> **+2 Faith Points!**

That prompt repeated in more or less the same way, one for each soul he'd consumed. In total, he had absorbed six spider drone souls and gained twenty-four Faith Points.

> **Total Faith Points:** 3,880

One thing that Fell noticed was that the max number of FPs he got from a spider drone was five. When he'd absorbed the souls of the murk dwarves, he'd been able to absorb up to eight. The prompt back then had said the upper limit on absorbed FPs was the maximum amount each being would have generated for their god each day. His own followers made 10 FP/day because they had reached devotion rank three, *Dedicated Believer.* Did that mean the spiders had a lower devotion level for Neith than his Chosen did for him? Or was it because they were monsters?

Again, more questions he couldn't answer… yet. Luckily, Fell wasn't one to dwell and wring his hands. If he survived another day, he'd have the chance to figure it out. For now, he had to link back up with his tribe. Unfortunately, the eaglebear cubs were proving an impediment to that.

The cubs had been a great help in the spider battle, but they were still young. Their stamina faded quickly. Not only that, but their green bars were less than half the size of the god and his clergy. The group had to make frequent stops, as the cubs would literally flop down on the ground and refuse to move. They were also too heavy and too numerous to carry. Each time, Fell's party would encircle the pups and look outward in four directions. Twice, low level creatures attacked while the cubs rested, but thankfully the attackers were alone and only level two. Together, the god and his acolytes dealt with them quickly. The cubs grumbled collectively when Fell kept the souls for himself.

Even with the stops, they made better time going back, as they were not searching for signs of the eaglebear's cave. There was also no need to backtrack. It only took three hours to get back to the spot of the murk dwarf attack. The signs of battle were obvious in the midday light: black stains on the ground, flattened grasses, and a still-smoking mound where they had burned the bodies.

The group waited for a few short minutes to let their stamina recover, then moved off again at a light jog. Walking, jogging, walking, jogging, they moved at a pace that let them both cover ground quickly and keep their stamina from bottoming out. They were still slowed by the eaglebear cubs, but made better time now that they were out of the forest. On the grassy plains, the chance of surprise attacks had also fallen. Still, they remained vigilant.

They continued traveling for another five hours. Fell started wondering if they might need to make camp for the night. If he were alone, he'd have kept going. The cubs, though, were near the end of their rope. Truth be told, his clergy were not doing much better. If not for the gift of the eaglebear's vitality, he might have been in the same boat. Thankfully, water wasn't a big problem. They had crossed two small streams and had topped up their water skins.

Fell was about to call a halt for the day when Midnight Dust came running back over the hill ahead of them.

"I have found the tribe, my lord," he panted. "They have made camp for the night about twenty minutes west, only two hills away."

Fell nodded to him and they went to join the tribe.

As he had instructed, the caravan had stopped early so they could institute some safety procedures. Every razin held a tool in their hand, and they were digging a trench using crude stone implements. He had told them to make a four-by-two-foot trough around the camp and pile the displaced earth on the inside of the excavation to make a soft earthen wall.

It must have taken a couple hours, but it would make them much safer in the night. As a pleasant surprise, the tribe's *Industrious* Characteristic had come into play. The 10% building bonus their tribe enjoyed seemed to apply even to field fortifications, allowing the razin to accomplish their goal much faster than should have been possible. The ditch wasn't finished, but it was nearly there.

One of the other precautions Fell had instituted was the sentries arranged around the camp. The guards noticed their god approaching, along with the clergy and the eaglebear cubs. Seeing twelve smaller versions of the monster that had nearly wiped the tribe out alarmed them to say the least, but their faith in Fell kept them relatively calm.

Minutes later, the god and his clergy were all catching their breath inside the impromptu fortification. Ghost, Dust and Sharp Leaf all fell on the offered food ravenously. Seeing their hunger, Fell noticed his lack of appetite for the first time. Thinking about it, he realized he hadn't been truly thirsty either. Drinking water at the streams had felt refreshing, but he hadn't actually needed to drink. He also hadn't slept since coming to Telos. He'd thought it might have been adrenaline, or a perk of his new body, but now he was sure it had something to do with his divinity. Had he moved beyond the basic needs of the flesh?

While his clergy told their fellow tribe members about the harrowing adventure they'd just been on, he walked over and grabbed a shovel. Autumn Ghost saw him and immediately began to stand. He waved her down. His clergy had worked hard. They all needed to rest. For himself, he walked toward the unfinished trench. There was work to be done.

CHAPTER 33

They made it through the night and the next day without an attack. The following night was not so kind. Two snakes, each more than a foot in diameter, killed two sentries in an instant. Then they sped through the camp. One grabbed another man and the other an eaglebear cub in their mouths before speeding away. The whole process took less than thirty seconds. By the time Fell had reached the boundary of the camp, he could just catch the monster fading away into the gloom. More pairs of bright eyes stared back at him from the darkness, promising a quick death to any that ventured out into the night.

Fell wondered if his spirit animal might react badly to the death of one of her children. When he examined the warm feeling inside him, however, what he felt wasn't exactly indifference, but more acceptance of the grim realities of the world. She had never expected all her offspring to survive. In that moment, he understood why the quest had specified that only half of the cubs needed to make it.

Telos continued to show them how dangerous it was. Three more tribe members died before morning. Not to a monster, though there was still blood. The trio had eaten berries they'd found. Sadly, the small fruit seemed to be a potent anticoagulant. Not even the collective healing of a god and his three clergy could save them.

An hour after the snake's attack, they started crapping blood. So much poured out of them that their hearts did not have enough left to keep pumping. The tribe burned the bodies, leaving yet another pyre in their wake.

While they walked the next day, the tribe started hearing strange sounds, like a distant hooting, but they could never find a source. The grass had grown taller over the past two days, from two to three feet. It wasn't over their heads, but it could easily hide all manner of dangers. Between the terrain and the sounds, the entire tribe's nerves were frayed, nearly fried; all except their god, who had long ago become accustomed to the stress of the unknown.

At noon, a series of long necks popped up out of the grass, forming a half circle around them. A member of the tribe called out in alarm and they all raised their weapons towards this new threat. The creatures continued rising until their six-foot-tall bodies were revealed. They were featherless birds, covered in short spiky brown hair patterned with purple zebra stripes. In the lilac-colored grasses it was perfect camouflage.

There were more than fifty of them spread out over a hundred-yard area. The distant hooting evolved into harsh squawking. The warning was obvious; the tribe was getting too close to something the birds valued. Fell guessed there was a nest hidden in the tall grass.

The giant birds looked strange to say the least. The short spiky hair seemed to move against the wind. What the tribe focused most on though were the wicked beaks and long claws. The rest of the beasts might seem strange, but their natural weapons were terrifying.

God's Eye showed Fell that while the creatures weren't predators per se, they were violent and territorial. The vitrotchs, as he found they were called, were all between level five and ten, a great deal more powerful than any member of the tribe, including their god. After the threat display, Fell deliberately moved away from the giant birds. It wasn't in the direction of the quest, but the detour wasn't an option. Zero had no doubt that the vitrotchs could tear through his people. He and his acolytes might survive, but the losses would be terrible if they kept moving toward the beasts' territory.

It turned out to be the right decision. The birds followed them for a full hour, herding them away, but they didn't attack. After they were far enough away, the long necks lowered into the tall grass again. The hooting resumed, reminding the tribe that they were still being watched. Despite being followed, the previous air of threat and menace was gone. A few hours later even the sounds disappeared, and Fell started guiding them back toward the quest destination.

It was a relief that the pack of birds didn't attack. Fifty higher level monsters might have wiped out the entire tribe. Despite that, Fell had received a clear message, not just from the birds but also from Telos itself. This new world was full of danger. If they didn't watch their step, it would consume them. There was also the fact that even though no lives had been lost, they'd burned half a day on the detour. With rations overtaxed because of the eaglebear cubs, tensions were getting higher.

The next day brought its own trial. Three hours after sunrise, the tribe started to feel a tremor in the ground. Fell thought it was an earthquake until several of the razin pointed into the distance with excited expressions. Zero's heart started beating wildly in his chest, a purely instinctual response to what he was seeing.

A giant, an honest-to-god giant, was walking in the distance, only a few miles away. Fell could barely wrap his head around the size of the figure. At that distance, he guessed it was at least four or five stories tall! The sheer devastation a creature that size could wreak was mind-boggling. Thankfully, it was walking in the other direction. Fell wondered if he was literally seeing his high Luck stat in action.

Most of the razin were dumbstruck. All except two men that were pointing excitedly and shouting. The second tribal Characteristic of the razin, *Curiosity*, was threatening to kill all of them. A second later Fell rushed forward and grabbed one of their wrists before hissing, "Are you bitches crazy? Be quiet!"

Thankfully they listened, and most of the tribe had sufficient intelligence to outweigh their curiosity. After that, they contented themselves with *only* pointing excitedly and gawking. Personally, Fell found the sheer immensity of the giant evoked a primal urge in him to just remain still.

He knew the damn thing wasn't a T-Rex and its vision probably wasn't based on movement, but motionlessness seemed like a pretty perfect idea all the same. Fifteen minutes later, the giant vanished behind a distant hill. Right after it did, Fell motivated the tribe to vacate the area with some wise words, "Quickly now. Let's go. Quickly!"

"Which direction, my lord?" Sharp Leaf asked.

Fell looked at him like he was insane, "The opposite direction, man. The *opposite!*" The new deity didn't stop looking over his shoulder for hours.

While they traveled, the tribe tried to ask Zero Fell questions. The topics ranged from the mundane to the fantastic. The most common question was where were they going. During their travels, they spotted several adequate locations to make a new home. Each had access to fresh water, nearby trees, defensible terrain or some combination of factors the tribe found attractive.

Fell's customary answer, "I'm not exactly sure," transitioned to "You just have to trust me," like so many gods before him. He was only a hair away from, "Quit bothering me!" when Autumn Ghost came to his rescue.

She told the tribe that their god was focused on matters of cosmic importance. Then she talked about how his divine will was difficult to understand and was often misunderstood. It all sounded like BS to Fell, but since it stopped the barrage of questions, he let her explanations stand. The new god did not realize it, but the fundamental principles of his religion were already being formed.

On the fourth night of travel, tragedy struck again. The grassland had slowly been transitioning back into forest. The vague pull of Fell's quest was growing stronger. He led them along the demarcation of the grassland and the woods. After his experience with the spiders and the skink, he was wary of entering a wooded area again. That night they made camp as usual. Just after moonrise, screams broke the stillness.

Fell jumped up and ran toward the sound. By the time he got there, all that was left of the sentry was a smear of blood on the ground. He looked around frantically for the attacker. Thanks to the vision enhancement from his spirit animal, he was able to just make out a quintet of birds winging away. These birds were no sparrows. Their wingspan had to be at least fifteen feet. Seven of his people were being carried away. Three of the birds had each snatched one of his Chosen and the two largest birds had a razin clutched in each of their claws.

All of his people were struggling and screaming, but they couldn't break free. In the blink of an eye, the tribe's population was whittled down to one hundred and thirty. In seconds, the birds and the screams vanished into the trees of the forest and were gone forever.

The god clenched his jaw. Turning back to his tribe, he saw looks of accusation in some of their gazes. A prompt appeared to affirm that it was not only in his mind.

Prayer Quest Update: **Save Us III**

Your bond with your Chosen tribe garners a large amount of Devotion, but the faith of your people is not limitless. More tribe members have died in pursuit of their new home. After having passed several locations that could have been their new home, some of your Chosen question why they did not settle before this life was lost.

Failing to complete a Prayer Quest has caused a drop in Devotion!

-50 Devotion Points

This is only the initial loss. A further **25 Devotion Points** will be lost each day until you found a proper settlement. If you do not assuage the doubts of your Chosen, the drop in Devotion may be severely aggravated!

Total Devotion of the Razin tribe: **+724**

Fell had brushed off the questions that had been coming his way, but this could not so easily be pushed aside. As far as he'd been able to make out, the razin's current Devotion was still in the third rank, *Dedicated Believer.* If their Devotion dropped below 500, it would decrease to rank two, and that would decrease the Faith Points they generated.

He also might lose one of his clergy slots which would reduce the tribe's strong fighters from four to three. There were serious consequences to losing his people's Devotion. What would happen if they were seriously attacked while weakened? He didn't know, but sure as shit was slippery, it wouldn't be good.

In this world of giants and monsters, his acolytes were his strongest fighters. Even the loss of one Chant might mean losing a battle. It would certainly mean losing lives if his people couldn't be healed.

The Machiavellian part of his mind also looked at his clergy as a resource. He now knew he could make more if they died, but it would take time and precious resources. Every swinging dick he'd come across on this world was trying to fuck him. Right now, he had an edge over them, and he had to keep it. Wasting Divine Points on making another clergy token would take days. Not to mention the Faith Points or souls he'd have to spend making the DPs. The creation Tokens had been single use. Fell had zero doubt that he'd need as many Faith Points as he could get his hands on in the very near future.

Bottom line, he needed his people to be devoted. Fell looked at the faces of his Chosen, and considered various approaches on how to respond to their doubt. He could lie to them. He could threaten them with his Divine Powers. He could even make an example of one of them. Fear was a powerful motivator. He was supposed to be a god now, after all. Even though he knew that wasn't really true, they didn't know that. God or not, he was a lot stronger than they were. Maybe they just needed to have "the fear of 'him' put into them."

These thoughts and more circled through his mind, each worse than the last. Truth be told, if all he saw when he looked at them was the doubt and recrimination, he might have taken one of those options. In his first life, he'd done far worse for less reason. Right now, these people had something he needed, faith, and they were threatening to take that away. When he was younger, that would have been the end of the equation. It was the lesson he'd learned from his father. When there was a threat, you removed it.

Then his eyes fell on Autumn Ghost. She was not looking at him with blame in her eyes. She was gazing at him in support. He could feel her faith in him like a palpable force. It was sunlight on his face. Warmth from the hearth. Her belief in him reminded Fell that he was not just the cold-hearted man that used to make prisoners piss themselves in fear. He was more than that now.

As a physician, he'd devoted the final years of his life on Earth to saving lives, not taking them. He could be better than he'd been before. He knew he wasn't really a god, but that didn't mean he couldn't be a good man.

He ran his gaze over everyone again and then spoke.

"I know you all have questions. And I don't have good answers. That makes you doubt me. I do not blame you for it. Your tribe has been uprooted from your home, survived attack after attack in this new world, and now you just want a place to lay your head in peace and safety." He looked at Autumn Ghost again before scanning the entire tribe again, "You deserve that. All of you do."

Some of the pantherkin started nodding to his words. A bit of tension left their faces.

"You call me a god. I was never really clear about what that meant, but I do know what it means to lead. I have a path that I am following. I can't tell you more than that, but the devotion you would give me as a deity has to come from the same place you would give me as your leader. Follow me," he beseeched. Words that had been passed down through his family for generations spilled from his lips, "I cannot promise you the future, but I can promise you that we will meet it together."

He met their gazes one by one. They each nodded to him, and another prompt appeared.

Prayer Quest Update: **Save Us III**

Your words have temporarily calmed your Chosen people. **Ongoing loss of Devotion Points has been paused!** Only finding an adequate home will fully remove the threat of losing their Devotion. Delaying too long in accomplishing this Quest or further loss of life may lead to further loss of Devotion.

Fell internally breathed a sigh of relief, though he kept his face impassive. He'd stemmed the bleeding. Thankfully, the initial loss of Devotion wasn't enough to change the overall rank. That didn't mean he was taking this lightly. He'd just been reminded that quests were a double-edged sword. They could lead to great rewards, but also to serious consequences. Apparently, the negative effects didn't only manifest if you failed a quest, but also if you took too long completing one.

The god spoke again, his face only half visible in the torchlight, "Settle back in, but tighten the perimeter. I will keep watch for the rest of the night, but we need to be moving again with the dawn."

"Ghost," he called, looking at his acolyte, "double the sentries."

She nodded to him and moved off to do his bidding. Increasing the guards on station wouldn't protect them from another flying attack, but it might make his people feel safer. Besides, most of the night was already spent, and he was pretty sure no one else was going back to sleep.

The group did as they were told. Fell remained where he was, thinking about what had just happened. Were they right? Was he crazy to keep following some vague instructions through this hostile world? It seemed like no matter where they went, or what they did, there were powerful predators around every corner.

They weren't even in the woods, and yet the fucking Eagles of Manwe had killed seven members of the tribe before anyone even knew they were there. There hadn't been a battle or a struggle. There had just been screams, a smear of blood, and it was done. What kind of world was he leading them through? Should he just settle in the next defensible area they came across, the quest be damned?

He always came back to the same answer. The world being dangerous was exactly why he had to keep going. So many things they had come across could have ended the whole tribe in minutes. The only edge they had, the only reason he himself was still alive, was because of the gifts his sponsor had given him.

The picture had given him the crazy idea to jump out of the tree. That had let him kill the eaglebear and had started the cascade of events that had led him to having a Chosen people, a spirit animal and a cadre of tamed monsters at his command. Without that message, he might have died in that tree. He'd either have been eaten by the eaglebear or the monkeys. Either way, it literally would have been a shit option.

The cultivation books would let him greatly increase his power. Over the past several days, he'd been experimenting with the *basic* faith technique. It let him turn 10 Faith Points into 1 Divine Point. It basically turned Faith Points into fuel for his cultivation. The process was more difficult than the *soul* technique, but he also had far more faith than souls.

The technique required him to mentally visualize each FP surrounding his Divine Core. The ten motes of light could be paired and a connection would form, turning the FPs into five strands of light. He then had to concentrate on all five threads at once, weaving them into a specific wreath-like pattern. If successful, it would form a red mote of light that changed the color of his white pyramid, just like with his *soul* technique.

It was a bit like standing on one foot, rubbing your stomach with one hand, tapping your head with the other while saying the alphabet backwards. It took intense focus. It was doable, but very easy to mess up, especially if you were distracted for even a moment. With the focus required, it was impossible to do while hiking. Sadly, if he failed, the Faith Points were wasted.

Fell found there was a definite upside to not sleeping. Each night he was able to devote time to cultivating. He still failed more than half the time. Even a momentary lapse in concentration could cause one of the strands to go awry, and the whole thing would be ruined.

Fell found that a successful attempt required at least two hours. In both speed and success rate, the *soul* technique was superior. A technique he wouldn't have without his sponsors, proof again that cheaters really could win. The downside, of course, was that he needed more souls.

One piece of good news came when he finally used the dwarf acolyte's soul. Braninon had been an *uncommon* spirit. It resisted his control far more than *common* spirits, but it was still within his ability to control. And though it took him three hours to "digest" it, the soul yielded four red motes of light, increasing his total number of Divine Points by the same amount. If that held true,

Over the past few days, he'd only managed to make nine points while cultivating. The ivory pyramid now had a decidedly pink hue. It had cost him his *uncommon* soul as well as 120 Faith Points. Fell hungered for a return to that higher state of being and would have sacrificed far more. A part of him recognized that both the thrill of capturing a soul and the hunger to cultivate could be addictive. A larger part of him didn't care.

CHAPTER 34

The next morning, Fell led them away from the forest. Even though the quest was pushing him to travel along the edge, he put about a mile between the tribe and the tree line. Thankfully, the next day and night passed without an attack. The air was still filled with horrifying cries and shrieks, but nothing came after the razin. The only real danger came from the tribe's own nature.

Halfway through the second day after the bird attack, three of the razin started vomiting and soiling their pants. Their condition was so severe that the tribe had to stop moving. Fell and his clergy kept casting *Soul Heal* as often as they could. It kept their health up, but did nothing to remove the symptoms. It was actually his medical training that saved the day.

The true danger of intractable nausea and vomiting was dehydration, in most cases. Even though the sick razin fought against it as strongly as a frat row drunk, he had other members of the tribe force water down their throats. Still, it was only when he threatened

389

them with water enemas that they saw the wisdom of taking the water from the top rather than the bottom.

After several foul-smelling hours, the sick razin stopped spewing everywhere. Miserable, they revealed that they had all eaten some purple fruit they'd found on a bush along the edge of the forest. When Fell shook his head incredulously and asked them why, good god *why* would they eat unknown fruit, *especially* after three of the tribe had already died from eating poison berries? They had just shrugged sheepishly. Only one responded, but she summed it up, "They just looked so tasty, Lord Fell! And how will we know if things are safe if we don't try?"

He'd rolled his eyes in disgust, but then a horrible thought occurred to him. "We haven't been next to the forest for over a day. That means you must have picked them then. Are you three the only ones who had the fruit?"

They looked at each other sheepishly again. Behind Zero's back came the sound of retching from a fourth razin, followed swiftly by a fifth. He just closed his eyes and rubbed his forehead, "Goddammit."

The good news was that the stank of forty-some-odd people vomiting and shitting made a stink cloud so bad that it kept animals and other predators away that day. The other good news was that the fruit wasn't actually fatal. The bad news was that Fell's pantherkin nose turned out to be much more sensitive than his human one. They also consumed half their water stores, cleaning and keeping the tribe hydrated. Worse, their food stores were dwindling.

The tribe had to stop traveling for the day. After digging fortifications again, they passed another tense night. Remy kept *Infuriating Enemy* activated, so hopefully, if a predator bird or any other dangerous creature attacked, it would come after him and not the tribe. With so many of the tribe incapacitated, he didn't dare risk cultivating. Thankfully, either his high Luck or the "senior-citizen bathroom on taco night" reek kept other creatures away through the night as well.

Fell confiscated the remaining fruits and examined them with *God's Eye.*

You have found:

Wurt Fruit

You lack the Herbalist Class. The information available to you is extremely limited.

That was all he got. Fell had hoped for more, but it turned out even his God's Eye had serious limitations. On Earth, there had been a gardener that had gotten a skill called *Herb Lore.* He'd said that looking at most plants had given him an idea about potential uses, from healing to poisons to furniture polish. Everyone had been pretty excited, thinking it might give them a better chance of survival during the apocalypse. Unfortunately, he'd been eaten by a vine monster only a few days later. Unfairly, people had started calling Fell an asshole after that, just for laughing at the irony.

It was becoming more evident that if he and his tribe were to survive, he'd need them to learn skills he didn't have. His God's Eye was a powerful tool, but it wouldn't have warned him against eating a poisonous fruit. He and his people would also need a way to identify useful herbs. Without medicines some of his people would definitely die from disease, maybe all of them. They couldn't always rely on Divine Power. There were just too many people in the tribe, and his acolyte's powers recharged too slowly. They might even come up again a sickness that his powers couldn't heal. Once again it was proof of how if he wanted to survive, he couldn't do it alone.

That meant, as irritating as it was, the razin had been right that they would have to try new things in this new world. It didn't change the fact that they'd been absolute fools to try the berries en mass. They definitely could have just chosen on person and waited to see the results. Still, their fearless curiosity was something he could work with. Between that and his own hard-won wisdom, the tribe could accomplish anything… if they survived long enough.

With the rising of the sun, every member of the tribe was ready to leave the soiled ground behind them. More than a few still felt nauseous, but they were all hale enough to keep going. They all heaved a collective sigh of relief at smelling fresh air. By the afternoon, they all noticed another change on the wind. The razin had been mountain and forest dwellers on their old world, so they didn't know what it portended. To Fell it was as obvious as the nose on his face: the scent of salt and water. They were getting close to an ocean.

They continued on for another half a day before the god saw it: an ocean, a deeper green than any found on Earth. While they had walked, the land had leveled out. The tall purple grasses had shifted to an ankle-deep "normal" green as well. After cresting a final hill, they could see a glistening body of water vast enough that the other side could not be seen. It stretched from horizon to horizon.

The razin exclaimed with their customary excitement over a new discovery. Fell's feelings were much more reserved. There was no doubt that the quest had led him here. The pull inside him had only grown stronger the longer they traveled. Now though, he could see that they were on a small peninsula. In front of them was grassland bordering a beach. The only deviation was a small, but thick, copse of trees at the tip of the headland. Where the hell was this "pull" leading him?

As far as he could tell, it was pointing him toward the end of the peninsula, but he just couldn't see why. The last freshwater stream they'd passed was more than a day behind them. There were no real resources here to build a settlement. He supposed fishing was a possibility, but the razin didn't know how. They also lacked any boats or nets. Where was this lost temple and where was this new home he'd been promised?

The god kept his concerns to himself. At this point, he was committed. It would only take a few more hours to reach the end of the peninsula. If they found nothing, they could backtrack to the stream to refill their water, the quest be damned. Then he'd lead the tribe back to one of the sites they'd passed. Food was already running out, but they would be alright if they rationed it.

If worse comes to worst, there were always the eaglebear cubs. Even one of them should feed the tribe for a day. That was another week and a half of life. He might lose his spirit animal and fail the quest, but keeping his faith supply alive was more important than anything.

Fell led his people forward. Hours later, they approached the stand of trees. The god was even more confused, as the pull kept growing stronger yet he still saw nothing special. After they moved into the boscage, however, a prompt appeared in everyone's vision.

Congratulations! You have found a **Minor Wonder** of the World!

You have discovered the **Great Bridge of Serathia**!

The Great Bridge of Serathia was made by the original race of Telos, so long ago that even the name of the civilization has been lost and forgotten. They are known only as **The First**. So great were their works, however, that they have lasted long enough for foothills to become mountains and those mountains to be ground into deserts.

This bridge offers fast travel between the various zones of Telos. For the knowledgeable it opens massive opportunities, but be warned; for those ignorant of its pathways, the bridge can lead to certain death!

While everyone was digesting that information, another prompt appeared for everyone, along with a sound like a crowd cheering.

YAH-YAH-YAAAAAHH!

Discovering the Great Bridge of Serathia is a notable Discovery!

By doing so you have honored one of your tribe's Characteristics: **Curiosity**

For finding a **Minor Wonder** your tribe has gained **1,000 Characteristic Points**!

Your tribe's **Curiosity** has progressed from **Level 0** to **Level 4**!

1,000/1,100 to Level 5.

Chance to find notable locations increased from **+5%** to **+25%**

Research bonus increased from **+5%** to **+25%**

Fell finally understood what "honoring" his tribe's Characteristics meant. The research bonus would definitely come in handy! He still wasn't sure what the point was of finding notable locations, but there was a secondary benefit to leveling up a Characteristic.

Increasing the **Characteristic** of your Chosen tribe has proven how much you honor your bond to them. This has impressed the tribe as a whole, and they have become more Devoted!

+125 (base +100) Devotion Points

Total Devotion of the Razin tribe: **+849**

Both prompts were good news, but neither could compare to what the stand of trees had hidden. Fell and the entire tribe stared at the structure, and the god couldn't help but think that the term *Minor Wonder* was inadequate. Even the normally rambunctious and playful cubs fell silent.

In the middle of the small grove was a bridge made of crystal and stars. About thirty yards across, the bridge rose from the grass. It was constructed of smooth clear crystal. There were no signs of tool work. It looked like a single solid piece, despite its massive size. What was truly amazing was that inside the crystal... under every step and floating beneath the jeweled decking, lay the blackness of space, dotted with stars and nebulae. The celestial bodies slowly moved to a cosmic pattern. It was like part of the night sky had been stolen and laid at their feet.

CHAPTER 35

The tribe oohed and aahed. Several rushed forward to touch the bridge, exclaiming that it was solid and cool to the touch. Others were staring at how the bridge seemed to disappear in midair. Indeed, it grew progressively more insubstantial after it rose from the ground. By the time it was halfway to the edge of the tree line, it had disappeared completely. Outside of the small grove, there would be no evidence of it at all. Fell checked the internal pull again. There was no doubt about it. The quest was leading him straight down the middle of the bridge.

Fell reviewed the prompts. This bridge led to other parts of Telos. It looked like the temple he was searching for wasn't even on this continent. As mind-boggling as the structure before him was, it also looked like it was his one shot to finish his quest. The only strange thing, besides again, well, *everything*, was what the prompt said about being "knowledgeable" about the "pathways."

Someone else might have hesitated over what to do. Fell was not that kind of person. He was not that kind of god. He merely raised his hand and randomly pointed at a tribe member, "Check it out." He'd learned long ago that you mustn't hesitate to spend lives if necessary. Spend, but never waste.

For once, the curiosity of the tribe played in the god's favor. The pantherkin woman agreed without hesitation. She walked onto the bridge, only stopping when Fell called out.

"Walk forward two hundred steps, look around, then come right back."

The bridge faded out of sight in less than one hundred yards, so that should be plenty, the god thought. With no hesitation, the woman walked down the bridge. After ten paces, her body looked less substantial. After fifty, everyone could see clean through her. After one hundred, she disappeared.

Everyone watched, breathless in anticipation. While they all waited, Fell cast glances at the razin. Not a one of them had a problem with his order. If anything, several looked like they wanted to follow her before she even reported back. At his command, a woman had ventured into the unknown. Not for the first time, Fell realized that devotion to a cause or ideal was a powerful thing.

Happily, it turned out alright. Minutes later the woman returned, speaking excitedly. She had lost sight of the tribe at the same time they lost sight of her. The sky and surroundings had disappeared as well. The only things she could see were the starlight bridge and a grey mist all around her. She had looked over the railing, but it was the same slate-colored nothingness. She could see the bridge stretching for only about a hundred yards in either direction.

Whatever the bridge was, it was their way forward. The other choice was failing the quest. That wasn't acceptable. Wasting no more time, and acutely aware of their dwindling resources, Fell had the tribe move out. Midnight Dust took point, hopefully able to see any dangers thanks to his *Keen Eye* ability. Soon they were all surrounded by the grey.

The tribe walked for what felt like an hour. During that time, nothing changed as far as Zero could tell. They kept marching on, but except for their feet moving forward, there was no way to gauge their passage. The grey enveloping them was a featureless expanse and no landmarks presented themselves. Even the razin's curiosity was dampened by the austere surroundings. More than one considered going back the way they'd come, but their devotion to their god kept them going. They were dedicated believers.

Their faith was rewarded minutes later. As they had walked, the bridge had formed in front of them at the same speed that it had disappeared behind. All of a sudden, a large doorway appeared out of the grey. Beyond it was a hub of sorts. The tribe walked forward onto a pentagram-shaped platform. It was comprised of the same crystal as the bridge, but there were no stars this time. It was completely clear. More than one razin staggered, feeling like there were standing on nothing at all, but the ground was firm and stable. Around them was no longer featureless grey. Instead, they stood under a blue sky with the sun beaming bright overhead.

Surrounding them on all sides was a green ocean, much darker than the waters they'd seen before leaving land. If things worked the same on this new world as on Earth, the color change indicated that the waters could be miles deep. The platform stood on one thick pillar of crystal, rising several stories above the ocean. The hub was about a quarter mile at the widest, and the five sides were equal in length.

The razin walked off the bridge they'd been on, looking around in fascination. There were four other bridges leading off the platform, one for each of the pentagon's sides. Fell looked back the way they had come. Just like when they had started their journey, the bridge grew more insubstantial the farther it extended out from the hub, until it disappeared.

No matter which direction he stared, he couldn't see anything but endless water. At the speed they had been walking, the peninsula should have been easy to see. The fact that he couldn't confirm that this bridge either greatly increased their speed or operated like some type of wormhole disturbed him.

Prompts had appeared as soon as they reached the hub.

> You have reached a **Crossroads** of the **Great Bridge of Serathia!** This is a nexus of the many paths that comprise this Wonder of the World.
>
> All who reach a Crossroads must reside there for a period of no less than one hour.
>
> At that time, the other pathways may be unlocked.
>
> Be Warned! Choosing the wrong path will lead to certain death!

That was the second time the term "certain death" had appeared in relation to the bridge. Now at least he understood how a bridge could have more than one destination. The various exits from the platform were going to require scrutiny.

Each of the egresses had an archway composed of star crystal. Fell tried to place a hand through the arch he'd just come through, only to be stopped by an invisible barrier. Even though people were still walking out of the passage, no one could go back. In fact, several of the razin walked to the edge of the pentagon and encountered the same wall. Thankfully, no one could fall off. With the way back blocked, Zero immediately feared a trap, but there was nothing and no one else on the platform. By all appearances they were safe. Testing the other portals brought the same result. All they could do was wait.

For him, choosing a path wasn't difficult. Fell was clearly being pulled toward a gateway two doors to his left. While the one-hour cooldown was elapsing, he examined each of the five arches. They were all the same, except for a glowing symbol at the apex. One outlined a tortoise, another a lion's head, the third a fish, the fourth a heron, and the one they had just come from was a bat. The portal he was being pulled toward was the fish.

The hour passed and the force fields disappeared. Fell led his people down the indicated pathway. Once again, they were in a grey mist tunnel. After a period of time, they came to another Crossroads, this one with seven sides and exits. Each arch was identified by a red jewel cut into a different shape. After the required hour-long wait, he led them down the path with the jewel cut into a heptagon.

The pattern repeated two more times, the only variation in the Crossroads being the number of archways and the way they were marked. There was one other large difference though. While they were surrounded by ocean each time, the position of the sun changed drastically. The second time it looked like it was 5pm, while the third was just after dawn and the fourth was at night. However the bridge worked; it wasn't just a straight line. Without his internal compass, there was no way he could have figured out the correct way to go.

Fell made sure to remember the markings to go back the way they had come. If the pathways were secrets, then he'd just be granted powerful knowledge. When they reached the fifth platform, the tribe finally saw something different than an endless expanse of ocean. One and all, they were immensely grateful for the invisible shielding. They were still suspended over an ocean, but above them raged a hurricane.

Streaks of lightning, miles long, sparked in the sky every few seconds. Never before on Earth had there been such a storm. The winds whistling by the Crossroads were so loud that it was almost an attack. Jagged hailstones the size of Fell's chest shattered against the dome. As they watched, everything turned blinding white with a massive flash of lightning. Snakes of electricity crawled across the force field before traveling down the central pillar and diffusing into the ocean. Thunder nearly deafened them, so strong the platform reverberated. Everyone knew that if they were exposed to this weather, only death waited.

They waited out the storm for the hour. The razin huddled together while several of the eaglebear cubs whined in fear. Only Fell stood by himself. He stared up at the natural fury with a delighted smile on his face. He had always loved storms. Being so close to such power could only be described in one way so far as he was concerned: true beauty.

When the doorways opened, they moved on to the next nexus of paths. Three hours later they came to another Crossroads that changed their perceptions of the world forever. It was then that the razin discovered that the dome protected them from more than just weather.

The tribe had been waiting fifteen minutes, when Dust noticed a disturbance in the ocean. Seconds later, everyone had their face pressed against "the glass" of the invisible barrier. What followed the strange ripples in the water strained Fell's ability to reason.

He'd seen the downfall of civilization on Earth. He'd seen monsters eat babies. Since coming to Telos, he'd found proof of the soul, been accepted as a god, and had seen a giant that was several stories tall. That "giant" would be nothing more than an ant compared to what he was seeing now.

A creature that was as large a mountain rose from the ocean. It towered higher than the tallest tree, higher than skyscrapers. Its head was the size of a small village. Five arms extended from either side of its body, and a single baleful eye rested in the center of its head. Its mouth was a mass of tentacles.

Waterfalls the size of buildings sluiced off its rising body. While everyone, Fell included, froze from a very real *Terrified* debuff, it reached a three-fingered hand toward the Crossroads. The hub was a quarter mile across just like the first, but the massive creature would be able to palm it like a basketball. Its bulk blocked out the sun and bathed the tower they stood upon in shadow.

Fell tried to move, even just a finger, but the debuff locked him into place. He hadn't felt so helpless since he was a child. When he'd read the warning of certain death, he'd thought the prompt was hyperbole. He didn't believe in no-win scenarios. In the shadow of this colossus, however, where its mere presence robbed him of his free will, he understood that there were beings that simply could not be resisted with his current level of power.

The massive hand grew ever closer. It had very nearly closed around the Crossroads when a bolt of orange lightning shot from the bridge toward the monster. It severed one of the reaching fingers free from the behemoth. The howl of rage that followed deafened every member of the tribe. The colossus fixed its one eye on the platform with a furious gaze.

Fell was sure it was staring right at him, but to be fair, everyone on the platform felt that way. Unwilling to test the Wonder's defenses again, it slowly slid back into the sea. It took minutes for it to disappear. Afterward, only their scarred psyches remained as proof of its presence. The gentle waves of the ocean lapped beneath them as if nothing had happened.

It took another few minutes for the *Terrified* debuff to wear off. Fell broke free first, followed by his acolytes. After that the tribe members came out of it in starts and stops. It didn't escape the god's notice that those with a higher energy value were able to clear their minds first. For Fell, as soon as the terror left, it was replaced with anger. It made him furious that he'd been so helpless.

Zero had always viewed fear as something to accept and overcome. There was no shame in it, there was only shame in it controlling you. What he had just experienced was different from anything he'd ever lived though. It was like being tied with real, physical chains, unable to move, barely able to breathe. And the effect hadn't only been physical, it had been mental and emotional. He'd barely been able to think. All he could do was feel.

Now that he was free of it, his fury surged. After a lifetime of life-and-death choices, of killing and situations that made other men weep, this was the first time he'd felt so helpless. For a man who held to one central tenet, that he could do anything, having his free will stolen was a violation. The experience engraved a new core principle upon the walls of his heart.

"I need power," he resolved, and he would do anything to get it.

The tribe remained quiet for the rest of the hour, unconsciously fearful that any noise might bring the colossus back. When the portals unlocked, they followed Fell quietly. For once, their excitement and ardor were depleted.

They took twenty more Crossroads before leaving the Great Bridge of Serathia. Sometimes when they exited a tunnel it was day. Other times, it was night. They had to sleep several times. Based on food consumption and the need to rest, Fell estimated that they traveled along the Wonder for about three days. Tensions were high, made worse by the fact that they'd been on half rations. When they exited the final grey tunnel, they were greeted with heavy humidity, thick-leafed trees, and a cacophony of life. It was a jungle.

As Fell's foot touched new land, a host of notifications appeared in his view.

CHAPTER 36

The bridge ended on the bank of a small stream. The ground was overgrown with underbrush, and vines as thick as Fell's wrist crisscrossed the trees. The tribe refilled their waterskins, and the god took stock. The pull inside him was stronger than ever, but he still didn't know how much farther they had to go.

The heat was oppressive, at least one hundred degrees, and the humidity was "Down South Georgia in August" thick, the kind of air you could chew, use as lotion, and maybe even lube if you were desperate enough. Between that, the huge leaves on the trees, and the fact that pool ball-sized mosquitoes found them in no time flat, it was clear that they'd all be having a case of the ol' swamp ass in no time.

The trees were so thick that it was hard to see more than twenty yards in any direction. Similar to the copse of trees on the old continent, the local flora hid the bridge entrance from view. This time probably even more effectively, seeing as how the jungle wasn't just an isolated stand of trees. With water so close by, Fell decided to bivouac for half an hour before traveling in the direction the stream led. It wasn't exactly in line with the "pull," but it would be much easier traveling down the waterway than Crocodile Dundeeing through untouched jungle.

Everyone ate a half ration. No matter what, they'd have to find more food soon. While the tribe rested, Fell went through the prompts he'd gained since leaving the bridge.

Congratulations! Your Chosen tribe has discovered a new continent: Home of the Three Kings!

Continents discovered: **Altidi's Cradle** and **Home of the Three Kings**.

They really had walked to another continent in just a few days. Of course, he knew that the bridge they'd been on was magical, but seeing the results of fast-travel was astounding. They had actually walked who knew how many miles to another continent.

The best he could estimate the distance was using the concepts of curvature and sight lines. Back on Earth, you could typically see about ten miles in every direction while at sea. With their elevated position on the platforms that would have been at least doubled. Of course, these estimations also depended on the size of the planet, but still, they had to have walked hundreds of miles in just days, and a lot of that time had been spent on sleep and waiting on each platform to cool down.

He now knew the name of both continents; even better, traveling to a new land mass had advanced his tribe once again.

Discovering a new Zone is a notable Discovery!

By doing so you have honored one of your tribe's Characteristics: **Curiosity**

For finding a **Minor Location**, your tribe has gained **100 Characteristic Points**!

Your tribe's **Curiosity** has progressed from **level 4** to **level 5**. 1,100/1,600 to level 6

Chance to find notable locations increased from **+25%** to **+30%**

Research bonus increased from **+25%** to **+30%**

+156 (base +125) Devotion Points

Total Devotion of the Razin tribe: +1005

The boost in Characteristic Points strengthened the tribe's Devotion again. This time it was enough to reach the next rank! Right after that, he heard the small cymbals ringing together again.

Cling! Cling!

The Devotion of your Chosen people has increased from rank 3, **Dedicated Believer (+500)** to rank 4, **Faithful to my God (+1000)**

"We have faith in our god."

Devotion Rank 4 Rewards

1) Faith Points generated increased from **+10** to **+15** FP/worshipper/day

2) 1 FREE Clergy creation Token (Single use item)

3) 4 Total Clergy Slots

4) +25% to max summoned population (Each successive Devotion rank achieved by your tribe as a whole will increase this by 25%. Max bonus 100%)

The rewards didn't disappoint. The amount of Faith each of his Chosen generated was increased by 50%. He also got another Clergy Creation Token and increased the max number of acolytes by one.

The final bonus, an increase to summoned population, was a bit of a mystery. There had been references to summoning before that he didn't understand. Now he knew there was a cap on that. He'd have to wait to understand more.

More benefits came with the next prompt. Back on Earth, a wise man had once told Fell that people only cared about was who did it first and who did it recently. Primacy and recency. It looked like the world of Telos valued the same.

For being the first tribe to discover a new Zone on Telos, every member of your tribe gains **+5,000 XP!**

Fell could barely believe it. Not just because it was a massive amount of experience, but because it affected every single one of his followers. The prompt made it clear it was a one-time bonus. Finding future continents wouldn't yield the same, but for now the survival chances of his people had just shot up!

One of his clergy was thinking the same thing.

**

Midnight Dust stared at his god in wonder. He'd lived twenty years in his first world before being brought here. Even growing up, life had been harsh. Death was an everyday threat. Fell had yet to learn this about his new people, but one reason they had adapted so well to this new world was that danger had been common on their old one.

At least now they had a chance to growing stronger. For the first time, Dust had real power. He could heal with a touch. Even more than that, Attribute Points made it possible to strengthen his body quickly, like the stories the elders used to tell around the night fires. There was also the possibility of cultivation.

He didn't understand it, but his god had encouraged all of the clergy to do it as much as possible. Lord Fell had promised it would unlock even greater power. All of this was because of the god standing before him. He'd heard of gods in his past life, but he'd never really believed. Now, he felt a connection to his deity that filled the emptiness inside him. The truth of Fell's divinity couldn't be denied.

Having gained another level, he set about distributing his points.

TRING!

You have reached level **2**! By following the teachings of your god Zero Fell, you have advanced in power! You are an **Uncommon** soul and will be awarded accordingly.

Attribute Points	+2 to Agility and +1 Dexterity +2 Free Attribute Points
Bonus Energy Slots	+10
Class Points	+25

He dealt with his Class Points first. There was no question what he and Sharp Leaf would spend their points on. They both bought the *Soul Strike* Chant. It exhausted his CPs, but now he could strike down the enemies of his god!

That done, he focused on his Attributes. For him, it wasn't a difficult decision. Dust placed both points into Agility, just as he had done with all his previous free points. He'd always been more flexible and light of foot than other members of the tribe. Upon arriving in Telos, he'd found that most of the tribe had a value of thirteen or fourteen. His had been seventeen. That was why after investing these two points, he was given a wonderful surprise.

Know This! One of your Primary Attributes has reached **25**!

You may make this your **Main Attribute** if you wish. Main Attributes provide extra bonuses, but you may only select one.

Do you wish to make **Agility** your **Main Attribute**? Yes or No?

Not even needing to think about it, Dust chose "Yes."

Congratulations! **Agility** is now your **Main Attribute** and by having a value of 25 it has reached its **1ˢᵗ Threshold**! You will randomly be awarded your 1ˢᵗ Benefit.

There are a number of Benefits associated with attributes, and two beings with the same Main Attribute have no guarantee of obtaining the same one.

The rank of 1ˢᵗ Threshold Benefits for a soul in the Mortal ranks ranges between *common* and *limited.*

A sound like dice rattling in a cup sounded in Midnight Dust's head before a rich blue prompt appeared.

412

A small vortex of wind surrounded Midnight Dust in that moment. It barely ruffled the grass, so tight was the effect. Before anyone else could notice, the wind sank into his body. To Dust, who already felt limber as a gymnast, it felt like he could literally run like the wind. With barely any effort he performed a backflip, to the applause of the other razin. When he straightened back up, a childish grin was on his face.

***

Fell looked at Midnight Dust with amusement. The acolyte wasn't the only one celebrating, but Dust was normally bashful and quiet. Seeing him so happy reminded the god of how much he had to learn about his new people. They had been traveling together for more than a week, but it felt longer. Of course, that might be because he was basically only a week old.

He resolved to get to know all of them better. For now, he just celebrated the windfall. Just like that, the entire tribe had advanced a level! The acolytes all had reached level two, and the rest of the razin had jumped to level one. Fell was immediately inundated with cheers from the tribe and bombarded with questions about what these points meant and what they should do with them.

The razin started hopping from foot to foot, enjoying the boost to their Dexterity and Agility. At their low levels, the two points that went into each constituted a 10-20% improvement. He advised every member of the tribe to place half of their free points into Constitution, earning everyone at least ten more HP. He informed them about the perks of having a Main Attribute, but told them to distribute their remaining points as they saw fit. After days traveling with the tribe, he'd come to understand that the razin weren't dumb. They just had such a love of discovery that they would sometimes do something reckless in the name of exploration.

While the boost to his people was great, it didn't feel nearly as good as hearing the sweetest of sounds!

TRING!	
You have reached **Level 3**! The power of a god is potentially without limit, but it must be grown. Your soul rank is the equivalent of **Limited**. Never forget, there are many forms of power and this is only one.	
Attribute Points	+2 to Agility and Dexterity per level +2 Free Attribute Points

Bonus Energy Slots	+20
Class Points	+30

The decision of where to put his free points was even easier this time. The second bonus from his spirit animal had increased his health and stamina by 50 points. He poured his points into Luck again, bringing him that much closer to the goal of 75 Luck and hopefully another powerful bonus.

The god pulled up his abbreviated stat sheet.

ZERO FELL	
Art: Soul	**Level:** 3
Energy: 418/668	**Cultivation:** Spirit Made Flesh (Tier 0) **Progress:** 9/100

STATS		
Health: 160	**Mana:** 120 *Regen/min: 7.2*	**Stamina:** 148/150 *Regen/min: 6*

ATTRIBUTES		
Strength: 8	**Agility:** 19	**Dexterity:** 19
Constitution: 11	**Endurance:** 10	**Intelligence:** 12
Wisdom: 12	**Charisma:** 11	**Luck:** 68 (34) (Leap of Faith: +100%)

He'd used up the majority of his Energy, but his other numbers were far better than when he'd first landed on Telos. His health was almost twice as high and his stamina had improved by 50%. His Agility and Dexterity were both increased by about 25%. There was no denying that he was faster and more flexible now. Of course nothing had changed as much as his Luck, but that didn't make him feel any different.

Closing his stat sheet, he found there was one more bonus to having found a new continent. While his people continued to celebrate, he looked at the last prompts.

For your act of discovery, your Chosen people have earned a *common* Tribal Title: **Explorers I**

Individual tribesmen can gain XP for discovering notable locations.

+10% Movement Speed of every member in the tribe.

Unlike Personal Titles, the Energy cost for Tribal Titles is only paid for by the leader of a civilization, in this case, their deity.

Equipping **Explorers I** will occupy 150 Energy Slots.

Know This! Tribal Titles can be adopted in addition to personal Titles.

Tribal Titles must, however, be assigned by the highest authority of the tribe and will apply to all members. Currently, only one Tribal Title can be activated at a time.

Do you wish to accept the Tribal Title **Explorers I** at this time? Yes or No?

The tribe had earned a Title, like his own *Infuriating Enemy* but on a macro scale. Unlike his title, *Explorers* could affect all his Chosen at once. The titles could even both work at the same time.

The obvious downside was that it would cost him another 150 Energy Slots. Fell still had several hundred slots free, however, especially now that he had used all his souls. The benefits of every single one of his tribe being able to move faster could be massive. He selected "Yes."

After that, he kept watch through the night. With the rising of the sun, he shouted, "Let's move out!"

The jungle growth was so thick that even following the stream was difficult. Without the waterway it might have been nearly impossible. They all immediately noticed the boost to their movement speed, however, which kept their spirits up. It wasn't that they had to push themselves harder, it was just easier to walk and their steps had a bit more spring in them.

The tribe followed the waterway until dusk. With the trees surrounding them the darkness should have been complete, but as the last rays of sunlight faded away, plants began to glow, a form of bioluminescence. It wasn't enough to navigate unknown terrain by, but it was better than torches.

They stopped for the night and the razin consumed their second-to-last half-ration. Fell saw more than one tribe member cast unhappy glances at him, but far fewer than had confronted him the last time. He had to assume that was due to the increase in Devotion. Devoted or not, it couldn't quiet a few grumbles.

His Chosen were all impressed by his power. He had also leveled them and honored their tribal Characteristics, increasing their

Devotion even more. Even the most stalwart believer would find their faith challenged, however, when they began to starve.

The acolytes showed their worth again. Led by Autumn Ghost, they spoke to each of the tribe, encouraging them and reinforcing their faith. Fell didn't see a prompt appear for it, but it was clear he'd found a hidden benefit to having clergy around. Their words had a noticeable effect and the grumbles faded away. Overall, the tribe stared at their god with confidence.

Thankfully, they made it through the night without an attack. After some sleep, they got on the move again. They followed the stream bed for another hour, until the pulling led Fell into the jungle. The way grew much harder, their copper blades barely able to cut through the undergrowth, but they didn't falter.

Fell led the way, with his clergy behind him. The entire time, bugs and heat made the trip unpleasant, but everyone picked up on their god's enthusiasm. He was starting to feel that their new home could be just around the corner. Still, those who had weapons kept them close at hand. It had been a miracle that they made it through another night without an attack, but no one expected their luck to hold forever.

With every step, the pull inside him grew stronger. It seemed almost frantic now. Traveling through the jungle was difficult, but the tribe was infected by Fell's excitement. With their god leading the way, their steps did not falter. They pushed through the trees, surrounded by bugs and the hooting calls of animals, until hours later, with hunger gnawing at their stomachs, they crossed into a small clearing. And then, at long last, they saw it.

In front of them was a grassy meadow. A cool breeze blew across everyone, eliciting sighs of relief. The field ended in a small hill whose backdrop was the ocean. It had been hard to smell the scent of the sea over the lush flora, but for the past hour Fell had been sure they were getting closer to a coast. It turned out that he was right and he was wrong. They weren't approaching just one coast; they were approaching two.

The meadow and the hill were bordered on the east and south by water. The east was higher in elevation, meaning the ocean ended against a set of sea cliffs. To the south, the land sloped down to a beach. As they walked through the meadow, they were able to see that while the eastern ocean was endless water, the southern direction hosted many small islands. A few were little more than rocky spikes, several yards across with lush plants growing from cracks and crannies. In the distance Fell could see larger islands though, some big enough to hold a settlement.

The north and west were bordered by jungle. Another stream ran along the northern border of the meadow. It traced through the meadow before cascading down the eastern sea cliffs. Now that the tribe was out in the open and climbing the hill, they could see isolated mountains popping up randomly above the canopy. Based on the direction, it appeared the stream was probably runoff from a small mountain several miles away.

Fell looked around, and could not fault his sponsors' judgement. This really was a great spot for a burgeoning village. The ocean offered an ample source of food. The jungle would supply plenty of building resources. Fresh water was close by and copious. For defense, unless Telos had the equivalent of Vikings, the coasts offered natural barriers, and the thick jungle would make it hard for large armies to travel quickly. It was isolated but with plenty of room to grow.

There was a great deal to take in, but everything else paled in comparison to what the tribe found after climbing the large hill. The top of the rise was flat, and it was littered with the remains of a black stone temple. Irregular lumps in the terrain showed how the grass had grown over some of the ruins, but a large portion of the structure still stood.

Before Zero Fell could investigate the temple any further, the tribe clustered around him. Autumn Ghost stared into his eyes with excitement on her face. Her auburn-furred ears quivered with emotion as she asked, "Is this truly to be our new home, my lord?"

Fell looked around again. At the clear space, perfect for building. The jungle and oceans, both filled with life to feed his people. There was also the fact that they'd been led here by his sponsor, so all the boxes seemed to be checked. He looked back at his head acolyte with a smile and told her, "It is."

Cheers filled the air, and a prompt appeared in Zero's vision.

CHAPTER 37

Prayer Quest Update: **Save Us III**

It appears you have selected a location for your Chosen people's first settlement. You must know that there are serious implications to this decision.

The current freedom you have enjoyed will come to an end. While gods are some of the most powerful beings in existence, their fates are bound closely to their followers. This is both their greatest strength and their greatest weakness.

Upon founding a settlement, you will be bound to the land. Unless special conditions are met, a bound god will only be able to physically manifest inside their domain.

Choosing a location for your settlement will provide a hexagonal domain that is 1 mile to a side.

> Fear not; increasing the size of your domain will also increase the area you can travel in. There are many ways to accomplish this. It is up to you to discover them.
>
> Knowing this, if you wish to found your first settlement, place your hand on the ground and exert your will.

Fell read the prompt and had to resist the urge to curse. He was about to be bound to one area like a goddamned criminal? Seriously? WTF?!

What. The. Fuck!

His sponsors had given him warnings and gifts, and had even taken the time to threaten him, but they couldn't tell him he was going to be trapped like some kind of goddamn queen bee? What the fuck!

Fell seethed quietly, and everyone saw the fury on his face. The tribe backed up, never before having seen their normally even-keeled god lose his reserve. Even Autumn Ghost backed away, not understanding what had just happened. Seeing the tribe so scared, he closed his eyes and took a deep breath. After making up something about a cosmic message, he told everyone to explore while he calmed himself down.

His immediate anger was because he hated being forced to do something almost as much as he hated being discounted or manipulated. The fact that he was about to be forced to stay in an area that was only a couple square miles was crap. That he hadn't been told by his sponsors beforehand was even worse. It reeked of manipulation. He took another deep breath. What was, was.

He absolutely didn't love the idea of being tied to one spot, but it also reinforced a theme he had already noticed. The rules of this new world seemed designed to create a symbiotic bond between him and his people, between a god and his worshippers. He'd already seen it in their faith production. Now it seemed that codependency would be taken to an even greater extreme. He would have to rely upon his people to explore this new world, and they would have to rely on him for the strength to survive while they did it.

His anger started coming under control. He read the prompt again. One thing that was clear was that he could increase the size of his domain, though he wasn't sure how yet. Maybe it wouldn't be as bad as he'd initially thought. Fell had thought his role would be as an adventurer, leading his people into battle. Now it seemed he would fill the role of a god-king, directing his people to grow from afar.

Emotions mastered, he looked around. If he really was about to stuck in one place, he needed to choose the right location. As soon as he thought that, something crazy happened. A light-green glow appeared, superimposed over the ground. Looking south, he saw it cut off over the water. He saw the same thing looking over the eastern ocean. The light disappeared into the trees to the north and west. He knew without being told that he was looking at the hexagonal domain he could claim.

So far as he could see, he was already in about the middle. It reached the beach to the south as well as a few small island spits, and it also included the jungle. It easily encompassed the entire meadow and the ruined temple.

He might be mad as hell at learning this latest reality of his new life, but he was still the same man he'd always been. When there was a decision to be made, he didn't wring his hands and hesitate. He got down to business. Fell slammed one hand down on the ground and exerted his will.

Congratulations! You have completed the Prayer Quest Update: **Save Us III**

You have founded your first **Settlement!**

You are now bound to this location.

Gods of Telos may only freely move within the domain of their religious influence. Discover ways to extend your domain, or make new domains, in order to increase your ability to explore your new world.

The rewards for finishing this quest are as follows:

5,000 Faith Points. Total Faith Points: 8,760

2,500 Experience Points

125 Devotion Points (base 100) for the Razin tribe

A new Quest: **Altar of Power**

> Congratulations! You have completed the Quest: **Last Wish III**
>
> You have founded a settlement and more than 50% of the Eaglebear's Cubs have survived.
>
> The rewards for finishing this quest are as follows:
>
> Permanent bonding of the Divine Eaglebear Bloodline to the service of you and your Chosen tribe.

He'd just finished two quests at once! The second didn't change much, but the rewards for *Save Us III* were all helpful. They weren't the largest he'd obtained, but each got him closer to another threshold.

When he closed that window, the next showed he'd gained another quest!

> You have been offered a Quest: **Altar of Power**
>
> You have founded a Settlement! This land is now yours as long as you can defend it. You are only half-finished, however. A Settlement is a hex of land. You must also form a religious Domain and claim the hex for your faith!
>
> Creating a Domain will unlock the tools of your divinity, but to do so you must possess an Altar. Without it, a god is merely a bird without wings.

Know This! Each deity is given this quest upon founding their Domain. The details of how the temple is constructed varies from god to god and race to race, but the focal point remains the same. You must create an Altar by using your Divine Powers.

250 points of Divine Energy must be invested to make an Altar.

In addition to the Divine Energy, a series of materials may be collected to provide bonuses to your Altar.

If it takes you more than **30 days** to construct your temple and Altar, your people will experience a 50-point drop in Devotion per day.

Success Conditions: Own an Altar

Rewards: Form a religious Domain

Penalty for failure of Quest: Loss of Devotion from your people.

This Quest cannot be refused!

Time until beginning of Devotion loss: 30 days, 0 hours, 0 minutes, 0 seconds

Fell breathed out heavily. 250 points of Divine Energy? Divine Energy was another name for the units of power he could create with faith. The same units of power that he'd only been able to make nine of over the past few days. Now he had to make hundreds?

Worse than that, he had to do it in thirty days. Admittedly, he hadn't given it his all before. Even at night, while the tribe was sleeping, he'd been looking out for danger. If he focused solely on cultivating, he could probably weave the strands of faith together faster. Could he do it at a pace of more than eight points of Divine Energy a day? It would also cost at least twenty-five hundred Faith Points, even without any failures, which wasn't going to happen. If he didn't improve his success rate, it would cost more than five thousand. Not to mention that he was averaging two hours per success. If he didn't improve his success rate then just accumulating the points would take more than a month!

A horrible thought occurred to him. Every god got this quest. And he'd been on this new world for nine days. He was behind!

He'd hoped to explore his new domain, maybe help his people settle in this new place. With needing to weave so much faith though, he wouldn't have time for anything else! Fell exhaled in irritation. He also wouldn't be able to replace his lost cultivation, not with funneling all his Divine Points into creating an altar. Though the feeling had been short-lived, he missed having a stronger State of Being. It was something that mere leveling could not replace.

Fell mastered himself. It was just one more thing that must be endured. Surviving unfortunate circumstances was something he had gotten used to, and had even come to excel at... until he'd died. But that was in the past. He pulled up the next prompt, and his stoic expression shattered into an evil smile. Until this very moment, he still hadn't understood just how good his sponsor was at cheating.

> Know This! An abandoned **Altar** has been discovered within your domain. If you wish to claim this Altar, you must place your hand upon it.

"Haha, yeah! Fuck those other guys!" Autumn looked at him in profound confusion, but he just waved her away. How could he explain that shit talking was great even if your opponents never heard you do it?

The last piece of the puzzle had fallen into place. The gifts his sponsor had given him had all been about keeping him alive and giving him an edge over his competition. If that was true though, why would they have had him walk across two continents before starting a quest that hundreds of thousands of other gods were racing to complete?

The days of travel hadn't only cost him time. He'd also lost followers, which meant he'd lost faith production. If the altar offered as much power as the quest hinted at, then he was in an arms race of sorts. He knew enough about military history to know that the losers of those races were never the ones who wrote those histories.

While it was true that the geography here was good, it wasn't much better than some of the other locations they had passed. Now though, he had a strong suspicion that the quest, the losses and the countless miles of travel had all been about claiming a hidden reward, the Altar! Rather than being ten days behind the unknown number of gods out there, he was twenty days ahead!

While he'd been reading his prompts, he'd still been walking around. Obviously, he'd been in a rush to finish his first quest, *Ruined*

Temple. He especially wanted to avoid the consequences of failure. Looking at the dilapidated building, however, he just heard General Ackbar, "It's a trap!" In every game, movie, or book he'd ever read, the lost temple just had to have a bunch of bad things waiting to jump out and kill him. That was why he didn't rush over even now. Instead, he gave orders.

First, he made sure that the eaglebear cubs were corralled. The monster babies had already started wandering around and wrestling with each other. Next, he ordered everyone to stay away from the border of the jungle. They would definitely need wood later, but after so many deadly experiences, he didn't want anyone approaching the tree line without the support of him and his clerics. Barring his clergy, everyone else was ordered to start making a defensive perimeter. After days of travel, they all knew what that meant, and they started digging a trench.

After everyone started working, Fell and his clerics walked toward the temple, ready to finish the quest and claim their destiny.

CHAPTER 38

Fell stalked forward, a copper short sword in his hand. A random hooting from the jungle made him freeze. His head darted to the left, his expression cold and ready. The noise repeated and he realized it was a bird call. That knowledge wasn't exactly reassuring, not when the birds in this world could swoop down and carry away a full-grown man. His eyes kept scanning the tree line until Autumn Ghost asked, "My lord?"

"Don't worry," he replied nonchalantly, giving the trees one more scan, "Let's get moving."

The four of them walked toward the temple, and Fell examined it while they did. The structure was made of reflective black stone. The midnight-black blocks tightly fit together in the two walls still standing. Whatever civilization had made the temple had made it to last. Fell tried to scratch the stone with the tip of his copper short sword. Other than an annoying screeching sound, there was no effect at all. Not even a faint groove was left behind. Which raised the question of just how the temple had been destroyed. How powerful would a force have to be to collapse a building made of this stuff?

Even more poignant than seeing the stone shattered was seeing how in some places it had been melted and frozen like candle wax. There weren't that many weapons back on Earth that burned hot enough to make stone melt and run. Even the fact that something had flung stones across the meadow didn't speak to that level of power. Fell's jaw tightened, but he didn't stop walking.

As soon as they set foot inside of the ruined structure, there was a rush of motion. Sharp Leaf and Midnight Dust took point. They rushed forward, weapons raised, chants hanging off their tongues. Again, there was nothing to fear. Something that looked like a hairless possum ran out from behind a piece of free stone. It scampered quick as a squirrel out of the building, running for the safety of the jungle as fast as it could.

"Dammit," Midnight Dust said under his breath. Fell looked at him in agreement and nodded his head.

"Should we go kill it?" Sharp Leaf asked. Autumn Ghost just rolled her eyes in response.

Fell ignored the question and kept walking forward. Whatever calamity had befallen the temple, one item remained unscathed. Near one of the remaining walls stood the altar. It was rectangular, three feet by four by five. Each corner had a stylized figure carved in such a way that it looked like they were holding the top of the altar on their backs. Even though a great deal of time must have passed since the altar had last been in use, the statues looked like they had been carved yesterday.

Even back on Earth, with its advanced technology, Fell would have been hard-pressed to find carvings with such fine detail. He was able to see the expressions of sadness and lost hope on the face of each of the figures. For the first time, he started to wonder what kind of being had owned this altar before he had.

Were they a "deity" like him, whatever that meant? Or were they something else? While the four figures holding up the altar top looked forlorn, there was another face, carved into the top of the altar. That head was horned, snarling and had many sharp teeth. It was just a guess, but it looked like a monster... or a demon.

As Fell continued to examine the altar, he also realized something very strange. The figures carved into the corners weren't holding the altar up. In fact, three of them had fingers curled over the top. Looking closer, his suspicion was confirmed. The statues weren't carved to support the top. Six sets of fingers were grasping the lid firmly, as if to ensure that it could never be removed. The fourth figure's hands were open and his reptilian face was full of fear.

None of this boded well for what was about to happen. Still, nothing had jumped out at him, and it was a beautiful day. His clergy had his back, and he had a quest to finish. Despite the creepy details, Fell reached out a hand and placed it on the altar.

Little did he know that the power he was about to unleash was not only a new beginning for him, but also the ending of a millennia-old battle.

CHAPTER 39

As soon as Fell's hand touched the altar, time froze. All sound vanished. He tried pulling his hand free, but found that he couldn't move at all. Before he could even try to shout, his vision shut off as effectively as his hearing, and everything blinked black. His heart thudded in his chest, and for long seconds, darkness and silence were all he knew.

Slowly, that began to change. He wasn't sure if it took a minute or an hour. There was no frame of reference. Over time, he realized he could see again though. Just blurry images at first, but then shapes began to resolve. It wasn't that a new source of light had appeared, it felt more like his eyes were acclimating to a light that had always been there.

He looked up and was struck by how beautiful the sky was. Several moons were in view, each a different color and in a different phase. He tried to open his mouth to speak, which was when he realized he couldn't. He wasn't frozen any more. He wasn't anything. With a faint sense of panic, Zero realized he didn't actually have a body. He was just a consciousness and a viewpoint.

Before Fell could ponder that further, a cry of pain tore through the night. Then another sounded but from a deeper voice. Besides the sky he couldn't see anything, but by focusing on the sound he found his viewpoint could change. His consciousness flew through the tall grasses surrounding him. In seconds, the godling was hovering above a familiar sight.

An endless jungle sprawled behind him. To the left and in front of him were coastlines. It was the same spot his tribe had just found but with some notable differences. Namely, the temple wasn't a ruin. It was a massive structure, many stories tall.

In front of it stood a creature of nightmares. Similar to the stylized monster carved into the top of the altar, Fell looked upon a demon that stood twenty feet tall. Serrated horns formed a crown upon his head and large muscles stood out in stark relief. His flesh was a nearly black red and four purple-feathered wings extended from his back. An agile tongue danced outside of his leering mouth as he looked at four endless lines of prisoners stretching off into the distance.

Row upon row of captured humanoid figures were being forced toward the temple. Some screamed, some moaned, but many just shuffled forward, glassy-eyed and resigned to their fate. Figures in black armor kept the captives in line. Fell cast his gaze about and realized that there must be thousands of captives. As he continued watching, he saw that the captives were made up of four different races.

One creature was tall and had pointed ears like elves in the movies. Another looked very much like minotaurs had always been described in books: human bodies with bovine heads. The third race was covered in scales and had sharp needle-like teeth, and their gills made it clear they would be at home in the water. The fourth looked like a mix of human and reptile, as if men had evolved from snakes.

No matter the race, they were shackled and shuffling toward a pit. Those at the front were stopped only long enough for white-robed priests to slit their throats and throw them into the large hole. Only the backs of the robes still showed their original color. Their fronts and sleeves were sodden with multicolored blood.

Each person they sacrificed sent a streamer of energy toward the demon standing in front of the temple. Sickly purple light throbbed beneath the monster's skin, growing stronger as it absorbed more death energy. Kneeling and bound before the demon were four figures, one from each of the representative races. As Zero's viewpoint shifted closer, he realized they were the same four figures that were carved into the corners of the altar. They stared defiantly at the demon, but bound as they were, they could do nothing to stop the carnage behind them.

The scene continued, and the new god couldn't do anything but observe. It felt like hours passed and hundreds were slaughtered. Fell was starting to wonder what the purpose of all this was, why touching the altar had triggered this memory, when something new finally happened. A commotion occurred out in the darkness.

Suddenly, four small armies surged into view, each led by a figure outlined in magical light. They rushed the black-armored guards, and a furious battle commenced. The demon's warriors were killed, but not without a price. The ebon-armored figures turned their blades on the bound prisoners, slaying dozens in moments, but even more were set free by the armies converging on the temple. The battle continued and the allied forces continued to liberate their people. Soon even the demon's priests were slain. All that remained were the four kneeling figures and the hellion.

For the first time, Fell heard someone speak, "Are you fools? Do you seek death? You dare challenge the great Asmodeus at the very heart of His power? Kneel!"

So saying, the demon reached out one massive clawed hand. Four tethers of energy shot from his palm to each of the kneeling figures. Fell heard him intone words in another tongue. They were heavy with power, and the sound of the guttural consonants would have sent a shiver up his spine if he'd had a body.

The armies shouted in alarm, trying to rush around the large pit filled with their dead. They ran as fast as they could, pushing their tired bodies to reach the demon before he could finish his fell magic, but it was hopeless. With a snarl, Asmodeus finished the incantation, and the tethers that connected him to each of the four bound prisoners swelled with baleful light. Each magical chain thickened from the size of a finger to the size of a wrist. They were black and writhing, with red swatches of color breaking through like a lava flow.

Each of the bound figures rose five feet into the air. Screams of utter agony issued from their throats. Magical auras of different colors emanated from their bodies and much weaker glows sprung into life around each member of the attacking army. It didn't take Fell more than a moment to realize the color around each soldier corresponded to one of the colors emanating from the bound figures.

Also, the auras seemed to be race-specific. The elvish soldiers and elvish prisoner were outlined in silver. The minotaurs were bathed in reddish-brown, like fresh rust. The fishlike race was surrounded in green energy with purple stripes weaving through it, like underwater plants swaying in a current. The reptiles were silhouetted in ochre.

The wailing cries of the bound figures were echoed almost immediately by the glowing soldiers that led each of the four armies. A tether of energy shot from the captives to several of the soldiers rushing to save them. Like chain lightning, it then spread to more members of the attacking force. With each jump, more tethers of energy appeared. In seconds, 10% of the soldiers were on the ground screaming. Blood poured from their eyes and the spell showed no signs of stopping. The demon continued to speak words of hellish intent. Moments later his incantation was completed, but the spell's effects continued on.

"Worms!" he bellowed, looking out at the armies he had single-handedly laid low. "You dare challenge a Tier 5 Duke of Hell? You are nothing more than scum. You are trash. You are filth! If your gods could not oppose the great Asmodeus, what hope did you have that you could?"

The demon laughed. The sound was horrible and thick with malice. "Enjoy this small taste of pain I am giving you now. Each of you shall burn endlessly in the soul flames of perdition. And in time you shall come to remember this as a sweet caress! Do not think death will free you. The pyres of hell shall burn you for all eternity without ever consuming you. Watch! Watch as the portal to your doom appears!"

As Asmodeus spoke, he unleashed his full aura. Zero felt like it would crush his consciousness into dust. Ever since seeing the colossus on the Great Bridge of Serathia, he'd reflected back on that moment. He had realized that it had exuded a feeling of menace and terror that was palpable. That was why he and the tribe had been so overwhelmed. What Zero felt now was orders of magnitude stronger. If he had been there in person, he would have knelt in supplication, all ability to resist repressed by the sheer horrible majesty of the hell duke.

While every other living thing writhed in agony, the demon began casting again. Whatever the spell was, it seemed to suck all light from the world. Fell could no longer see the armies, he could only see the tethers of hell power and hear their agonized screams. A triangular portal of malevolent energy appeared in the air. It siphoned energy from the demon, the same energy he'd stolen from the sacrifices.

Zero realized that wherever the doorway led, it was why thousands of men, women and children had just been butchered. More death energy flowed into the portal with each soldier's death. The demon's heart thrilled. The armies were the last ingredient he had needed. The fools! Their vain attempt to save their gods had marched them into his trap, and now their deaths would open the way.

Fell didn't know what the demon was thinking. He wouldn't have cared if he did. Not when he could see horrible shapes on the other side of the opening portal. Even the outlines of the monsters were so disturbing that they made the demon look like a fresh-faced maiden. Fell turned away, the power coming through the gateway threatening to destroy his sanity.

He now knew that the bound figures were gods. Not only that, but the demon was a Tier 5 being. Fell could barely wrap his head around that. The single step he'd taken in cultivation had increased his power significantly. His Energy had increased by one hundred points from a single step. How much Energy would a Tier 5 being possess? What terrible powers could a demon command if he filled every Energy slot?

With all the power he had come to possess, Zero was still only a Tier 0 godling. Despite that, he had the capacity to overcome vicious monsters. Fell couldn't even conceive of what it would mean if he reached Tier 1, let alone Tier 5.

Just how powerful was a Tier 5 demon? Fell had no idea, but apparently it was an existence great enough to bend four gods to his will. Not only that, the demon lord was somehow destroying entire armies through their connection to the deities. The hellion was living up to its name. To slaughter people using their own faith… Fell realized that this was a betrayal and a perversion of the greatest magnitude.

Fell continued to watch the scene play out. Asmodeus fed more power into the portal and the hell beasts on the other side started pawing at it. The membrane between dimensions began to stretch and bend. They weren't able to cross the boundary yet, but the shapes on the other side were becoming clearer. Zero watched, powerless to affect events. He still wondered why he was being forced to see this. Based on the fact that the temple was intact, he assumed he was watching a scene from the past.

Other than that, he had to guess. The demon had utterly defeated the armies by using their connection to the captured gods. More than half the soldiers were dead, and the rest continued to writhe and scream on the ground. It could not be long before all of the demon's enemies were drained dry. Zero didn't see any way for the gods to prevail. Asmodeus was thinking the same thing but then something happened that shocked him. There was something strange about seeing surprise on a two-story-tall demon's face.

One of the deities, the elvish goddess, mastered her pain enough to crane her neck and stare at the demon. She remained suspended in the air. Veins stood stark under her skin from the strain she was withstanding. Suddenly the aura of power around her surged, silver light combatting the tether of black-and-red demonic energy. Her people continued to writhe in pain, but Fell could see that the tether leading out of her body was a bit thinner and weaker than before. She screamed in the face of the seven-meter demon, "You shall not have my people!"

Asmodeus was not impressed by her display of strength, "Hmph. You are merely a radiant. Your paltry third-tier power means nothing in the face of my dark majesty. Even burning your cultivation will not save you, and as you lose your tiers you shall become even easier to control. Do you think that you can resist me?" He gestured behind her with a spiked arm, "All who believe in you shall serve me! After I claim their souls, then I shall take your essence as well. You shall die alone!"

Tears flowed down her dirty but perfect face. It was a struggle even to speak, but the goddess managed to defiantly spit out two words.

"Not alone!"

CHAPTER 40

The demon looked confused, but then the other three gods raised their heads as well. The mantles of power surrounding them flared and the demon took a step back in surprise and caution. The black chains holding the gods burned away in response to their surging power. Each aura fought against the demon's energy until they gradually matched it and surpassed it. The tether of black-and-red energy dissipated. The attack on the armies of the faithful ended.

Despite seeing the new strength of the gods, the demon remained undaunted. He knew the poor state the four were in. Asmodeus beckoned with a clawed hand. "Come then," he laughed, his tone sounding like the gurgling of filth. "Come if you think you can challenge a prince of the Red Curse Dynasty!"

He flexed his massive hands and dreadful flames appeared. His right hand held a blaze the color of glowing lava. The left wielded a bonfire as dark as the center of a singularity. The raw power was harnessed in an instant, the fires turning into a glowing red mace and a pitch-black shield.

Instead of immediately attacking, however, the four gods turned toward the armies of their worshippers. No words were spoken aloud, but the eyes of every fighter were trained on their individual god. The glowing figures leading the armies spoke first. Each uttered words in a different language, but they were easily understood by Fell. The exact wording varied but the meaning was the same.

"In this, as in all things, I serve the divine."

"All that I am is yours, my lord god."

"The horns have blown, the bells have rung, take me to Tovock!"

"May I serve you in death, even as I have in life."

After each leader spoke, staring into the eyes of their gods, they took their own lives. Keen edges slashed throats. Sharp blades pierced hearts. Red, green and black blood sprayed into the air as the lives of the four religious leaders drained away. The auras around their figures dimmed, but before they winked out the power in their dying bodies streaked toward their respective deities. The gods' own mantles of power grew stronger.

Like a tragic series of dominoes, the officers of the armies sacrificed themselves. They were followed by every soldier. Entire armies paid the ultimate price for their gods, until the only living beings were immortals. Endless streams of light flowed into the four deities. With each life claimed, the bedraggled appearance of the gods improved. Their auras strengthened until they were each a beacon in the night.

Asmodeus finally lost his composure upon seeing how the willing sacrifices were strengthening his enemies. He bellowed in rage and the ebon shield turned into a four-pronged spear in an instant. He threw it immediately after. Hellfire enveloped the weapon as it flew, the flames eagerly reaching out to incinerate the gods. The four were no longer bound and weakened however. While the demon had thought the armies had fallen into his gambit, in truth, he had fallen into theirs.

In normal circumstances, the gods knew that the hell duke would have been correct. It was pure folly to think that four Tier 3 gods could destroy a hell duke in the seat of his power. Now, however, much of the duke's power had been sacrificed to open the gateway to the demonic realm. By burning their foundations and the lives of their armies, they had bought themselves one chance to defeat him. It came at a horrible cost, but every one of their followers had known they would never see another dawn. They had sacrificed themselves for their gods and the members of their tribes who would survive them.

Now brimming with power, the gods sacrificed their foundations to temporarily boost their State of Being to Tier 4. It would not last long, but it gave them a chance. The deities pooled their power and formed a shield. The hellfire spear struck the shield with a crack like thunder. The weapon exploded and black fire cascaded across the surface of the barrier, eager to consume divine flesh.

The four immortals all grunted and were pushed back. Their feet gouged furrows in the ground, but their defense held. The fires died, and their hands dropped, the shield winking out of existence. Each of them stared murder at the demon, united in a single thought.

My turn.

The elven goddess stepped back, but the other three harnessed their power and attacked. A blast of black lightning shot from the hands of the lizard god, and a wave of fire, white as snow but hotter than

Hades, billowed from the minotaur's mouth. The fish god held both palms forward, and energy that looked like purple water formed a broad shield. While the black and white energies blasted into the demon's body, the shield protected the gods from the demon's counterattack. Even this had been planned by the deities long before that night. They each had a role to play if they were to survive.

The demon bellowed, summoning two spears that were twice as thick as the first one he had thrown. The lava mace in his hand struck at the black lighting, destroying the attack. He could only tank the minotaur god's white fire though, letting it spill over his demonic body. While the heat did little, the holy energy scalded the fiend's skin. That did not stop the duke's retaliation. While the gods' power had increased, it had only brought them to the lower part of the fourth tier. They were still a full tier lower than him. Weakened or not, Asmodeus was not easy prey. All he had to do was wait them out. Burning cultivation would give a surge in power, but it did not last long. Similarly, the energy stolen from their worshippers' sacrifices would fade. Once it did, he would feast on their entrails!

The hell duke threw his two spears, hellfire blazing around them. In response, the gods burned more of their cultivation. That let them oppose the hellion's strength and even surpass it. Lightning and fire attacked both spears in flight, reducing their attack enough for the fish god's water shield to block them. The purple water gushed forward like a geyser, defense turning into attack. The minotaur and lizard deities redoubled their efforts. All three attacks landed at once, blasting the demon. Asmodeus snarled in pain. The duke held his lava weapon out in front, blocking the worst of the attacks but also taking damage. He was forced to take several steps back before he could begin a new incantation.

While gods and demons battled, the elven goddess had cut her own stomach with a blade of pure silver light. Reaching inside her divine body, she removed a small item she'd hidden within her own flesh. To Zero Fell it looked like a circle of silver mesh festooned with multicolored gems. Still bloody, she forced her fingers through holes in the item, interweaving the individual chains like a cat's cradle. Her own aura of godly majesty poured into the artifact, trusting the other gods to hold the demon back.

Time passed, the three male gods fighting against Asmodeus while the elvish goddess cast a long, slow spell. Time was not on their side. Burning their own divinity had given them the power to suppress the hell duke for a time, but that fuel was being spent too quickly. Every minute consumed more than a year of accumulated power, painstakingly cultivated. The power they blazed through had not only required time to accumulate, but also rare and precious materials that could not be easily replaced. Even if they won, it might take centuries for them to reach such heights again.

The demon, on the other hand, had deep reserves of power. Even with a great deal of it invested in the incomplete portal, he had oceans to draw upon. The battle went on, and the auras around the gods began to dim. Their defenses began to fail and hellfire started to burn not just their bodies but their souls as well.

The minotaur's skull leered, exposed to the air, and the other two male gods suffered equally. Only the elf goddess was spared, her allies using their own bodies to protect her. Asmodeus had noticed she was doing something furtive and attacked even harder, but the deities fought back with equal ferocity.

The struggle continued. Despite the strength of their resolve, the three deities were finally forced to abandon all attacks, focusing only on defending themselves and their elven ally. The demon took a step forward, his sharp-toothed leer mocking the gods and his hellfire seeking to consume them. One hand shot a beam of concentrated energy at their shield while his four wings flapped, each beat summoning razor-sharp wind blades to pummel their sides.

"Sagiina!" the fish god yelled. "We cannot last much longer!"

The jewels of the item in the goddess's hands had been lighting up one after another as it absorbed her power. The last finally kindled, and she replied with a sigh of relief, "We need no more. It is ready." Her voice carried profound exhaustion, and her aura had almost disappeared. Fell wasn't sure, but he also thought he heard notes of pure sadness. Still, she stood tall and intoned, "Our time has come."

The battle raging between the demon and the three gods had not been merely to stall the hellion. If that had been the case, the deities could have preserved their strength and only defended from the beginning. It would have been a much wiser use of their fading power. Though they had expended a great deal of energy, their attacks had succeeded in putting the hell duke off balance. The cost for occupying the demon's attention was high, but it had hidden the actions of the elf goddess for precious minutes. By the time Asmodeus noticed, it was too late.

Revealing the Relic, Sagiina threw the silver net over the heads of her fellow gods. As it flew through the air, it expanded in size, from a single foot to ten yards in diameter. The flare of hellfire against the gods' combined defense hid the net until it had crossed half the distance. By the time the hellion saw it, and his demonic face began to twist in appalled realization, there was no escape.

The silver mesh landed on him. It wasn't until it began to twist around his body like a mummy's bandages that his expression turned to fear. As he began to succumb to the item's power, he realized that all of this had been an elaborate trap. The damned deities had a Relic. A Prime Relic!

"No!" Asmodeus bellowed. "Curse you! Where did you find the Prison of Almaphus?"

"Quickly," the minotaur god ordered, ignoring the question. "Take your positions."

The elf goddess and fish god moved to the east and west corners of the silver net. The minotaur stood at the north, but the serpent god hesitated. The minotaur bellowed at him to move, but still the reptilian deity held back. Truth be told, his fear was not unwarranted.

Black-and-red hellfire surrounded the hell duke's body. The demon now burned his own cultivation in a desperate attempt to escape. Never had he thought that the radiants he was using as fuel could ever threaten him. He had not been this vulnerable in nearly ten millennia. With that helplessness came a long-forgotten emotion: fear.

In the face of concentrated Tier 5 power, some of the smaller strands on the silver net had already begun to melt. The Relic possessed nearly unimaginable power, but only nearly. It was also being fueled by pseudo Tier 4 energy. Compared to the demon's enhanced State of Being which had reached the peak of Tier 5, there was no guarantee it could last.

The four gods had not put their hopes in the relic for no reason, however. The Prison of Almaphus was one of the strongest Relics of their age, able to bind any being of any tier. If the elven goddess hadn't paid a terrible price to obtain it, the other three gods would never have agreed to this plan, the world be damned.

The silver net that had originally been no larger than a handbreadth was now large enough to contain the two-story-tall demon. Hundreds of silver chains crisscrossed to bind him, and thousands more were growing before their eyes. The demon's rage had also caused the weakest to snap, however, and the rest were beginning to glow red-orange with heat. Without all four gods feeding their power into the Relic, sooner or later the demon would break free. When that happened, the hell duke's wrath would be horrific.

Even knowing that, the snake god still hesitated. Looking at the other three, he lisped, "You know what this will mean. We will lose nearly all of our power if we use this item." His concern was not idle. He had no idea what price Sagiina had paid to retrieve a Prime Relic, and not just any Prime but a pinnacle item like the Prison of Almaphus, but he did know the cost to use it would be devastating to him and the other gods. It would bind the demon, but it would also consume the very essence of the gods, making them lose almost all of their cultivation. If they were unlucky, it could even fracture their divine cores, turning them into only quasi-immortals. The snake deity's fearful selfishness kept him from making that sacrifice.

Both the fish god and minotaur started to yell at him as he hesitated. The other three gods had started to feed their power into the net, but without him, it was not enough to contain the demon. Even now, Asmodeus was showing signs of breaking free. It was not their threatening yells that reached him, however. It was Sagiina's soft voice.

"We all know what we are going to be sacrificing, Ishstae. You also know that this is the only chance for any of our followers to survive. If Asmodeus breaks free, he will bind us, devour us, and then consume all of our worshippers. At least this way, some may survive." Ishstae's face still looked reluctant, but he moved into position as

Sagiina reminded him, "If even one of our followers survive, so shall we." Her gentle voice soothed his turbulent soul. He nodded at her next words, "It is time."

The snake god looked like he'd tasted something vile, tongue darting in and out of his mouth rapidly, but he moved to the southern part of the silver net. Seeing that all the gods were now in position, Asmodeus screamed in fury. He burned an entire tier of his State of Being all at once. The influx of energy could not even be contained by his body, and gouts of red flame shot out of his arms, legs and torso. He gained three feet of height. Two nodules appeared on his back, struggling to grow into a third set of wings. His eyes glowed bright, like baleful spotlights, and raw demonic power raged around him.

The silver strands popped in quick succession. *Ping, ping, pingpingpingping!*

The entire net glowed neon red and Asmodeus strained with his impressive body. The glow on the net began to turn orange-yellow and all the gods caught their breath. Would the hell duke break through even this? For a long minute, the strands of silver snapped at the same rate that they formed. The gods' veins stood stark under their skin and scales, and their bodies withered, so great was their power loss. Finally, the fiery glow subsided back to a dull red. If Ishstae had not joined the others the demon might have broken free, but with all of them working together, the relic reached Tier 5 power.

The demon still did not give up. He burned even more of his cultivation, trading thousands of years for moments of power. The gods had to give more power to keep him bound. The deities chanted and their auras flared once more. Their faces all grew strained. Minutes passed and the gods' cheeks hollowed. Their visages grew gaunt as if they were starved. The power they were using to bind the demon was literally consuming their bodies.

Cost aside, it was working. The glowing heat of the silver chains faded, replaced by a metallic gleam. The net also continued to grow, more strands appearing and wrapping the demon even tighter. It was obvious to Fell that the gods were succeeding in suppressing Asmodeus.

The demon's power surged several more times, but whatever techniques had been used to forge the Relic, it was able to withstand his hellish power. The captured hellion even began shrinking as he burned his own State of Being. That made it easier for the gods to suppress him. The four continued to feed their power into the net, the demon fighting like a giant fish. More time passed until Asmodeus was fully bound like a mummy. His struggles had weakened considerably, and he was only three meters tall. The gods wasted no time and threw the bundled duke onto the temple's altar.

"Now!" Sagiina shouted. "Begin the final incantation and bind him to the altar!" The silver net could not only bind a powerful being, it could also trap them in an item of sufficient power. Asmodeus had slaughtered thousands to feed his desecrated altar, and had advanced it all the way to *Grand* rank. His own obsession with power had created the very prison that would bind him for eternity.

Fell had watched all of this as a passive observer. He did not understand any of the intricacies of what was occurring but the overall theme was clear. The four gods had trapped the demon, but at the cost of their own power. Despite the sacrifice, it looked like it had worked.

The gods looked exhausted, but the demon's struggles had also very nearly subsided. As Zero watched, the gods hoisted the ensnared demon and placed the cocoon on the altar, never letting go. They began a new chant, each exhausted but speaking in sequence. Their auras began to feed the altar. The ambient power surrounding them was significantly weaker and less colorful than before. They all assumed their sacrifice had paid off and they just needed to finish this final rite. It became apparent, however, that the demon had one more card to play.

Asmodeus had not been completely overcome. No being became a duke of hell without power, knowledge and cunning. As soon as he'd seen what the elf bitch had thrown at him, he'd identified it as truesilver. Any hellion would know that accursed metal by sight. Still, he'd been confident that he could quickly break free of the trap.

It was not until it had snared him that he realized it was actually the legendary relic, the Prison of Almaphus. Many demons knew of this infamous item. It had been forged by a grandmaster smith and was strengthened with countless gems of power. The Tier 3 god must have traded almost all her wealth to obtain such a powerful item. In fact, it was probably more valuable than a single radiant god's treasury. Whatever had been sacrificed, they had indeed found an item that could contain the essence of a duke of hell.

It had quickly become clear that he would not be able to destroy the powerful item that was binding him tight, not with the four gods supplying it with their power. That did not mean he was without options.

For long minutes, the Duke of Hell had marshalled his strength. His "struggles" had just been theater, to lull the gods into a false sense of security. Now that their guards were down, Asmodeus released his accumulated power all at once. For once, his goal was not to destroy.

Instead, he used his advanced understanding of his Art, the power of Perversion. It could not completely change the nature of a thing, but his demonic identity could "alter" it in a meaningful way. The truesilver of the item resisted his hell-based powers of course, but the change he was attempting was so small that he still succeeded. The gods themselves remained unaware until it was too late.

The chant of the gods reached a crescendo. Binding Asmodeus had cost them dearly, pushing their cultivation all the way back to the very beginning of Tier 0, but they knew they could recover, given enough time. The demon, however, would be bound and trapped until the end of days. The fires of success burned in their immortal hearts... just before their joy turned to ash.

Just before the end of the gods' spell, Asmodeus acted. Black-and-red demonic energy exploded from the center of the altar. His power of Perversion did not weaken the legendary relic in any way. Instead, he merely increased its area of effect. Items of sufficient power could develop their own rudimentary consciousness, and the Prison of Almaphus was indeed such an item.

If he'd been attacking or attempting to weaken the item, the Relic itself might have opposed him. It was not an easy or simple task to change the nature of a thing. If it had opposed his will, that could have been enough to stop the demon's efforts, but Asmodeus showed his cunning. He didn't make the item weaker. He made it *stronger*, and that was something the item would have encouraged if its intelligence were high enough to do so. In fact, Asmodeus made it just powerful enough to entrap the gods along with him.

The explosion of demonic energy faded, swallowed by the truesilver item. For a moment the gods thought it had been the last futile roar of a caged beast, but then terror gripped their hearts even as the truesilver chains shot out to grip their bodies. The Prison's chains wrapped even tighter around the demon, but it also began to entomb the gods!

The truesilver chains that each god held wrapped around their own hands in an instant. Less than a second later, the chains snaked up their arms. As the bonds moved, more chains spawned, like the tributaries of a river. Each one birthed many, and each child was as strong and thick as the parent. To their horror, the relic quickly wound itself around their arms, making it look like they were armored in silver. The four gods struggled, and the demon's muffled laughter boomed out from his silver cocoon. The truesilver burned him down to his bones, but his malevolent heart thrilled at the thought of damning the gods along with him.

"You may have snared me, but you will share my fate. Even now, I offer you a choice, however. Break the bonds that hold all of us, and I will set you free!"

The snake god screamed, "No!" Not in response to Asmodeus' pyrrhic offer, but instead in futile protest of the Relic that was entombing him. He yanked his arm away in a futile attempt to break free. He even drew a dagger from his belt to cut off his own limb, but before he could strike, the chain wrapped itself around his chest and then his other arm. "No!" he screamed again, his voice shrill with denial.

He had made his peace over losing most of his power, but that was only because the other option was losing all of his followers. He didn't actually care about his worshippers any more than he cared about the world. Sagiina had been correct though. As long as just one follower survived, he'd be reborn in time. If the demon had been willing to kill everyone except for his own followers, Ishstae would have left him alone.

It was only the hell duke's endless appetite that had driven the craven god to act. Losing decades of work was very different than being trapped, bound and powerless for all eternity. To be imprisoned with the demon, away from the comforts and adoration of his people? That was something he could not accept!

The elf goddess and fish god cursed as well. Only the minotaur god remained calm. This was not because he was happy about his fate. It was only because his Art was fire, and he had come to understand that any blaze required fuel. The fact that the binding of the demon would require a sacrifice from them as well served as no surprise.

Seeing his calm, the fish god shouted, "Help us break free, Rigon!"

The minotaur god just looked back placidly, not deigning to answer. Instead, he closed his eyes and began to chant a prayer. Not one of power, but instead merely a hopeful blessing that his people would survive without him. The fish god cursed him again.

In direct opposition to Rigon's calm, Ishstae felt suffocating panic. When he saw that struggling would not work, he shouted, "I agree!" to Asmodeus, and tried to reverse his flow of energy into the relic.

No matter what happened to the other gods and the worshippers, his own included, it was better than being bound. Why should he care about anyone else? He was a god! His faithful existed only to serve his own magnificence. He didn't even blame Asmodeus for his actions. If he could grow his power by consuming the strength of others, then he would have slaughtered billions!

Ishstae's efforts, however, were for naught. Now that he was a target, the Prison of Almaphus took his power for its own. It no longer needed his consent. That didn't stop him from trying. It did not stop tears from falling from his serpentine eyes.

Despite anger and sadness gripping the hearts of the other gods, none broke as Ishstae did. They remained resolute to binding the hell duke. They also understood that even if they had wished it, their chances of breaking free were nil. The binding magic had progressed too far to be denied. The power of the relic had surpassed Tier 5, and they had all burned their cultivation down to Tier 0. A mouse might as well lift a mountain.

Seconds passed and all four gods continued to be entombed. Sagiina and Tritor joined Rigon in accepting their fate. The power in the relic continued to grow and bind them. It was then that Fell saw why the temple was destroyed in his time. Although Ishstae had no hope to get free, he didn't stop struggling. By luck or fate, one of the Prison's gems of power was positioned directly above him.

That particular gem held the one flaw in the entire Relic: a small crack, invisible to the naked eye, nestled in its heart. A surge of power interacted with the near limitless energy in the Relic, energy that was approaching Tier 6, in just the right way to destroy that one gem.

It did not free any of them, and the rest of the Prison almost immediately compensated, but it did allow a bolt of horribly destructive energy to be released inside the confines of the temple. The mana feedback caused by Ishstae's actions caused a torrent of multicolored magic to rage and roil across the truesilver relic.

A moment later it zipped through the air, back and forth like a living thing, before slamming into the hard black stone of the temple wall. Despite the great strength of the black rocks that made up the house of worship, the blast of raw energy devastated the structure. The dark blocks at the site of impact simply vaporized, while those farther back from the center melted into slag. It destroyed that entire wall and the walls to both sides. Debris was flung hundreds of miles away. That one errant wisp of power between higher tiered beings caused the destruction of a small city when a boulder of void stone struck it at twice the speed of sound. It answered why the temple was destroyed, and also gave Fell the barest idea of the staggering power the gods were wielding.

That one blast was a herald of the end. The gods were drawn farther in toward the altar and the bound figure of the demon began to shrink. Amidst screams, bellows and the roar of magic, all five powerful beings sank into the altar. A wave of pure magic shot out in all directions like a stone thrown into a pond.

A moment later, there was only silence. The bodies of the slain, the trees surrounding the temple, even the grass on the land were scoured clean by the shockwave. The devastation reached outward in a circle for miles around. The only thing left standing was the final wall of the temple. Afterwards, there was only a profound silence. The truesilver net, the demon and the gods had all disappeared. All that remained was the altar, three of the corners showing gods holding the top of it closed, keeping the demon contained, but the fourth depicting a god with open hands and a look of fear on his face. Asmodeus' leering visage was now embossed on the top.

With that final scene, everything went dark again. Moments later he was back in the present, without a second having passed. Prompts appeared in Fell's vision.

CHAPTER 41

> Congratulations! You have found an unclaimed Altar. Several Beings of Power are trapped within this Altar, and they must be expelled before you can claim it. To claim this altar they must be destroyed, removed or forced to them to relinquish any claim to the altar. Otherwise, you must do battle and the victor will claim the spoils. Do you wish to free them? Yes or No?

There wasn't really a choice. He had to claim an altar. Everything that had happened since coming to this world, everything he'd survived and been subjected to, had been just to get him here.

He also had to remove any "threats." When he'd first read the quest given by his sponsors, he'd assumed that meant some goblins, another tribe, maybe even some badass monsters. He *hadn't* thought it meant a goddamn duke of hell and a quartet of gods who were probably more than a little bit cranky!

If it were up to him, based on what he had just seen, he might choose "no." He knew how to make his own altar now. Even being ten days behind some of the other gods was less of a threat than having to face five immortals. Even if the deities weren't enemies, it was clear they each had their own motivations and personalities. He couldn't count on all of them opposing the demon, not when they were divided on the issue before they were even imprisoned.

The point was, it wasn't up to him. His sponsors must have foreseen everything, even his hesitation. The penalty for failing the quest had always seemed a bit... excessive. Fell suspected this particular moment might be why. They had pushed him into a corner.

He wasn't a huge fan of letting five trapped immortal entities go, but his sponsor had led him here and hadn't left him another option, something he'd have words with them about if ever given the opportunity. Also, irritation aside, as much as he hated being pigeonholed, he had to admit that the cosmic beings responsible for bringing him here had known their stuff so far. He looked at the prompt again, his mind made up. A few short orders formed his acolytes up behind him, weapons raised.

Fell chose "Yes."

A *whoosh* sound swept through the ruined temple, and the altar began to glow. Several colors battled for dominance within it, flashing through a spectrum faster than his eyes could follow. The final glow was a mix of red and black. Waves of power radiated off it, and Fell took a step back. A few moments later this radiating energy coalesced into a semi-translucent form, horrific to view.

It was the demon, now two meters tall and still heavily muscled. Skeletal black wings spread out behind him. His body was smooth and dark, like a beetle's shell, but there were gaps in his exoskeleton that were covered with a thick gray tissue. Pulsing red light shone through these gaps, darker than blood. A large cock hung between his legs. The fact that it was two feet long was bad enough, but there were actually barbs sticking out of it. They pointed in multiple directions, ensuring it would be a bad time coming or going.

Fell was pretty sure he was looking at pure evil. The demon didn't approach him though, merely staying atop the altar. A second later, the reason became clear. Silver chains phased into existence, wrapping around his black body.

After it coalesced, more waves of energy rolled off the altar. Four more times, beings were born from the power the dais was shedding. They each stood at one of the corners and held a silver chain that connected to the bonds surrounding the demon. Like the hellion, their forms were ethereal. The five beings stood tall and unmoving for a single moment, before the demon threw his head back and bellowed. The sound was horrific.

Fell, Autumn, Dust and Leaf all winced involuntarily at the sound. The pantherkin god was able to remain standing, but his clergy all fell to their knees. The combined mental pressure of five deities raging about their release was too much for their mortal minds.

Unbeknownst to any of them, a furious conversation had begun as soon as Fell had chosen to release the deities. To the pantherkin god and his acolytes, it took ten seconds for the five immortals to appear. To the prisoners, however, the process lasted one hundred times as long. More than enough time for ancient enemies to find common ground.

The countless ages they'd been imprisoned in a pocket dimension had not passed in a blink. The five of them had been aware

459

and able to converse the entire time. Being psychically connected had kept madness at bay, for the most part. Their many years of confinement had had another effect, however, creating two distinct groups.

At the speed of thought, three gods communicated. They excluded the fourth figure from their conversation, as he had long ago pledged himself to shadow. As soon as the four gods appeared, the one to the north, a beautiful elf maiden, sent an urgent message, "Asmodeus is trying to escape. We must stop him!"

"We can't, Sagiina," one of the other figures responded in a deep voice. The ghost-like figure had the head and horns of a bull. He shook his head, "We are barely spirits now. We have lost all of our tiers."

"He is just as weak. He is Tier 0 like the rest of us now," she argued back.

"No," the third figure denied. "He made a pact with Ishstae long ago, the Fates curse his traitorous heart. As soon as he breaks free, Asmodeus will enact the deal the two of them agreed upon. With them working together, we are not assured victory. It could cost the little we have left if we oppose him as we are. Our divine cores could be destroyed."

He sent the mental equivalent of a hand held up to forestall her objection, "We are not willing to sacrifice any more than we already have. This battle has gone on long enough. We are so weak now that we cannot even fully materialize on the material plane. You see the truth as well as I."

The elf goddess wanted to argue back, but her tongue was stilled as she reread the prompt they had all received as soon as they had escaped their aeons long imprisonment.

> You have escaped the **Prison of Almaphus**. Your long imprisonment
> has absorbed all your power. More, it has left you in a *Weakened*
> State. **-50% Energy**
>
> This state will worsen by 5% per day unless you resolve the energy
> deficit. Reaching -100% risks dissolution of self.
>
> Your physical form is also *Insubstantial* until your Energy deficit is
> resolved: **-50% Physical Damage** given and received.

Tritor, the snake god, was not wrong. They were in serious jeopardy. Not only were they *Weakened*, but their condition was also worsening. In ten days their Energy would drop to zero. That could cause their core to fracture, or trigger True Death. Not even gods could come back from that.

The reason deities were able to revive after apparent death was because even when their physical bodies were killed or destroyed, their core self would maintain their energy pattern. Given enough time and power, their body, mind and soul would coalesce around this pattern, allowing them to be reborn. The time until rebirth would be significantly shortened if there was an altar to tether themselves to or if they had followers to generate Faith energy. Both would help them coalesce their pattern much faster.

Even without those factors, a god should re-coalesce given enough time, though that might take centuries without help. That was why Sagiina could not rebut what Tritor was saying. There were many benefits to being a god, but this *Weakened* debuff threatened them with True Death.

461

"We have sacrificed enough," the minotaur god agreed. "We must find new followers and rebuild our strength."

Sagiina tried again, "If we do not stop him, here and now, all our sacrifices will have been for nothing. He will escape back to a hellscape, but sooner or later he will return. Asmodeus will not forget what is buried beneath this temple. Even if we find new followers, we shall simply have to fight him again, but this time without the help of Ishstae and without the power of a Prime Relic."

She was absolutely right. The power matrix of the relic had been compromised when Asmodeus had altered it. Between that and having contained them for so long, the Relic would be destroyed as soon as they were set free. They could all feel that ages had passed.

How many they did not know, but each new age brought new Relics and weakened nearly all that had come before. As soon as they had rematerialized, they had also felt the silver net coming apart. Even if Asmodeus did not struggle, he would be free in a short period of time.

Rather than her words convincing Tritor, he answered even more vehemently, "My exact point. The net is destroyed. The very Relic which was our only hope of defeating him is now almost useless."

"That is only because we unbalanced its energy and because we were trapped for so long!" Sagiina snapped back, "If we don't help now, Asmodeus will kill this new god."

"Let him die!" the fish god snapped. "He has followers here. He could very well reconstitute in a matter of days or weeks."

"You know what the penalty for that would be!" Sagiina reproached. "Especially for a new god, unbound to an altar." For the three old gods, they could easily read the truth of Zero's State of Being.

462

"If Asmodeus kills this god, he will absorb his power, Tritor. You know this." the minotaur interjected, the voice of moderation. He was not overly moved to fight Asmodeus or help Zero, but he was extremely wary of the demon they had been bound with for so long. Rigon did not like the idea of Asmodeus regaining even a sliver of his old power.

"Exactly," the fish god responded. "No matter what Asmodeus once was, he is weakened like the rest of us now. He will not want to risk fighting the three of us, not when he can make an easy kill and absorb the young god's power."

"Easy kill?" Sagiina echoed doubtfully. It was true that Asmodeus had once been a powerful Duke of Hell, but that time was long past. Even though the new god was young, he wasn't suffering under the terrible debuff that they all were.

"Yes, easy… if we were to help him." Tritor responded in a wheedling tone. "Our debuffs limit the power we can release, but it also decreases the physical damage we receive. With surprise on our side, no matter what attack the pantherkin god can muster, we will be able to win the day. Then, while Asmodeus gets the body of the cat god, we can feast on the altar. There is just enough residual energy in its structure for the three of us to share."

"You would actually treat with our sworn enemy?" Sagiina asked in shock. "Not only that, you would feed a young god to him? You know that would not be a simple death. His soul would be consumed over centuries, twisted and hollowed into a horrible mockery of itself."

The fish god did even bother to deny her words. His fury was evident in every word, "Feel the energy around us, Sagiina! Ages have come and gone since we were trapped in this damned altar. Trapped because you convinced us to attack a being that was stronger than all of us, using an item that was too powerful for us to wield! Where are your tears for our followers that were left without their god? What happened to them when our enemies closed in? You know the answer. They were slaughtered and their bones have turned to dust! We no longer have time for your sentiment and honor. We must think of ourselves!"

"The Pact- " the elf goddess began weakly.

"Screw the Pact!" Tritor spat. "We have to survive! We need the power of the altar to regain even a sliver of our old strength. Rigon knows the truth of this as well as I do." His voice turned cold. "The only question is, will you truly turn against comrades who have been imprisoned and suffered with you for countless centuries? All for the sake of a battle we cannot win? For the sake of a godling we do not know?"

Sagiina turned her thoughts to Rigon looking for help, but the minotaur god's decision was written on his bovine face. Confronted with the betrayal of Ishstae, the united front of Tritor and Rigon, and her own guilt from having bound them in quasi-eternal purgatory with the demon, she bowed her head. "I will not stand against you."

The message was clear. She wouldn't help to attack the new godling, but she wouldn't oppose them either. That was good enough for Tritor.

Tritor was not bothered by her answer. Despite their *Weakened* state, between the demon, himself, and Rigon they should still be able to slay a new god. He was sure she would partake of the altar's energy after that. For good measure, after he'd drank of its power, he would kill all of the new god's followers and feast on their energy as well. It was true this would ensure that the pantherkin god would not be able to reconstitute for centuries, if ever, but concepts such as right and wrong had long since ceased to matter to him.

Sagiina would protest again about the rightness of it all, he was sure, but by that time he would have absorbed enough energy to no longer care. In fact, by that time perhaps she would have outlived her usefulness as well. His fish eyes flashed to her for a split second before looking away.

After the three of them spoke, Tritor brought the demon into the conversation. It took no time at all to convince Asmodeus. The hellion hadn't been able to hear their earlier conversation, but after countless years of taunting his fellow prisoners, Asmodeus knew them well.

He had only been able to fully corrupt Ishstae, but he had wheedled his way into the hearts and minds of the others as well. Only Sagiina had remained more or less unsullied by him. He agreed to attack the godling with them and then share the energy of the god's followers.

Asmodeus even meant what he said. He was suffering under the same *Weakened* debuff as they were. It was not the time to settle old scores, not when he had finally been freed after all this time. The only caveat he placed was that Ishstae would not join the battle. He fully intended to absorb the reptile god's energy as soon as he was free. That was a debt that had been promised him long ago. It also ensured that Ishstae would not be able to gain enough power to attack him or break the covenant they had made.

Tritor momentarily argued that Ishstae could still help in the battle even if he wasn't given a split of the energy, but Asmodeus refused. The fish god agreed soon after on behalf of their coalition, just as the demon knew he would. Through it all, the snake god remained quiet. He'd agreed long ago to serve the former duke of hell.

All this communication happened in mere seconds. What Fell and his acolytes saw was just the theater the five immortals put on, the demon struggling and the gods trying to keep him contained. The immortals conspired even as the silver links began to snap.

The psychic conversation continued, fast as thought. The main point was to keep the new god from attacking until after Asmodeus absorbed Ishstae's power. There was enough juice left in the snake god to increase the demon's State of Being. Not by a full rank, but enough to increase his combat power by a significant degree. Demons fed on battle and suffering. After Asmodeus was powered up, he'd use a small amount of it to open a hell rift, which was basically a much smaller version of the hell gate he'd tried to open in the past. This one would only allow one-way passage from the material plane to a hellscape. It would also be unstable and would last bare minutes.

Tritor would have preferred for Asmodeus to not waste any energy before attacking the young god, but the demon was adamant. Hellions needed to either be tethered to the material world or to expend a large amount of energy to stay in it. Depleted as he was, Asmodeus would be drawn back into a random hellscape if he did not open a rift. Knowing the number of demonic planes and how many locations in them would be termed "hellish" even to hellions, the demon wasn't willing to risk being sent to a random destination.

Even after opening the rift, the demon would still have enough power to deal the pantherkin godling serious damage. All Tritor and Rigon had to do was keep the pantherkin and his clergy out of the fight until the duke was ready. Less than a minute after being freed, the battle would be over.

466

CHAPTER 42

The four figures holding the demon's bonds "struggled" to keep him contained. As Fell watched, the silver chains themselves began to vibrate. The demon's wailing also increased in volume. The tremors in the chains grew until Fell could barely see them. They looked like a silver blur. The sounds of snapping metal *pinged* off the ruined temple walls.

Soon after, all the chains shattered. There was no actual shrapnel. The link disappeared like smoke. The drama continued to unfold as three of the figures grouped together, taking a step away from Asmodeus and Ishstae.

"Stay back if you value your lives," Tritor shouted to Fell and his clergy. His tone conveyed warning and care. The fish god even complimented himself on his performance.

With a sneer at the stupidity of the young god, the demon held his hand out to Ishstae. The snake god took his master's hand and then started to scream. Hellfire washed over his ethereal body. It transformed the snake god into a more twisted version of himself. Spikes of bone shot out of each of his vertebrae, branching out to either side like a cobra's hood. His shoulders broadened, but also gave him a hunched stature. The figure's mouth widened and filled with twisted fangs. The reptilian god became a nightmare of what he had once been.

The process did not take long. In only a few seconds Ishstae's conversion was complete, and the snake man had turned into a demon. His body also grew more translucent. The newly transformed demon's hold on the mortal plane faded as his new hellish nature took hold.

In contrast, Asmodeus's ethereal body solidified slightly. The corruption of Ishstae's divine core gave him the power he needed for what came next. The hellfire spread from the snake god and up the demon's arm. Asmodeus pointed his arm down and hellfire shot out like a phoenix's tongue, rending the ground asunder.

What appeared at the bottom of the trench wasn't dirt, or even the darkness of a previously hidden ravine. The demon had torn reality itself. Oppressive heat washed over everyone present. Fell could see something impossible through the schism. A landscape of flowing lava and black basalt hills somehow existed only a dozen yards beneath the floor of the ruined temple.

A fell wind blew out of the rift. It stank of sulfur and something else Zero couldn't place. He felt the wind, but it didn't so much as ruffle a single hair on his head. The effect on the demons, however, was profound. Ishstae's arms flung out as if he was resisting gale force winds. He lost the battle and was carried by unseen currents into the rift.

Asmodeus leaned against the pull. It grew stronger by the second, but he had time to claim a bit more energy before joining his new follower. It was always best to wait a bit after opening a rift anyway. His aim wouldn't be better than a general location in a hellscape. He might have to fight for his life as soon as he entered the demon realm. Luckily, Ishstae should have served his purpose as bait and distraction by then.

All he needed to do now was kill the godling. It should be easy with his fellow prisoners helping. Sagiina would probably not actually join in, but after millennia together he knew her well enough. Her guilt would keep her from opposing them. Asmodeus smiled to himself. Guilt was always so delicious.

With his back turned to all of them, the duke began chanting an incantation. His wings hid the movements. Even if the godling did not see that he was preparing to attack, Asmodeus was confident. No matter if the pantherkin god threw lightning, fire or the powers of darkness, the demon should be able to shrug off the damage and finish his own attack, even in his *Weakened* state. At that point, it would be time to feast!

Tritor and Rigon prepared to attack as soon as the demon's spell was completed. Sagiina looked away, but she did not interfere, bound by guilt as surely as she'd been bound by the Relic. The demon's bloodlust flared as his spell grew closer to completion. With only one syllable left, he turned to throw the dart of hellfire he'd conjured.

There really were no words to describe the surprise he felt at finding Fell standing right in front of him. That surprise was followed by pure agony when Zero's *Soul Strike* cut two feet of spiked dick off his body. Tritor called out a panicked warning, but it was too late. The deed was done.

It was true that Fell had no idea the immortals could psychically plot together, but he was no fool. Even before his first war, he'd found battles on the streets outside of his house. Where he'd grown up, there had been plenty of bullies. You could always smell 'em.

He'd found that they often riled themselves up before throwing the first punch. They'd jump around, talking shit, make bad jokes that their cronies would laugh at, and basically psych themselves up. Fell had found a pretty good solution when he was confronted with an impending fight he couldn't avoid. Go for the dick punch.

Before the immortals had even finished their traitorous plan, Fell had summoned his *Soul Strike.* Light blue energy surrounded the short sword that he'd held behind his back. His clergy standing behind him had positioned themselves to hide any telltale blue glow.

Before Asmodeus's chains had snapped, Zero had already fully powered his attack. Still, he wasn't going to attack the group of immortals first. Between Tritor's obviously bullshit warning and the demon lighting one of the gods on fire though, it was obvious things were about to get real for him.

Before the other gods could register it, he was on the move. With the razin's racial bonus to Agility and Dexterity, his reactions and speed were well above theirs. Being able to act without hesitation made him faster. The insubstantial deities might once have wielded great power, but now their levels and tiers were all zero. By the time they had registered his intent, Fell was already behind Asmodeus. Tritor barely managed to yell, "No!" before the copper blade swung. In the next moment, the world's scariest Japanese eggplant fell to the ground, and for the first time, a demon's face went white.

"Ah. Ah." Only squeaks of disbelief came out of the demon's mouth. He stared in horrified shock at his severed penis. His addled mind felt like the stump stared back in accusation. Asmodeus' gaze traveled to Fell's callous face, then back to his lost buddy again. One more step backward and the hell winds sucked him through the portal. The tear in reality closed a moment later.

All was quiet, while acolytes and gods alike stared at Fell in shock and fear. Zero gazed at the spot of the disappeared gateway for a few moments, making sure it wouldn't pop back open, before bending down. Asmodeus's member had become substantial upon being severed from his body. Fell had expected it to just fade away, but there it was, sad and lonely. He picked up the fleshy black foot-long, careful to avoid the spikes. Then his eyes met Tritor's.

"You were saying?"

CHAPTER 43

Asmodeus fell dozens of yards, his body becoming more substantial as it absorbed the infernal mana that was ubiquitous to hellscapes. That same mana removed the *weakened* debuff of his long confinement. His body becoming solid also let sludge-like blood flow from his ruined crotch. Pain skyrocketed in his mind. Even as he fell, the demon's hand reached for his oldest friend, still not comprehending that it had pulled a Wilson. There were only five inches left of his sheared stump rather than the two-foot-long dangle he was so proud to swing.

"Where are my inches?" he screamed in agonized fury. His anguish was so great that he didn't even notice he was falling until his body landed on a spike of jagged rock. The basalt speared through his body like a lance.

More black blood geysered from Asmodeus's mouth in a violent cough. His mind reset, putting his feminization to the side for a moment. The lovely stink of the hellscape triggered old survival instincts. He was wounded in a demon dimension. The wounded were eaten. He was in trouble.

If he had jumped through the portal uninjured, Asmodeus would have landed safely even if he'd fallen from a much greater height. He might only be a Tier 0 demon spawn now, but he'd once been a Tier 5 Duke of Hell. His knowledge and ability to manipulate infernal mana remained, albeit greatly diminished.

As it was though, he was in real danger of dissolution. His Demon Core had kept his consciousness intact through the long millennia of his incarceration, but he was not a god. He was not bound to a certain location, guaranteed to be resurrected at some point. He was a demon and there was only one rule for an existence such as his. The weak are meat, and the strong do eat.

Despite the pain in his body, the demon forced himself to focus. He had to get off this rock, and then find hell creatures weaker than himself to feed upon. As long as he did not encounter anything more powerful in the short term, he could heal his injuries. He could even regain his missing inches. His hell spear would rise again!

Yes, he thought to himself, I survived entrapment by those damnable gods, and even managed to pervert one of them. He would not be outdone by a godling and a piece of sharp rock. He was the great Duke Asmodeus. He could do anything! He just needed a bit of luck in the short term, and then he would wreak vengeance on those gods that had dared to bind him for millennia. He would exact an even worse retribution against the pantherkin god that had dared to assault him so savagely!

Asmodeus comforted himself with dreams of the bloody acts he would perform. He even knew the godling's name. He repeated it like a mantra. Many of the demon's powers were locked away due to his tier reduction, but his Demon's Eye could still analyze the information

473

of opponents provided their Energy did not greatly eclipse his own. "Zero Fell," Asmodeus intoned with pure hatred.

"Enjoy your short-lived victory. For I, the great Duke Asmodeus, do now swear! I shall rise from the infernal depths and only the tears of your people shall comfort you against the fires of m- Oh, fucking shit!"

DEMONIC BLUE BILE SCORPION	
Level: ???	Monster Rank: ???
Energy: ???	Soul Rank: ???

The basalt ground only fifty yards away from where Asmodeus was impaled broke apart. A giant scorpion rose through the opening. Lava dripped off its body, not discomforting it in the least. It turned its gaze toward him, pincers quivering in ravenous hunger. The fact that Asmodeus could only gain its name with his Demon's Eye showed just how much stronger it was than he. With his vast knowledge of hellscapes, he knew it was probably not only many levels above him, but possibly even several tiers. He also knew something else with grim certainty. If he was eaten now, it would absorb his remaining power, and it would mean the True Death!

The bus-sized creature rushed toward him. It closed the distance between them in the same time it took Asmodeus to heave his body off the sharp spike of rock. As he prepared to throw hellfire at it in a most likely futile attempt, he cursed his latest enemy and the reason for his current weakened state.

"Damn you, Zero Fell! I will survive this and then I will turn your world to ash!"

On a nearby hilltop, a former god turned demon watched the battle, deciding what he should do.

CHAPTER 44

Back in the material world, Fell continued to stare at Tritor, demon dick in hand.

The silence grew, the insubstantial fish god pinned by Zero's implacable gaze. Tritor wondered just what Fell was thinking. Was the godling going to take retribution for his shouted warning? He hadn't said a name, so he should be able to play it off. Yes! He would say that he had been trying to warn the pantherkin god. That should work! His eyes flicked to the acolytes, and the fish god could not help but dry swallow at seeing a blue crystalline glow around all of their weapons. He had to talk himself out of this. If only Zero would speak! Just what the hell was the godling thinking behind that cold, dead gaze?

Tritor would have been surprised to discover Zero's thoughts were something along the lines of…

Why the hell would a dick have spikes on it? Is it just because that makes it more evil? Like kill-a-mockingbird-level evil? Is blood… demon lube?

In a game, this would be where the penis turned into a weapon of some sort. Maybe with god-level damage, though he supposed that didn't mean as much as it used to, seeing as he himself was a god. It would probably also have a cool name, like, The Diggler, or something. No matter how much he looked at it though, no prompt appeared.

It was just meat as far as he could see. Maybe if he had the Cook Class, he might be able to make a nice osso buco out of it to gain a buff, but if so, that was currently beyond him. More idle thoughts and more demon-dick names ran through his head while Tritor sweated bullets, wondering if Fell would feminize him as well.

The silence grew. Autumn Ghost kept her eyes pinned on the three remaining gods. The fact that they were deities mattered to her not at all. If they tried to hurt her master, she would bash their skulls in.

After what she had seen, she was not willing to take any chances with unknown beings standing so close to her lord. Her club was raised threateningly. Midnight Dust stood next to her holding his short sword. Zero walked closer to the newly released gods, all three staring at him in shock and fear. The being they had sacrificed everything to defeat, and had ultimately failed to actually overcome, had just been banished in a matter of seconds. Not only defeated, but mutilated in a spectacular fashion by this merciless godling.

Now they were confronted by that very same deity, along with his acolytes, while still in a *Weakened* state. Not only that, but Tritor had seemingly betrayed their intentions by shouting a warning before Asmodeus was dealt with.

All three of them had watched uncomfortably as the pantherkin god had picked up the dick. Looking at Fell holding it, Tritor couldn't help but psychically ask his fellow deities, "Is he," the fish paused as if mentally licking lips he didn't have, "is he going to eat it?"

477

Fell was *not* planning on eating it, but he did plan on keeping the three gods off balance. He had already analyzed them with his God's Eye, and so knew about their *Weakened* status. If there was one thing that combat had taught him, however, it was not to underestimate a potential enemy. They might be *Weakened,* but there were three of them, and they were gods.

He had indeed heard Tritor's shout of "No," and he seriously doubted it was meant for him. Zero didn't know why the fish god would help Asmodeus, especially having seen their past, but the why didn't matter. What mattered was showing these three that he was the biggest dick-swinger in the room.

That was why he let his clergy raise weapons against them. It was also why he put the demon dick in his other hand, leaving the first slick with purple blood. That was the hand he placed on Tritor's shoulder… and then cupped the side of his face with. Staring deep into those fishy eyes, he said, "Thank you for your warning."

Dick blood ran down the side of Tritor's face, and the fish god's already large pupils widened even more. He didn't attack though, merely nodding slowly, Fell's hand still on his cheek before replying, "You- you're welcome."

"I'm assuming," Fell asked softly, only a foot between their faces, "that you're not with them?" His eyes flicked to the disappeared rift. There was no way Tritor wasn't smelling his foul breath. Fell hadn't brushed his teeth in almost ten days.

"N- no," came another stuttered response.

Zero met the eyes of the minotaur and elf who also shook their heads. He put a broad smile on his face and stepped back, but not before wiping his hand clean on the ruined shirt Tritor was wearing. He left behind a long smear of purple dick blood.

"That's good to know. I'm so glad I could help all of you." He hopped up and sat on the altar; it looked like a simple block of white stone now. Drawing his short sword, he held it against the demon dick. With a deft movement, he skinned a barb off. The hard spine fell to the stone floor with a soft *tink*.

The eyes of the three *Weakened* gods moved in unison. Not to Fell using their former prison as a stool, but to the bloody piece of penis on the ground. As if they'd rehearsed it, they looked back up at the same time. Fell didn't repeat himself, he just stared back then cut off another barb. This one also fell to the ground with a faint *plink*.

It was Sagiina who spoke, "We are not allied with either the demon or his apprentice." The other two gods nodded.

Fell just kept dick skinning. *Plink. Tink. Plink.* "You said that." *Plink. Plink.* "And you know what," he finally continued after a time, "I believe you. At least I believe it's true… now." *Plink.* He smiled at all of them again. "I'm sure you all feel you owe me a great debt for freeing you, but doing good is its own reward, so don't worry about that." His grin would have given them diabetes had they been fully corporeal. The god decided to ignore Autumn's overly dramatic eye roll.

"I just want to know what your plans are now that I've freed you. It's not that I want to be rude, of course, but this is my land now, and I'm not ready for guests." *Plink.*

The three gods shared a wary glance and it was the goddess who spoke again, "We can all feel the remnants of our prior followers. We must return to them. Let them know their gods have returned."

"Going to walk, are you?"

"No," Sagiina responded. "We have a spell that will return us to our places of worship, wherever they may be."

"Okay. I'm fine with that. I guess you should get going then, shouldn't you?" Fell kept smiling, but only a blind man would miss that it did not reach his eyes. Those were as cold and gold as a distant star.

It wasn't easy reading the fish god's face in light of his features, but to Zero, it looked like the guy was ready to chew glass. He still hadn't wiped the blood from his face, probably not wanting to risk provoking this clearly unstable godling. Sagiina nodded graciously though, and the minotaur just stared with no expression on his bovine face. At least, Fell didn't think he had any expression. The three gods raised their hands to begin the spell, and Fell's clergy raised their weapons in return.

"We are only trying to leave," Tritor spat angrily.

Fell held up a hand to his people. "Maybe one at a time. And why don't we do this outside. You," he said, hopping off the altar and walking close again, "get to go first." He punctuated the point by whapping Tritor lightly on the chest with Asmodeus's former tip.

"Who are you to tell me-" the god began angrily before gulping in fear. Once again, Fell had used his superior attributes and readiness to do violence to act before the other gods could respond. His blade was at the fish god's throat.

Zero slowly called upon his Soul Art. The forming crystalline energy made a razor-sharp incision on Tritor's throat and white blood began to slowly dribble down the god's scaly throat. It ran alongside Asmodeus's purple blood, twin rivers, one holy, one hellish.

Fell whistled sharply. An eaglebear cub with mottled brown coloring skidded into view like a puppy on a tile floor, before waddling closer. Without breaking eye contact, Fell calmy tossed the skinned dick into the air. It flipped on three axes before being snapped up and eaten loudly, mere inches from the wide-eyed fish god. His legs began to tremble in cadence with the meaty smacks of the still-chewing eaglebear.

"This is my house now," Fell spoke quietly, but with intensity. Then he looked around at the shattered rock and debris, and shrugged, "My ruined temple. Whatever. The point is, I make the rules. And let me make another point, chum."

Zero paused a moment to see if that joke had landed, but no one laughed so he kept going, "I think you were going to attack me. I think all three of you were, but I'm pretty sure you were the ringleader. Which leads me to my third and final point. I'll let you go to whatever shithole your followers are hidden away in, but if you ever come back here looking for trouble, I'll find a way to kill you permanently." Tritor had to resist the urge to swallow as it might cause himself further harm.

The last thing Fell wanted was to leave an enemy standing, but he had seen the power of the gods in his vision. He knew they were weaker now, but if he attacked Tritor there was every chance the other two would join the fray. If that happened, there would probably be casualties on both sides. Now wasn't the time to even the score. That would come later.

Zero withdrew his blade by an inch, "After you."

The fish god stared bloody murder at Fell, but walked outside nonetheless. Zero followed, moving in lockstep. When they were all outside, the gods began to leave one at a time. First the fish god, then the minotaur. Their ethereal bodies grew more insubstantial until they

481

disappeared. When it was Sagiina's turn, she gazed at him consideringly before extending a hand.

"A gift of knowledge," she intoned softly, "if you wish it."

Fell stared at her. Part of him screamed not to trust her. He had no idea what powers gods had. Touching her hand might kill him. It might be a trick. Fell had seen countless killers with the face of an angel and many that he'd killed had seen him smile before they were claimed by the black. He wouldn't discount someone because she was a woman. On the other hand, having endured so much death and danger had also honed his instincts. Right now, he didn't feel any threat. Still, he hesitated. He'd already died once, and he'd died screaming.

Fell stared a while longer, then he took her hand. When their fingers touched, a faint green glow appeared.

For freeing her and for showing the ability to trust, the Goddess Sagiina extends her thanks. **+500 Relationship Points** with Sagiina and her tribe, if she finds one.

Relationship Rank increased from **Neutral (0)** to **Kind (+500)**

"You like me more now?" Fell asked, underwhelmed. He'd freed all of them from eternal imprisonment. A "'preciate cha" seemed a bit small.

Sagiina spoke again, "You may not know, but the friendship of a god is not to be taken lightly. My cordiality is also accompanied by a warning. The altar you have found once held great power, but power is never without peril. The hell duke will not forgive your attack, and I think my fellow gods may covet your new riches as well.

"As we have survived, other gods from previous eras may have as well. That means others may also possess the knowledge I am about to share with you. Long ago, Asmodeus sought to open a permanent doorway to a hellscape. While it is true that a demon needs no special reason to do so, I always suspected it was part of a larger plan. There were rumors that a great secret is tied to this altar, a secret that can only be revealed when it has gathered enough power. I have always believed that the true purpose of the hellgate would be to build an army great enough to advance the altar to its final rank. What would happen after that I cannot say, but in my time, empires were burnt and mountains crumbled in pursuit of power. No matter how much time has passed, I doubt that has changed."

The two held each other's gazes for a few more seconds before she cast her own spell and faded from view. The only beings left were his people and a few of the eaglebear cubs that had wandered in. Silence reigned in the ruined temple, until…

"Our Lord scared them all away!" Sharp Leaf shouted. "Lord Fell is the best! Woohoo!"

Autumn Ghost flinched. It had been dead quiet and she was still tense from nearly having fought a god. Having Sharp Leaf shout in her ear didn't help. She was only a second away from yelling at or possibly beating the shit out of the acolyte, but he had already run back to share the story with the rest of the tribe. The eaglebear cubs ran happily behind, screeching merrily and making enough ruckus to put a pack of hounds to shame.

Not long after, Fell started getting prompts alerting him to small boosts in Devotion from those who heard Leaf's story. From what he could hear, his actions got bigger and more profound each time his acolyte told the story. Rather than have Autumn Ghost stop Sharp Leaf, he figured he might as well just let him spread some propaganda. The increases in Devotion weren't much, but they were something.

Midnight Dust's eyes were trained on his god. "My Lord. With only seconds to react, you foresaw that the gods and demon would attack us. How did you know?" Even with his increased Perception, he hadn't picked up on anything.

Zero shrugged, "Assholes always think they're clever. They come up with complicated plans to betray you after they get what they want. To beat them, just remember that, and make sure you hit them first." Dust nodded slowly in thought. "Also, that was a fucking demon. I'm not an idiot."

A prompt appeared showing he'd finished his sponsor's quest.

> Congratulations! You have completed the Quest: **Ruined Temple**
>
> You have shown you can follow directions. You are now qualified to be a god or a golden retriever.
>
> **Rewards:**
>
> A new home.
>
> A message.

That was it? He'd been expecting some experience at the very least. His sponsors had put him through hell and they couldn't squeeze out a few more rewards for literally crossing oceans? Shaking his head, he pulled up the message.

Fell actually growled. To his surprise, he didn't even need to dismiss the prompt. It just disappeared on its own, and he couldn't pull it back up when he tried. He guessed it was his sponsors covering their tracks. He didn't forget their bullshit message though. It was true they'd been helpful, but what assholes!

He also had no idea what the postscript meant. They could never just let him know, could they? The god's eyes and seething nostrils turned back toward the altar. After days of stress and frustration, after terrifying attacks from monsters that hungered for their spilled blood, and relentless attacks from evil gods, they had finally found a place they could call home. He placed his hand on the altar and a prompt appeared before his eyes.

Greetings, god Zero Fell! Do you wish to claim this **Altar** and begin to form your empire? Yes or No?

CHAPTER 45

Fell's only resentment was that there wasn't a third option called "Finally!" That was how he felt. Without ceremony, he exerted his will and claimed the altar. A clear and visible ripple flowed outward. It looked like a colorless bubble of water, but caused no sensation on his skin as it passed. The wave moved impossibly fast, passing through him, the standing walls of the temple, and then beyond his sight in a millisecond. He looked around, but didn't see any other physical manifestation. A moment after that though, his mind was assaulted with information.

Even with his high Mental Aegis, it was too much to bear. It felt like fingers had roughly shoved themselves into his corpus callosum and were ripping the lobes of his brain apart.

"Arrrgghhh!" he screamed. He fell to his knees and both hands grabbed the sides of his head. He was so distressed his talons unsheathed, one nicking his ear. A bright scarlet drop of blood welled from the site. Fell didn't notice. His brain was literally being ripped apart to accommodate a new level of consciousness. It was an awareness that would have already sundered a mortal mind.

For agonizing seconds, he was intensely aware of everything within his new domain. He heard every mewling cry of young animals and beasts, saw every small creature scurrying through the underbrush, felt the rubbing of every tiny insect sawing their legs together, tasted the cool water of every stream and smelled the thick musk of every member of his Chosen tribe. He experienced each sensation separately and together, a potpourri of existence that overwhelmed his understanding of his own concept of self. His new awareness extended around him in a perfect hexagon, one mile to a side. His five senses were laid raw, nerve endings flayed, salted and uncaringly left open while a new sixth sense developed overtop them.

Zero's screams embedded a seed of fear in the heart of the tribe. It was a terror they had never known before, not even facing the attacks of dark dwarves or fearsome monsters. Autumn reached out a hand, half timid to interrupt or touch her god without permission, but half driven to try and help her beloved deity in some way, anyway. Thankfully, as quickly as the pain came, it stopped.

The pantherkin god blinked in astonishment, not only at the agony suddenly disappearing, but also at the feeling of truly seeing the world, any world, for the first time. It was like having been colorblind and seeing the deep green of lightning through trees. It was never having heard music, then experiencing Schubert. Having only eaten gruel, then tasting your first kiss.

In that moment, he understood that he'd barely scratched the surface of existence. Zero understood and knew things on a deeper level than he ever had before. For a moment he wondered if he had gained a new sense or awakened a dormant one. Whatever the case, he felt like his senses were unlocked. Zero frowned for a moment. That word felt wrong. Not unlocked… awakened.

The torrent of sensation faded away. His astonishment grew into pure wonder as he realized he could see and sense what was happening around him much farther than he should have been able to just through his eyes. For about half a mile in every direction, he could focus and know what was happening. He saw fish jumping in the ocean. He saw something that looked like a jaguar but much larger, running away from the temple through the jungle. He saw a mound of grey stone glowing slightly in the jungle to the north. On an instinctual level, he knew that he could choose to see anything that was happening inside his domain.

Unlike before, he wasn't being overwhelmed with every sensation, but instead was able to focus his will and consciously move his awareness to view specific things. Quick experimentation showed that he mostly had an aerial view, but he could shift it to a lower or higher elevation. The treetop canopy of the jungle was no impediment, but he could not force his viewpoint into the ground or even too far into a cave that he saw in the western cliff face.

Zooming out, he found his vision stopped at well-defined borders. Everything within an equilateral hexagon was clear and easy to see. Even with his eyes closed, he could focus on Autumn's still-concerned face just a few feet away. He could just as easily extend his view to the boundaries of his new domain where he saw a slightly glowing tree on one of the small islands to the south.

Beyond his domain, however, the lands he had already traveled could be seen, but they looked like they were blanketed in grey mist. He couldn't make out any details or movement. They looked like a static painting, not having the life, movement or real-time updates of the hexagonal area around him.

Everywhere else, the places he hadn't explored yet, was an impenetrable black. Some people might have been intimated or fearful of what such a sea of the unknown was hiding, but Fell looked at it with mouthwatering anticipation. His own curiosity peaked. Just what amazing discoveries awaited him and his people?

Prompts were waiting for him, notifications that he easily ignored in lieu of exploring his newfound awareness. He would have kept exploring, but then he got the greatest shock of all: a voice spoke to him.

"Are you done playing around?" The voice had a distinctly British accent.

"Who is that?" he spat in surprise. The god raised his short sword and looked around wildly at the ruined temple. He'd been distracted so it was possible someone could have crept up on him, but he didn't see anyone besides his clergy.

His sudden motion made Autumn's heart start thudding wildly once again, and she raised her own club, looking for whatever threat had filled her god with unease. Neither of them were able to see anything. Fell blinked and thought back to the voice once he saw he wasn't in imminent danger.

His analytical mind played back the question, the lack of inflection, and realized something interesting. The voice hadn't come from any particular direction. In fact, it seemed to have come from exactly where he was standing. Wondering if he was crazy, but willing to take the chance, he forcefully thought, "HELLO?"

The response was immediate... and British, "Alright. Alright. No need to shout."

Curious now, he tried again, out loud this time. "Who are you?" Autumn was still looking around fearfully, but relaxed slightly at seeing her god lower his own weapon. She started to wonder if her life would be filled with unexplainable events that she would just have to attribute to the unknowable divine.

The voice answered inside Zero Fell's head again, and the response made him huff in surprise.

"I am you, God Fell. I am your awakened God's Eye."

CHAPTER 46

"What?" Fell asked.

"What?" echoed the response in a distinctly British voice. The tone was more than a bit mocking.

Zero's gaze became a bit lidded and with some heat in his voice he repeated, "What?"

There was a pause, then the response, "What?" in the same tone.

Fell took several deep breaths before asking, "What do you mean you are my God's Eye?"

"Oh, right. Upon forming their first territory, gods have access to large amounts of information. This is a reflection of their connection to the worlds they occupy. The typical way to access this new info is by viewing their domain via their new sensory input. This is typically called a 'heavenly' sight, as it is a bird's eye view. Now that you are bound to a location, you will be able to see anything inside of your territory, also known as your 'Zone of Control' or 'Domain.' Gods typically experience this as the awakening of a new sense, similar to sight or sound."

All of that made sense and checked out, but it still didn't answer the fundamental question, "What does that have to do with you though? Why are you talking to me? And what do you mean that you are 'me'? And why the hell are you British? In fact, answer that last question first. If you're me, why do you sound British?"

The answer was as simple as it was infuriating, "Why don't you?"

Fell nose furrowed and his mouth was stuck partly open, not sure what to do with that. He settled on, "What?"

"What's wrong with how I talk? What's the problem?"

"It's not a problem. Not exactly. But why would you sound British? I grew up in the Western Confederation, the former US. In the south, for god's sake. It makes sense that I speak the way I do. I'm a product of where I grew up."

"Oh," the voice replied with disdain. "So what I'm hearing is that it's easier for you to talk like a gutter rat, just because you grew up around hill folk. Yeah. That makes sense." The voice paused before adding, "Let's just not try, eh?"

Fell didn't respond, but in his head he thought, whatthefuck? Whatthefuck? Whatthefuck? Rather than literally argue with himself, he went back to his original questions with a heavy sigh. "Just tell me more about how this 'new sense' explains why there is now a voice in my head."

Annoying or not, the voice answered promptly, "As a god's heavenly sight develops, it can, over time, develop its own awareness to help in the administration of the territories in a god's dominion. The amount of time this takes is a mix of chance and intention. You just lucked out enough for me to develop immediately. That is why there is 'a voice in my head'." The last couple words sounded like the British voice was faking a dumb American accent while it repeated the god's words.

Zero's left eye twitched. If he were to believe what he was hearing, the voice really was a piece of himself. The fact that a voice in his head was mocking his own manner of speaking was way too strange though. Almost as strange as having a voice in his head... Almost as strange as being reborn in a new world as a god...

Yeah, he thought. I need to reset my definition of strange, but still, this is strange! He had a voice in his head, and if he had to label it with a personality trait, the answer would have to be a resounding "asshole." Not that that would be a big stretch from his own personal quirks, but still. Rather than think about the existential implications, he went back to his questions.

"Who are you though, really?" the godling asked.

"I am you, Lord Fell. I am a new sense that represents your connection to Telos, the Lattice, and even the Labyrinth."

The concept just didn't make sense to him. It wasn't like his nose could hop off his face and go smelling around. It wasn't like his tongue could go tasting, despite what several exes had said about it having a mind of its own. This new sense he'd just developed was saying it could not only do things on its own but could also think and make its own decisions? And it did it with a snarky UK accent?

If it could act on its own, that raised another important question, "Can you do anything to harm me?"

"On the contrary," the voice responded, "I exist only to make your life easier. I am here to help you and further your ends. I could no more harm you than you could harm yourself. I am you." It waited a few seconds before adding, "Plus, if I did mean you harm, I certainly wouldn't tell you, now would I? Think a bit."

The first part of the answer might have made Fell feel better except that he could easily rattle off a top ten list of ways that he'd hurt himself in the past, starting with a little brunette named "Susie Rider" with flexible hips, big thick lips and two oceans of crazy for eyes. Even if that had made him feel better, the voice's latest dig would have taken that cozy feeling away. He realized that he'd just have to hope this new side of himself was here to help and not hurt him.

"Look," the voice added, "I was going to save this for a bit later to give you a nice feeling, but it's clear you're feeling uneasy about having developed a second, smarter consciousness."

Definitely could have done without that, Fell thought.

"So let me just tell you now," the voice continued unabated, "that the moment a deity's God's Eye achieves sentience is normally a celebrated milestone. You can see that for yourself."

Without Fell willing it, a prompt appeared in his vision.

Congratulations, God Zero Fell! Your God's Eye has evolved to the Rank 2, **Basic Sapience**. It will now be able to independently monitor your territories, follow general commands and answer basic questions. It is provided with basic knowledge from the Labyrinth and your host worlds.

That all sounded amazing. It also answered why the voice knew things about this new world and his own nature as a god that Fell didn't know. It was plugged into some sort of mystical internet. As useful as that was however, Fell was seriously bothered by the fact that the voice could access his prompts before he did. "You have access to my information?" he asked with a touch of accusation in his voice.

There was a silent pause, "I am you, Lord Fell. *You* have access, so *we* do." Then the voice started muttering to itself. Himself? Ourself? The pure inanity of the concept gave Fell a headache, but just as he was about to interrupt it the voice continued, "I think I know something that could help. I will need to access older memories to provide a context. Alright?"

Before Fell could even respond, the deep dive into his memories was apparently done. He hadn't felt a thing, which worried him even more. The voice's next words did help him understand though. "You are familiar with how Siri and Alexa evolved into Geneva. I am what Geneva would one day evolve into if given infinite resources and limitless time."

"Hmm," the god responded musingly. Everyone on Earth had used Geneva. She'd been the perfect assistant: organizing, reminding and keeping track of everything from birthdays to a first date's name the next morning. It was a personalized operating system that was completely unhackable and, most importantly, utterly loyal.

Back on Earth, Geneva was heralded as one of the greatest inventions of the millennia. There had been a few people that never stopped shouting about how AIs would one day rise up and wipe out humanity, but after a couple years everyone realized they were nutcases. In contrast, most of humanity had come to accept that using

AIs could elevate their minds to new heights. That was actually one of the worst parts of the Forsaking for some people. Like almost all advanced technology, Earth linking to the Labyrinth had made Geneva go kaput.

Fell didn't like that his memories had been invaded, but he had to admit that referencing the AI had helped him wrap his mind around the concept. Not that he trusted the voice, but if it was telling the truth, and that was a big if, then having an awakened God's Eye might not be so bad.

Still, he asked, "Can I get rid of you?"

In an irritated tone, it responded, "Alright, alright. I've been trying to be nice. Trying to speak in small words for you. But you just want to be rude, eh?"

Fell was about to explode on the voice when it continued in a banal tone, "No. I could just stay quiet and not offer my help while you bumble around this new world, leading to the death of all your people, but you cannot 'get rid of me.' You cannot remove your ability to smell, hear or feel things either, if you were curious."

The voice paused, "Actually, that is not completely true. A dumbass like you could get rid of your sense of touch by burning your body so badly that your nerve endings were destroyed. Does that sound fun?"

"No," Fell began lamely.

"Oh, would you like to shove peppers up your nose and ass? That might get rid of your sense of smell if you're trying to cripple yourself."

"Why up my ass?"

"Because fuck you," was the calm response. "You could also rub sharp rocks in your eyes if-"

"I get it!" Fell spat. A simple 'no' would have sufficed, he thought.

Trying to get back on track, he asked, "You said that a god's new sense would take time to develop its own awareness. I'm guessing that means advancing their God's Eye to the second rank, like you. Why were you able to talk with me immediately? I can't believe it's just because my Luck stat is high."

The voice didn't answer immediately, and Fell knew instinctively that it was, as crazy as it sounded, pondering his question. How a part of him could be pondering a question posed by another part of him seemed insane, but then again, it was only crazy until you remembered that he was currently a cat god on a new planet.

Finally, the nonplussed voice admitted, "There is a lot I do not know. Over time, if you continue to evolve me, then I believe I will be able to give a more concise answer, but for now I feel confident saying that any god has a chance to evolve their God's Eye. The odds of that happening spontaneously and without the aid of powerful energies..." It paused, "I think the chances would be very low. In summation--"

"I got lucky," Fell finished for it. On his HUD, he looked at his insanely high Luck of sixty-eight again.

"Yeah," it agreed, but it didn't sound fully convinced.

"Hmph," he replied, sucking his teeth and nodding. Having a second voice in his head was ridiculously weird, but it was what it was. If nothing else, maybe he could use it to his advantage. "We should get to it then. What can you do for me?"

"While we have been conversing, I have perused your waiting notifications and organized them in a way that will be most convenient for your specific method of processing information."

"My specific method?" he asked.

"Yeah, a bit like short-bus Sesame Street."

"Listen," Zero began sharply before he realized he didn't know what to call the voice. He couldn't very well call it his own name. Calling it God's Eye would also get old real quick. As he thought about it, an idea popped into his head. The voice had said it was like Geneva and it was his new sense, as insane as that was. Why not just put the letters together for Royally Insane God's eye?

"I'm going to call you Rig. That work for you?"

The voice was silent while it thought about it. "Could be worse, I suppose."

"Good," Fell responded, before continuing his previous response. "Listen, Rig, I don't need your lip! Just answer my questions and give me the damn prompts!"

Surprisingly, the voice complied. While it started speaking, the god walked over to a hole in the temple's walls and looked out over his tribe. His gaze went farther. Standing on the hilltop, he could see distant mountains, thick jungle, countless islands, large swaths of grassland and to his left, endless ocean. There was a world waiting for him and it was his to explore, battle and conquer. All that would come soon enough though. For now, he needed information.

CHAPTER 47

The first prompt was about the altar.

> Congratulations, Lord Zero Fell! You have claimed an **Altar**! This has allowed you to form your first religious domain!
>
> Countless souls, limitless blood and inconceivable magics were consumed to create it. Sadly, the power of this priceless object has been drained to low levels due to the aeons-long imprisonment of several Beings of Power. It currently is the lowest rank, *Basic.*

Fell stopped reading for a second. Did that mean his new altar was broken? "Thanks, jabronis," he muttered to himself. He focused on Rig. "Are you telling me that demon and those dickhead gods broke my altar?"

"Checking," came the response. A few moments later, Rig responded, "The altar is not 'broken' per se. It is instead severely depleted. I have been provided with a basic understanding of altars that I can share, if you like."

At Zero's assent, the God's Eye continued, "Altars are structures that focus a god's power on the Prime plane. By 'Prime plane,' I mean this world you're currently on."

"Altars, not temples?"

"Temples house altars. They can channel the power the altar has, provide protection and add certain bonuses, but the altar is the true power. A loose analogy would be that altars are engines, and temples are the cars around those engines. It is not a perfect association as engines would merely be lumps of metal without the car, but it is a close enough approximation. Do you understand?"

Fell wanted to shake his head at the inanity of a new, and therefore younger, piece of himself explaining things, but he just assented once more.

Rig continued his previous explanation, "Altars have seven major ranks: *Basic, Improved, Advanced, Empowered, Great, Grand,* and *Supreme*. Each rank can vastly increase the power it offers both its god and its god's worshippers. The altar that you have found was once the second highest rank, *Grand*, but its energy has been depleted to the rank of a *Basic* altar."

"Then why does it even matter that it's *Grand*?"

"Checking," Rig answered.

After a few seconds of silence, Fell asked, "What are you doing when you're 'checking'?"

"As your awakened God's Eye, I have access to information that you did not before you claimed your altar and bound yourself to the land. Access or not, however, all of this is new information. Meaning that though I can call it up, I do not have mastery of all this knowledge. I do not believe it would be possible for me to actually master the massive amount of information, at least not at our current tier. When I am 'checking,' I am both searching the data available to us and finding the best way to communicate it in a way that you would understand."

"That 'I' would understand?" Fell asked with a bit of incredulity. "Aren't you me?"

"I began as you," Rig answered. "I am more advanced at this point."

"What do you mean 'at this point'? You just came into being a couple minutes ago!"

"True," Rig admitted slowly, "but a good deal has happened since then and, to be honest, it wasn't too high of a bar to jump over, was it?"

Did Fell just hear snark? Was that snark? He was sure that was snark. Arguing with himself was the definition of futility though, so he just said, "You were telling me about the altar?"

"Indeed. You asked if there were any benefits to having a *Grand* altar in light of the fact that its energy has been depleted to the *Basic* rank. Simple answer, I don't know. We'll have to find out. One thing I can tell you is that a *Basic* altar might cost as much as buying a reasonably priced car. Advancing it to the second rank might cost as much as a house in a nice part of town."

Quite a jump, Fell thought, "How much would it cost to make a *Grand*?"

"The materials and magics required might cost several times as much as the island of Manhattan."

"How much is that supposed to cost?" he asked, confused.

"I believe you already know," Rig answered simply.

Fell's brow furrowed searching his memory. Then it was almost like a dimly remembered thought remnant was lifted from his distant past, a news report he'd barely been paying attention to twenty years before his death on Earth. It had said that the real estate of Manhattan was worth, "Two trillion dollars?"

"Yes," Rig responded simply.

That amount of money was so massive it was hard to conceptualize. When he was a kid, a hundred dollars seemed like a fortune, let alone anything more. Those "-illionaire" words had all been interchangeable. It was only later in life that he'd understood the vast difference.

It had happened at a dinner party. He'd found himself sitting next to an economist. The woman had been dry as a nun on Christmas, but she had said one interesting thing. She'd talked about how people didn't really understand the difference between the three levels of wealth. She'd put it in simple terms. One million seconds ago was about a week and half. One billion seconds was three decades. One trillion seconds, and he still remembered his shock when he'd heard this, was thirty thousand years.

That meant that one trillion seconds ago on Earth, the pyramids hadn't been built. Humans hadn't invented pottery. No one had ever even woven a rope. It would be twenty thousand years before man domesticated the first animal. It would be another seven thousand years after that before the Sumerians created the first written language. That was the magnitude of difference between a million, a billion and a trillion.

Rig had made his point well. Constructing a *Basic* altar would require hard work over time and access to the right resources. Finding the materials and mastering the power needed to make a *Grand* or *Supreme* altar would require an organization the equivalent of a global superpower.

"It used to be priceless. How does that help me now? Does it have powers I can unlock over time?"

"Checking… no. It looks like whatever abilities it had have fully degraded over time. It is a blank slate. I feel like there is… something. It feels more like a residue of its former power. Whatever it is, if anything, isn't something we can access now. Perhaps its secrets will be revealed if you restore its former power."

"Its former power?" Fell repeated. "The power that is worth tens of trillions of dollars?"

The ghost sent the mental equivalent of a shrug.

Putting that aside, Fell had something even more important on his mind. "I barely remembered that fact the next day. How were you able to bring it back so vividly?" Was the God's Eye not only able to access his memories but improve his recall as well?

Rig stayed quiet for several seconds. "I am not sure. I do have a feeling that as time goes on, I will be able to increase your capabilities. At present, it seems I can help you access your memories to a greater extent than you are able to alone."

Fell wasn't sure how he felt about that but asked, "Can you do anything else to augment me?"

"Sadly no, Lord Fell, but I suggest you gather the resources to strengthen the altar as soon as possible. While I do not know what made this altar so special, it triggered a war with a Tier 5 demon. There are at least three gods in the world now who at least have an idea. If they tell others, your enemies could be endless."

The godling nodded. Rig was making sense. He already knew that at least some of these other gods were hostile. The dwarves of Vúr and the spiders of Neith were proof of that. If there was one thing he was sure of it was that he needed to get stronger as quickly as possible. Otherwise, the next time he encountered an aggressive force might be the last time. "What is the point in even having an altar?"

"That is the correct question. Even a *Basic* altar is a tool of massive power. If you are ready, I can show you the benefits of your new domain and dais."

"Let's do it," Fell replied. His vision was flooded with prompts.

CHAPTER 48

> Congratulations! You have claimed your first **Altar**! At its current *Basic* Rank, it offers the following benefits:
>
> **Maximum Faith Points:** 100,000
>
> **Divine Powers:** Increased by 10% while within religious domain
>
> **Sea of Souls Summoning Limit:** 10,000
>
> **Lattice World Connection**

Fell was confused by the very first line, "I didn't know I had a limit on the Faith Points I could hold."

"There is," Rig replied simply. "It is determined by your State of Being or the max altar rank in your domain. Initially, as an unbound god you were capped at 10,000 FPs. When you took your step down the Rainbow Path it increased to 20,000. When you sacrificed that progression, it went back to ten."

Having an altar greatly increases your cap, as you can see. A Tier 1 god would actually have a cap higher than 100,000 by themselves, but until you reach that point, your altar will significantly improve the Faith you can call upon. That will allow you to wield devastating powers that have a greater cost."

"Do I have access to any of those powers now?"

"No."

"Predictable," Fell harrumphed, but then he had another thought. "The altar is a bank for my Faith Points. Does that mean my acolytes can use them?"

"No, perhaps in the future, but currently it's impossible."

Zero huffed, "Predictable!"

Rig ignored him, "The next lines is just what its sounds like. Gods and their clergy have a boost to their powers while in range of their altar."

That could come in handy, Zero realized. "What about the last two benefits, the 'Sea of Souls' and 'Lattice World Connection'?"

"They are the most important," the voice echoed. "The Sea of Souls is a resource that you will share with every other god that has access to an altar. There may be other immortals who can access it as well, I am not sure. What you need to know is that you will be able to summon new followers if you can pay the price."

Fell blinked, trying to process what he had just heard. "I can make more razin?" It sounded insane.

He was really getting tired of thinking that.

"Yes. Specifically, you can summon souls to serve you. Once summoned, the altar will give them bodies. In essence, you can create new members of your tribe. For now, you can only create members of the razin, but I have a feeling that capability can widen and improve in the future."

"I..." Fell was still struggling to understand this. Wielding powers, consuming souls, even being reincarnated was easier to believe than this. "I can actually create new life?"

"You can create ten thousand of them, Fell. You are, technically speaking, a god. What did you think that meant?" Rig replied simply.

The godling shook his head. He'd seen some amazing things, before and after his death on Earth. He'd fought monsters, used magic, and wielded powers that defied imagination. If he'd said he'd believed in any of that just ten years before they would have locked him up. Called him schizo.

Since coming to Telos, he'd even come to believe that he was a "god," with very heavy quotation marks, and was tied to the razin. The term was still just a euphemism in his mind though. When they called him "divine," "holy," or "lord," he'd just taken it as them calling him "boss," "jefe," or "sir." The fact that he might very well be able to create life out of thin air... that was something he just wasn't quite willing to accept yet. To be honest, it wasn't something he felt overly comfortable with.

"I truly am... a god." His mind still rebelled at the thought. He tried to argue against it one more time. "If I'm really a god, why do I feel pain? Why do I bleed?"

"Why wouldn't you?" Rig countered

Ask a stupid question, Fell thought. Still, he tried again, "Gods are supposed to be all-powerful, all-knowing, aren't they? I've gained power, but nothing like that, so am I a god or not?"

"You are," Rig responded definitively, before adding much less assertively, "Technically."

"What do you mean by 'technically'?"

"Well, you are a god, yeah? But only a Tier 0 god. A godling. So you are indeed a god, but sort of in the same way a child's finger painting is art. It isn't, not really. And when you really look at it, it's just awful, but you still put it up on the refrigerator, don't you? Because if you don't, the child," Rig paused as if to indicate Fell was 'the child,' "will throw a tantrum and smear shit on the walls. So, you are a god, technically, just the finger painting equivalent."

"I wish I could slap you so hard right now," the godling seethed.

CHAPTER 49

After a few moments of silence, Rig brought the conversation back on track.

"As I was saying, the Sea of Souls is the main way you will grow your tribe initially. Every tenday you will be able to summon new followers, for a price. Each follower will start at Level 0 and Tier 0. This may not be true of higher ranked souls, but is most definitely true of the lower ranked."

Fell was still irritated, but there were things he needed to know.

"Ranks? Like *uncommon* and *limited*?" Sharp Leaf and Midnight Dust both had *uncommon* souls and Ghost had a *limited* soul. His own level up prompt said his soul was the equivalent of Autumn's.

"Yes, but those are only the first three ranks. They make up the *mortal* ranks. There are six higher ranks as well. I suggest we move on to the topic of Lattice worlds for the moment, however."

"Why?" Zero asked. His own Art was of the soul. The Sea of Souls sounded like something he'd want to know more about.

Somehow he heard a faint smile in Rig's voice, "Because you're not as trapped as you think you are now that you're bound to this place." The God's Eye summoned a hologram to float in front of Fell's face. It was the same image he'd been shown before by Sariel, before coming to Telos. It had Telos nestled in the center of a vast array of stars, planets and moons. "I know you hate the idea of being tied to one place. While that is true on Telos, the altar lets you explore all the worlds of the Lattice!"

Fell looked at the model again. It was impossibly complex. If he had to describe it, it would be as a spider's web, but as a 3D structure… and the spider had probably been strung out on PCP for a month. There was no way to tell how many planets and moons there were. Each time he focused on one section, he noticed a detail he hadn't seen before. There had to be thousands of worlds.

"I can go to any of these?" If that was true, then being bound to his domain on Telos really didn't matter that much.

"Well, not all of them, not at first," Rig corrected. "The worlds of the Lattice are many, as you can see. Some are small, while others will be larger than Earth. At present you will only be able to travel to the worlds closest to Telos, the worlds of the First Shell. In fact, you only have access to one right now. Each major zone gives access to one world. You must discover ways to reach the others. Once you do, you will be able to instantly travel to those worlds from your altar."

"Are you saying this altar," he gestured to the now featureless block of midnight-blue stone, "is a stargate?"

Rig sighed heavily, "Yes. It is also a divine artifact that allows you to create sentient life from raw energy, but yeah, let's call it a stargate."

Even with his God's Eye's mocking tone, Fell was starting to feel better. If there was one thing he'd hated in his whole life, it had been being forced to do something. Finding out that he was imprisoned, confined to an area two miles wide had triggered him. He'd even started to feel "hot" anger. His ability to go cold in response to danger hadn't always been his default. He'd been taught to do so from a young age because his anger was such a volatile and dangerous thing. Dangerous to him and those around him. That was why he'd been taught to stay rational even in response to anger.

"Even on Telos," Rig added, "you can have more than one religious domain."

That immediately got Fell's attention, "Tell me more about that."

"Your Chosen tribe will serve many purposes. One of the most important is spreading the word and worship of your name. They, your clergy in particular, will be able to make shrines and altars in other locations. A shrine is similar to an altar but gives far less benefits. The religious domain it creates will only be measured in yards rather than miles, for instance. Still, shrines can be upgraded and new altars can be created. Either will increase your domain."

"This is sounding better. How do I make more altars?"

"I have no idea."

Was there a phone ringing? That had to be impossible, but Fell could swear he could hear something ringing in his head!

Some time passed. After a bit he calmed down again, "Do you have any idea how we can find out?"

"Of course, Fell. You will need to advance the village's research to unlock those Blueprints."

It was such a simple statement, but to Zero, it just underlined the symbiotic relationship with his tribe again. If he was going to grow his power, he would need to grow the power of his people. He had already saved them several times. Despite that, he needed them. Maybe even more than they needed him.

CHAPTER 50

This new world was far more complicated than he'd thought. He still couldn't wrap his head around the fact that tomorrow was his tenth day on Telos, or the tenday, which meant he would be creating life from thin air.

Fell was eager to explore the area around his new settlement. Not only that, but also the Sea of Souls and the Lattice worlds, but Rig told him there were a few more prompts to be reviewed. The fact that he was in a ruined temple with no defensive structures around it was weighing heavily on his mind so he asked if the other prompts could wait. Rig told him he would be happy that he'd seen these. It turned out the God's Eye was absolutely right!

> Congratulations! You have created your first religious domain.
> **+5,000** Faith Points

The 5K increased his total FPs significantly. Rig told him every god would get this bonus, Telos's way of jump-starting their initial settlement.

Rig wasted no time suggesting that Zero use some of his new Faith Points. "For 1,000 FPs, you can make me a body. I won't be able to touch anything, but others will be able to see and hear me. I would basically be a hologram."

Fell thought about it. Having others see Rig could come in handy, if only to run messages around. And he had just gotten a windfall. His FPs decreased by one thousand, and suddenly a mirror image of Zero appeared, at least from the waist up. The ghost had the same brown skin and gold eyes, and black round ears poking up through even darker cropped hair.

Instead of legs, there was just a wisp of grey smoke like how genies used to be drawn. Rig floated so that their eyes were at the same level. Seeing an identical twin staring back at him immediately made Fell uncomfortable.

"Can you pick another form?"

"Like this?" Rig asked without missing a beat. The face stayed the same, but two lady lumps started swelling under the bloody shirt the ghost was wearing. In just a second, they'd reached "C" size and were showing no signs of stopping.

"No, fuck this!" Fell spat. He pulled up his interface looking for the option to cancel Rig's body.

"Wait, wait. I was just joking! How about this?" Rig swept a translucent arm down his body and his features and coloring changed. His skin became white, his ears and hair turned mouse-brown and the face filled out… a lot.

Fell blinked, trying to understand where he'd seen that face before. Then it hit him. "You're that comedian guy. Ricky Jury. No. Juree. Jurve? No. Gervais. Ricky Gervais. Why the hell do you look like that old comedian?" Now that he thought about it, even the British accent fit now.

"Well, no reason," the ghost said. Fell could have sworn he added "that's important" under his breath, but then Rig said, "As long as this form doesn't offend you, I can go back to providing critical life and death information free of charge. Would that be okay?"

Fell glared at the ghost suspiciously, but he did need to finish going through his prompts. He motioned for the ghost to continue. Zero didn't know if Rig had timed it like this to distract him, but the next rewards made his recent faith bonus look like nothing.

It turned out that even though he'd spent more than a week traveling, putting trust in his sponsors was continuing to pay off. He'd not only found an Altar, but he'd been the very first one to accomplish that feat on his new continent!

Know This! The world of Telos has many major continents and major ocean zones. Being in the top 7 gods to claim a domain in any of the major continents or major oceans will provide a unique bonus.

Congratulations! You are the 1st god to establish a religious domain on **Home of the Three Kings!**

<u>1st of 7 Rewards</u>

+1 FREE Hex

+7 Scientific Great Spirit Points/day

+700 Research Points

+100% Devotion gain with natives of Home of the Three Kings

<u>Lattice World Connection now available</u>

Azure Forest

Rig apparently got the same prompts, because the God's Eye started explaining.

"The free hex increases your religious domain. It will take up the same amount of space as the hex you're on now."

Fell liked that. It meant he'd already increased the area he could travel in by 100%. "Can the hex go anywhere?"

"No," the spirit said, pulling up a map of the surrounding lands. It was the same fog of war map as before. "It has to be connected to a hex you already own. Right now, you have six options." In quick succession, Rig highlighted each of the hexagons contiguous to the one he was standing in.

Zero nodded, "Take me through the other rewards before we claim the next hex."

Rig had a distracted look on his insubstantial face, but nodded. "Great Spirit Points let you summon a soul with special properties."

"Like a *legendary* soul? From the Sea of Souls?"

"No," Rig said slowly. His eyes moved like he was reading something only he could see. "It looks like great spirits are a special category. You can't summon them from the Sea of Souls. A *legendary* soul might very well be more useful to you than a great spirit, but the great spirits have unique powers."

"Like what?"

Rig looked like he was reading again, "I'm not sure. We'll have to wait until you earn one. I do know that unlike the Sea of Souls, the cost to acquire great spirits goes up for each one claimed. It will cost 1,000 points to gain the first scientific great spirit. After that the price might increase to 2,500 or 25,000, for all I know. The increase in cost will apply to every being on Telos."

Fell was starting to get a clearer picture. Whatever the great spirits were or did, earning them was a race. Those seven points a day might have just put him in the lead.

"The next reward gives you free Research Points. You can use those to make some scientific advances all at once. Lastly, it looks like you'll have an advantage trying to gain new worshippers on this continent. How you go about doing that, I do not know."

"What about the Lattice world?"

"As I said, each major zone is connected to a different starting world of the Lattice. These starting worlds all belong to something called the "first shell," as they are all directly linked to Telos. When you gain a religious domain in a zone, you can access the corresponding world. It appears the world connected to Home of the Three Kings is called the Azure Forest."

"A different world for each zone?" The idea of so many worlds being somehow connected to this one seemed crazy.

"Yes, and that is only the beginning. More worlds branch off from those. You will have to find your own way to them." Rig paused, "There is much I do not understand, but I do know that these worlds hold the potential for great power. While your tribe develops on Telos, *you* must develop on the Lattice. There could very well be problems the tribe will face that will only be solved by what you find out there." Rig motioned to the sky above.

"I believe that is true, but I cannot tell you much else about them. It was not until these prompts appeared that I was given information about these three Lattice worlds. It appears that while I am made privy to knowledge, much of it must be unlocked by your actions."

Once again, his sponsors had come through. Being able to advance the tribe's technology quickly was a definite edge. He turned his attention back to the map, and tried to decide where to place his free hex. He was leaning toward one of the areas to the north, mostly because the east and south were over water and they had no boats. To his surprise, Rig gave him a suggestion.

"I have found something interesting, my lord. The map provides more information than just what we see. It also shows that the hex you have claimed borders other major zones. Let me show you."

The map didn't change in the detail it showed, but the hexes were divided into three different colors. The one Fell had claimed and all the hexes to the north and west were shown in orange. The deep ocean tiles to the east were in green, and the island waters to the south were colored pink.

Fell quickly understood the significance, "We are sitting on a confluence of major zones. My sponsor didn't just choose this spot because the altar was here. It was also because if I extend my domain into those zones," a smile broke across his face, "maybe I can get even more first-of-seven bonuses!"

Zero wasted no time and chose the hex to the east, extending his domain past the cliffs and over the deep ocean. If not for Rig, he never would have chosen that direction. Having a voice in his head was still strange, but the benefits of his awakened God's Eye were obvious. He'd been hoping he'd be in the top seven again, but he got the number one spot for the second time!

Congratulations! You are the 1st god to establish a religious domain on **The Fathomless Deep!**

1st of 7 Rewards

+1 Hex

+7 Explorer Great Spirit Points/day

+700 Exploration Points

+100% Devotion gain with natives of the Fathomless Deep

Lattice World Connection now available

Dark Sun Dunes

He was right! He'd not only gained another hex, but also more Great Spirit Points, an explorer type this time. Rig wasn't able to tell him what that great spirit could do either, but he was able to explain the Exploration Points.

"Any hex you claim in your Domain will reveal its secrets to you. You already noticed the first hex you claimed has Grey Stone. It is a building resource that will increase the durability of your buildings." Fell remembered seeing a slightly glowing patch of stone on the northern side of his first hex when he'd claimed it. Apparently, it was a special building resource.

"Hexes that are not within your Domain, however, can hide many secrets. To uncover them you will have to send your tribe into them to explore. Every day that a member of your tribe is in an unclaimed hex there is a chance they can gain an exploration point. If you gain 100 points in any one hex, you can consider it fully explored. Even if it is not fully explored, the more Exploration Points you have, the more likely you will discover rare resources.

"If you reach 100 points though, there will be nothing hidden from you, even if the hex is not in your domain. Exploration will not only let you know about powerful resources, but it can also help guide your decision about which hexes to acquire in the future. If used on unexplored hexes, it will reveal that part of the map. It will still have the fog of war, however."

Fell could see the usefulness of Exploration Points as well. It was the equivalent of having satellite recon of the surrounding lands.

"These will let me know if there is iron, gold or oil hidden in the surrounding lands?" he asked. If so, back on Earth, governments and corporations would have literally killed for

Exploration Points. Fighting over natural resources had triggered more wars than love.

"Yes and no," came the noncommittal response. "Exploring a hex will reveal resources, but you will only understand what is revealed if your tribe has researched the technology to utilize it. If you discover a vein of gold ore, for instance, but have not researched *Mining* yet, then it will only be labeled 'unknown ore' or something similar."

"What? I'm no geologist, but I've seen gold ore before. It's kind of hard to miss." That was thanks to a fourth-grade field trip to a ghost town. He'd learned that iron ore could look like almost anything, but gold ore looked like, well, gold.

Rig was adamant in his response, "Even if you pointed it out to a member of the tribe, even if you put your hand on it, your tribe still wouldn't be able to see it if they hadn't researched the right tech."

"That's ridiculous."

"More ridiculous than being a deity in a fantasy world with a bunch of anime panther people worshipping you?"

Zero sniffed. Fair point.

"Much of my information is incomplete, but this is one message that has been made clear to me. A god cannot artificially advance their tribe, no matter the knowledge they personally possess. By using mechanisms already built into the Labyrinth, you can speed their understanding; using Research Points to gain knowledge, for instance, but not by just telling them."

That made no sense, but arguing would literally be fighting himself, so instead he placed his second free hex. After placing one to the east of the central one, Fell could have added more in that direction, but it was just the deep blue sea. It also wouldn't extend his domain to a new zone. Claiming the grid to the southwest, however, brought more sweet, sweet rewards!

Congratulations! You are the 1st god to establish a religious domain on **The Shattered Archipelago!**

1st of 7 Rewards

+1 Hex

+7 Merchant Great Spirit Points/day

+700 Trade Points

+100% Devotion gain with natives of the Shattered Archipelago

Lattice World Connection now available

Liberated Isles

At this point, everything was self-explanatory except for the Trade Points. Rig explained they were basically universal chits that would be accepted in deals. They would even work in places where gold, silver or copper wouldn't be accepted. Just exactly how valuable they were was influenced by your relationship with the other trader, and other variables. They could definitely come in handy, especially for a burgeoning settlement.

Rig suggested placing the last hex to the northwest. The basic reasoning was that the hex was completely on land, and so covered the most physical area. The god's domain ended up looking like a gear key or a fat Mercedes symbol. Placing the last hex didn't unlock a new domain, but he had a feeling that his sponsor had already cheated him to near the top of the rankings. He had nearly ten square miles that he could range in now. A quarter of that was over the eastern ocean, and another quarter was a mix of small islands and water, but it was still four times as much area as he'd had before.

The advantages of being in three different zones at once were obvious. It looked like his sponsors had come through for him again. He did wonder what price there could be for all these advantages down the line. Time would tell.

Fell was grinning ear to ear. His sponsors might be some sandbagging assholes, but they had really set him up right. "I can't believe I was the first of seven in all three domains!" Sariel had made it clear there were other sponsors, so he assumed they would have hooked their respective deities up as well. It wouldn't have surprised him if another god had managed to beat him to the punch through a different shortcut. After all, no matter what world you were in, there was the way they said you should do things and the way winners got it done.

"It's actually not surprising," Rig told him, "Not when you realize that you established the very first domain on all of Telos."

Fell's grin grew greedier, which should not have been possible but was. "Does that mean I get even better rewards than I earned for being first of seven in the zones?"

"Hmmm, about that," Rig replied carefully. "This is one of those bad news, good news situations. And here comes the bad."

A baleful gong resounded in Fell's ears three times. As he read the prompt, the joy drained right out of him.

CHAPTER 51

> **GLONG! GLONG! GLONG!**
>
> Worldwide Announcement! Congratulations to God Zero Fell for establishing the first religious domain on Telos! **Home of the Three Kings** is now--

Fell stopped reading. His mind was wholly occupied by the implications of the first line of the prompt. "When that says, 'worldwide announcement'..."

"It means that it was announced to every immortal on the entire planet."

Zero bared his teeth. "You're kidding me, right? Please tell me you're kidding me. Please tell me that every power-hungry bastard out there doesn't know my name. Please tell me that they don't know where we are!" He was already seeing armies of murk dwarves and those blasted orbweaver spiders attacking them along with who knew how many other aggressive tribes.

525

Rig shrugged his ghostly shoulders, "It is what it is. No need to be a little girl about it."

Fell snorted in irritation. Rig's blunt words had the intended effect though. He focused back on what was and quit worrying about what wasn't. The god brought the prompt back up.

> Worldwide Announcement! Congratulations to God Zero Fell for establishing the first religious domain on Telos! Home of Three Kings is now known as the **Religious Cradle** of the world!
>
> To celebrate this, a **Prime Relic** will be hidden in this zone!
>
> Great power awaits any immortal who can claim it!
>
> Be guided by these words:
>
> "Brightest Night shows Darkest Light"

Great, Zero thought sourly. A riddle. I can't wait to waste days trying to figure this out. He'd never been a big fan of brainteasers. They always seemed like nerdgasms. He wasn't bad at riddles, it was just when you'd had the "o" variety, you didn't waste time with anything else. Despite his feelings, the back of his mind was already teasing it out. Did "Brightest Night" mean a full moon? Only problem with that was that there were three moons on this planet...

He caught himself noodling it and focused instead on the prompt, making sure he hadn't missed anything. That was why he asked, "What does it mean by 'Prime Relic'?" That was how the trapped gods had described the item that had bound Asmodeus.

Rig brought up another prompt.

There are many items of power in the worlds of the Lattice, but Relics number only **1,001**. The closer a Relic is to the number 1 position, the greater its potential. Each has unique powers and most have a bitter cost. These vestiges of power from ages gone can lead you to grace or damnation.

Among the Relics are various ranks. The top 3 Relics of each rank are Prime.

Basically super-powerful items, Fell thought. The prompt didn't tell him much more than he'd guessed before. And now every immortal on the planet knows that somewhere on this continent, one of the most powerful Relics is just waiting for someone to find it. Not only would it make the other immortals on the Home of the Three Kings aggressively expand, but it might draw heat from every other zone as well. In effect, his reward for being first was to have a big damn target painted on his back.

As weak as his tribe currently was, he wasn't even sure if he would want a Relic. Grabbing power and holding power were two different things. More than once in his old life he'd seen weaker groups wiped out after they gained something valuable if they weren't smart enough to hide it or sell it immediately. In any world, the only thing that mattered was power and its application.

"You said there was good news?" Zero asked resignedly.

"I did," Rig replied with a happy tone, and he brought up the rewards for being first in the world. As Fell read the first line, he thought about how Rig was supposed to be a combination of him and the world of Telos. If that was true, then either he or the world itself was an asshole.

Actually, probably both of us are, Zero thought sourly.

Congratulations, Lord Zero Fell! For founding the 1st religious domain on Telos, you are awarded:

1) **Free Relic**

   To honor your achievement, you will be awarded a random Divine Relic. This can greatly magnify your power, but will also make you a target for every other immortal who desires the power you wield!

"I'm fucked," Fell reflected aloud before reading the rest of the bonuses.

---

2) **Free Acquisition from the Sea of Souls**

   1 spirit can be obtained from the Sea of Souls at no cost and with no qualifiers.

   This soul will have the same level of Devotion as the average of your Chosen tribe. You must choose this soul within one day of founding your first settlement. Choose well!

3) **1 Dimensional Space** – 5 x 5 x 5 yards.

4) **Free Resources** (These will be kept in an extra-dimensional space for 7 days. After that time, this space will disappear and all of these resources must be stored or used)

    a. 500 units of Wood

    b. 500 units of Stone

    c. 500 units of Food

5) **5,000 Fame Points**

6) **100,000 Faith Points** (You are currently above your maximum Faith cap of 100,000. Use the excess within 1 day or it will be lost.)

Total Faith Points: **112,760**

7) **10 Gold Coins** (Each Gold Coin is worth 100 Silver Coins or 10,000 Copper Coins)

Reading the very first line made Fell blink rapidly. "Tell me this wasn't a worldwide announcement too."

"No," Rig assured him.

"Thank god for small favors," Fell breathed out in relief. Even his zero fuckedness wasn't zeroey enough to not care if every other god knew he had a Relic.

"I see what you did there," Rig quipped.

"No," was the god's deadpan reply. "Don't do that."

Zero fuckedness reacquired.

CHAPTER 52

Rig started explaining the rewards. The Relic was something he already knew about. The God's Eye said there was no telling what kind of item he would get. 1 to 1,001, it would be random. To Fell, it sounded like his Luck might come into play. He had seven days to claim it, so he decided to hold off. If he could gain another level, that would be another four points in the attribute.

The next bonus brought him back to the Sea of Souls. According to Rig, the first three ranks of *common, uncommon* and *limited* were known as the *mortal* ranks. They only required Faith Points to recruit, and there were usually more than enough of these souls for every deity to recruit as many as they wanted.

The next three ranks of the Sea comprised the Heroic ranks. These souls required more than Faith Points to summon. Typically, they would only be interested in civilizations known to have performed great deeds. That was why Fame Points were important. Rig told him that even if you could pay the recruitment cost, there were a finite number of Heroic souls that would appear every tenday. If two or more immortals tried to recruit the same soul, they would compete auction style, greatly increasing the cost.

The final three ranks were known as Sagas. These souls would typically not appear in the Sea of Souls on an average tenday. When they did, they might demand great things in return for their loyalty. They could even issue quests that were nearly impossible to complete. Saga-ranked souls were named that for a reason, however. While Heroic-ranked souls would be great leaders in any tribe, the power a Saga rank brought to a tribe could be enough to change the course of history.

"That is why," Rig told him, "the ability to grab any soul from the Sea is incredible. The only downside is that you have to use it within a tenday. There probably won't be any Saga-ranked souls so soon after Telos connected to the Labyrinth, but you might be able to claim a Heroic."

Fell nodded in appreciation. While he still hated the idea of drawing attention to himself without the power to back it up, having a powerful Relic and a powerful helper were indeed great bonuses. He told Rig to keep explaining.

"The next few are more self-explanatory," the God's Eye continued. "The third bonus," the God's Eye continued, "is basically a bag of holding without the bag."

Zero had played enough games in his life to understand that.

"You can't put anything living inside of it. Apart from a few other special cases, however, it is very versatile. All gods will gain a dimensional space upon founding a domain, but yours is much larger. I believe the default is one cubic meter. The only downside is that every kilogram you place inside it will temporarily take up one Energy slot. When you shed the weight, the slots will free up again."

A dimensional space could definitely come in handy. It wasn't a complete cheat like in some games he'd played. He couldn't put an army in it and have them sneak attack from inside an enemy's walls, but there were still plenty of options having a separate dimension opened up. Especially seeing as how he was starting with more than one hundred times as much space as other gods. It also showed again how important Energy was. He'd need to find a way to increase his max as soon as possible.

"The next perk will give you a jump-start on building your settlement. You have been given 500 wood, stone and food. It looks like you can summon any of that at will, but only for the next week. If you haven't used it up by then, it will just materialize in a pile. Might be a good idea to make a storage shed before that happens."

Fell nodded. He'd been thinking the same thing. A pile of stone might be in the way, but that shouldn't be a big issue. Having a pile of wood rotting in jungle humidity, however, would be a waste. The best bonus though was the food.

"How do food units work?"

"Each of your Chosen will consume one unit of food a day. You can halve that, but it will affect the tribe's health and morale immediately, with more negative effects down the road. Conversely, you could double their rations, which might increase population growth but you might also invent diabetes."

Zero ignored the British ghost's dry humor. Having the food was great, especially seeing as how they'd just run out, but five hundred units wasn't a lot. They'd blow through that in less than a week. He needed to find another source of food for the tribe or there would be a problem soon. "At least there's water nearby."

"Yeah," Rig cheerily agreed. "And nothing bad ever happened from drinking water running through a jungle." The ghost threw a finger up, "Giardia! Party of one!"

Fell put his hand out, but it went right through Rig's neck. Nope, he thought. Can't strangle him… yet. He spun one finger in a circle to tell the ghost to keep going. He also made a mental note to find a way to boil the tribe's water from now on. They'd been lucky so far, but he'd be a fool to think this new magical world didn't have diseases, especially as they were now in a jungle. He'd also have to choose a tribe member to drink from the local stream.

Rig highlighted the next bonus, "I have already mentioned that Fame helps you recruit Heroic souls. It has multiple other effects, but the only other one you need to know about now is Influence. The way you claim new hexes is to have your tribe's Influence increase. As a god, your mere existence affects your environment. As your State of Being increases, your passive influence will also increase. As of now, you are producing 1 Influence Point per day. Once you gain enough IPs, you can claim a new hex."

"But the new hex still has to be connected to the old ones?"

"Yes, and the farther away a hex is from your central area, the higher the price. Also, the more hexes you own, the higher the cost." Rig checked something, "We're lucky. Normally, with four hexes under your control the next one would cost 400 IPs. As three of them were awarded though, it looks like the rules of this world are treating you as if you haven't claimed any except the central hex. You only need 100 IPs. Fame helps with this as it can increase the amount of IPs you generate every day."

"The more famous I am, the faster my influence spreads. But the more land I already hold, the harder it is to spread more. Makes sense."

"The last benefits are pretty obvious. You've been given gold. It should be in your dimensional space."

Fell searched his HUD and found a new icon. It looked like a translucent cube made of orange and purple light. Focusing on it brought up an inventory list. Just as Rig had said, it now contained ten gold coins and nothing else. It looked like the wood, food and stone were stored somewhere else, which made sense because even one hundred and twenty-five cubic feet might not be enough to store large amounts of building materials.

"There is only one common currency in all the worlds of the Lattice," Rig told him. "Remember what dad told us, 'Money doesn't buy happiness, but it's damn hard to be happy without it.' The coins should make things easier and help us keep our head start."

Fell had no arguments there. His dad had been right. *His* dad, but it wasn't worth correcting the ghost. The point remained. While money might not buy happiness, money's true power was buying people out of unhappiness. If your car broke down and you couldn't fix it, or if your daughter was sick and you couldn't afford the medicine, then the lack of money might be all you thought about. If you could just write a check though, suddenly the good things in your life didn't have to compete with another horrible stress. Cumulatively, the person was generally happier. It wasn't fair, it wasn't right, but it was the truth. The only people who thought money didn't matter were people who had too much of it.

"The last one is also easy," Rig told him, finishing up. "You've been awarded more faith. In fact, they gave you enough to reach your cap. Luckily, it looks like the system is letting you spend the overflow. I wouldn't count on that in the future. If you reach your cap, anything else you earn will just be wasted."

Waste was not in line with Fell's frugal heart. He took the warning seriously.

"Can I increase my faith cap?" Fell asked. The main benefit of his tribe was their faith production. If he was already maxed out, it was being wasted.

Rig nodded, "The main way is by improving your altar. I don't even know how to do that yet. It is something we will have to discover. I sense there are other ways to improve your faith cap, but we'll have to discover them as well. It is important, however. There are many things that cost more than 100,000 Faith Points. One example is an altar core. If you ever want to expand your religion past this corner of the world, you'll need to make another altar."

Fell waved his hand. Making another altar was a tomorrow problem. A long time ago his uncle had told him it was better to learn how to handle one before you moved on to two. Of course, his uncle had been talking about whores in Tai Pei, but the advice was still sound.

"For now," Zero continued, "I just need to use some of this faith so we don't lose it. Which is the question I need answered. Except for summoning the eaglebear, what am I supposed to do with all this faith before the Sea of Souls opens tomorrow?"

Rig graced him with a ghostly smile. "You're a god," he stated, and for the first time without derision. "If you're willing to pay the price, you can do anything."

CHAPTER 53

Fell pulled up his Faith total.

> Total Faith Points: **112,760***
>
> *Faith Point Cap exceeded! Special circumstances allow you **1 day** to reduce total FPs to **100,000**. Any excess faith will be lost when time expires.

"You have nearly 13,000 points to spend, though you should spend more. The tenday is tomorrow, which means your followers generate more faith. Now put your hand on the altar."

Fell did and a new interface appeared. It had an overwhelming cascade of tiles.

"One second," Rig said, looking at it as well. "Let me order this and remove some of the locked info."

What Rig replaced it with was much easier to follow.

Rig gave him a moment to peruse before speaking again. "You can use your Faith to rapidly build anything you have the Blueprints for. You gain those through science and technology. As I said before, the buildings you can construct are limited by the technologies you possess. Every humanoid race starts with the same tech, *Stoneworking.* Each tribe also gets another free tech. The razin's free science is *Basic Building I.* Focus on both, and descriptions will appear."

Fell followed the advice.

You have Researched:

STONEWORKING

Description: Allows the creation of the most basic stone tools and weapons.

Resource Revealed: Stone

Unlocks 2 Blueprints: *Quarry (level 1)* and *Rock Totem (level 1).*

Unlocks 3 Techs: *Basic Building I, Gathering I* and *Fighting Skills I.*

Fell checked each Blueprint. The quarry would let him harvest more stone. It was also necessary to utilize the special resource,

Grey Stone. Once a quarry was built, there would be a civilization-wide bonus. The rock totem would increase the Influence Points his settlement produced, increasing his hex acquisition. The next tech, *Basic Construction,* unlocked three more blueprints.

You have Researched:

BASIC BUILDING I

Description: Provides a rudimentary understanding of constructing buildings.

Perk: Increases Building Speed and Durability by **10%.**

Unlocks 3 Blueprints: *Palisade (Level 1), Longhouse (Level 1)* and *Storage Shed (Level 1).*

Unlocks 3 Techs: *Basic Building II, Mining I,* and *Woodworking I.*

Fell focused on the Blueprints one at a time. The storage shed did just what it sounded like: it stored goods. It also reduced degradation of what was put inside by 25%. That could come in handy in a balls-hot jungle. The longhouse was a form of housing that gave a morale boost, and the palisade was a rudimentary wall that increased the defense of his people. This tech was definitely crucial as well. It did make him wonder though.

"Those orbweaver spiders were the Chosen of another god. I can't imagine a mason's shop or logging camp would come in handy for monsters. Will they unlock the same tech?"

"Every tribe has a different tech path," the God's Eye responded. "For other humanoids, the differences might be slight. For a monster race, they probably learn better ways to fight or increase their population. From what I feel, our tech tree is about average, not good or bad."

"As you can see," Rig continued, "technologies can give bonuses to a tribe, called 'Perks.' They can also unlock new knowledge. In this case, Blueprints. Before we get into that though, let's claim your free tech. Right now, you have six options." He waved a ghostly hand and a prompt appeared listing them.

"I was thinking about that. Am I able to get information about the techs before they're researched?"

"Just focus," Rig replied.

Looking at each one supplied the description.

GATHERING I

Cost: 70 RPs

Description: Can identify and gather edible foodstuffs

Resource Revealed: Various *common* grains

Class Unlocked: Herbalist (*common* rank)

Perk: Effect of herbs increased by **10%**

Unlocks 1 Blueprint: *Herb Hut*

"Do all the techs have the ability to level up?" Fell asked

"I don't know about all, but I think most do. You're now seeing how technologies are a bottomless research pit. You can keep mastering an old one, but that means you might fall behind other civilizations. Of course, there might be amazing benefits to specializing as well."

"I'm not seeing any indication of this tech unlocking more branches of research. Is it a dead end?"

Rig paused searching his information, "No, but the next tech requires two techs to be researched before it is revealed. The farther you go down the tech tree, the more this might happen." Rig told him that he "felt" that technologies progressed in a logical way. If Fell wanted his people to be able to grow crops, for instance, then he'd probably need to research *Gathering I*. That was how they'd get seeds, after all.

"More importantly, it says it unlocks a Class," Rig continued. "Once you build an Herb Hut, you'll be able to recruit Herbalists."

Thinking about the several poisonings that had already happened, that was very attractive. Zero went back to looking at his options. The next tech was extremely tempting.

FIGHTING SKILLS I

Cost: 78 RPs

Description: Teaches your people the rudiments of combat

Perk: Increases Damage by **5%**

Unlocks 1 Blueprint: *Fighting Pit (level 1)*

Those were the three that came off *Stoneworking*. Fell was tempted to grab *Fighting Skills I* immediately. It would let him increase the combat ability of his people. Right now, they were brave, but basically clueless as to how to fight. As important as battle was though, he couldn't ignore the need for a little thing called eating. His tribe would run out of food in a few weeks. He kept reading. The next three techs had been unlocked by his knowing *Basic Building*.

BASIC CONSTRUCTION II

Cost: 117 RPs

Description: Provides a basic understanding of constructing buildings

Perk: Increases Building Speed and Durability by **15%**

Unlocks 3 Blueprints: *Mason's Shop*, *Logging Camp* and *Elder Circle*

The mason's shop gave a bonus to quarrying stone, while the logging camp increased the speed of wood acquisition. Thanks to the glut of starting materials he'd gotten for being first to establish a Domain, resources weren't an issue yet, but he could see both of these buildings being crucial in the future. The Elder Circle increased the science output of his settlement, also useful.

Fell dismissed the prompt and looked over the last two techs.

MINING I

Cost: 110 RPs

Description: Allows your people to identify *common* ore and harvest it from the earth

Resource Revealed: Various *common* ores

Perk: Increases chance to find rare minerals by **5%**

Class Unlocked: Miner

WOODWORKING I

Cost: 109 RPs

Description: Allows the creation of the most wooden buildings and products

Perk: Wooden buildings and products have **+10% Durability.**

Class Unlocked: Carpenter

Unlocks 2 Blueprints: *Sawmill* and *Carpenter Workshop*

Now he had to decide how to use his free tech and his Research Points. It made the most sense to use his RPs to purchase as many techs as possible and use the free one for an expensive and, as of yet, unrevealed technology. What should he buy first?

This world might work by game principles, but this wasn't a video game. Even though he'd found and claimed the altar, they were all still in the middle of a hostile world. The focus had to be on food, shelter and defense. That narrowed it down to *Basic Construction I* or *Gathering I.*

Access to stronger Blueprints, especially for a stronger wall, was tempting but not as important as food. *Gathering* had the added benefit of identifying useful herbs. He used some of his Research Points and removed any information he already knew.

Congratulations! You have researched: GATHERING I

...

Unlocks 3 Techs: *Gathering II, Fishing I* and *Agriculture I.*

Rig had been right. Gathering opened up two more pathways to feed his people. Fell immediately grabbed them along with *Fighting Skills I, Mining I* and *Woodworking I.* He'd spent 513 Research Points, but knowledge was literally flooding the minds of his people.

Congratulations! You have revealed: FISHING I

Cost: 71 RPs

Description: Allows your people to gather food from the sea

Resource Revealed: Various *common* aquatic resources

Class Unlocked: Fisherman

Perk: Chance to catch fish increased by **10%**

Unlocks 1 Blueprint: *Fish Hut*

Unlocks 2 Techs: *Nets I* and *Fish Traps I*

Congratulations! You have revealed: AGRICULTURE I

Cost: 75 RPs

Description: Allows your people to plant crops

Resource Revealed: Various *common* grains

Class Unlocked: Farmer

Perk: Crop yield increased by **10%**

Unlocks 2 Techs: *Animal Husbandry I* and *Fertilizer I*

Each tech unlocked more. He scanned through them and they all had their appeal, but it was the tech coming off *Fighting Technique I* that was what he was looking for. It cost 184 RPs, but he purchased *Basic Combat I* and gained the ability to make Warriors!

Congratulations! You have researched: BASIC COMBAT I

Description: Introduces the Warrior Class to your society

Class Unlocked: Warrior

Blueprint Unlocked: Barracks

Perk: Attack and Defense **+5%**

Unlocks 2 Techs: *Bow Making I* and *Spear Fighting I*

He then used his free tech bonus to obtain *Bow Making I* and gained the ability for his people to engage in ranged combat!

Congratulations! You have researched: BOW MAKING I

Description: Allows your tribe to create crude bows

Skill Unlocked: Archery (requires Warrior Class)

Blueprint Unlocked: Archery Range (requires Barracks)

Perk: Ranged Damage **+5%**

Unlocks 1 Tech: *Archery I*

He'd used up almost all his Research Points, but his tribe could now feed themselves, protect themselves and make shelters.

With all the freebies done, Rig revealed that their settlement could currently assign up to five razin to the temple to make Research Points. Each would produce between zero and one Research Point a day, for a maximum of five points. Rig said there might be a benefit to the five having high Intelligence, but he couldn't be sure as it didn't always reflect a higher intellect. Put another way, having points in the Intelligence attribute didn't necessarily make you smarter.

Fell told Rig to assign the five villagers with highest Intelligence, and to have them start researching *Basic Construction II.* He wanted to unlock the Elder's Circle Blueprint.

"I still don't see what this has to do with my faith," Fell stated. "Can I buy tech with FPs?"

"Now you're getting it," Rig replied with a smug grin. "And if you didn't have the Research Points, I would have advised we do that. Instead, I think we can dive into that later. For now, we have Blueprints and buildings to create. It's time to change the face of Telos."

CHAPTER 54

"Of all the Blueprints we have, I believe the most important is the palisade," Rig began.

PALISADE
A 7-foot-tall wooden wall that can slow some enemies but will not stop stronger foes.
Effect: +10% Defense against enemies on the other side of the palisade. Has Defense +5.
Quality: Average
Durability: 50/50
Building Cost: 50 BPs per 100 yards
Resource Cost: 50 Wood per 100 yards

After reading the prompt, Fell held up a hand, "Why do I need a blueprint to build some of this stuff? A palisade is just a row of sharpened trees, isn't it? Pretty sure I can figure out how to shove a stick in a hole. I've had plenty of practice."

"You could indeed, but you would miss the extra effects. Though the buildings produced by these Blueprints are all Tier 0, they are also Level 1. Level 1 buildings will have additional effects and bonuses. The palisade you would build by 'shoving sticks in a hole' would be Level 0, and so would not give the +10% defense to your fighters. It would also probably be easier to tear down, having a lower defense and durability."

"You're saying Blueprints magically make a building better?" Zero asked in disbelief. He'd seen some amazing things, but a building was a building. Back on Earth, everyone had been too busy running for their lives to construct anything. He'd met an engineer that had been babbling about how the structural integrity of certain materials was starting to change, but the man had been off his nut. Of course, seeing your daughter eaten by a monster while you ran away from both it and her screams for help could do that to a fella.

"Yes," Rig answered with more than a bit of snark. "I know that might be hard to believe for a god whose powers are fueled by the captured souls of your slaughtered enemies."

Once again, he was losing a battle of wits to himself, which annoyed the hell out of him.

"What about BPs? What are those?"

"BP stands for Building Points. It is a measure of how much effort is required to construct things. Dedicating a member of your tribe to building a structure will generate one BP/day. If any of them have the Builder Class, that can increase."

Zero's eyes scanned over the prompts, "The logging camp costs 75 BPs. Does that mean that if I assign seventy-five people to build it, it should only take a day?"

"Good thought, but no. Seventy-five virgins wouldn't get you happy faster than one freak, would they? No. There'd just be a lot of elbows, tears and feminine disappointment, wouldn't there?"

Fell breathed heavily, but didn't interrupt.

"Using unskilled labor," Rig continued, "you don't want to use more than five people to build a basic building. Those five have a fifty-fifty chance of following the Blueprint correctly. If you add more people past that five, then the chances of failure increase."

It made sense in a way. Adding more people to a situation rarely made it safer or more sensible. That was especially true if they didn't have any idea what they were doing or talking about to begin with. That was a lesson he'd learned from the internet. As a compendium of all human knowledge, it should have made everyone smarter. Instead, it just gave a pulpit to every idiot who otherwise could have been ignored. The resulting noise was so loud it drowned out logic and good sense.

Rig continued his explanation, "Even if a Blueprint is followed successfully, it is highly likely that the quality of the building will be low. There are several quality ranks ranging from *slum* to *masterwork*. Anything that is *slum* quality has a chance of spontaneously collapsing or being blown down in the first storm. If we build a structure like that, I recommend tearing it down and starting again."

Not a bad idea, the godling agreed. He'd worked construction one summer, and the first, second and last thing anyone talked about was job safety. Of course, women and money occupied a couple of the middle slots. There were lots of opposing opinions about those two, but everyone agreed on safety. He certainly didn't want to be buried under a collapsed structure.

"We can worry about all of that later. For now, the most important thing is the palisade."

At Fell's prompting, Rig pulled up the bird's-eye view. "We'll use the topography to our advantage. The eastern and southern cliffs provide a natural barrier." At least he hoped they did. If there was something that could scale wet cliffs, then a seven-foot wall probably wouldn't slow them down much either.

"With that in mind, we only need to build two sections."

"How long will each side be?" Zero mused. "With how small the tribe is, we can't cover a large area." He rubbed his chin and looked up at the sunlight coming through the ruined temple roof. "Maybe half a mile to a section."

"We'll need to tear it down when it's time to expand," Rig warned.

"The tribe needs to survive long enough to expand," Fell countered.

Rig conceded the point. He altered the virtual image of the settlement to show where the wall would go. It looked good to Fell. The God's Eye focused for a moment and another prompt appeared.

> To build **1,760 yards** of a **Level 1 Palisade,** there is a building cost of **880 Building Points** and a resource cost of **880 Wood**. Do you wish to pay the building cost with **8800 Faith**? Yes or No?

It looked like the building-to-faith ratio was 1:10. With his Faith Point slush fund, he didn't see any reason why not. Fell chose "Yes."

The sound of churned earth echoed out, followed by exclamations from the tribe. Looking out across the hilltop, Fell saw columns of sharpened wood emerging from the ground. Fast enough that you could keep a beat to it, more treated wood emerged, close enough to not leave a gap. Starting at the exact spot it had been on Rig's map, the wall began to take shape.

"At our current altar level, the settlement can construct at a rate of 10 BP/min. The entire wall should be done in less than an hour and a half."

As amazed as the razin were, Fell was just as much in awe. He watched for several minutes as more wood emerged from the ground. It reminded him of waking up in the morning to find that a whole crop of mushrooms had grown overnight. Such a blatant manifestation of power, seeing the very landscape change only because of his will, was mesmerizing.

And seductive.

"Yes," Rig intoned quietly beside him, "this is the kind of power you wield now. The power to change the earth and the land itself. Yet this is only the barest inkling of what a god can do. It all comes down to if you are willing to pay the price."

The columns continued to pop out of the ground, perfectly level with one another at seven feet each. It looked like his first use of faith in the settlement was proceeding well. With a grin on his face and a thrill in his heart, Fell asked, "What else can I do?"

"These are all the Blueprints we have."

QUARRY

A simple wooden structure that allows stone to be harvested. Must be built near stone.

Effect: Allows stone to be harvested

Quality: Average

Durability: 50/50

Building Cost: 50 BPs

Resource Cost: 100 Wood

ROCK TOTEM

Can construct a basic religious structure with quarried stone. This Totem will increase the influence of your religious domain.

Effect: +1 Influence Point/day for the settlement in which it is built.

Quality: Average

Durability: 75/75.

Building Cost: 35 BPs.

Resource Cost: 10 Stone.

HERB HUT

A wooden structure that increases the potency of herbs and increases the speed of training in the Herb Lore skill.

Effect: +10% Potency to all Herbs.

Quality: Average

Durability: 50/50.

Building Cost: 50 BPs.

Resource Cost: 35 Wood.

LONGHOUSE

A wooden structure that houses your population. Base capacity: 20 people.

Effect: At base capacity, +25 Morale. If at half-base capacity, +50 Morale. If overcapacity, no morale bonus

Quality: Average

Durability: 50/50

Building Cost: 50 BPs

Resource Cost: 50 Wood

STORAGE SHED

A wooden structure that decreases resource degradation. Can hold 1000 storage units.

Effect: +20% half-life of resources.

Quality: Average

Durability: 50/50.

Building Cost: 100 BPs.

Resource Cost: 75 Wood.

Fell scanned through the options. They seemed pretty simple. The palisade was already being built. The quarry would let his people harvest more stone, but that could wait. The longhouse was a must. It looked like he'd need to build several of those. We've got almost 130 people to house, and who knows what the weather is like here.

The rock totem would increase the village's influence, which translated into more area for him to claim and to walk around in. That would probably be his next build. The storage shed was also practical; the bonus resources he'd been awarded needed to be stored in 7 days. It was actually the storage shed he had a question about.

"What does 'storage units' mean?"

"It references how much space a resource takes up. One food unit is about a hundredth the size of a wood unit. A wood unit takes up two storage units, so food takes up 1/50th of a storage unit. Each unit of stone, on the other hand, takes up four storage units."

Fell did some quick math, "Then I'll need at least two storage sheds. I have more than enough Faith Points. I can purchase those as well."

"You can," Rig agreed. "Do not forget your people are natural builders, however, thanks to their *Industrious* Characteristic. You have also unlocked the Builder Class, which means you can give it to any tribe members who meet the requirements. Having a Builder make the storage sheds, rather than buying them with faith, will provide an increase in durability. Faith is powerful, but skilled artisans will always provide a better product.

"Also, you must remember that the altar can only generate 10 Building Points per minute, total. Which means that if you want two projects going at once, they'll manifest twice as slow."

That made sense. Better to build one thing at a time and have it done. There was another option though, "What about the other perk from having such high Soul Resonance with the tribe? The bonus that lets me create any building and that I have to use within seven days of founding my settlement."

The God's Eye smiled, and looked over his shoulder. Zero followed his gaze but all he saw was the ruined temple, grass, rocks, the cliffside and the ocean. What could he-

Fell's eyes widened and he pulled up the exact wording of the bonus.

1 Free Building or **1 Free Repair of an existing Building** (must be used within 7 days)

"We can repair the temple?" the god asked in surprise. Fell looked around at the ruined building in amazement. It was several stories high and more than half of it had been blown to bits. Not only that, the Blueprints he'd unlocked all looked pretty simple. They were just structures made out of wood and rock. Meanwhile, the temple was made of some sort of impossibly hard stone. Could he really have it repaired, just like that?

In response to his doubts, Rig responded, "It wouldn't be nearly so large or grand. You're right in that we don't have enough of this type of stone to fully repair it, but we could give you four walls and a roof. That being said, it is still a building in your domain that can be repaired."

Rig sent him a prompt.

RUINED TEMPLE

A temple created from Void Stone. This impossibly hard stone is resistant to most magics and has a very high defense. Due to its destruction by an unknown force, it has lost all qualities.

Effect: n/a.

Quality: n/a.

Durability: n/a.

Fell smiled. "Let's do it." There would be definite benefits to having a building made of this black rock.

Before Rig could trigger the restoration, however, a sense of foreboding swept through the both of them. A moment later, Fell realized it wasn't a vague feeling. It was targeted. In fact, he could point a finger at the source of it. That finger pointed North by Northwest, and he knew without being told that there was trouble coming from that direction.

A red warning prompt appeared.

An Enemy has entered your domain.

Fell didn't even have time to ask before Rig told him in an urgent voice, "An unbound god has entered your domain." There was no trace of mocking in his voice. Instead, his tone was deadly serious. With a wave of his hand, he summoned an aerial view of the settlement. More than a dozen humanoids had entered the northwestern hex. They were all eight to ten feet tall, and were built like walking refrigerators with tree trunks for arms and legs. Their mouths sported long tusks set in faces ugly enough to make a mother cry.

Rig focused on and identified the enemy, "The god's name is Svaroth. His Art is Earth, which probably means he can increase defense and health."

"Do you know what his Divine Powers are?" It would make a big difference if the god could increase the defense of his whole tribe or just himself. The invaders were already double the height and quadruple the size of the razin. If they could be further augmented by Divine Power…

"I can't say," Rig replied. "I think your States of Being are the same, and the Energy difference is negligible, so I'm limited in the information I can gather. I can tell you that his Chosen are ogres." With a grim tone, he summed up, "That means fifteen eight to ten-foot-tall enemies are running directly at us. The terrain is slowing them down a bit, but we only have minutes before they arrive. Finally, the god has at least one acolyte. He's the one that's twelve feet tall."

Turning north, Fell bared his teeth.

CHAPTER 55

Seven days earlier.

"Move, you stupid lumps! Move!"

A guttural voice like a coal miner's thirty-year rasp still somehow managed to reach the volume of a bellow. The slow moving but powerful ogres had been berated by it for days. The tribe did not respond beyond slightly picking up the pace. To the dim-witted giants, violence and bloodshed were as natural as breathing. When ripping an opponent's arm off was a normal occurrence and eating your dinner while it screamed was the height of comedy, mere words couldn't bother them. Not even when they were spoken by their new god.

Svaroth cursed, quietly this time. He wasn't afraid they'd hear him. He just knew that yelling again would have little effect on his stupid Chosen. He'd known that choosing ogres as his worshippers meant they'd have low intellect, but this was worse than he'd imagined. Even their massive physical strength was barely a trade-off. As they plodded through the jungle, he comforted himself that he could convert smarter worshippers after his Chosen murdered a few weaker tribes.

Still, if the god had known they'd be this stupid, he would have made a different choice, advice from his sponsor be damned.

The tribe continued to tromp through the jungle. Nothing about their travel could be called stealthy. The hulking ogres made enough noise to wake the dead. Not only had the sounds drawn countless beasts and monsters to them while they'd made their way through the thick trees, but the damn ogres seemed incapable of walking away from a fight or even employing the most basic of tactics. Admittedly, their skin was thick enough to serve as armor. Coupled with the fact that the smallest member of his Chosen was eight feet tall, and that the weakest could rip a tree out of the ground and use it as a club, they'd killed all the monsters they'd come across so far.

Drawing in jungle beasts had actually served Svaroth's purposes at first. A few ogres had died but the rest had grown stronger. The entire tribe had reached level one after just a few days. It also meant food was not an issue. Unfortunately, the god had soon learned just how dangerous their new world was. After five days of travel, they found an enemy they couldn't overcome.

A jaguar-like creature, three feet at the shoulder and white as snow, had leaped out at one of his ogres. It had been hiding in a tree and moved in near silence. The sneak attack had let the cat bury its giant fangs in the ogre's throat. Not even his worshipper's thick skin could stand against the beast's incisors. Blood had sprayed in a fountain, painting the jaguar like a canvas. The ogre had died within seconds of hitting the ground.

The rest of the tribe had immediately retaliated, but even outnumbered the creature had proven difficult to take down. The panther had been much more agile than the strong but stiff ogres. It had evaded the first blows they threw at it. Its counter attacks caused more injuries. After all of his Chosen had joined the fray, however, they had pounded the beast into a meat paste.

If that was all that had happened, Svaroth wouldn't have given it another thought. The loss of one of his worshippers was like the loss of an arrow. The ogres were a resource, nothing more. They only had value in how they served him, and he had more to spare. On his path to power, he'd surely sacrifice countless worshippers. Besides, once he reached the location his Sponsor was directing him to, he would be able to summon plenty more.

Only moments after the panther was slain, however, they heard an ear-splitting *yowl*. Another sounded right after. Then they heard two more roars to the left and another to the right. Jaguars stalked out of the jungle, white-furred just like the one they had killed. More and more came, until he counted twenty. The tribe was surrounded. The two groups stared at each other. Even then, Svaroth wasn't concerned. His God's Eye had shown him that all the beasts were levels one and two, no better than his tribe, and he had far more fighters.

Also, his Art was Earth. He could harden his skin to be as tough as rock and summon spikes of stone that could skewer opponents. Even more importantly, being an Earth god made him extremely resilient.

EARTH ART

Your power is most in tune with Earth. The consequences of this will grow vastly over time. At your current State of Being, it has the following effects:

Enduring Earth meant that any debuffs, from poison to burning to mental attacks, would have a reduced effect on him. Basically, he was one tough bastard. *Earth's Bounty* was even better. Both the damage he could endure and his ability to fight were increased. At his current State of Being the effect wasn't too dramatic, but in time it would become substantial.

Finally, his Profound Act had boosted his Constitution. Upon the suggestion of his sponsors, he'd eaten a poisonous flower called Scarlet Widow's Tears. The pain had been horrific. For a full day, he'd writhed on the ground, blood leaking from every hole, eyes to anus. Svaroth was convinced that the only reason his tribe hadn't turned on him during that day was that he'd killed one of his worshippers immediately after claiming them as his Chosen. It was not his first time as a god. No matter what world he'd found himself in, eating a steaming heart fresh from someone's chest cavity had a way of establishing dominance.

If it hadn't been for the two effects of his Earth Art, the poison flower would have killed him. He'd managed to endure, however, and had gained a *Major* boost to his Endurance and a *Meaningful* boost to his Constitution. His Endurance had increased by +10, and his Constitution had gone up by +15. The attribute changes had made his health and stamina skyrocket.

His Profound Act and *Earth's Bounty* meant that he had the health and stamina of a level ten ogre. Even though the monsters of Telos were rapidly absorbing mana and growing stronger, he could easily be considered a heavyweight in these early days.

While his stats and his Divine Powers were mere parlor tricks compared to the power he would wield when his Art evolved, they were more than enough to deal with *common* monsters like these. His acolyte, Grimshaw, could also use the Chant *Stone Skin* and should be nigh-invulnerable to the beasts.

With nearly fifty ogres at his command, Svaroth might take losses, but his surviving warriors would gain more experience and, hopefully, levels. He didn't view this prowl of panthers as a threat, but more as a whetstone to hone his people.

The god's confidence fled though when he heard a roar deeper than any he'd heard before. A black panther had stalked out of the thick trees, staring death at the ogres. It was a foot taller than the other cats, and its muscles were much larger and more well-defined. It padded forward, moving soundlessly as it approached the tribe. An invisible but almost palpable change occurred between the two groups. The fact that the ogres weren't immediately attacking told its own story. His tribe loved blood, battle and destruction. They weren't bright, but they could be cunning. They knew this new panther was far stronger than the one they'd already killed.

Svaroth knew the same, and he even knew why. His God's Eye confirmed what he'd already suspected. "Damn the luck," he cursed.

It was an *elite*.

The god might have been new to Telos, but he was an old god of the Labyrinth. More than that, he belonged to a half-star pantheon that had conquered a world. Not only did he have experience, but he possessed knowledge that rogue deities, those that did not belong to a pantheon, did not. Though this new world would have many secrets and magics unique to it, there were some things that almost always remained true.

When it came to monsters, being higher ranked didn't just mean that a creature was stronger than the lower ranks. *Elites*, even lesser *elites,* would be able to fight smarter and possibly even strategize, greatly increasing their effective combat power. Greater *elites* could have powers that could turn the tide of a battle.

Svaroth's worst fears coming true, the black panther started rumbling deep in its chest. It wasn't a roar so much as a purr, but there was nothing comforting about it. The sound built in volume until the god could feel it thrumming in the air. Then the panther let loose a bloodcurdling *YOWL* that nearly deafened him. The god wasn't concerned about his ears though. His eyes were trained on the jaguars that were reacting to the magic in their leader's battle cry.

The hair of every panther stood on end like they were electrified. The muscles under their pelts swelled and their talons lengthened. Red glows kindled in their eyes. The attributes of the entire prowl surged, and they went mad with anger.

Svaroth barely had time to curse before the now-*Enraged* panthers attacked. Before the *elite* had buffed them, each of his ogres could probably have killed a panther in a one-on-one fight. Now, however, the beasts' power and speed had increased dramatically. The prowl of cats fell upon the ogres like mice. Soon, the scent of blood was heavy on the air.

The ogres roared to meet the challenge, not intimidated in the least. They swung fists the size of boulders and uprooted trees to use as clubs, but the agile panthers were able to attack with impunity. Not only were they much faster, but the terrain strongly favored them. While the heavy-footed tribe were slowed down by the thick undergrowth, the panthers dodged, rolled and bounced off of tree trunks before attacking again. In the first minute of the battle, seven ogres lay dead and more were wounded.

After a savage battle, Svaroth's tribe ultimately did kill the twenty *common* panthers, but the *elite* escaped. The creature was just too strong to overcome. Even when the god used his Divine Power, *Stone Spear,* the *elite* had only been wounded. The agile cat had managed to twist out of the way of the rock spear, receiving only a gash across its side.

By the time the battle was done, only twenty-five members of the god's tribe still breathed. Three of them were so heavily wounded that they wouldn't make it through the day. Another three were maimed badly enough that they would only slow down the tribe.

Svaroth didn't have any healing powers. His own Divine Core and higher energy would heal most wounds in a matter of hours, but his tribe could make no such claim, so he ordered the six put to death immediately. The tribe fell upon their injured fellows without qualm or hesitation. The god let them eat to regain their strength while he assessed the situation. A few cannibalized their dead, though most seemed to prefer panther meat. Other races might hesitate or at least get an upset stomach after eating the raw flesh of beasts or their former comrades, but the ogres showed no such squeamishness.

Svaroth begrudgingly admitted there was a good reason he'd reached the fourth rank in Soul Resonance with the massive brutes: they did not trouble themselves with insipid questions of right and wrong. For both the god and his Chosen, there were only the strong and the prey they fed upon.

Night had fallen during the battle, so he had them make camp. The ogres' vision was average during the day, but worse at night. Coupled with the fact that they were not exactly agile, traveling through the jungle after sunset was a bad idea. It had only taken one-night march punctuated with a lot of, "Ow, me foot!" "Stupid tree keep moving front of me!" or "Back hole only 'in' when sun in sky!" before the god stopped trying to travel after sundown.

The next day the greatly-diminished tribe moved forward again, following their god. Only Svaroth knew why they were rushing through the jungle. Only he could feel the "pull" from his sponsor's quest.

More than once, he'd thought back to how strange it was that he'd gotten a sponsor. He was by no means weak, but his standing in his pantheon was not very high. Even if it had been higher, his pantheon was weaker than one star. New immortals might not know how much it cost a sponsor to help on new Labyrinth worlds, but he was an old god, and well-versed in such matters.

The gifts of a sponsor cost trillions more than they were worth. It was not an exaggeration that millions might be slain to provide the energy required to gift a simple note. That was why Svaroth had been so thankful to receive instructions before arriving in Telos. It was a bit strange that he did not know the identity of his sponsors. The note had only been signed with an unfamiliar image of seven shining jewels. There was no doubt however, that the advice it had contained had served him well.

That was why he was now pushing his Chosen tribe toward the last objective he'd been given. He didn't know how much farther he needed to go, but according to the quest orb it would be a great starting location. With the benefits the quest provided, he'd swiftly expand his domain and grow in strength. With any luck the other members of his pantheon would establish themselves nearby, and the Shattered Curse empire would rule another world!

First, he needed to survive, however. Unfortunately, before noon that day, he found himself wishing his Luck stat were higher. Just before the sun reached its zenith, he heard it again: a bone-quaking *yowl* that pierced the humid jungle air. Answering cries echoed out behind the tribe. The *elite* had found more *common* beasts to follow it. Svaroth had ordered the ogres to run faster. For once, they eagerly agreed.

For the next two days, the tribe had been hunted. They not only had to fight the jaguars, they also had to fight the environment and elements. While on the march, one ogre had reached for a red fruit only to be ensnared by vines as soon as he touched it. He was pulled out of sight faster than the rest of the tribe could react. A surprisingly high-pitched scream echoed out from the thick jungle undergrowth and was abruptly cut off. Svaroth had no idea what kind of plant monster was able to kill a nine-foot-tall wall of muscle in less than a minute, but he had ordered the tribe to circle around it.

Another of his Chosen had made the mistake of touching a thorny plant. She only made it five steps before orange-red blood poured from her eyes, nose, mouth and ears. The ogress choked to death on her own fluids seconds later. The jaguars also claimed the lives of another two tribe members. One, they took at night. A fading cry and a smear of blood was all that was left of an ogre sentry that had not paid enough attention.

The cats avoided another straight fight but still managed to claim one more life. During the day, one of his tribe had lagged behind. In a flash, five panthers attacked. A hard swipe across the back of the ogre's thigh had hamstrung the fool. He went down with a cry, and the cats started tearing pieces of flesh off his struggling and screaming form.

The ogre hadn't died quickly. The rest of the tribe had started to rush back to help him, but the black-furred *elite* had stepped forward in challenge. It bared its teeth at Svaroth's people, a deep growl building in its throat. The message was clear: if they tried to save the fallen ogre, it would trigger its power and start another battle.

To make matters worse, the Labyrinth itself was strengthening their tormentors. In their first confrontation, the *elite* had been level three and the *common* panthers level one or two. Now the black-haired panther was level six and *common* beasts were between levels two and four. Battle could not explain the increase. Even though only a few days had passed, the Labyrinth was pouring mana into this world. The world of Telos, and all of its beasts, were drinking it up like a man lost in the desert.

Svaroth had bared his fangs at the black panther, but he still backed down. Fury and shame had filled him as he and his tribe left the ogre to his fate. Again, Svaroth didn't actually care about his worshipper, but the fact that an old god like himself was being thwarted by a damn jungle cat made his blood boil. Anger or not, it didn't change the fact that he couldn't afford to lose more followers.

He had led his Chosen away, the captured ogre's screams echoing behind them. The cruelty of cats was obvious. He heard his abandoned Chosen screaming for at least a mile.

As the tribe had run away, they came upon a ravine. At first, it had seemed like their luck was still against them, but they found a fallen tree large enough to form a narrow bridge. After crossing, Svaroth had ordered the tribe to push the tree down into the crevasse. It took their combined strength, but they managed it. That night, for the first time in days, the sounds of hunting cats had not followed them.

As the stars had danced above them that night, Svaroth had looked out over his tribe. When he'd first come to Telos, he'd had nearly sixty tribe members. Now he only had fifteen. He cursed his sponsor for leading him down this path. It was enough to make him wonder if his unknown benefactor was actually trying to harm him.

He put that thought out of his mind though. Sponsors were all cosmic beings of universe-ranked power. They would have to be completely mad to waste resources helping him, only to trick him later. Almost no existences at that level were both powerful *and* insane enough to do such a thing. No, he counseled himself, it must just be bad luck.

Also, it wasn't all bad. He was still powerful and in peak condition. The days of constant battle had leveled his remaining Chosen to level two. His acolyte had even reached level three. Most of the tribe had died, but those that remained were stronger for it. He further comforted himself with the reminder that once he had an altar, numbers wouldn't be a problem anymore.

The next night, the ogres camped with their backs against a boulder. On the morning of his ninth day on Telos, he started moving his tribe forward again. After nearly a day of travel, excitement filled Svaroth's heart. They had crested a hill and caught a whiff of salt in the air. His sponsor had left a clue that when they saw the ocean, he'd be close. The Earth god opened his mouth to urge his tribe to pick up the pace. The end was in sight!

Before he could speak, however, a loud sound reverberated in his mind. It sounded like a gong being struck three times.

> ### GLONG! GLONG! GLONG!
> Worldwide Announcement! Congratulations to God Zero Fell for establishing the first...

Absolute fury filled Svaroth's heart. Some other god had managed to establish a religious domain. He didn't recognize the name. Being part of a pantheon, even a half star, meant he knew the names of thousands of Labyrinth gods. He did not know them all, of course; the Labyrinth was a super-dimension that encompassed countless planes of reality. Still, the number of powerful gods and pantheons was small in comparison.

The fact that he did not recognize the name opened up the possibility that a new god had somehow outperformed every other old god. The idea of such an upstart already growing in power while he, the mighty Svaroth, was having to traipse through a jungle was infuriating! If not for his ill luck in running into those damn cats and having to search for a way to cross the ravine, he might have already reached his quest location. As he seethed, he realized the hate he felt for the god Zero Fell was only matched by his anger toward the panthers. He fucking hated cats!

As he read the rest of the prompt, his anger burned through his soul to reveal pure incandescent fury.

> ... the first religious domain on Telos! **Home of the Three Kings** is now known as the Religious Cradle of the world!

Home of the Three Kings? He was on Home of the Three Kings! That was his continent! Gaining the First bonus was why he'd marched through sweltering jungle and had his balls stung by giant mosquitos, why he had lost more than half of his followers! Now some pissant unknown immortal had claimed the bonus? The benefits for being first on a new Labyrinth world were always considerable. Svaroth immediately resolved to destroy this new god who had taken what was rightfully his!

He was about four breaths into what would be a truly amazing rant when a horrible thought occurred to him. What if this Fell Zero hadn't only taken the First prize? What if he'd managed to do it by taking the very location that Svaroth himself had been struggling to reach? As if summoned, a blinking light at the corner of his vision showed there was another prompt waiting for review.

As he read, his seed of worry sprouted tendrils of despair.

571

> **You have failed your Quest:** Slaughter the Lambs.
>
> Another god has claimed the altar you agreed to obtain! You have **FAILED!**
>
> Your Penalties are as follows:
>
> Your Chosen have lost faith in you! **Devotion decreased by 1 full rank.**
>
> You have betrayed the trust of Telos! **50% decrease in any gained experience for 1 month.**
>
> You have betrayed the trust of the Labyrinth! **50% decrease in any gained Faith for 1 month.**
>
> Take the altar from the god that owns it to remove these debuffs.
>
> You have 24 hours.

The god's eyes widened in shock. The penalties for failing this quest were way too harsh. They basically ensured he would be weaker than every other immortal on Telos! The only ray of light was the last line. He could still redeem himself.

"They've stolen from me!" Svaroth bellowed. "Run, you dumb meat sacks! Run! There is blood to spill!"

The ogres did not understand what was happening, but the promise of carnage made their legs pump like pistons. Their high endurance and monumental strength forged a path through the dense jungle. An hour later, they were able to see cliffs and ocean far to the left. Twenty minutes after that, Svaroth felt himself cross an invisible barrier. Even without the prompt he'd have known he was in the domain of another god. Minutes later they reached a clearing with a hill at the far end bounded by sea cliffs. At the top of the hillock he saw a tribe of humanoids standing in front of the ruins of a black stone temple.

To his right he saw a wooden wall rising from the ground. It was irrefutable evidence that this group of small men and women had indeed stolen his prize. To his delight, he also saw there was no way the fortification would be completed before his Chosen could attack.

The enemy tribe were dressed in simple furs and were only half the size of his ogres. The tribe was most likely a hundred strong. Even though his Chosen were outnumbered, compared to his ogres, the five-foot-tall men and women looked like children. The fact that they were all holding weapons and were arranged in two distinct blocks didn't please him, but their wooden spears should pose no real threat to his tribe. He doubted they could even pierce his ogres' thick skin.

What was slightly concerning, however, were the auras of Divine Power surrounding three of the enemy. The female's glow was also stronger than that of the men. Svaroth seethed seeing that. It could mean only one thing. Not only had this god managed to make three acolytes, but the woman's power had somehow been increased. They could be problematic.

Those acolytes were nothing compared to the figure oozing Divine Power. At the forefront of the enemy tribe was a black-skinned man with black-furred ears. His stature was no different from the others, but he stared down at the ogres as if all he surveyed was under his control. At his side stood a golden-skinned figure leaning against a large white bow. They both had energy levels far stronger than the others.

One was obviously the god of the enemy tribe. Svaroth's God's Eye named him as Zero Fell. The archer had no Divine Power, but Fell had undoubtedly found a powerful ally. Seeing the battle formations and high energy figures made the Earth god feel a moment of uncertainty, but that feeling was quickly brushed aside. These bastards had dared take what had been promised to him! Worse, coming out of the top of each of their heads were round furry ears. His God's Eye identified them as pantherkin. That meant they were cats. And not only cats, but panther cats! It was like this new world was mocking him.

Cats! Panthers!

Panthers! Cats!

It was a cruel joke!

Svaroth's eyes went bloodshot, but he still controlled himself. He followed the forms of godhood and shouted out a warning and declaration. The response he received drove him mad with fury. Pointing a thick finger at the tribe, he commanded his Chosen.

"Kill them! Kill them all! I fucking hate cats!"

CHAPTER 56

Twenty Minutes Before…

The moment Svaroth's tribe had crossed the invisible boundary of Fell's domain, it had filled Zero with a sense of danger. When Rig had shown him what was rushing toward his tribe and his defenseless altar, that feeling had hardened into something sharper.

"How long until they get here?" he asked curtly.

Rig watched the enemy on the virtual map. They showed up as figures outlined in red pushing their way through the thick jungle. Their large size worked against them in the dense trees, but their massive strength made up for it. After watching for a few more seconds, the apparition responded, "They'll be here in twenty minutes, maybe less."

"Will the wall be done in time?" he asked tersely.

"Not even close," Rig said, zooming back to the village. Less than a quarter was built. "Even it was-"

"Even if it was," Fell finished, "those things are as tall as the wall. Without ranged weapons, it'll be as useful as a comb holding back the tide." The god searched for options, flipping through prompts as he considered different scenarios.

"Repair the temple, Rig. Even if those ogres are as strong as they look, hopefully they can't beat their way through that black stone. It will buy us time to figure out how to kill them. There are only fifteen. Maybe I can murder them one at a time once night falls." His nightvision was perfect now. If theirs wasn't it would give him an edge.

Rig did as he was told, but a moment later had more bad news to share.

Do you wish to use your **FREE Building Repair** to restore the **Ruined Temple**?

This will cost **0 resources**, but will revert the building to Level 1, Rank 0, Tier 0.

It will take **1 hour** to complete. Yes or No?

Fell could see the same prompt. A muscle in his cheek twitched. One hour was way too long. He wasn't sure what the full importance of the levels, ranks and tiers would be in this case, but he knew that this battle would be joined long before the temple was restored. Comparing his hundred-and-twenty-eight tribe members -- the tallest of which was five feet and the heaviest probably one hundred pounds -- to these eight-to-ten-foot walls of muscle didn't promise a happy ending. Especially not when his people were fighting with sharpened sticks. Some of those ogres were *carrying*, not dragging, uprooted trees as weapons.

The god considered his options for another few seconds but not more than that. Battles were won and lost before they began. Every moment counted, and he had long ago learned not to waste time. Without an edge, throwing his people at the ogres would be like pitting a hundred toddlers against fifteen bodybuilders. Even if victory was achieved, it would be pyrrhic.

There was a lot he still had to learn about this new world, but he'd already internalized the lesson that his people were his power. If they all died, his faith generation would be crippled. Also, he would lose access to the altar. He wouldn't be able to summon more. A glorious death was not an option.

Maybe if he challenged the ogres by himself he could do some damage with his *Soul Strike* until the charge ran out. Zero put a hand on his chest. Maybe it was even time to bring his little friend out to play. That might buy enough time, especially if they would chase him into the forest. He could only go as far as the borders of his domain, but that was at least a mile from the temple. If he could stall for an hour, then his tribe could hide inside. If not, his people could scatter into the jungle, or maybe even retreat back down the bridge.

Rig knew him. The God's Eye *was* him, after all, so he knew what Fell was thinking. Before the godling rushed to meet the enemy, the apparition spoke up, "There are other options to consider. You are forgetting the benefits from being the first in this world to create a domain."

With a mental flexion the God's Eye pulled up two prompts.

Free Relic!

To honor your achievement, you will be awarded a random divine Relic. This can greatly magnify your power, but will also make you a target for every other immortal who desires the power you wield!

Free Acquisition from the Sea of Souls

1 spirit can be obtained from the Sea of Souls with no cost and no qualifiers.

This soul will have the same level of Devotion as the average value for your Chosen tribe. You must choose this soul within one day of founding your first settlement. Choose well!

"Which one of these is supposed to save us from the army of giants?" Fell asked doubtfully.

"Both," came the British reply.

Fell didn't understand how one item or one person could change the tide of battle, but there was no time to hesitate and it wasn't in his nature to do so anyway. He focused on the first award.

Do you wish to claim your **Free Relic**? Yes or No?

He chose "Yes" and a pillar of light descended from the sky. It was visible from miles away. The beam centered on the altar, pencil-thin at first but rapidly expanding into a column of yellow luminescence. Fell's Luck manifested just as this was happening. At that exact moment Svaroth's tribe was passing under thick foliage, and so they had no idea what they were now running into.

The light was bright enough to leave an afterimage in Fell's sight. He turned his head away and raised a hand to ward off the glare.

The beam vanished as quickly as it had come. In its place was now a metal cup, resting on its side. It was an ugly thing, about a foot long, all sharp edges and dark iron. The mouth of the cup was square rather than round. The four planes of the vessel each sported a face, and all were frozen into varied expressions of agony.

Thumbnail-sized clear gems were embedded around the rim. They were occluded like weathered plastic. The lip of the cup looked sharp and unwelcoming. It would probably cut his mouth if he drank from it. Nearly black stains were sunk into the dark metal handle, and more decorated the rim. At first, he thought the discolorations were rust, but then he realized the color was too dark for that.

The cup was ugly and disturbing. It spoke of forbidden horrors. Just being near the thing made Fell feel like he'd found a map to a door that should never be opened. As small as it was, the entire thing screamed of violence. It felt like looking into the eyes of a killer who enjoyed their work. Despite that, Fell stepped forward and picked it up. If this is what could defend his new home and save his followers, he would use it. He'd done worse in war than murder, and he wouldn't get squeamish now. Battle was not the place to worry about right or wrong or the way the world should be. He only had time for what was.

As he used his power to identify it, the sound of soft exaltation filled his ears.

579

CHAPTER 57

In addition to the Relic, he was awarded bonus points for obtaining such a powerful object.

> **+50** Divine Points
>
> **+10,000** Faith Points
>
> **+5,000** Fame Points. Total Fame Points: **+10,000**

All of the points were welcome, but the increase in fame actually advanced him a level, something he hadn't known was possible.

> ### CHIME!
>
> Congratulations! You have advanced from Fame Level 0, **"Who the hell are you?"** to Fame Level 1, **"Your deeds have caught my attention."**
>
> New quests and opportunities will become available to you! It may be easier to convert new worshippers and attract stronger souls for summoning.

You have found:

The Cruel Grail

225th of the 1,001 Relics

Better to count the flickers of a world on fire or the stars on a moonless night than to tally the lives claimed by the Cruel Grail. This forbidding cup was once owned by the Demiurge Blood God Mendat. Using this beacon of power, he created an army that shook the firmament of the Lattice. The Cataclysm which shook this world caused the Cruel Grail to be lost to the ages. In the interim, it has been damaged and has lost much of its power, but it can be repaired. Only Blood of sufficient strength will make the Cruel Grail whole.

Remember! Relics cannot be lost, only won or taken.

Requirement: User must have Energy Level of 500 or greater

Durability: Indestructible	**Relic Rank:** Limited

Traits: Great power hides within the blood of all creatures. The strength of giants, the healing of trolls, the fire of ifrits; all can be traced to the lifeblood of these creatures. In some cases, even greater power can be gleaned from the distant ancestors of the Cruel Grail's victims.

At *common* rank, The Cruel Grail has 2 Powers:

1) **Siphon** – Killing an enemy with the Cruel Grail will absorb some or all of that creature's Bloodline. This Power can also remove a bestowed Bloodline.

2) **Vestment of Blood** – When a Bloodline has been completely absorbed, drinking from the Cruel Grail offers a chance to absorb that Bloodline. Each attempt will permanently decrease the health of the imbiber; each attempt risks the life of the imbiber. Chance of death is based on the Energy of the imbiber and the strength of the Bloodline.

The Cruel Grail has 2 basic forms at its current power

1) **Form 1:** +10 Dagger. This thirsty weapon will absorb the blood of an enemy. Each strike that draws blood will inflict a bleeding status of 5 Damage/second for 7 seconds. Can stack 5 times.

2) **Form 2:** Chalice. This cup can fill with the blood of a fully absorbed Bloodline.

Fell not only absorbed the information, but also went over it a couple times. If this thing was going to be his ace in the hole, it was worth sixty seconds to really understand it. As per usual, the description raised more questions than it answered. It was the bottom tile of the description that seemed the most relevant right now.

When he'd seen the cup, he'd felt the menace it exuded, but still… it was a cup! While it was entirely possible to kill someone with a mug, it is even more probable you'd get your ass kicked by the guy holding the sword or club. The description said there was more to it than met the eye though.

"Two forms?" he repeated softly.

Picking it up, he examined it carefully. It was hard to see how this ugly cup could become a dagger. That thought triggered a change. The surface of the bloodstained goblet flowed like water. He almost dropped it in surprise, but the liquid metal held tight to his hand.

The stem became thicker, and each face of the square cup sunk inward until all four touched. The mouth of the cup disappeared and the edges grew razor sharp. In only seconds, the grail had turned into a dagger. The base was still wide enough that it could stand straight up like an obelisk.

The blade had four edges, as if two different daggers had been seamlessly fused together into a cross. The weapon quivered slightly in his grasp. To Fell, it felt like an animal unsure if it liked being held. Flexing his will, he got it to change back from a weapon to a cup, and then into a weapon again. Each change took only seconds and happened smoothly.

"Not a bad weapon," Fell remarked. "I don't think it will stop monsters like the ogres though."

"Do not be so sure," Rig responded. "A +10 weapon will overcome the natural armor of most sentients. Coupled with the armor penetration boon provided by your Soul Art, it will be able to draw blood. The stackable *Bleeding* status can drain 25 HP/second. It is true that the Cruel Grail's real potential seems to lie in being a support item at this point, but providing Bloodlines to you and your people will lead to great power."

"Seeing as we are running short on time, let me just ask, does your connection to the Labyrinth tell you anything about Bloodlines?" Zero was pretty sure the prompt didn't mean the bullshit nobility definition they used on Earth. Could it be talking about genetics?

Rig summed up his knowledge, "All I can say right now is that Bloodlines can offer a wide range of benefits. You must be careful, however. If you attempt to add a Bloodline to someone whose Energy Level is too low to absorb it, I believe there will be an unfortunate reaction."

"Like a mutation?"

"Like they will explode."

Even with the threat of looming battle, Fell paused for a second, "What do you mean 'explode'?"

"Bloody chunks all over the place. 'Explode'," Rig repeated simply. His tone made it clear that for once the chubby ghost wasn't joking. "That includes your body. I wouldn't try absorbing the Bloodline of any ancient dragons until you level up a bit. Preferably not until you get to a higher tier."

Okay. Good safety tip. The point was, Fell finally felt like he had a real weapon. The damage was way better than his battered copper short sword that was on its last points of durability. The Relic had *Bleeding* abilities to boot. This might let him bring more pain to the ogres, but one little dagger wasn't enough to tip the scales. That left the last bonus. "Is there anything I should know about this free summons from the Sea of Souls?"

Rig placed a ghostly hand on the altar. "It's time you finally saw it."

A vortex appeared on the surface of the altar. What had been a solid surface now rippled like water. The center indented, deepening like a hollowed mountain growing down. As it got deeper, the color shifted. A blue layer appeared, followed by a green. Within each layer there were motes of light swirling endlessly. Ultimately, seven layers mirroring the colors of the spectrum were revealed. Each layer had fewer lights. The bottom layers had none.

"This," Rig pointed to the top white level, "is the *common* level of the sea. Each deeper rank has more powerful souls. As you can see, the deeper you go, the less souls there are to recruit. While the *common* rank has an endless number, more powerful souls will always be in short supply. The deepest rank you can currently see is rank nine, *Legendary.*" He indicated the orange-colored level.

"Every god has access to the Sea of Souls. At the end of every tenday, you'll compete to recruit the strongest spirits. Obviously, stronger souls cost more. The effects of having stronger followers cannot be underestimated. You've already seen that Autumn Ghost gains more points each level than the other razin. That is because of her rank-three soul. Over time, she will be vastly more powerful than your other Chosen."

"Are there other differences between the layers?" Fell asked.

"Plenty, but..." Rig nodded to the floating map. The red figures were still running and were getting closer, "We're running out of time."

Fell grunted and waved for the God's Eye to continue.

"What you need to know is that there is an exception to the ranking in the sea. While weak souls cannot dive deeper, occasionally stronger souls may swim up. What I'm saying is that while a *common* soul cannot appear in the second rank, an *uncommon* soul will occasionally appear in the first. That means you can get lucky sometimes and get a higher-ranked soul for the price of a lower rank."

"Alright," Fell replied, not sure why this mattered at this particular moment. The ogres had already crossed a quarter of the distance to the temple.

"I'm sure you're wondering why this matters," Rig continued.

That's going to get old quick, Fell thought. His flaring nostrils answered for him, prompting the ghost to continue.

"As you can see, there are countless *common* souls, but on the bottom three ranks there are none. Those are the Saga ranks. In the sixth rank though, the orange one, there are five souls. That means they are at least *epic* strength. I've been keeping a watch on the Sea of Souls since I came into existence. When you initially claimed the altar, there were no *epic* souls. After you got the Fame bonus for making the first Domain, there were four. After you claimed the Cruel Grail, however, a fifth soul appeared."

"After I claimed the Relic," Zero repeated with understanding, "and after my Fame advanced a rank."

"Yes," Rig continued, knowing they were of the same mind now, "which raises two possibilities. Claiming the first Domain on Telos and a Relic might have attracted the attention of another *epic* soul. Or-"

"Or it might be from an even deeper rank," Fell finished. "Is there any way to know?"

"Not at your current State of Being and with your Domain so new, but a powerful soul will be a boon either way."

"No argument here," Fell confirmed. He cast his own view at the Sea of Souls and saw the five spirit lights in the deepest region of the *heroic* ranks, swimming through the pink light. "Which one is the new one?"

"No idea," the ghost replied, not making eye contact. "Take a shot."

Zero's nostrils flared one more time, but he cast his gaze back into the pink zone. He couldn't tell any difference at all between the five lights. He was just about to pick one at random, when he saw, just for a second, a gold aura around one.

Your **Golden Sight** has randomly triggered and identified an

opportunity!

A big smile crossed Fell's face. In the words of his cousin, "I'd rather be lucky than ugly. Let's do it."

Do you wish to claim your **Free Soul** from the **Sea of Souls**? Yes

or No?

He chose "Yes" and a ring of light appeared on the ground in front of the altar. With a blinding flash, a razin man appeared in the middle. A new prompt appeared, and Fell's heart thudded in excitement. The prompt that accompanied his new follower wasn't pink. It was amber!

Congratulations! You have summoned a **Fabled** Soul!

CHAPTER 58

Congratulations! You have summoned a **Fabled** soul, **Minamoto Tametomo**, the Crypt Ranger.

Saga-ranked souls arrive with their own identities and have the potential to progress to among the most powerful creatures of the Lattice!

MINAMOTO TAMETOMO		
"The Crypt Ranger"		
Level: 0 (0/2,500 XP until Level 1)	**State of Being:** Mortal (0/7)	**Class:** Ranger
Ability: Bone Crafting	**Energy:** 258	**Soul Rank:** Fabled
STATS		
Health: 100	**Mana:** 130 *Regen/min: 7.2*	**Stamina:** 120 *Regen/min: 6*

PRIMARY ATTRIBUTES		
Strength: 9	**Agility:** 14	**Dexterity:** 17
Constitution: 10	**Endurance:** 12	**Intelligence:** 13
Wisdom: 12	**Charisma:** 11	**Luck:** 13

Congratulations! You have recruited your first soul!

Souls recruited from the Sea of Souls will begin with the same characteristics (e.g. Devotion, Morale, Health) as the average of your tribe.

Know This! Souls recruited from the **Saga ranks** (Fabled, Mythic, Legendary) will inspire your entire civilization.

By recruiting **Minamoto Tametomo**, the following effects are now active:

+2 Warrior Great Spirit Points per day

+25% speed of learning and advancing ranged combat-related skills

+25% Attack Speed and Damage for ranged combat

-25% cost of producing Rangers

Loss of this soul by death, lack of Devotion, etc, will remove these effects.

You have also gained the following one-time bonuses:

+500 Devotion Points. Total Devotion Points: 1,608.

+1,000 Fame Points.

You have gained a Blueprint: **Ranger's Lodge**

You have gained a Ranger Cultivation Technique: **Wandering Life**

Fell absorbed all the prompt information in an instant, but his attention was on the man standing before him. Minamoto was taller than he was, a giant for the razin at five and a half feet tall. He had yellow skin like a tanned Japanese man, and his panther ears were covered in green fur. His tail was also green but with black stripes, looking almost like forest camouflage. His eyes were a shining yellow. All the razin had jewel-colored eyes, but looking into his, Fell felt like he was actually staring into the eyes of a hunting cat.

Minamoto had a disquieting gaze. It was piercing, but he also had small pupils and irises, making each eye look like a bullseye. He was garbed in simple clothes that appeared the same as the ones the rest of the tribe were wearing. For the first time, Zero wondered if he was looking at the "starter gear" for creatures newly summoned to Telos.

As intense as Minamoto's gaze was, it was the white longbow in his hand that stole the show. It matched the gleaming arrow shafts sticking out of the quiver on his back. The weapon had strange knobs on it that struck Fell as "wrong" somehow. Looking closer, Fell discovered why. The bow was made of bones that had been fitted together. He used his power to identify it.

The archer knelt before his new deity; bow held out to the side.

"I, Minamoto Tametomo, do swear my life and service to you, Lord God Zero Fell." His voice was somewhat husky, with the heavy accents of formal Japanese.

"I'll need that service," Fell responded. Inwardly, he cheered. They had an archer now. With the ogres having to run up a hill to reach the temple, they also had the high ground. It also sounded like Minamoto's arrows would add extra damage. He thought back to his Ammo of Light skill back on Earth. If Light magic could shred enemies, what would Death magic do? It was time to find out. "Rig, how do I show him what's coming?"

"Place your hand on his temple."

Fell did so and Rig facilitated the share of information. Not only the encroaching army, but also the resources and personnel they had to call upon. Zero thought Minamoto might question such a wondrous ability, but the *fabled* archer just took it in stride.

Seconds later, the information had been shared. Minamoto nodded and looked at his god, "If you introduce me to the troops, I can take control of them. I believe we have a high chance of defeating this enemy, though there will be casualties. I will rely on you and your clergy to counter the powers of their god and acolyte." His voice had the steady surety that Fell had only seen in the very best of military commanders.

Fell glanced back to the map. The ogres had covered half the distance now and had almost reached the central hex. He considered his options. The Relic greatly increased his personal strength and Minamoto increased the strength of the tribe overall.

If only the wall were completed. Even if it slowed the ogres for a few moments, every second would let his people throw spears and let the Ranger shoot arrows. Without a wall, the ogres would be up the hill and into his people only seconds after they were in Minamoto's range. If they could stall them for a couple of seconds, to whittle down the numbers more…

Something occurred to Zero at that moment. There was more than one type of wall. He shared his idea with Minamoto. A predator's smile grew on the *fabled* archer's face as he listened. His response was "Hai!" He had started to run out, when Rig raised a ghostly hand.

"Let's level him up first," the apparition said with a smile. He gestured and another prompt appeared.

For a Tier 0 being, Faith to Experience Point ratio is **1:1**

Note, you cannot increase a devotee's level higher than the highest obtained average level of your tribe.

Highest Average Level: 2

Do you wish to increase the level of your devotee **Minamoto Tametomo**?

Cost to reach Level 1: 2,500 FPs

Cost to reach Level 2: 7,500 FPs

Fell chose to bring his new Ranger to level two and watched light flash in Minamoto's golden eyes. He accessed the archer's information and was shocked by what he saw. Zero already knew that stronger souls could gain extra Attribute Points and Energy. Dust gained an extra point in Agility, and Autumn gained an extra point in Dexterity as well. Minamoto put them to shame.

TRING! TRING!

You have reached level **2**! By following the teachings of your god, Zero Fell, you have advanced in power! You are a **Fabled** soul and will be awarded accordingly.

Attribute Points	+6 to Agility and +4 Dexterity +10 Free Attribute Points
Bonus Energy Slots	+120
Class Points	+100

Fell finally saw the power of a higher-ranked soul. The average razin only gained four total Attribute Points every level. Minamoto gained ten! Those two levels had increased the Ranger's overall points by 20%. Fell could literally see his worshipper's body getting leaner as the points took hold.

His total Energy had also skyrocketed. In just a few levels, the Ranger's total would be higher than Fell's. That meant *fabled* souls would have more than enough slots to learn multiple skills, even multiple classes.

Finally, the man's Class Points advanced 66% faster than Zero's own. Minamoto wasted no time investing his points. He became a level 2 Ranger and bought two bow-related attacks. At Fell's suggestion, four Attribute Points went into Dexterity and the bowman claimed it as his Main Attribute, gaining a *limited* bonus. The rest went into Constitution. The Ranger's chest broadened again. After that, Minamoto ran off to organize the tribe. As he did, Fell couldn't help but reflect. It was wonderful having the Ranger on his side, but he'd have to make sure his higher ranked followers stayed loyal. If he wasn't careful, their power could outstrip his own.

For now, however, he had a powerful new ally. In the next few minutes, Minamoto arranged the tribe into three blocks. In the eyes of every razin, there was only fierce resolve. On every face was the promise of pain to any who would attack their god. They had found their new home and would be damned if anyone would take it from them!

They didn't have to wait long before the ogres reached the tree line. Fell stood slightly in front with his clergy, Minamoto by his side. The invaders paused upon seeing them, but only for a few moments. Before long, an ogre with greenish skin bellowed in a guttural tongue. Only Fell and his acolytes could understand the words, but every razin there understood the intent and the snarl on his face.

Still, Svaroth hesitated to attack until he knew one more thing. He used his God's Eye to gain info about his foe. The knowledge he could gain was just as limited as Zero's, but it was enough. The cat god wasn't affiliated with a pantheon. His enemy was alone, a rogue god. That was all he needed to know.

"I, Svaroth of the Shattered Curse pantheon, am here to claim this land." As soon as he finished speaking, an illusion appeared above his head. It was a pillar of ice wreathed in blue flame. It was the mark of his pantheon, and proof of his claim. He didn't need to formally declare his intentions, but he liked his victims to know who was killing them.

Fell looked at his acolytes to one side, then to Minamoto standing to his other side. He looked back at Sharp Leaf and nodded his head solemnly. The acolyte grinned wildly and took a step forward. He air jacked at crotch level three times before throwing imaginary knuckle children at the invaders, "Claim this!"

Svaroth's vision turned red. So much anger surged through him that his voice went high-pitched, "Kill them! Kill them all! I fucking hate cats!"

CHAPTER 59

Fifteen ogres rushed across the three-hundred-yard space between the tree line and Zero's tribe. Svaroth's acolyte ran right at their heels. From eight to ten feet in height and weighing five hundred to seven hundred pounds each, nothing could stop them. They were a tide of death. Their bellows sounded out like the charging hounds of hell. Behind them, a vengeful god shouted his hate and anger.

Svaroth stared at the pitiful army of beastkin atop the hill and couldn't help but smile. The fools! Meeting a charge from his mighty Chosen was no different than throwing away their lives. His ogres wouldn't even need to slow down as they ran though the enemy. The only thing more pathetic than these peasants were the crude weapons they were holding. The wooden spears were toothpicks compared to the uprooted trees some of his people wielded. He ran at the back of the ogre pack, and his smile grew into a bloodthirsty grin. This was going to be fun!

Anyone looking at the field would have agreed with the Earth god. They would have seen the seventeen attackers and concluded that the lives of every single razin was about to be extinguished. In minutes, if not seconds, every man and woman of Fell's tribe would be dead. Even with superior numbers, no one would bet on Zero's tribe. The ogres were linebackers charging a group of children. Their war cries were bloodcurdling. Their visages were horror-inducing. Their eyes were mad with battle lust.

Nothing could stop them.

In the face of the ogres' charge, fear finally overcame the curious spirit of the razin. Almost all of their hands shook. Their mouths were dry and their hearts fluttered in their chests. Only Minamoto and Zero stayed steady in both heart and hand. Despite their fear, however, not one member of the tribe fled. They stood by their people, and they stood by their god.

The distance between the two armies closed, and Minamoto assessed the enemy with a cool eye. In no hurry and with absolute smoothness, he nocked a bone arrow to his bow. As the ogres ran forward, the Ranger's trained eye knew when they reached the one-hundred-and-fifty-yard mark. His level might be pitifully low compared to the other lives that he had lived, but his combat expertise had not suffered. Before the first ogre's foot had crushed grass at the halfway mark, the *master* of the Diamond Hawk archery style began to fire.

Two arrows shot from his bow in under a second as he used one of the two Class upgrades he'd bought: *Double Shot*. Again, the attack was paltry compared to the powerful capabilities of his previous lives, but in this newly connected Labyrinth world, he was literally the instrument of his god's wrath.

Double Shot decreased his overall accuracy in exchange for firing two arrows nearly simultaneously. The penalty didn't matter. For a trained archer, and at such a short range, the chances of him missing approached zero percent. Before the surging invaders even registered his movement, two arrows were in flight.

The bone shafts thudded into a nine-foot-tall ogre with a staccato *thwump-thwump!* The behemoth stumbled and looked down in surprise. Both arrows had sunk deep into his powerful body. Despite the ogre's skin being as tough as leather armor, the arrows had penetrated nearly a foot into his torso. That still would have been nothing more than a moderate injury, but then the Death magic in the bone arrows triggered.

The ogre's surprise turned into panic and pain. Like snakes burrowing through sand, angry purple tendrils raced outward from the impact sites. The tissue around the wounds blackened and began to slough off. When the two areas of necrosis met, the process accelerated rapidly. Two seconds later, the top half of the giant humanoid's body folded down over the bottom half, like a closed book. The two pieces fell to the ground unmoving.

In the seconds it took for the first ogre to die, the rest of the horde had kept running. Of course, the Ranger hadn't stopped firing.

Every step the ogres took was bought in blood. If Minamoto had had more arrows, he might have been able to destroy the attack force by himself. If he had gained a few more precious levels or had been able to pick better terrain, he might still have been able to rout them. On that hot jungle day, however, with the flies buzzing loud in anticipation of the gore, the ogres were too many, and his arrows too few. The ten shots in his quiver were spent quickly, and *Double Shot's* cooldown was too long to use more than once against the charging invaders.

Limited or not, every one of his arrows struck their targets. The *fabled*-souled Ranger's combat expertise was beyond reproach.

Where his shots landed, Death energy spread. Sadly, the ogres were not so easily undone. They may have been stupid, but they were born fighters. Each arrow stole dozens of points of damage a second, but the invaders ripped the bone shafts out as soon as they were struck. The arrows were snapped in their meaty paws and left behind on the battlefield. Too soon, Minamoto's arrows were spent.

Through the rain of arrows, the ogres continued to run. Rather than show fear, the giant invaders became even more excited for battle. Every step of their tree-trunk legs devoured nearly ten feet. The distance closed between the two armies. One hundred yards. Seventy-five. Fifty. The mouths of the ogres filled with saliva, their large jowls slavering at the thought of fresh meat and bones to crunch. Forty. Thirty.

They stared at the tightly clustered razin, and even their pea-brained intellects wondered if the beastkin were fools. The ogre leading the charge raised his small sapling like a club, and his massive heart thudded in anticipation. There was nothing he loved so much as the *pop* when he smashed the body of something smaller than him. If he was smarter, he might have written a poem about it. Something like, "Smash, smash, bash, bash," before giving up because words were hard.

Mere seconds before the ogres would have harvested the lives of nearly the entire razin tribe in just their first push, Minamoto bellowed, "Now!" The ranks of razin split apart, every single pantherkin's heart beating hard enough to launch it out of their chest. They didn't let their fear conquer them. Their ruse had worked.

Many of them had thought it wouldn't. Only fools would cluster together when faced with an unstoppable force like an ogre charge, after all. It would take a bigger fool though to believe that the razin were that foolish. But the real fools are the ones being fooled! Even lacking military experience, the razin had assumed the ogres would suspect a trap. As the followers of Fell stepped aside, they shared the same thought as their deity.

Thank god for stupid.

The front line of razin stepped back simultaneously, revealing the eaglebear cubs that had been hiding behind them. The tamed beasts opened their mouth as one, letting loose their *Sonic Screech*. The palisade might not have been completed, but the wave of sound was as good as a wall.

Everyone on the battlefield learned the truth of an old female adage: softness can destroy hardness. Almost the entire invading tribe was caught in the sonic attack. Giants or not, they were not immune and were stunned for precious moments. The effect only lasted one to five seconds, but Minamoto didn't waste a single heartbeat.

The momentum of the ogres made them faceplant and slide in the grass, delivering themselves literally to the razin's feet. With almost no space remaining between the two armies, Minamoto's first command of 'Now!' was followed by a second.

"Attack!"

The razin released war cries of their own, stabbing their wooden spears into eyes, mouths, noses and ears. For a couple glorious seconds, the pantherkin inflicted one-sided damage on their enemy. Only four ogres hadn't been in the AoE of the sonic attack. They kept running forward, bellowing in rage. The tribe bravely ignored them, knowing they had to inflict as much damage as possible on the fallen enemy before the *Stun* status wore off. Though they were small, the razin showed that their hearts were huge.

Fell and his acolytes tried to intercept the four ogres, but lives were lost. Every time an ogre fist, foot or club fell, a life fled the world of Telos. Even as some of their fellows were smashed and pulped by the ogres still on their feet, the rest of the tribe kept inflicting as much damage as possible on the fallen.

If the razin had had better weapons, they might have won the day right then and there. If their spears had been tipped with cold iron or sharp steel, they could have pierced through the ogres' leathery skin. Rather than being stopped by eye sockets and dense skulls, their weapons could have stabbed hearts, lungs and livers. Instead of small trickles of blood, their sharp blades would have opened large vessels and spilled life's blood.

There was no world that was fair, however, least of all the worlds of the Labyrinth.

Four ogres had been killed and another three seriously injured by Minamoto's arrows. The eaglebear cubs' surprise attack had let the razin kill two and moderately injure several more. The two slain were those already damaged by the Ranger, though. The kills would not have even been possible if those enemies hadn't already been weakened by the Ranger's Death mana. His shots had opened gaping wounds in the ogres' bodies, leaving their organs exposed and vulnerable.

That still left nine bloodthirsty giants, not including Svaroth's acolyte or the god himself. As *Stun* wore off, the razin bravely continued to thrust their wooden spears. Even when the ogres growled and pushed themselves up off the ground, Zero's tribe showed their mettle.

Sadly, without easy targets, their weapons splintered and shattered against the invaders' thick skin and rock-hard muscles. Conversely, with each ogre attack the razin bled, squished and exploded. The invaders wasted no time in claiming revenge for the eaglebears' sneak attack. The monster cubs themselves had been led away by one of the tribe as soon as they had used their *Sonic Screech,* leaving the pantherkin to pay the butcher's bill.

The eaglebear cubs' special move had helped the razin even the odds, but Minamoto had known there would still be a cost. Indeed, even though two ogres had been killed, five razin had been ripped limb from limb by the few ogres still on their feet. As a great and cruel man once said, 'In chess, the pawns move first.' Minamoto knew that one law of nature ruled supreme: Jaku Niku Kyō Shoku.

"The weak are meat and the strong do eat."

Even as the Ranger, clergy and god raced forward, a young razin, only sixteen years old, cried out in fear. His gaze was glued to his brother and sister, who were facing off against an ogre that was three feet taller than they were and weighed three times as much. At first, the more agile razin were able to avoid the invader's powerful but clumsy blows. In return, his siblings were able to land blows almost at will. With their rudimentary wooden spears, however, they accomplished almost nothing.

The stalemate went on for several seconds, the razin narrowly avoiding death again and again. A second ogre joined the fray, however, and the razin's sister was knocked to the ground hard enough to daze her. One of the ogres grabbed her feet. The teen's cries of fear morphed into wails of horror. "Stop it! Stop it!" he screamed.

The only response were guffaws of laughter as an ogre gleefully used his sister as an impromptu weapon. The giant swung the beastkin like a club and knocked her brother to the ground. Several powerful, wet and sticky blows later, neither member of Zero's tribe were identifiable as anything other than churned meat. The young razin showed his true nature, anger overriding both fear and reason as he ran to help his dead brother and sister. A second later, his soul left Telos as well.

At another spot in the fray, a spear-wielding razin scored a lucky blow against an ogre's neck. The attack broke through the leathery skin and earned him a small trickle of orange blood. The ogre responded not by grabbing the spear, but by ripping off the offending arm. The razin screamed as he fell, drenching the ground in salt and red. The ogre munched on the bloody end of the appendage, enjoying the flow of blood like a fine wine. A heavy but almost absentminded stomp of the invader's foot ended the life and story of the mutilated razin; the ogre was already reaching for his next victim.

At every point where the tribes met, a version of these stories played out. If there was only one ogre, the razin might have been able to wear the giants down, albeit with casualties. With multiple ogres fighting together, however, the razin's superior mobility was neutralized. The ogres had almost nothing to fear with their great strength and natural defenses. In each mini-battle, it was only a matter of time before the larger fighters won. Every victory for the invaders was a tragedy for the razin.

In the first ten seconds of contact, seven pantherkin were killed. In the first minute of battle, more than ten percent of the tribe died. Many more were injured. The ogres surged forward, wreaking destruction and stealing lives. The fact that the razin were now spread out lessened some of the devastation, though it would have been more accurate to say that the death rate slowed than to say it decreased.

Svaroth licked his lips in anticipation. He had failed his quest, but all he needed to do was kill the rest of this tribe, and his path to ascension would be restored. When that damn archer had cut one of his tribe in half, the Earth god had cursed. He'd known the man would have power, his energy and aura had foretold that, but he hadn't expected Death mana. Thankfully, the archer had limited shots.

The sonic attack had been a surprise as well. Even with both trump cards played though, most of his fighters were still hale. Now they were wreaking absolute devastation on the enemy. It looked like the beastkin were out of tricks, and the archer was out of arrows. It was time to end this.

Even if every one of his Chosen died, it would be a good trade if he wiped out the enemy tribe. He could just summon more worshippers once he claimed the altar. After all, what was the point of worshippers if not to die for their god? As Zero Fell and his clergy rushed forward, Svaroth and his acolyte Grimshaw did the same. The battle would be decided here and now.

CHAPTER 60

Autumn Ghost sprinted toward her enemy, the acolytes flanking her like a "V." As Fell had ordered, they didn't angle toward the center of the battle. Instead, they targeted invaders that had been separated from the pack. They had to claim kills as quickly as possible. Their objective was an ogre fighting six razin singlehandedly.

Two pantherkin already lay on the ground, unmoving in pools of blood. As they approached, the giant kicked a razin female. The ogress's foot made a *crunch* as it collapsed her enemy's chest, the razin flying through the air and landing meters away. She did not move after she hit the ground. One forearm was snapped past the angle it should bend. The fact that her fingers were in unmoving claws made it clear that life had left her body. The ogress turned her attention to the clergy with a leer, her sagging breasts swaying this way and that in the open air.

Autumn bared her sharp teeth and held a hand up as she approached. Words of Power fell from her lips as she used her Chant, "Fear the fury of Zero Fell!"

The Divine Power made her faith pool drop by fifty, but thanks to her Head Acolyte bonus, she had plenty to spare. What mattered was that her copper club now had +5 soul damage for the next several minutes along with 10% armor negation. Anger flowed through her veins over the deaths of her people. It burned so hot that the edges of her vision turned red.

The last syllable of the chant fell from her lips and a crystalline blue fire enveloped her weapon. A light as bright as the sun to the unfaithful, but gentle as a sunset to the Chosen of Lord Fell flew toward her enemy's face. The ogress's leering laugh stopped, and orange blood fountained from the giantess' nose. Ghost's target had tried to dodge, but the razin's highest attributes, Agility and Dexterity, improved both her aim and attack speed. Pain worse than any the ogress had ever felt before turned her vision white. Her disorientation would only last seconds, but in another way, it would last the rest of her life.

The ogres were indeed powerful, and their skin was as good as leather armor. Against a weapon strengthened by Divine Power, however, none of that meant much. The club not only destroyed the invader's nose, but also crushed her upper jaw. Autumn's weapon became embedded in the ogress's head so the acolyte rode her victim down to the ground. A hard yank and a second blow drove bone shards into the disoriented ogress' brain.

The other razin cheered. It was the first kill they'd claimed after the sonic attack. Their jubilation stilled on viewing what came next. Autumn opened her mouth and inhaled. A blue furnace light appeared in her throat and the ogress' soul flew out of her body to be consumed. In the light of Ghost's active Soul Art, both defenders and invaders could see the screaming soul being consumed. The head acolyte's mouth snapped shut and a vicious grin spread across her face.

For just a moment, the battle froze as everyone understood the horror of Fell's acolytes. Not even death was a release. The ogres stared in instinctual fear, and the razin stared with the same emotion. Was this the power of their god?

The acolytes didn't pause, each hungry to reap more souls. Sharp Leaf and Midnight Dust teamed up to take down another ogre. Dust's *Zephyr Body* let him avoid attacks with ease while Sharp Leaf's *Shrewd Fighter* ability gave him an almost precognitive sense in battle. Crystalline blue fire surrounded their dagger and axe.

Their target was dismantled more than slain. A feint caused the ogre's punch to swing wide of Sharp Leaf. The acolyte's axe cut off three fingers in response. At the same time, before the ogre could even scream, Dust's dagger had cut through both of the invader's Achille's tendons.

The ogre collapsed forward. Sharp Leaf's keen-edged axe cut through the front half of his neck while the giant fell. The invader had only just started bleeding out when both of his hands struck the ground. He collapsed down to one shoulder after his mangled hand blasted a bolt of agony into his brain. With his neck bent low, Leaf couldn't help but oblige. A heavy swing of his enchanted axe freed the ogre's heavy head to drop to the ground with a dull thud.

The two acolytes, covered in orange blood, grinned at each other, and Dust made a magnanimous gesture with one hand. Acquiescing with a wide smile, Sharp Leaf consumed the ogre's soul in just under two seconds. And just like that, the duo was off to hunt their next prey.

Autumn watched her junior acolytes with pleasure. She placed a foot on the dead ogress' neck and pulled her club free. It took two strong heaves to reclaim it from the invader's ruined face. There was a sucking sensation as she reclaimed her weapon. The Divine Power enveloping it burned the blood away, leaving the copper pristine even as it degraded the weapon.

The sounds of battle surrounded her. As she looked around, her joy at slaying a foe drained away. More than half of the tribe was dead. Autumn motioned for her fellow acolytes to follow her. There were more enemies to slaughter. Quite specifically, she wanted to kill the largest ogre. Her god had said he was an enemy acolyte. Cruel Thorn had escaped her, but this time she would claim the enemy's life. This ti- "Gack!"

Autumn looked down in shock, seeing a three-inch-wide spike of stone jutting out of her abdomen. She'd been struck in the back, and the projectile was strong enough that it was sticking a foot and a half out of her stomach. She coughed involuntarily and a large cupful of dark red blood flew out of her mouth. As she fell to her knees, she thought she heard someone scream, "No!"

Ghost crumpled to her side and everything went black.

Svaroth smiled grimly. He could admit that the enemy acolytes were powerful. Despite that fact, the woman had fallen to his magic. Of course, that was to be expected. How could a low level being with no natural armor withstand his divinity? His *Stone Spear* had been more than enough to take her out of the fight. With a hole that large, she should bleed to death in seconds.

The Earth god looked at the two acolytes rushing to her side and figured this was a great opportunity to remove all the enemy clergy at once. He could have sent another stone spike, but the damn pantherkin were too agile. Now that they were expecting it, he might miss, and he only had two more uses of his Divine Power without recharge. He might need his attacks to defeat the enemy god. Besides, that was why he had followers.

A bellowed order to his own acolyte sent the twelve-foot-tall ogre rushing toward the two pantherkin. One of the enemy acolytes was already kneeling next to the unconscious woman, trying to pull her off his stone spear. The fool thought he could still save her. That was fine. Fools were easy prey. Still, Svaroth couldn't even allow for the chance that she could be healed. "Use your power and kill them quickly, Grimshaw. Kill them for your god!"

"Yes, me god," came the guttural and imbecilic reply. Then the giant ogre rushed forward. While he did, he used his Chant.

"By power of Svaroth, me hard skin!"

The idiotic prose still triggered his Divine Power. While he ran, his green skin turned the color of grey stone. It grew rougher and flaky as if he was armored in rock. This was the effect of his Divine Power, *Stone Skin*.

It was a defensive chant that should make him impervious on this battlefield. He rushed over from several dozen yards away, each footfall shaking the ground and leaving a four-inch imprint in the ground. Each step brought him closer to where Autumn's blood was soaking into the ground.

Midnight Dust was still yanking on Autumn Ghost's body. "No!" he screamed, again and again. He wasn't able to accept that the woman he loved, the woman he'd never had the courage to admit his feelings to, was dying in front of him. The sounds of battle and screams of pain filled the air as both tribes fought in a life-or-death struggle. He heard none of it.

Some razin tried to stop Grimshaw's rush, but if their weapons couldn't even pierce the normal leathery skin of the ogres, how could they possibly harm his divine rocky armor? The ogre barely noticed their attacks, absentmindedly backhanding razin as they got in his way.

Even without taking the enemy seriously, Grimshaw left devastation in his wake. One punch snapped a razin man's neck. Another kick shattered a spine. Fell's worshippers collapsed like puppets with cut strings and more souls rose into the air. Each second they slowed the ogre was bought at the cost of a life.

"Stay with us. Stay with us!" Dust sobbed. Snot and tears streaked down his face. He managed to pull Autumn off the stone spear. Bright red blood fell from the wound, along with loops of intestine. Her eyes stared glassily up at the sky. Midnight pushed loops of intestine back into the gaping hole in her body and chanted *Soul Heal*.

His faith dropped and blue healing energy sank into her body. The edges of the wound started pulling together, but she continued to bleed to death. Desperately, he kept his hand over the wound, but the 5 HP/sec of healing was not enough to compensate for the damage she'd suffered. The ten-second duration ended and he tried to continue it, but his faith was already nearly bottomed out. His own body rebelled against Midnight's unreasonable demands, forcing him to vomit.

The spew fell inside the gaping hole marring Autumn's body. Dust looked down in pure horror, seeing his bile coating the viscera of his dying love. In that moment, he learned that no matter how much you believed, you could not pull water from a dry well.

Dust didn't know if the stone spear had crushed her spine or pulped her organs. All he knew was that his healing magic was not enough. The tide of blood that had begun to ebb began to flow again.

"Sharp Leaf," Dust screamed out desperately, "I need you!"

The other acolyte looked at his friend, his expression torn. He knew Autumn Ghost was almost certainly a lost cause, but he also knew of Dust's hidden feelings. He wanted to comfort his fellow acolyte, but the battle still raged around them and their people were dying. Should he waste his remaining faith trying to heal someone who most likely couldn't be healed, or should he save it to keep *Soul Strike* active as long as possible? A moment later, a harsh bellow told him his time to choose had run out.

"I going to smash kitties, hur hur hur."

The voice was deep and guttural, and Sharp already knew who had spoken it before turning his head. Barreling down on them, the ogre acolyte was closing in. Grimshaw looked like a giant boulder imbued with life and hatred. Stealing another glance at his bereft friend, Sharp cursed and ran toward the living wall of stone.

Seeing their clergy struggling, more razin threw themselves at Grimshaw. It was tantamount to throwing their bodies into a meat grinder. Each life only bought Sharp Leaf a second, perhaps two. He didn't waste them.

Leaf sprinted the short distance to Autumn and placed his hand on her ruined stomach. His faith dropped to nearly zero. His Divine energy flowed into her, and the hole in her abdomen began to close once more. It finally shut, leaving only unbroken skin. The clean area looked strange surrounded by the gore on the rest of her body. Autumn still did not wake up however, and her breath remained ragged.

Behind the three acolytes, the cries of their people told the tale of Grimshaw's delighted slaughter. Baring his teeth in anger, he picked up Autumn's copper club. Focusing for a second, he poured his Class Points into increasing his cleric level. In an instant, he was a level three Cleric with another one hundred Faith Points to use.

That meant he could keep *Soul Strike* active on one weapon for half a minute or active on both for ten seconds. Seeing his armored enemy, his ability let him know instinctively which he had to choose. Sharp Leaf took a deep breath. It would be enough. It had to be. As prepared as he would ever be, he looked at Dust with an uncharacteristically solemn expression.

"Keep her safe," was all he said, then he ran to meet his fate.

Sharp Leaf sprinted toward Grimshaw and his heart ached at seeing nearly two dozen razin lying dead in the ogre's wake. The enemy acolyte who was laughing with abandon at the devastation he had wrought. The uprooted tree Grimshaw held was coated red and dotted with fur of different colors. He lashed out at any razin that came within reach, but steadily made his way toward Autumn Ghost's body and Dust's helpless form. If the ogre had been a bit less bloodthirsty or a bit more intelligent, he already would have reached and killed the priest. The imbecilic glee he felt at crushing and stomping on living creatures, however, delayed him.

Only twenty yards from Dust's wailing form, Sharp Leaf and Grimshaw met in battle. The ogre acolyte was holding a razin upside down in one large fist. His arm went up and down, driving the woman's head into the ground. Her skull shattered and her brain turned into paste.

She was probably dead after the first hit, but the ogre was enjoying himself. Nostrils flared and teeth bared, Sharp Leaf wielded two weapons, Ghost's club and his axe. Blue soul light surrounded both as he swung them in quick succession at the back of his target's thigh.

Even enhanced with *Soul Strike,* the club couldn't overcome Grimshaw's *Stone Skin.* The blunt weapon impacted with a dull thud, and only the razin's momentum kept it from just bouncing off. That was why Zero's faithful had swung both weapons. Sharp Leaf's ability, *Shrewd Fighter*, had come into play and guided his actions. Though it meant he only had 10 seconds of boosted power, he had covered both weapons in crystalline blue light.

The brawny razin hadn't known consciously why he was led to attack with both weapons at once, but the answer became clear. Even though *Stone Skin* could block one *Soul Strike,* it couldn't block two. Between the armor negation and extra damage, Leaf's axe drove past the stone and into the meat of Grimshaw's thigh. Orange blood sprayed across the grass.

The ogre bellowed and tried to turn, but Sharp Leaf's copper blade had cut too deeply into the thigh muscles. Two of Grimshaw's quad muscles were severed. The enemy acolyte only managed to fall to one knee and use his treeclub to block Leaf's next attack. The agile razin didn't let up.

Dropping low, Leaf bellowed in rage and swung both weapons again in a one-two combo, this time targeting the knee of Grimshaw's injured leg. Both weapons landed less than a second apart. The ogre's knee dislocated, completely crippling the leg.

The giant howled in pain, his eyes widening in disbelief. How had this little thing managed to hurt it? *Stone Skin* coupled with his own large physique and great strength had made him think he was invincible. Unfortunately for him, his small mind had never understood that others could wield great power as well.

For ten seconds, Sharp Leaf held the initiative. He moved faster than ever before, putting every point of his Agility and Dexterity to greatest use. With the ogre's mobility severely hampered, Leaf's combo attack was able to whittle away at the larger acolyte's health. Blow after blow rained down, the tattoo of strikes sounding like a drummer's masterpiece. Red flashed in the corner of the Grimshaw's vision as his health was whittled away.

You have lost 7 health!

You have lost 8 health!

You have lost 4 health!

From the outside, it looked like Leaf was absolutely dominating his enemy. Sadly, Sharp knew the truth. He was only causing minimal damage, and that was only thanks to *Soul Strike*. Grimshaw's divine defense was too strong. Some attacks failed to even penetrate Grimshaw's strong defense, causing no damage. With the ogre's large size and racial Constitution bonus, at level three the enemy acolyte had nearly three hundred max health. The smaller razin, weighing nearly a ton less, even gifted and blessed with a battle ability, just couldn't harm his enemy in any meaningful way.

Grimshaw had no such difficulties. He missed almost every attack he launched against Sharp Leaf, but he didn't miss them all. A backhand from the ogre hit Leaf like a sledgehammer. It was a glancing blow or the damage might have been worse, but the hit still knocked Leaf down.

Sharp tumbled head over tail, rolling twice before laying on the ground partially stunned. It was either instinct or his *Shrewd Fighter* ability that made the confused man roll to the side. That saved his life. Grimshaw's follow-up strike was an overhand swing of his treeclub so strong that the weapon sunk into the ground several feet. It was only stuck for a few seconds, but that let Sharp Leaf shake his head clear and get back up. This time, it was the razin who had a red warning prompt.

*You have lost **34 health**!*

That one offhand blow from Grimshaw's rock-covered fist had cost Leaf nearly a third of his health. It would have been more, but the razin had been investing his free points into Constitution. Still, one or two more strikes like that would end him. Stumbling back onto his feet, Leaf looked at Grimshaw. The ogre glared back. With a wink, Leaf gave the ogre a bloody grin.

"You think you're dangerous?" he taunted. "I am a faithful of the god Fell. In his holy name, and by my mighty hand, I will smack the bitch out of you!"

There was a reason Fell's Soul Resonance was nearly perfect with the tribe.

The true tragedy of being knocked down was that his dual *Soul Strike* had elapsed. The good news was that Grimshaw's *Stone Skin* had elapsed as well. With his grip tight on both copper weapons, Sharp Leaf ignored his wounds and rushed back into battle. Grimshaw roared back in defiance despite his two ruined legs.

Sharp Leaf danced around the ogre and began to whittle away his enemy's health once more. He actually caused more damage now that both of their Divine Powers had disappeared. The damage he caused was small, but it started to stack up. Without healing powers, the ogre continued to be impaired. Leaf kept up his two-point attack, each club strike followed by an axe fall. *Thun-ssshink! Thun-ssshink! Thun-ssshink!*

The attacks were so close together that it often sounded like a single impact. Leaf increased his tempo, pushing his body to the limit. He kept up the attack, chipping away at the ogre's health, but also maneuvering his foe to be more and more off balance. Without even fully understanding what *Shrewd Fighter* was guiding him to do, he stepped inside of the ogre's guard and finally was in position. Launching himself off the ogre's own bent knee, his axe swung in a perfect slice that would tear through Grimshaw's neck.

The ogre's eye opened wide in panic, but he couldn't move fast enough to stop the ability-boosted acolyte. With a cheer in his heart, Sharp Leaf twisted his body, adding a strong acceleration into his blow. He was only a split second away from winning the battle. Sadly, that was one second too long.

Striking Grimshaw's stone skin earlier had whittled away the ogre's health, but it had also eroded the copper weapons' durability. Channeling *Soul Strike* through them had worsened the damage. Only a single point of durability was left in the blade and just two in the club, as Leaf tried to decapitate his enemy.

In the next instant, Leaf learned that though his Luck was high, it could never overcome the inevitability of time. His axe blade bit into Grimshaw's neck and orange blood spurted, but the axe head shattered and snapped free of the haft. The energy left was not enough to reach the major vessels in the ogre's neck, let alone cut through the iron-hard muscle. The shattering axe also threw Sharp off balance, robbing him of his battle tempo. A single use of *Soul Strike* would have made all the difference. Sadly, his faith had run dry.

So close to Grimshaw, this time there was no escape. The ogre wrapped him in a bear hug and laughed in Leaf's face. The giant's breath stank of the days-old spoiled meat that Sharp could see hanging between rotten teeth. The pantherkin struggled to free himself, but the ogre just laughed at his puny efforts.

"Now me crush," the enemy acolyte chortled.

With a savage squeeze, Leaf's spine fractured in three places. The ruined fighter's legs kicked spastically in response to severed nerves. Blood poured from his eyes, nose and mouth. Broken ribs stabbed through his lungs and the airs sacs filled with blood. Death was instantaneous. Leaf's soul flew free along with the others he'd collected, unseen by his killer.

Grimshaw stared into the vacant, bloodshot eyes of his enemy before dropping the body like a tattered doll. The ogre acolyte picked up his treeclub again and began limping toward the corpse of Autumn Ghost and her small protector, Midnight Dust.

So ended the story of Sharp Leaf, acolyte of Zero Fell, a man who had healed a friend and died because of it.

CHAPTER 61

"No!" Dust cried out for what felt like the hundredth time. His gaze was locked onto Sharp Leaf's mangled corpse and his hands were covered in Autumn's blood. Leaf had managed to stabilize her, but her breathing was still ragged, her skin pale. Midnight could not bear to look at her, she was so pale.

He searched frantically for his god, only to see Fell fighting single-handedly against half a dozen ogres. If his deity had not occupied so many, the razin would have been wiped out already, but it also meant Zero would not be coming to his aid. Dust mechanically smoothed Autumn's blood-soaked blond hair. He wanted to tell her still form it would be okay, but he couldn't force the lie past his lips.

After Sharp Leaf had saved his love, Midnight had dared imagine things would work out. Watching the battle, and seeing his friend triumphing over an enemy three times his height, Dust had even started to believe it. For a few great moments it had seemed like they were all going to be fine. His friend's mangled body showed that for a lie.

Grimshaw smashed his own dislocated knee back into place with a heavy fist. His inhuman, ogre constitution locked the bones into the correct position. His other leg was still mangled, but he was back on his feet, bloody and grinning. He turned that leer on the last two clergy. Using his club as a crutch, he limped toward them faster than his wounded legs should have allowed. All around them, the fight was continuing, but the ogre paid it no mind. The deaths of his fellow ogres, the death of the razin, none of it mattered. The only thought in his small mind was how much he would enjoy breaking, smashing and crushing these two beings that worshipped a false god.

Even an imbecile could enjoy his work.

Midnight Dust was not the fighter Sharp Leaf had been, but he would not allow Autumn to be killed in her sleep like an ailing pet. After gently laying her head down, he stood with his hand wrapped around the hilt of his copper short sword. With an anguished cry, he ran at the ogre, his blade glinting in the fading light of day.

Grimshaw's response was simple and brutal. He stabbed at Dust with his treeclub. The bottom of the uprooted tree was at least two feet across. The roots sticking out in every direction increased that to four. At the distance they were apart, Dust should not have been able to dodge. The roots even gouged the ground, but Dust's *Zephyr Body* was not to be underestimated.

Without breaking his stride, but timing it perfectly, Midnight jumped and grabbed a root sticking out from the bottom of the treeclub. With a twist that no human on Earth could have managed, he flipped up and landed atop the giant's weapon. Dust ran along the club until he could swing his shortsword at Grimshaw's face. Grimacing, the ogre tucked his head. Dust's blade struck with a *ting!*

You have caused **1 damage!**

With his faith pool empty, Dust couldn't chant *Soul Strike*. He might as well have been tickling his enemy. His blade bounced off the top of the ogre's skull, barely drawing blood. The only real effect was a small dent in the dagger and a one-point drop in its durability.

Grimshaw's eyes had widened at seeing Dust's impossible movements, but he just chuckled darkly upon realizing how the razin couldn't hurt him. The ogre reached up to grab Midnight. The black-furred pantherkin dodged, his body collapsing bonelessly underneath the giant hand and rolled off the treeclub. As soon as his feet touched the ground, however, he struck like a snake. His blade darted into the softer skin of the ogre's groin.

That got a bit more of a reaction.

You have caused **11 damage!**

You have mutilated **Grimshaw**!

Dust bared his teeth, more a bloodthirsty leer than a grin. Meanwhile, Grimshaw screamed like a tea kettle. Flipping backwards, Midnight shouted pure bile at his enemy.

"What's wrong? It's just the tip!"

Grimshaw's scream turned into a roar of rage and he threw himself at the razin. The ogre swung his club three more times, but missed with each attempted blow. Dust's high attributes and ability made him hard to hit, and the dodge bonus of *Zephyr Body* made it nearly impossible.

Dust was just as helpless. Despite his one low blow, his sword just couldn't penetrate Grimshaw's thick skin. Even if it could, the enemy acolyte wasn't letting him get close again. The ogre had finally learned his lesson about underestimating his smaller enemies. Midnight contemplated throwing his blade, hoping for a lucky blow to an eye, but as big as the ogres were, their eyes were small and recessed in their massive skulls. Even if he did land the strike, it wouldn't be fatal.

It was only because Dust was staring at Grimshaw's face that he saw it, an evil and calculated narrowing of the eyes. In the next moment Dust learned why the ogre race had claimed so many victims. Just because they lacked intelligence did not mean they lacked cunning. The giant raised his treeclub high overhead, but then turned toward Autumn Ghost's unconscious body.

Eyes widening in fear, Dust abandoned all defense and sprinted forward. That was what the ogre had been waiting for. With a sneer, he dropped his club and swung a barrel-sized fist at Midnight. The razin realized too late he'd been played for a fool. He took the hit head-on and lost consciousness immediately. Even while his mouth filled with his own teeth, he lay still on the ground, senseless.

A gap-toothed grin spread on Grimshaw's face. He lifted his treeclub again. He almost swung it down on Midnight Dust, but then a horrible thought occurred to him. It was so horrible, in fact, that it filled his giant heart with glee.

Grimshaw grabbed Dust by the neck and dragged him over to where Autumn Ghost lay. The ogre pressed one fingernail, broken and jagged, into Dust's chest hard enough to draw blood. The razin roused with a scream. The ogre forced his captive's head toward the sleeping priestess even as thick red ran down Dust's chest.

"Watch," Grimshaw commanded, his voice guttural and grim.

Midnight Dust could only do as he was told. He couldn't even manage more than a weak cry thanks to his wounded mouth. Without

623

preamble, Grimshaw slammed his treeclub down on Autumn. Once. Twice. Three times.

Dust screamed and clawed at the branch-sized fingers around his neck. He accomplished nothing but ripping one of his own fingernails loose. Tears, fears and hopes could not bring back the dead. Seeing her ruined body, something snapped inside him. It felt like a part of him sank deep inside his own mind to hide and never come back into the light. What was left saw the world with new eyes. A prompt appeared and was accepted, perverting the divine gift he'd been given.

So ended the story of Autumn Ghost, a woman whose death gave birth to a monster.

CHAPTER 62

Grimshaw held Dust by his throat and lifted him until they were eye-to-eye. The razin's feet dangled more than a meter off the ground. The ogre was prepared to taunt his prey right before he killed him, but what he saw in the man's eyes made him hesitate for some reason. It wasn't hate or anger or even hopelessness. It was the look of a man who had already died and been welcomed in the shadowy vale.

The ogre didn't understand, but he paused all the same. That hesitation saved Dust's life. Two events happened in quick succession after that. An invisible force seemed to pass over the battlefield. It stole the attention of nearly every ogre and seemed to both confuse and enrage them.

Grimshaw continued to hold Dust aloft, barely allowing the razin to breathe, but it seemed like he'd forgotten the kill he was about to make. Instead, he cast about for the source of his new anger. The second event occurred barely seconds after. A ghostly figure of translucent blue light hit the ogre like an avalanche and Zero's last remaining clergy was flung free.

Less than a minute before, Svaroth had just finished crushing a razin's skull in his bare hands. Not bothering to shake the gore free, the god had assessed the battlefield with a hideous grin. Two of the enemy clergy were dead, and the last was about to die. The powerful archer had disappeared during the ogre's initial rush and could be presumed dead. Scarcely a dozen of the enemy tribe remained on their feet.

The beastkin god had killed three ogres, but was barely fending off the rest of his worshippers. Soon, this Zero Fell would be left without allies. Meanwhile, he still had five powerful worshippers in fighting shape, including his acolyte.

Svaroth was more than pleased. He hadn't wanted to risk a confrontation with the enemy god, not until the pantherkin was worn down a bit. The cat deity followed the Art of the Soul. It wasn't as directly powerful as his own Earth Art, but it could be annoying versatile depending on what soul Fell had captured. It was well known in the Labyrinth that Soul Art practitioners were unpredictable. Before Svaroth risked himself in direct combat, he wanted his enemy tenderized.

Thankfully, the six ogres he'd tasked to keep the enemy god busy had done just that. Half were dead, but they'd forced Fell to burn a divine charge. As expected, Fell had an attack strong enough to instakill one of Svaroth's worshippers. Fell had also managed to slay one more, but after that the remaining three ogres had been able to keep the small deity busy.

This type of tactic was only possible in the early days of divinity, before a god's power truly manifested. In the future, the idea of two basic worshippers, even ones as large as an ogre, suppressing a god would be insane. Now, however, it was enough to keep the greatest threat at bay.

Svaroth knew they had the same cultivation and nearly the same Energy. As long as he didn't give his enemy a chance to rest, he should have more charges than his opponent. That edge would let him crush the cat god. As always, it was the application of power that mattered more than just power itself. Soon, very soon, the cat god's allies would be dead and his Divine Power would be depleted. At that perfect time, the god would be alone and Svaroth would take his life and the altar!

The Earth god focused back on his acolyte. Grimshaw was dumb as a box of rocks, but he'd done his job well. Not only smashing two of the acolytes, but now about to snap the neck of the last one. Victory was at hand!

Before the Earth god had even finished that thought, however, an invisible force swept across the battlefield. Svaroth found himself struck with an inconsolable rage. He immediately cast about for the target of his ire, and quickly found that it actually came from the enemy god.

Svaroth might have been a new god on Telos, but he'd existed in the Labyrinth for millennia. It was not the first, or even the thousandth time, his mind had been assaulted. As was often the case with mental attacks, they became much easier to fight if you were aware they were occurring. Of course, being aware of a psychic or emotional attack was a trick in and of itself. For the old god, however, detecting such a rudimentary assault was only to be expected. With sheer force of will, he fought it off.

You have resisted a negative Title effect: **Infuriating Enemy**!

His followers were not so lucky. With their Energy values so much lower and without any natural resistances, every last one of his worshippers had been caught, in thrall to Zero's power. They stopped their actions and turned as one toward Fell, even ignoring attacks by the pantherkin.

At first, Svaroth thought the enemy god must have somehow unlocked a third Divine Power. Observing the battle, he'd learned that his foe had a healing and melee attack. A potentially troubling combination, but nothing that couldn't be handled. When he saw his status prompt, however, he knew it was worse than that. Even though immortals had only come to Telos less than a week ago, somehow that damn cat had already earned a Title!

Worse, between the effect it was having and its name, it was obvious that the Title gave him the ability to attract the aggression of enemies. Every ogre seemed to forget that they were fighting anyone else and only had eyes for Zero Fell. Even Grimshaw, who literally had a defenseless enemy in his hands, was only focusing on the Title holder. If the razin weren't so puny, just a few seconds of distraction might have cost him this battle. As it was, the ogres' physical advantages were so large that the razin could not harm them significantly. In fact, a couple of the smaller tribe were killed accidently as the ogres rushed to kill the cat god.

Svaroth shouted at his worshippers to snap out of it and ignore the rage that had overtaken them. He knew it was a lost cause. The ogres had great physical prowess, but that strength was only matched by their low intellect. Still, he tried bellowing once more before realizing it was useless. There was no way his moronic followers would even recognize they were being manipulated, much less be able to resist.

The Earth god was about to rush over and try to kill the cat god, waiting be damned, but then his eyes narrowed cunningly. Just how bad was this? After thinking, he realized he didn't need to be overly concerned. Nearly all of the cat tribe were dead. Less than two dozen were still able to fight.

Even if all of his followers died taking out the enemy god, he could mop up the rest of the enemy himself. The last clergy wasn't a problem either. He would lose all power when his god died. That other cat man, the one with the bow, was nowhere to be found. The archer was probably just one more pile of flesh on the battlefield.

Svaroth's ragged teeth showed in a gleeful grin. Even in a worst-case scenario, if the enemy god should manage to kill all of his tribesmen and survive, he'd be heavily damaged. At that point it would be easy for Svaroth to finish him off and claim his prize! It didn't matter to him how he won. All that mattered was the altar.

The other god's followers weren't even worth mentioning. He had the same ogre body as his Chosen after all, and he was larger than most of his tribe. Any who stood against him would be ripped limb from limb. Any who fled would be killed by the jungle. The tenday was tomorrow. By using the Title, the cat god had just sealed his fate!

The green-haired Earth god started to realize that even though this battle was costly, it was good that he was killing the cat god now. There was no way a rogue god with no pantheon could have accomplished this much without a sponsor. Svaroth had no idea who they could be, but they had to be powerful.

If he hadn't met this Zero Fell now, and his enemy had been allowed to grow in strength, their future battle could have turned out very differently. In a way, he was almost lucky that events had turned out as they had. Svaroth chuckled to himself in satisfaction. I have a patron too, he thought, and they delivered you to me on a platter. It was time to "Slaughter the Lambs!"

Svaroth might have been a Labyrinth god for ages, but there was a reason he only belonged to a half-star pantheon. It was the same reason he had a high soul resonance with ogres. He was an idiot who had never learned a simple law of the Universe, one that every man on Earth learned on the playground.

Don't talk shit until the game is done.

CHAPTER 63

Fell had killed three ogres since the beginning of the battle. He had to give it to Rig, the Cruel Grail was an amazing weapon. The piercing power was high, but it was nothing compared to the *Bleeding* effect. Even the smallest scratch literally drained the life out of his foes. With his level higher than the average invader, he was able to prick them time and again. Meanwhile, his high Agility and Dexterity let him avoid every blow. A single hit from an ogre might have done him in, but a lifetime of battle before his godhood made the invader's attacks seem like slow-motion jokes.

The +10 weapon cut through an ogre's skin and muscle like butter. It was amazing how easily the rusty and simple-looking blade split his target's skin. The ogre cried out and yanked his arm away. His combat log assigned his enemies a number depending on how many he was fighting at a given time.

*Fell strikes Ogre 1 for **4 points of damage!***

*Cruel Grail **siphoning 5 HP/sec** from Ogre 1. Stack 1/5.*

631

To both Fell and the ogre's surprise, as the Relic came free from his enemy's torn flesh a tether of blood floated in the air between the blade and the wound. Blood flowed out of the ogre and into the grail along a pencil-thin red rope. With a savage grin, Fell finally understood the power of his Relic. Time would show that that thought would be one of the greatest understatements of his life. In the moment, however, he just resumed his attack on the ogres with bloody glee in his heart.

Each hit drew blood, and each strike increased the flow of blood between the ogres and the Cruel Grail. It was a fast-paced battle, and Fell didn't escape unscathed.

*Fell strikes Ogre 1 for **5 points of damage!***

*Cruel Grail **siphoning 10 HP/sec** from Ogre 1. Stack 2/5.*

*Ogre 2 strikes Fell for **14 points of damage!***

*Fell strikes Ogre 2 for **7 points of damage!***

*Fell strikes Ogre 2 for **5 points of damage!***

*Cruel Grail **siphoning 20 HP/sec** from Ogre 2. Stack 4/5.*

*Ogre 1 strikes Fell for **20 points of damage!***

The first injury was thanks to a mistimed dodge; the god was clipped by an ogre's backhand. The second bout of damage happened when Fell spun to avoid a tire-sized punch, but still got clipped in the shoulder. A popping sensation accompanied the pain. That one blow had dislocated his arm.

Agony felt like it was literally pressing on the boundaries of his cold assessment like a hydraulic press, but he remained dispassionate. He triggered *Soul Heal* from his bound soul and healing energy flowed through his body. It took several seconds, but he restored all of his lost HP, leaving the smallest bit of one charge in reserve. Fell pressed the attack.

After nine successful attacks, the Cruel Grail was absorbing 25 HP/sec from one and 20 HP/sec from the other. Mighty or not, the ogres were still flesh and blood. Within seconds they were feeling woozy. Fell marveled at the relic, but also knew he couldn't stop the attack. The *Bleeding* effect was powerful, but only lasted for seven seconds after it drew blood. The giant invaders had health to spare.

As he fought, he knew his Chosen were dying, but he didn't let it make him panic. There was always death in battle. Getting upset about it was just a waste of energy. He didn't do anything to provoke this attack, and he wouldn't carry the weight of the deaths it caused. Instead, he focused on the only thing that mattered: slaying his enemy.

More ogres closed in and Zero knew he had to even the odds. The first kill had been a one shot thanks to *Soul Strike*. Wrapped around the Relic, for the first time his Divine Power didn't damage his weapon. Instead, his celestial energies let him deliver two +30 strikes back to back. They'd literally ripped through his first enemy, dropping him in his tracks. The ogre collapsed, nearly cut in half.

His next kill was thanks to bleeding an invader nearly to death. After it had gotten lightheaded, it tripped. A fast roll brought him next to it, where he buried the grail in its ear. After claiming his second life more ogres attacked him, and things got more difficult.

Contrary to what Svaroth believed, instead of only having two divine charges left he still had all three basic charges as well as the remnant of a healing charge, thanks to his bound souls. He wasn't willing to spend them all in the first minutes of the fight, however. Even if he did, there would still be plenty of enemies left to fight.

With so many attacking him at once, Zero had to dodge and run far more than he attacked. It didn't help that the ogres were twice his size. That meant he wasn't able to stack the Cruel Grail's *Bleeding* effects efficiently. Each bleed only lasted seven seconds. With the ogres having hundreds of HP, he needed to strike them seven or eight times each. Not an easy task when his dagger was only a foot long and they were triple his mass and wielding tree trunks for clubs. Still, he was wearing them down, and the more blood they lost, the slower they moved. Indeed, he claimed his next kill when one fell over due to blood loss. Not wasting his chance, he stabbed it prison-style, landing five blows in half as many seconds. Fell claimed its soul seconds later.

He would have kept up the battle of attrition, but then red prompts emblazoned across his vision nearly back-to-back.

Your Acolyte, **Sharp Leaf**, has died! **- 100 Devotion Points** for all worshippers!

Your Head Acolyte, **Autumn Ghost**, has died! **- 150 Devotion Points** for all worshippers!

Total Devotion has fallen to **1,358**. Devotion rank remains... unchanged!

In the heat of battle, he couldn't care less about the drop in Devotion, but losing Ghost and Leaf were hard hits. Of all the razin, his acolytes were the ones he'd become closest to over the past few days. While his heart was hardened after years of battle, losing close comrades could still pierce his emotional walls.

Even as he dodged and stabbed, his mind couldn't help but think how he would never again hear another of Sharp Leaf's stupid comments or see the unwavering strength in Autumn Ghost's eyes. He flipped backwards, gaining himself a second of respite from the constant attacks. Scanning the battlefield, he saw that the largest ogre was about to snap Midnight's neck.

That was why he dodged past his two opponents and ran as fast as he could toward Dust. Even as Grimshaw was lifting Dust to look into his eyes, Fell brought the two of them into the maximum range of his Title. He'd been saving *Infuriating Enemy* as one of his final trump cards.

Fell had no illusions about being able to stand up against all the ogres at once. It was only thanks to the sacrifices of the razin fighting alongside him that he'd managed to survive so long. If he had been mobbed by the entire enemy tribe all at once, he definitely would have been overwhelmed. In this wide-open meadow he wouldn't even be able to outrun the enemy, not with every enemy being more than twice his height.

When he saw that Midnight Dust was about to be killed as well though, he couldn't hold back any further. That was why he'd activated his Title, *Infuriating Enemy*, and went for broke. He activated *Soul Strike*. Crystalline blue energy surrounded his Relic, a nearly invisible jewel of deadly power. Fell dodged for the four seconds required to fully power it up then dove at his closest opponent.

There was no guarantee that even *Soul Strike* would ensure a kill. +30 made for a powerful attack, but it'd only be fatal if he landed a head shot or struck the right spot on the body. The Relic's *Bleeding* effect was only useful in a prolonged fight. With two more ogres rushing to kill him along with the three already driven mad with fury, he needed stopping power and he needed it now. Even putting it all on the line and burning his remaining divine charges, he'd need luck to survive the next few minutes.

That was okay.

He made his own luck.

All three of the ogres he'd been fighting lunged toward him, driven crazy with rage. Two others howled their fury and pounded the ground toward him. Only extreme contortions, movements that would have been impossible in his human body, let him dodge the attacks. His tail gently caressed the face of one of the ogres as he performed a final back handspring. It caused zero damage, but Zero felt that psychologically the effect must have been just as devastating as it was disrespectful.

With a moment of breathing room, and hoping nothing would go wrong, he searched inside himself and triggered a power for the first time. His internal monologue went on a loop.

Don't eat me. Don't eat me. Don't eat me. Don't eat me.

Time froze and cerulean light surrounded his left hand. Fell could actually see the thick yellow-white drool dripping off an ogre's fangs, its face frozen only a couple yards away. Even though he and the rest of the battlefield were locked in stasis, he was able to perceive the light pouring out of him.

The speed of the fountain increased and power raged through him. Unable to stop, both his arms were thrown back and he roared as another existence was torn away from his own. The violently churning light pooled on the ground in front of him like liquid. From this sapphire cauldron rose the shape of his old Mortal Enemy, the eaglebear.

Somehow taking minutes and no time at all, his spirit animal was summoned for the first time. He now had a powerful ally who had the same armor penetration as his Soul Art. Time sped back up, but only from his perspective. To everyone else on the field of battle, one moment the god's hand had blazed with blue light, and the next a massive, spectral monster stood before him.

Congratulations! You have summoned a Spirit Animal: **Divine Eaglebear**!

This phantasm carries the power of your Soul Art: **+10% Armor Negation**

The eaglebear had the same shape that it had had in life, even down to the barbs on its feathers, but in other ways was wildly different. Rather than being constructed of feathers, fur and muscle, it was comprised of a deep blue light. The edges of its body were distinct, but it was also translucent. The energy of its body was a thick azure haze. It was real and solid, however, its heavy claws sinking easily into the grassy ground.

Not even ten seconds had passed since Autumn Ghost's death, but Fell wasted no time. Dust's life could end at any moment. The spirit eaglebear read his mind and his desires. Whatever animosity it had felt before, it was purely devoted to its god in death. Without hesitation it sprang down the battlefield, leaving a sapphire afterimage in everyone's eyes. One of the charging ogres was in its way, but that was fixed by a swipe of its razor-sharp claws. The invader fell to the ground screaming and minus one eye.

The turquoise spirit barely slowed. It struck Grimshaw broadside, its weight greater than the ogre's nine hundred pounds. Midnight Dust flew free from the ogre's grasp, landing in an unceremonious pile of arms and legs. The two behemoths started rolling on the ground, Dust completely forgotten, each trying to gain the upper hand.

Seeing the spirit animal, Svaroth finally lost his calm. Fell had not only managed to recruit a powerful archer and tame beasts, he'd also gained the service of a powerful spirit! Not only a spirit, but one that had been touched by Divine Power. The energy signature was unmistakable to his eyes. A younger immortal might have missed the signs, but for an old god there was no confusing the magical emanations of the thing. The cat god probably didn't even know the power of the spirit he was commanding, but Svaroth knew its potential was almost limitless! He had to end this battle and the enemy god's rise to power. He had to do it now!

Fell was unaware of Svaroth's panic. He was too busy playing his last trump card. With five ogres bearing down on him, it was time. All chess players knew that winning meant taking the king. Nothing else mattered. If the invaders killed him, then the razin would be erased from the surface of Telos. With a mental flexion, he triggered another power for the first time.

Do you wish to activate the 2nd Secret Benefit of your Luck:

Tough Luck? Yes or No?

Fell chose "Yes" even as he dodged another attack. Time froze again for a split second and he heard the sound of dice rattling around inside his head. Time resumed as another prompt showed the random reward he'd gained.

Congratulations!

Your defense has increased by **+43** for **4 minutes**!

The god's savage grin showed his sharp fangs. He went on the offensive, absently noting that Svaroth was finally rushing to fight him. I'll be with you soon, he thought with grim hunger. His fully powered *Soul Strike* surrounded the Cruel Grail. For the first time he fully committed to an attack. His weapon slashed through an ogre's neck. The head flew into the air, and blood followed it in an orange geyser. The attack ended one of his enemies, but left him wide open. A fist the size of a barrel struck him hard enough to shatter stone. Zero shot through the air like a bullet.

For a moment, Svaroth's heart thrilled. Was that it? Had the god been slain? He knew the strength of his Chosen and a hit like that should have broken most of the bones in the cat's body. Even if Fell used his healing, it would take time to knit bone back together. Time that the ogres could use to finish the kill!

That hope died after Zero, rolling end over end, stopped his own backwards movement and landed back on his feet. Furrows carved into the ground before he stopped moving, but he was standing upright. The god twisted his neck until he felt a pop and deliberately leaned over to spit out a bloody wad. Then he gave the ogres the same savage grin as before, only this time his white fangs were coated with red.

Holding the Cruel Grail in one hand and his unsheathed claws extending from the other, he laughingly shouted at the giant enemies staring at him in both anger and disbelief.

"Who's next?"

CHAPTER 64

Fell didn't wait for an answer. His increased defense would only last so long. He sprinted back toward the ogres, eager to claim another life. The enemies he'd been fighting were the easiest targets. Thanks to the Cruel Grail, they'd already lost a lot of blood. Their healths were down past the halfway mark and one was unsteady on his feet. Zero didn't hold back.

When one ogre punched at him, he rolled under the blow, completely ignoring his attacker. He was focused on another invader. Seeing Fell suddenly pop out of nowhere, the ogre couldn't react in time. Zero didn't hesitate, plunging his dagger just left of the giant's groin. He twisted his wrist hard, all four of the blades widening the holes.

One of them shredded the equivalent of the ogre's femoral artery. Pulling the weapon out, orange blood liberally showered Zero. Seeing the spout, the ogre panicked and tried to block the flow with his snow shovel-sized hands. It was no use. The ogre was already dead, he just didn't know it yet. Fell didn't wait around for him to find out.

Fell placed one foot on his opponent's knee. He backflipped high into the air, passing over his first attacker's head. As he flew over, he sank the Cruel Grail into the ogre's shoulder, as stable as a climber's cam. The invader's mouth opened to bellow in rage and indignation, but the sound was cut off, literally. Blue energy surrounding the talons on his free hand, Fell swiped his claws across the ogre's throat.

His divine energy sheared through the ogre's neck, the head flying free, netting him his second decapitation. Confusion and surprise were frozen on the invader's face. Zero rode the body down before yanking the Relic out. Turning, he looked at the three ogres closing in along with their god.

One full charge left, he thought, plus a little change. A battle-hungry smile grew on his face. No problem.

Zero met the ogres' attack head on, trusting in his Tough Luck defense. With *Soul Strike* wrapping the Grail in pale blue power, his blade glinted, now honed to an impossible edge. His smaller body and high Agility made all the difference once again.

He slid under the swing of a tree club. Easily regaining his feet, he was inside the ogre's guard. Jumping across, Fell buried his dagger into the ogre's chest. The invader bared his teeth in defiance, but only for a moment. Then, heart punctured, the ogre let out a soft sigh and slid to the ground.

Fell twisted his body and placed both feet on the dying ogre's chest. Pushing off as though it were a springboard, he somersaulted to land five feet away. The other ogres were only seconds away from him, their eyes bloodshot with rage, but Zero wasn't alone. The enemy had forgotten about his tribe in their Title-induced fury. His people had not forgotten about them.

The few remaining razin threw themselves valiantly at the ogres. One giant was taken down not by a fancy combat technique, but because a brave catwoman threw herself at his legs. The ogre tripped over her and his own feet, landing with a heavy thud. Pure luck saved the catwoman's life. She somehow managed not to be squashed while the ogre tried to catch his feet. Nearly every remaining razin fell on top of the downed invader: stabbing, clawing and even biting. While the ogre was by far stronger, he could not resist the fury of more than a dozen razin protecting their god.

That just leaves two nuts and a hardon, Fell thought. His eyes flicked over the ogre rushing toward him and then to Svaroth, and ended where Grimshaw was fighting his spirit animal. The eaglebear was tearing pieces out of its enemy with abandon. The enemy acolyte was out of the fight for at least the next couple minutes. Large splashes of orange blood painted the ground around his spirit animal and the ogre. Good girl, he thought. Fuck'em up.

An ogre worshipper dove toward him, the same invader that Fell's spirit animal had partially blinded. Zero leapt back, once again relying on his agile body and finding it was equal to the task. He bounded back in a one-handed reverse handspring. His attacker faceplanted, its depth perception ruined. Ramming the ruined socket into the ground nearly made the ogre pass out, something that was almost racially impossible.

The one-eyed ogre had been hurt so badly that his pain and fear had started to override the effect of Zero's Title. That was why he hesitated, waiting for his god to arrive. What he did not know was that Svaroth was rethinking things as well. The ogre god had slowed his roll.

Fell could see all of it and was quick to capitalize on his enemy's fear. Dodging from side to side, he kept moving into the ogre's blind spot. The advantage of having a smaller size was being harder to keep an eye on. After one hard feint, the giant stumbled in fear.

The ogre had flinched a bit, having seen the power the god could manifest. To anyone watching, it might have been funny: a five-foot-tall man with a panther tail making an eight-foot-tall behemoth flinch. Of course, to enjoy the joke you'd have to ignore the nearly one hundred dead and mangled bodies around them. Zero wasn't laughing. He was driving the Cruel Grail, a full foot of divine metal, into his enemy's knee.

The ogre screamed and punched down, but Fell had already reclaimed his weapon. The god danced back, easily avoiding the blow of the crippled ogre. The two of them locked gazes and a sadistic grin broke over Fell's face. This was one of his favorite parts. Seeing the realization of hopelessness in an enemy's eyes. He was going to enjoy this.

As he'd pulled the weapon out, a pencil-thin rope of blood had remained attached. Zero was used to seeing this by now, but for the first time there was nothing and no one blocking Svaroth's view. He'd known Fell had a weapon strong enough to kill his followers, but he hadn't known it was enchanted. Using God's Eye, Svaroth suffered his largest shock yet.

The cat had gotten a Relic... How the hell had the cat gotten a Relic? Not only a Relic, but a powerful one from what he could see. Unlike normal items, gods couldn't just glean in-depth information if a Relic belonged to another immortal. They could just identify that it was one. Indeed, the stats of Relics would be treated like a high-level military secret by gods, no matter what world of the Labyrinth they ruled.

Seeing the powerful item brought a craven fear back to Svaroth's heart, but it was quickly replaced by greed. Even without the altar, if he could possess a powerful Relic so soon after this world had connected to the Labyrinth, he could build an empire even without his fellow pantheon members. He might even take the preeminent spot on this world, and one day ascend to the heights of godhood!

The cunning Earth god had started running to the side while Zero was finishing off his follower. As the death stroke fell, he was in the enemy god's blind spot. He kept running; he had no intention of engaging in a melee battle, not against a Wielder. Instead, he prepared to use both of his divine charges at once. Agile or not, once he got close enough, his *Stone Spears* should take the enemy deity out. Svaroth raised both arms, his heart thudding hard in gleeful anticipation. It was time to end this.

It was in that moment that two bone-white arrows struck him less than a second apart, and Svaroth's heart started to fibrillate for an entirely different reason. One of the arrows landed high in his chest, and the other sank deep into the meat of his thigh. Pain ricocheted through the god's body. Svaroth turned his head in the direction the arrows had come from. What he saw was the archer holding his bow of bones. The razin's yellow skin was stretched around a cocky grin. The Ranger had another arrow nocked on the string and one more in the quiver on his back.

Death energy started necrosing the god's body immediately. It spread slower than in the other ogres thanks to the god's *Enduring Earth* Divine Skill and higher Energy, but the purple-black magic was deadly all the same. Tendrils of Death mana eroded through the deity.

With a disappointed cry, Svaroth's arms fell, his *Stone Spears* uncast. He hurriedly ripped the arrows from his body. Blood arced into the air from the violent manner he removed the enchanted bones. The act of yanking them out caused further loss of HP, but it was better than leaving the poison pills in his body. The necrosis slowed perceptively as the bone weapons were removed, turning a one-shot kill into a moderate injury. The attack had still served its purpose.

Even as he'd ripped the arrows out, Svaroth had grabbed a treeclub from one of his fallen ogres. The uprooted tree still had leafless branches on one end. The limbs didn't hide him from view, but moving side to side, they could easily foil a shot. It wasn't much, but it was enough to ensure that an archer would have to calculate a great deal more before firing. The old god glared murder at the catman. The archer returned his gaze coolly.

Svaroth wanted nothing more than to rip the limbs off every member of the beastkin tribe, slowly and with great pleasure, but he forced himself to think. The fact that the archer was still alive changed everything. Coupled with the fact that nearly all of his tribe had been killed, including his acolyte… the situation had changed.

Even though it filled his throat with bile, the old god had to admit the truth. He'd lost. That didn't mean he couldn't escape. The archer was a problem, but Svaroth's powerful Earth body made him hard to kill. Not only was his health insanely high, but his Earth Art was already combating the Death mana. The Ranger was definitely a threat. With his treeclub, Svaroth should be able to block at least one shot, however.

Svaroth decided to flee.

Even as he did, he started plotting his revenge. The accursed cat god was stronger than he'd thought, but this was only a minor setback. The penalties for failing the quest would be terrible, but nothing he couldn't endure. Better to have a late start on this new world than no start at all. He would just found his settlement somewhere else.

With his powerful body he could survive in this new world, and once he had created his altar, he would give birth to his tribe once again. Sooner or later, he would reconnect with the other gods of his pantheon, and then, *then*, this cat god would know true despair. Svaroth had shed divine light upon many worlds. He'd met powerful rogue gods before, but they always fell to the collective power of pantheons.

Svaroth also had something incredibly valuable now: information. A rogue god like Zero Fell most likely did not know the true importance of a Relic, but as an old god, he did. That knowledge could be traded for power. Gods would burn entire cities to claim even a weak Relic, and Zero's looked strong, very strong indeed. By spreading that information, the Earth god would not only earn resources to rebuild, but would also earn the cat god powerful enemies. It was gain-gain.

By the time Svaroth had firmly decided to run, a cruel smile was on his lips. The very strength Fell had shown this day would ultimately bring him down. While the cat god stayed smugly in one place, he, the great god Svaroth, would endure! In time, he would pay back this grave insult.

This was only a setback, and one that wasn't even his fault. The cat deity had somehow claimed an altar, grown his powers at a nearly insane pace, and, awe-inspiringly, had even laid claim to a Relic. It was no wonder Svaroth had lost the battle. There were too many things arrayed against him. He could not be blamed!

He was no weak young immortal. He was an old god. Where a new deity might only see disaster, he saw opportunity. This was not his first stumble. Truthfully, he'd stumbled more often than not for some reason.

Fell was not the first enemy that had enjoyed a small triumph before a final and total defeat. He was Svaroth! One day, he would make mountains crumble! He had survived the explosions of stars! There was no way he would be undone by a kitty with round fluffy ears! He would prevail… just as soon as he got by this damn archer.

Svaroth started his retreat. He took a step forward, but Minamoto drew back on his bow in response. Svaroth settled back, and the archer eased tension on the bow. The Earth god ground his teeth in irritation while he calculated. He had the treeclub in his hands, so he might be able to block one or both of the cat's arrows. If both shots got through though, the consequences could be dire.

The white arrows clearly possessed Death magic. If he was struck in the eye or the heart, he might die before his body could neutralize their malignant power. Taking an arrow in the knee might be just as bad. Dying did not completely faze him, he'd died before. He did not know the laws of this new world, however. While the True Death was not likely for a god, at the very least he'd become untethered. Who knew how long it would take for him to respawn? And in an untethered god, destruction of his Self might actually trigger the True Death. To a being that had lived hundreds of thousands of years, a final death was perhaps even more terrifying than to a mortal.

On the other hand, his opponent only had two shots left. If Svaroth could block both, he could kill the Ranger before fleeing the battle. That would greatly reduce the combat power of this accursed tribe. He still didn't like his odds though. The Death magic from the first two shots was still chipping away at his health and destroying his body. The two combatants stared at each other, locked in a stalemate in the middle of a battle. Svaroth's eyes were furious. He didn't have much time! Minamoto only smiled faintly in return, never blinking.

Seeing that the enemy god was neutralized, Zero's own face split into a feral grin. For the entire battle, he had tried to be aware of the whole battlefield. Doing so had made him split his focus between his personal fights and the battle as a whole. Now, however, all he had to do was focus on the enemy before him.

The ogre Fell was fighting didn't know he had been abandoned by his god. It was the only reason that the giant still had hope. Four blood tethers led out of his body. The evil god he was fighting was obviously a god of suffering and pain. He seemed to grow stronger and more excited the more blood was spilt! Fear rose in the ogre's heart, overriding the thrall of Fell's Title.

The ogre threw a punch which Zero ducked beneath while stabbing upward. The dagger form of the Cruel Grail wasn't long enough to do real damage even if he'd plunged it into his enemy's chest, but that wasn't the point. Zero claimed a few points of health with his stab and the *Bleeding* effect gained another stack. All five tethers of blood pulsed as the ogre was drained dry.

For the next minute, he traded attacks with the invader. Each strike the ogre attempted was weaker than the last. By the time Fell's tribe had finished the ogre they'd tripped, his opponent was weaving like an unsteady drunk.

Before the giant died, he fell to the ground, too weak to even move. His face was wan and pale. Even his thick skin couldn't hide the blood loss. Fell didn't waste time gloating. He stabbed the Cruel Grail violently into the dying giant's face multiple times. Each impalement refreshed the *Bleeding* effect, but the debuff was no longer necessary. To the music of tearing flesh and splintering bone, the ogre died. A pale blue furnace appeared in Fell's throat as he consumed a new soul.

Standing tall, orange blood coating his black skin, he looked over to where Svaroth and Minamoto remained locked in a standoff. His own thoughts mirrored his enemy's. It was time to end this. He started jogging toward the enemy deity. While he did, he stared at the Relic in his hand.

One thing he'd noticed was that as the grail had absorbed blood, the jewels around the rim had flashed with ruby light. Each new source of blood had coincided with a prompt that he'd minimized. As he moved toward his enemy, he absorbed them one by one.

Know This! Each **Bloodline** is composed of **Sequences**, but a Sequence must be pristine to be collected. It is rare for an entire Bloodline to be pristine in any one individual.

Each new blood source the Cruel Grail bathes in allows the Relic to collect any pristine Sequences that are present.

Once all the Sequences of a Bloodline are collected, the Grail will be able to bestow that Bloodline upon the worthy!

It sounded like genetics to Fell. Every species had a progenitor. Every descendent would have some of that DNA, but it wouldn't be identical. It sounded like the sequences were the grail reconstructing the original genetic code.

Zero didn't know it, but he'd grasped the basic concept without understanding the power at all, like a caveman using a railgun as a club.

The next windows showed him the sequences he'd gained so far.

The Cruel Grail has tasted a new blood source!	
Bloodline: Ogre	**Blood Rank:** Common
Sequences Consumed: Rik', kri	
Total Sequence: Rik' ___ ___ ___ Kri	

The Cruel Grail has tasted a new blood source!	
Bloodline: Ogre	**Blood Rank:** Common
Sequences Consumed: Rik', ala	
Total Sequence: Rik'ala ___ ___ Kri	

Despite the lives he'd claimed, he still hadn't completed a bloodline. Fell surveyed the battlefield. There was no shortage of blood sources.

It was a charnel house.

The bodies of his Chosen dotted the meadow like horrific wildflowers. Spaced here and there were the much larger bodies of the invaders. His people had managed to kill every ogre except for Svaroth and Grimshaw. The ogre his worshippers had tripped lay unmoving on the ground, two wooden spears sticking out of its eye sockets like railroad spikes. The bodies of six razin lay on the ground next to him, just as dead.

His people had obtained victory, but only by paying in blood. He'd lost two of his acolytes. Barely a tenth of his tribe that had started the battle was still breathing. Even less were standing. A few more were injured and moving weakly on the ground, but the truth was, his tribe had been massacred.

The enemy acolyte was still screaming as the eaglebear ripped pieces off him. All the remaining razin were staring at the scene, heart-dead. The eaglebear had ended up on top of the ogre and was now, slowly and deliberately, biting off the ogre's arms and legs. His spirit animal was clearly as sadistic in death as it had been in life.

Fell saw that Midnight Dust was finally back on his feet. The razin had jogged over to Grimshaw's screaming form. He'd approached from the right. The eaglebear had already torn that appendage free. The blue spirit snarled at the acolyte, but then pulled back at a silent command. Without ceremony, Dust slid his copper blade into a wound on the ogre's neck.

With the thick skin already broken, the shortsword slid in easily, smooth as butter. It must have hit an artery due to the resulting spray, but blood loss made the spurt weak. The acolyte's screams turned into a wet burble. More orange blood splashed over Midnight's soiled clothes and face, but the invader still clung to life. Dust absently licked his lips. *Bitter*, was all he thought distantly.

In the last moments of Grimshaw's life, Dust stared deep into his enemy's eyes. Whatever the giant saw made him kick his one remaining leg in panic. An unmistakable stream of piss shot out from beneath the ogre's loincloth. Grimshaw's heart beat its last, his face frozen in terror. Dust looked at the corpse dispassionately. With a come hither gesture, he pulled the soul from the body. He didn't claim it though. Instead, he tossed it to the spirit animal.

The azure eaglebear opened its mouth and inhaled the struggling orb. A manic smile crested Midnight's face as he imagined the pain his most hated enemy felt even after death.

The death of his acolyte caused physical pain in Svaroth. He turned his head to the right, gazing at his acolyte's dead body. As he looked, he realized that in the short time he'd been focused on Minamoto, the last remnant of his followers had been slain.

Since his standoff with the Ranger began, the Earth god had been sidling closer to the tree line, keeping the treeclub's branched end pointing toward the archer. His hope was to move around the archer and then run into the jungle. Even if his opponent moved with him, the god would still be that much closer to the safety of the trees. It wasn't a bad plan. Minamoto couldn't afford an errant shot. The branched end of the ogre god's club was as good as a shield.

Grimshaw's death provided an opportunity, however. For the split second Svaroth was distracted, Minamoto wasn't. The Death archer shot with unerring precision, at the perfect moment. Pain tore through Svaroth for the second time in as many moments. The bowman had chosen his target well. His arrow tore through the meat, bone and tendons of the god's knee. Death magic immediately began to spread, but even without the necrosis of the baleful magic, his shot would have ended Svaroth's paper dream of escape.

"Yoraba taiju no kage," the archer intoned.

Translation: If you seek shade, do so under a large tree.

Paraphrase: Don't try to fuck me with such a little dick.

The Ranger will fit in well with his new people.

A moan, more denial than pain, escaped Svaroth's lips. Zero's face broke into a feral grin at the sound. Who the hell needs giant ogres when a badass archer has your back? If gaining strong allies was how his high Luck manifested, he'd take it over high Strength any day.

Svaroth dropped his club in agony and ripped the arrow from his knee. At least, he tried to. The jagged edges of the arrowhead had caught on something deep inside his leg, and his skull-crushing hands lacked the dexterity to remove it. Instead, he snapped the shaft free, leaving the Death head inside. Minamoto, slowly and deliberately, took hold of his final arrow and walked closer to the distressed god. Watching the ogre attempt to stop the rot spreading through his leg, he began to speak.

"You may want to know that it is not easy to create these arrows. Each one requires an entire body. All the bone, from the toes to the top of the skull, are condensed into this perfect weapon of death.

That is the only way to make them so strong. It is why, even as I speak, death is spreading through the body of a god." With a chipper smile, he added, "Through your body."

Svaroth cried out in frustration, still trying to dig the head out of his leg. His *Enduring Earth* ability couldn't remove a negative status that kept renewing itself. If he couldn't take out the arrowhead, the decay would never stop. A wail of desperation escaped the god's throat. It was as useless as trying to pick up a pencil with loaves of bread.

The rot kept eroding the bone it had embedded in. The agony was unrelenting. A fresh wail ripped from his throat, hopelessness having vanquished hope. Minamoto continued to speak with the tone of a factory owner proud of his product.

"I must also pay one hundred mana to sculpt the bones. One hundred mana, at least! At my low level, that is no small thing. After I used the skeleton of one of your worshippers to make one of my quietus arrows, I had to scrounge the battlefield for the others I shot. Your thug worshippers had destroyed nearly all of them." The archer *tsked*. "Do you feel bad about destroying my art?"

Svaroth screamed like a tea kettle as his knee finally rotted away. Minamoto's calm speech had gouged out the last remains of his sanity. He bellowed like a mad animal, mouth opening and closing as his powerful body released unintelligible sounds. "Ahh, gaaaahhh, gwaaahhh!"

The bottom of his leg fell to one side, Death magic still spreading black tendrils through the below-the-knee amputation. The god reached into his own mangled stump and finally dug out the arrowhead. He threw it away, the tips of his fingers already blackening, but it was too late. The Death poison traced up his leg, through his balls and penis, and across his stomach. The old god had lived countless years and had seen water wear down mountains. At that moment, he was little more than a wounded animal. A beast snarling at the inevitability of its own death.

Svaroth half knelt, half collapsed to his remaining knee. The ground drank the lifeblood of the Earth god, and beneath the surface his divine blood started a reaction. No one on the battlefield was aware of this.

With the arrow not actively spreading Death mana, Svaroth regained some semblance of sanity. His divine ability, *Enduring Earth,* fought against the purple-black magic spreading throughout his body. The god looked at the archer and the arrow resting lightly against the bowstring. Teeth bared in defiance, the deity reached over for his dropped treeclub but stopped as the bowstring tightened and Minamoto *tsk*'d.

After having just been driven mad by the Death poison, something deep within Svaroth feared the touch of those bone arrows even more than actual death. The ogre's eyes remained locked on the quietus arrow. His large hand fell to the ground, defeated. He wasn't willing to invite another attack in exchange for a weak and meaningless gesture. A fool he might be, but he was smart enough to recognize the end.

Minamoto's cool gaze took in the final moments of a god's life. He could not remember his previous lives clearly, but he felt sure that he'd never seen a god die before. The Ranger was unimpressed, which made him frown. Then he realized that if he survived long enough in the service of his new god, the dying moments of deities would probably not be rare. Maybe the next one would be more interesting. That thought brought a smile to his face.

Watching the play of emotions across the archer's face threatened to break Svaroth's sanity again. Why was he smiling?

Seeing Svaroth's fear, and, more importantly, who was approaching from behind the Earth god, the archer chose to share just a few more words. His tone was not mocking this time, but instead spoken with quiet understanding, "The road we take to avoid our fate often leads us to it."

Svaroth frowned, not understanding. Then he felt a sharp pain at the base of his neck. Quick and lethal agony speared into his brain, fast as lightning. Then he was falling, having lost any control over his body. As he fell, he wondered how the pain could have been both searing hot and freezing cold.

The Earth god remained confused, still not understanding why he couldn't move. That was because he still didn't know that for the last minute, Minamoto had just been the decoy. While Svaroth had focused on his own pain and his fear of the Crypt Ranger, the god Fell, his true enemy, had run silently behind him. The Cruel Grail had penetrated Svaroth's skin at the base of the neck, piercing first through hardened vertebrae and then the soft spaghetti of the god's spinal column.

It had happened so quickly that Svaroth did not have time to understand, not in his pain-addled state. Even when his eyes focused again seconds later and he saw Fell standing on his chest, he still didn't understand. It was only when he saw a thin ribbon of blood stretching from behind his head, past his field of vision, to the ugly iron blade in Zero's hand that it finally clicked. A wave of prompts had flashed in his vision at the same time the pain hit. Looking up at his enemy, he finally absorbed them and confirmed what he already knew. He was paralyzed and it was this cat bastard that had done it to him!

With his last, weak breaths, Svaroth looked up at Fell with hate in his eyes, "Enjoy this victory now, rogue! Clah, clah, clah!" he coughed, orange blood flecking his large ogre lips.

"Count your days and cherish them, for my pantheon will come looking for me. No matter what you do with this body, they will know what you have done! This world may be newly reborn, but the gods that have come to it are older than the stars. They are stronger than the primordial forces of the Universe!"

The Earth god's voice got stronger as he used his last energy to spit defiance at the dark-skinned cat deity, "My people will know what you have done and their collective might will smite you and your horrid tribe. They will cut the cock off every man, and desecrate every woman!"

The Earth god went on like that for a minute with Fell watching impassively. Fell was actually impressed at how resilient Svaroth's body was in light of the multiple injuries, blood loss, and loss of limb. Even the *Bleeding* effect of his Relic didn't last the full seven seconds. Fell knew because he counted, feeling like it was a better use of his time than listening to the ogre's monologue.

Svaroth's final words ended with a wet and undignified, "*GACK!*" The world of Telos would never know what else he might have said because his vocal cords were severed by a large spike of bloodstained iron sticking out of his throat.

"Wow. That guy could talk," Fell commented disdainfully. Then he twisted his hand hard. The four blades of the Cruel Grail shredded blood vessels, depriving the ogre god's brain of oxygen. Zero stood up, divine blood and flesh slipping off the edges of his blade. His feet remained on the chest of Svaroth, and he watched the light die in the eyes of a god.

658

The Last Blood of a newly born god fell onto the ground, more powerful than all the blood that had been spilled before. The raw potential of the first drops mixed with the potent strength of the last, and something powerful began to form.

At the same time, with his enemy's last breath, a prompt appeared in Fell's vision.

The Cruel Grail has tasted a new blood source!	
Bloodline: Ogre	**Rank:** Common (rank 1)
Sequences Consumed: Rik', ala, hom', oto	
Total Sequence: Rik'ala hom' oto~Kri	

Not even Svaroth had possessed every sequence, but he had far more than his followers. It was also enough to finish the code! Another prompt appeared accompanied by a forlorn wail.

MOOOAAANN!
Congratulations!
You have claimed a complete Bloodline: Ogre
Bloodline Rank: Common

There were more prompts, but Fell minimized them. His eyes were trained on the large soul that was rising from Svaroth's body, dark green with lighter flashes of energy dancing inside like swirling leaves.

CHAPTER 65

This soul sphere was different than any Fell had seen before. Not only was it larger and more colorful, but it didn't behave like the other souls. First, it rose from the body almost immediately and of its own accord. Second, other souls that he'd seen rise from bodies had just wanted to move on to whatever came next. There had been no real intelligence behind them. Even their struggles against his control felt more like an animal reaction than a conscious decision.

The god's soul acted with intent. It floated above the body for a moment before rising to hover in front of Zero's face. The sphere had no organs, no eyes, and nothing about it spoke of an orientation, but the god was sure it was looking at him. That was confirmed a moment later.

<<HAHAHA! YOUR ONLY HOPE WAS THAT THIS WORLD DELIVERED THE TRUE DEATH TO IMMORTALS! NOW YOU KNOW THAT YOU WILL NEVER BE SAFE! I WILL COME FOR YOU, GODLING! WHETHER IT TAKES DAYS, WEEKS OR CENTURIES FOR ME TO RESPAWN, I WILL HAVE MY REVENGE UPON YOU!>>

The voice spoke directly into his mind. It was changed, deeper now than the Earth god's voice had been in life. It also echoed, as if it were speaking through a wide tube, but it could still be recognized as Svaroth's voice.

Fell looked at it impassively. There was a lot he didn't understand about this new world, but if he'd kicked this guy's ass when he was a big ol' ogre, he wasn't about to be afraid of a nightlight. Instead he responded, "Funny you should mention revenge."

Without any further warning, he swung his blade at the large green soul. He was out of divine charges, so *Soul Strike* wasn't an option. His Soul Art gave him a bonus against spirits, though. The way Fell saw it, attacking was worth a shot.

The blade struck the soul with a blow hard enough to cause a shockwave of spiritual energy to ripple over the orb's surface. Midnight Dust, his god and the spirit familiar watched the soul shoot backward.

<<AARRGHHAHAHAHAHAHAAA!>> The soul bellowed briefly in pain, but that almost immediately turned into cruel laughter. Zero's attack had landed, but had caused barely any damage. In defiance, Svaroth's spirit floated back toward his foe and taunted Zero.

<<THIS? THIS! THIS IS THE EXTENT OF YOUR POWER? DON'T YOU FOLLOW THE ART OF THE SOUL? HAHAHA! ANY EXPERIENCED DEITY WOULD KNOW THAT YOUR TIER 0 POWERS COULD NOT HARM A DIVINE CORE!

YOU MAY HAVE DEFEATED MY BODY, BUT IN THIS WORLD MY SOUL PERSISTS AFTER DEATH! YOU CANNOT EVEN KEEP ME HERE UNLESS I WISH IT. I WILL TAKE

MY LEAVE NOW, BUT SPEND YOUR DAYS AND NIGHTS FEARING THE DAY THAT I RETURN. FOR WRATH AND RUIN SHALL COME WITH ME!>>

"You have *got* to stop monologuing," Fell sighed. He exerted his will, and used his Art to keep the soul in the same position. Every other spirit he'd controlled had barely been able to resist. This time was different. As soon as Svaroth realized what Zero was doing, he started to struggle. One moment the soul was held quivering in place, the next it would jerk a foot away before Fell gained control again. Svaroth mocked Zero again, voice a bit strained, but also full of confidence.

<<YOU CANNOT CONTROL ME! YOU WILL NOT HARM ME EVER AGAIN!>>

"Good god, you're dumb. Don't you ever learn?" Fell asked. "I'm just the decoy."

By the time the words had registered with the disembodied god, the eaglebear had already attacked. With its translucent beak opened wide, it inhaled the energy of the Earth god. A bright blue light appeared in the eaglebear's gullet, like a sapphire star.

Streams of green energy immediately began flowing from the floating soul into the spirit animal's beaked mouth. It was true that Zero's attack hadn't harmed Svaroth's soul. That hadn't come as a surprise to Fell. It had been worth a try, but his enemy was a disembodied deity. The whole "god" title wouldn't have meant too much if his basic attack could wipe his enemy from existence.

Siphoning power from the soul to grow his spirit animal though, well, he'd been hoping that was another matter. The fact that his pet was now consuming Svaroth's energy, and the fact that the ogre god's soul was spinning like a disco ball on crack, seemed to indicate that he'd been right.

<<**WHAT ARE YOU- NO. NO. NOOOOOOO!**>> Svaroth's voice shifted from confusion to panic in a second as power was siphoned from his Divine Core. Such a thing should not have been possible, not based on his countless years as an immortal of the Labyrinth, but he learned what many gods and demons would learn in the years to come. The worlds of the Lattice, perhaps Telos most of all, were more brutal than the worlds of paltry danger the immortals had survived in the past.

The flow of energy to the eaglebear cut off abruptly, and a quest prompt appeared.

You have received a Quest: **Birth of the Divine I**

Your spirit animal was changed by tasting your Divine Power. Countless roads sprawled in front of it. Now that it has fed off a second source, a new divine path has appeared.

Your spirit animal has the chance to develop a Divine Core!

Doing so will elevate it to a godlike existence and will provide you with a deity loyal to your cause.

Success Conditions: Supply your eaglebear with divine energy from three different sources

---

Rewards:

The allegiance of a newly born god

XP

Unknown

Penalty for failure of Quest: None

This quest cannot be refused!

Svaroth had screamed the entire time. The sound was so piercing that Fell could barely react to the fact that the eaglebear could become a god. Before Zero could even think about that, Svaroth's soul spoke again. The timbre of his voice had noticeably decreased and was pathetically forlorn.

<<How could you… How could you! My Divine Core! What chicanery is this? What have you done?>>

The green spirit sphere, considerably smaller and dimmer than before, sped away. Fell could not have kept hold of it had he tried. Not that he did. It was clear there was nothing more he could do with his current level of power. The soul shot into the jungle, wailing all the while. All of the tribe's enemies were defeated... at least for now.

CHAPTER 66

The tribe had won the day, but the cost… the term "butcher's bill" had never been more accurate. The grassy field in front of the ruined temple was no longer a verdant green. Now it was only mud and muck. It was the specific mix of grey-black-brown that is only made by mixing dirt and gallons of blood. The hue was slightly different where the ogres' orange blood stained the ground.

Everywhere you looked were broken bodies, pulped flesh, and scattered viscera. Smashed livers sat in puddles of nearly black blood. Ropes of intestines spooled out of bodies, stretching yards longer than should have been possible. Bowels and bladders had released, adding the scent of bloody shit that was the same in any world, like a hot copper penny jammed up your nose.

The first thing Fell wanted to do was pour Faith Points into Dust. As his only remaining acolyte, Midnight was the only one left who could heal the survivors. Now that the battle had ended, Fell's own power could recharge, but some of the wounded would die before ten minutes passed. He found his acolyte sitting in the mud, Autumn Ghost's ruined head in his lap.

Her single remaining eye stared sightlessly up at the sky. Almost all of her was bloody and half of her face had been crushed by Grimshaw. The other half was strangely preserved, and a single lock of blond hair lay against her cheek, only spotted here and there with blood.

Zero had expected that Dust might rebel, be comatose or just weep uncontrollably. It was obvious that Autumn's death had hit him hard. To the god's surprise, Midnight had just looked at him with a deadpan stare, not challenging, just lifeless, and had responded, "I cannot heal them anymore. I made my choice."

Not understanding, Fell used God's Eye, and a prompt explained the choice Midnight had made.

Your acolyte's soul has been damaged by extreme loss. The Labyrinth has recognized his **Ultimate Suffering** and gave your acolyte a choice, to continue on as he was or to focus his powers in one direction, to share his suffering with all those who deserve it.

He has gained a new ability: **Soul Scarred**

His Chants may now be silent. His soul energy will be silent and unseen.

He has lost the ability to heal others.

Divine damage he inflicts is increased by 200%.

Fell had just looked at Dust then, and the acolyte had gazed back calmly. The god knew well that battle left scars. Even before the Labyrinth that was true. It was no real surprise that this world of hidden mechanisms would formalize that effect. Midnight had made his choice and only the future would tell what it meant. Zero just made a simple offer.

"I can store her body," he said. "I can keep her preserved until we can bury her in her own grave later." It went without saying that the more than one hundred other bodies would have to be burned in a mass pyre. The ogres would be dealt with separately, but it was the best that Fell could manage. The dead outnumbered the living ten to one.

Midnight shook his head, answering in a strangely detached voice, "She would want to be with our people." He took hold of his battered copper blade and cleaned it on his own shirt. With the sharpest edge, he cut that lock of nearly pristine hair free. It went carefully into a pouch before Dust stood, nodded to his god, and walked off to help the few razin still alive.

He didn't look back.

Fell gazed after him for a moment, but didn't speak up. He'd never tell someone else how to grieve or deal with death. Life left marks on them all. Midnight deserved his. Instead, the god made sure all his enemies were dead.

His people had been thorough. Every ogre was indeed dead. Fell saw more than just rotting meat, however. He could see their souls stirring inside their bodies. As he walked the battlefield, he methodically consumed them all. Each absorbed ogre provided Faith Points.

667

> For absorbing energy from a **faithful of the Fallen God Svaroth**, you have gained **+4 Faith Points**!
>
> **Total Faith Points:** 103,994*

The prompts had the same warning for him to spend the extra Faith Points or they would be lost. They also informed him that Svaroth was now "fallen." It looked like even though the ogre god's spirit had fled, his spirit animal's attack had taken a toll.

Zero took a moment to walk over to Grimshaw's body. He stared down on the giant ogre's body in contempt. The bastard had killed two of his acolytes. Initially he wished that he'd been able to consume its soul himself, but knowing his spirit animal had made the ogre suffer in both this life and the next, he made his peace with it. The god spit on the body before moving on.

Fell continued walking the battlefield. As he passed the bodies of his people, he murmured thanks. It was a ritual he'd done far too often in the past, thanking the dead as he kept living. The part of him that would feel true sadness over their loss had long ago shriveled.

One of his people approached him.

"What should we do, Lord Fell?" the razin asked. Less than two dozen were left. More than one hundred of his people had died.

"We honor our dead," the god replied. "Start gathering the bodies of our people. We will put them to rest."

"What about the invaders?" another worshipper asked.

"Minamoto?" Fell looked at the Crypt Ranger.

"I will put them to good use."

The god turned his gaze upon the bodies of his fallen tribe, and asked the question he'd been avoiding because he was already sure of the answer. In his own mind, he silently asked, "Can I bring them back?"

"No," Rig responded simply. "Even your Soul Art does not have that power, at least not yet."

Fell nodded. It always came back to power.

Time passed quickly. Cleaning up a battlefield was never pretty, but it was necessary. Bodies and pieces of bodies were laid next to each other. The wood in his storage space came in handy. By the time night was falling, they had built a pyre. While they worked, the fence was finished, and the first structure of his empire was completed.

One moment there was only a ruin. The next, sparkles of light spun in the air. Through the flickers, a fully constructed building phased into existence. The structure was two stories tall and made entirely of the impossibly black stone.

Congratulations! You have constructed your first building!

You have made a **Level 0 Temple**!

Durability: 5,000/5,000

Each tenday, your Chosen will now generate 10% more Faith Points if they are within your religious domain.

Fell gazed at the building. It was so dark it looked like a hole in the universe. Light didn't seem to hit it. Instead, it felt like he could only see it by the negative space around it. *Void stone*, he thought to himself. It probably has some interesting properties. For now though, I'll just take the high durability and the promise of safety.

Rig had shown him some large creatures prowling along the edges of his domain. It appeared as if the beasts felt something when they crossed the invisible boundary and that unknown feeling had been keeping them back so far, but more were testing the boundary as time went on.

Zero turned his attention back to the pyre. Night had well and truly come by the time the fire was lit. Nocturnal sounds of the jungle filled the air. Fell, Midnight Dust, Minamoto and the few remaining members of his tribe watched the fires consume the bodies of their fallen. Dust's eyes were trained on two still forms in particular. His cold gaze never deviated and the warmth of the fire could not reach him.

The scent of blood hung heavy on the air. Now that it was combined with the aroma of roasting meat, the predators could no longer hold themselves back. The beasts crossed into Zero's domain, marked red on the minimap.

One of the monsters, something that looked like a cross between a large dog and a mole, burst from the ground just past the tree line. Two arrows from Minamoto turned it into black ooze. That scent made the predators cautious again. They didn't leave, but the beasts stayed back in the jungle. There may have been a banquet beckoning them, but clearly a dangerous monster was guarding it.

With the coming of night, however, the strongest jungle predators had awoken. They followed the scents just like the lesser beasts. These were apex predators who would not be frightened off by a strange smell.

In the past tenday, mana from the Labyrinth had made them even more powerful, both in levels and ranks. One of the smaller predators was eaten as an appetizer. High-pitched dying screams echoed through the jungle. Zero looked over and saw the tops of trees undulating. Whatever had come was still hidden by the thick jungle, but it was big enough to push hundred-foot-high trees out of the way. He knew that their new wall would not slow something like that down. To get to the buffet, these monsters would turn the wall into kindling.

Zero pointed at five men to help him open the wooden gates of the palisade, hoping that would keep the monsters from destroying it in the night.

"Everyone get inside," he commanded. It had taken several high-tier immortals to break the temple in the past. Even then, it hadn't been completely destroyed. With the stone's high durability, he couldn't imagine that the approaching monsters, even after days of absorbing Labyrinth energy, could break the temple's walls. Not yet.

The tribe quickly complied, all except Minamoto, who stared at the remaining ogre bodies with regret.

"It would be a shame to waste such good raw material," the archer lamented in his thick samurai accent.

Rolling his eyes, Fell touched each body in turn and used his storage space to save them. It was only enough to store two, but that was two more magic arrows for his strongest follower. The Ranger smiled in appreciation and ran over to open the gates. As soon as the doors were flung open, the two sprinted for the safety of the temple as well.

Fell was the last one inside. As he was closing the doors, he caught a glimpse of what was coming out of the jungle. For just a moment, his mouth dropped open in shock. Even after everything that had happened, he was surprised.

It was a dinosaur!

That is, if there had ever been a dinosaur that looked like a cross between a T-Rex and a centaur. Its head was three stories off the ground. The monster's hungry eyes met Fell's, only a few hundred yards of churned, bloody earth between them. A horrible cry, loud as a fog horn, issued from its throat, and Fell used God's Eye.

RITALOSAUR		
Level: 14	**Monster Rank:** Elite	
Energy: 501	**Soul Rank:** Limited	
STATS		
Health: 3570/3571	**Mana:** 709	**Stamina:** 1901/1902
DESCRIPTION		
Ritalosaurs are powerful reptiles that can imbue the element of Fire into their attacks. At higher levels they gain the ability to use Fire mana for ranged attacks.		

The monster had the highest Energy he'd seen in a wild creature. Its level was high as well. The greenbacked skink he'd come across on the old continent had only been level seven. The ritalosaur was also an *elite* with a health in the thousands.

To Fell though, nothing mattered so much as its soul rank. *Limited*, he thought with a gleam in his eyes and a growl in his throat. Imagine what I could do with you!

Numerous prompts were begging to be read.

Your domain has captured the **Last Blood of an Earth god**. Would you like to invest Faith Points to manifest this power?

Your **FREE resource** is waiting for you to claim it. Which hex would you like it to appear in?

The **Tenday** comes on the morrow! Are you ready to recruit more **souls**?

You have captured a complete **Bloodline**! Would you like to see the **powers** it offers?

Those and more were waiting for him. Fell pushed them all to the side. Instead, he kept his eyes trained on the roaring dinosaur, his mind swirling with possibilities. A rank three soul… What could that do for my *Soul Strike*? Would it gain a Fire element the same way Minamoto's arrows held the Death element? He was due for an upgrade after all, he thought with a smile. What could it do for my State of Being?

The ritalosaur roared again and began to charge the open gate on its four powerful legs. Fell stared back at it as he closed the door. It roared again at seeing its living prey escaping. To Zero, it almost sounded like a challenge.

The beast was proclaiming its dominance and majesty. It was saying, "Who are you to even look upon me? I will consume you and make your strength my own!"

The god just smiled in response thinking the very same thing. He closed and secured the temple door. A few seconds later, there was a dull boom from the monster ramming its body against the void stone. A quick check showed that not a single point in durability had been lost. Fell chuckled to himself and stared at the blank doorway. Silently he made the monster a promise.

I'll see you soon.

After a few minutes, the thuds of monsters knocking against the walls faded. Even beasts were smart enough to not slam their bodies into stone repeatedly. There were also ogre bodies for the larger predators to feast on and countless scattered body parts for the smaller ones. The noises were unsettling for the tribe, but the thick temple walls muted most of it. Rig was able to help morale by summoning faint lights to see by.

Fell sat upon one of the steps, while Minamoto worked his abilities on the two ogre bodies Fell had saved. The god was getting ready to start cultivating, when Dust walked up to him. Whether by fate or chance, the acolyte looked upon Zero with his cold eyes and asked the same question the god had been asked twice before.

"What are you going to do, my lord?"

His entire life, Zero had been conflicted. His father had taught him to be a killer. His mother had commanded him to be a protector. For the first time, Fell didn't feel pulled in two directions. At long last, his path was clear.

"We are going to save the world," the god responded with a content smile.

Dust blinked, not expecting that answer after seeing his people slaughtered. It warred with the darkness that had taken root in his soul, but he still mustered the strength to ask, "How?"

Zero ran his tongue across the roof of his mouth, tasting the words before releasing them, "By conquering it."

~ The Story Continues ~

Thank You

I am so very honored that you spent your precious time with me. Thank you for walking in my worlds!

I started writing 5 years ago and it never occurred to me that I would connect with so many wonderful people spread all around the world. It's amazing!

There are many more stories to come and I hope you continue on the journey with me.

In appreciation of my wonderful fans, I've had some artwork commissioned. I hope you enjoy it!

Thank you again, and as always…

Peace, Love, and the Perfect Margarita!

Aleron

I LOVE hearing from my fans so feel free to reach out!

 - I try to respond to every email.

- (FB Page) Join 22,000 awesome people and get updates on new books

- 10,000 Strong. If you'd like to see me practicing my memes skill and the artwork of the Labyrinth, I hope you'll join us on Instagram

- (FB Group) Join 14,000 other Mistfits who have a great time every day joking around. No politics, no religion, no stress, only fun!

- No more than one newsletter a month and only for new releases and special updates. I respect your privacy

- If you want to help me write the books and raise money for charity, please consider becoming a Patron

- The LitRPG Website

- Funny, ridiculous videos and Live AMAs

  - You must really love the Labyrinth! Just random thoughts by yours truly

About the Author

Dr. Aleron Kong is an Internal Medicine physician by training, best-selling author by love. He writes in the new genre of LitRPG, Literature Role Playing Game. He is based in Atlanta, Georgia and can often be found grilling the perfect steak and mixing the perfect margarita. Best known for his series "The Land", Aleron has published nine titles in the last five years, and continues to write passionately. He has a lifetime goal to publish fifty books and a movie or TV series. He hopes to break the mold of SciFi writers, bringing more diversity to the genre.

His latest novel, The Land: Monsters, became a Wall Street Journal Best Seller and reached #5 out of all books sold on both Amazon and Audible.

His work has been chosen as Audible's *Customer Favorite* of the Year out of their hundreds of thousands of titles.

The Land series has also earned more than 100,000 ★ ★ ★ ★ ★vs. If you turn the page, you can find out why!

Try the Land
(If you've already fallen in love with The Land, you can skip forward HERE)

EARTH, North America, 2037

"I swear to God, Silk. If you get caught on the way in just because you're trying to steal some cheap loot, I'm going to nail your nuts to a stump and kick you backwards."

"Calm down, Crush. Jesus! Where the hell do you get this stuff?" Silk put down the gold candlestick he had picked up, hearing the sound of chuckles over the group chat. "I'm on it."

The rest of the party watched safely from behind a grove of trees several hundred yards away, nearly invisible in the dark. The only reason they could see what was happening in the castle was that Jewel had cast the spell *Shared Vision*. Now a small magical window showed them everything that Silk could see.

"I will not calm down," Crush protested. "You're messing with the big payday."

"He's not wrong, Silk," Loki said. "It took us forever to even find this castle, then fight through the wilds, and finally break through the defenses to allow you a small window of time to get in. No one on the forums has even heard of the Castle of Transition. The loot we could get from this place will probably be artifact!"

"Okay, okay, fearless leader. I'm on it." As Silk spoke, he looked down and gave his four party members a great view of him scratching his virtual balls.

"You're a dick, Silk!" Daliah spat.

A low chuckle came over the group chat as Silk made his way down the stairs to the lower levels, "That's not what you said the other n-"

The rest of the comment was lost to everyone as Daliah sent a psychic pulse through the spell connection. It was the mental equivalent of stubbing your toe in the middle of the night on the way to the bathroom, minor but insanely irritating.

"Enough, Silk!" Loki commanded. "And cut that crap out Daliah. I hate that." The rest of the group was nodding and glaring at Daliah, who had the good grace to look down and away.

Silk, for his part, stopped the chatter and continued down the dark hallway he found himself in. There were no torches or other light sources in the castle. If not for his Senses of the Bat subskill, that Rogues only gained upon reaching the lofty level of one hundred and thirty, he would have been knocking into walls. Luckily, their entire party was ranked in the top one hundred groups in The Land, so none of them were noobs.

What was strange was the complete lack of monsters and NPCs (non-player characters) in the castle. The lands surrounding the castle were teeming with high-level creatures and difficult terrain. It had taken Jewel a solid day to burrow a hole in the shield covering the castle, burning through countless replenish-mana potions. It meant that the castle shield had an ungodly number of HPs (hit points). And the hole had barely lasted a few seconds before shutting again. Silk had managed to wriggle through, but no one else had been able to follow. It meant that if he got in trouble, he was totally hosed.

He had yet to encounter any resistance, though. The layout had no hidden traps he could detect, no mazelike corridors and no enemies. It was like it was inviting him in. *Hopefully inviting me into the treasure room*, Silk thought gleefully. He would love some *artifact* level gear, like those Gloves of Dark Beckoning that Chinese kid had posted he'd found in a secret labyrinth. *Lucky a-hole!*

As Silk made his way down a fifth spiral staircase, green light welled up from the lower level. The entire party caught their breath in anticipation. Months of work were hopefully about to pay off. The Rogue stepped into a round room, and they saw the source of the light. It was coming from an arch of black crystal.

Within the arch was a rippling Dartmouth green energy field. Looking at it was almost like staring straight down into a deep and limitless ocean on a stormy day. In front of the arch was a short column with the indentation of a handprint on top. In the rest of the room there was… absolutely nothing.

"Are you effing kidding me? Where is the loot?" Crush shouted. The rest of the group kept quiet, but they all shared the same disappointment.

"Maybe it's back up top," Jewel said hopefully. "Probably down another corridor?"

"What do I do here," asked Silk, "do I put my hand on it? Do a little dance maybe?"

"You could make a little love," Loki suggested.

"Maybe get down tonight," Crush finished. Light chuckles came over the chat line.

"Uhhhh, I say touch it," a voice said.

"Was that you, Daliah?" Silk asked, exasperated. "I don't know why I keep expecting you to be smart just because you're psychic. Loki, what should I do?"

"Uh… touch it," Loki replied.

"That's what she said," Crush plugged quietly in his gravelly voice.

"Thanks, oh fearless leader," Silk exclaimed, responding to Loki. "You're about as useful as a Swiss cheese condom… and good one, Crush." More chuckles came over the chat line.

He braced himself to touch the pedestal. He was really hoping there wasn't any pain. Even though the game muted it down, even a minor burn or electrical shock could ruin your whole morning. Still though, they hadn't come all this way for nothing. Silk placed his hand on the imprint.

"Are you the agent of your people?" a deep voice boomed, seeming to come from all directions at once. At the same time the only door leading out of the room clanged shut.

Immediately lowering his body and drawing both daggers, Silk quickly looked around. There was no place for anyone to hide. They could always be cloaked or veiled, but his True Sight Talent had maxed out more than forty levels ago, and no players or NPCs had been able to hide from him for quite a while. Assuming it must have been a game prompt, he tried to chat with his group, but no one responded to his queries. Shrugging, he answered.

"Uhhhh, yeah."

The voice spoke again, "Do you embrace a life of adventure and danger, love and betrayal, power and wonder?"

"Yes," the word came out stronger, Silk's greedy little heart imagining the top shelf loot they were about to get.

"Will you be among the first to move forward, preparing the way for others?"

"Hell yeah!" Silk shouted, throwing both fists in the air.

Silence greeted his proclamation. After a few seconds, he realized that unless you are an Asian time traveler who had saved a cheerleader, you just couldn't pull this stance off. Before he could lower his arms though, he heard another voice. It was quite different from the previous deep bass, and it said in a self-satisfied tone, "Thrice heard and witnessed."

The world flashed white and…

Thank you so much for giving The Land a shot. I hope you enjoyed it as much as my thousands of other loyal and wonderful fans!

That was just the first part of an eight book series that
- Is a **WSJ Best Seller**
- Has sold over **1 MILLION** copies
- Has more than **100,000** 5-star reviews
- Became Audibles **Customer Favorite** of the Year
- Reached the **Top 5** on both **Audible** and **Amazon** out of the millions of books they sell
Find out why!

Just click HERE or on the image below:

How to Make a Difference

This is Joe!

Joe leaves book reviews

Joe also upvotes reviews he likes

Joe helps indie authors like Aleron

Be like Joe 😄

As an indie author I don't have a publishing company behind me.

I have you!

As far as I'm concerned, that's more than enough.

Nothing helps as much as leaving a Review.

60 seconds of your time it would help me for a **FOREVER!**

Even leaving some stars or clicking "LIKE" on votes you agree with helps so much.

Thank you again!

I am honored to share my world with you.

Review Awakening

GUILD MEMBER HONORABLE MENTION

I would like to give a special thanks to everyone who supports me on my Patreon Page! Specifically, I would like to thank:

Assistant Deputies

Michael Clack

Luke Clack

Patrick

Officers

James King	William Haviland
JQ Phillips	Keith H Anderson
Thomas Adams	Christopher Payne
Aryeh Winter	Spencer Lee
Nate B	Mitch Van Winkle

Sergeants

Michel Noris	Jadeghost	Ryan Galle
Michael Gomez	John Osborn	Ben Peacock
Andrew Blumer	Tyler Schibig	Mike Lyons
William Akin	Mark French	William Gibbs III
	Johnny K	

Thank you ALL for helping me make this dream a reality!!!

Books of The Land

The Land: Founding

The Land: Forging

The Land: Alliances

The Land: Catacombs

The Land: Swarm

The Land: Raiders

The Land: Predators

The Land: Monsters

I want to thank my wonderful and tireless Beta Readers who have made this all possible!

Steven "The Sieve" Fleischaker

Sandy "The Syntax Witch" Berg

AND WELCOMING THE NEW MEMBER

James "Beatle" Kelly

Ya'll are the BEST!!!

If you want to stay connected and know when my next work comes out, the BEST way is by NEWSLETTER and my AUTHOR PAGE.

Unfortunately, Amazon doesn't update you when new works come out some of the time, but if sign up for the newsletter or like my author page, you'll know immediately.

GNOMES RULE!

CPSIA information can be obtained
at www.ICGtesting.com
Printed in the USA
LVHW082318060222
710426LV00006B/59/J